TROS—son of Perseus, Prince of Samothrace, must lead a strange expedition to a primitive, mist-shrouded, unreal Britain.

CASWALLON—the doughty chieftain, fearless of all men save Druids.

FFLUR—Caswallon's queen, whose clear gray eyes see very much more than what is before them.

GWENHWYFAR—treacherous and ambitious, offers TROS her greatest possession—herself.

BRITOMARIS—as devious as his wife, he might have been a man had he taken a different woman.

. . . and a bizarre CAESAR—lurking always in the background—is the most convincing and diabolical figure of evil in all fantasy fiction.

The First Book of
TROS OF SAMOTHRACE

TROS

TALBOT MUNDY

AN AVON BOOK

AVON BOOKS
A division of
The Hearst Corporation
959 Eighth Avenue
New York, New York 10019

First Avon Printing, August, 1967

Cover illustration by Douglas Rosa

AVON TRADEMARK REG. U.S. PAT. OFF. AND FOREIGN COUNTRIES,
REGISTERED TRADEMARK—MARCA REGISTRADA,
HECHO EN CHICAGO, U.S.A.

Printed in the U.S.A.

TO

ROSE WILDER LANE

WITH SINCERE GRATITUDE FOR HER
PERSISTENT INTEREST AND ENTHUSIASM

Contents

TROS

CHAPTER I

BRITAIN; THE LATE SUMMER OF 55 B.C.

These then are your liberties that ye inherit. If ye inherit sheep and oxen, ye protect those from the wolves. Ye know there are wolves, aye, and thieves also. Ye do not make yourselves ridiculous by saying neither wolf nor thief would rob you, but each to his own. Nevertheless, ye resent my warning. But I tell you, Liberty is alertness; those are one; they are the same thing. Your liberties are an offense to the slave, and to the enslaver also. Look ye to your liberties! Be watchful, and be ready to defend them. Envy, greed, conceit and ignorance, believing they are Virtue, see in undefended Liberty their opportunity to prove that violence is the grace of manhood.

FROM THE SAYINGS OF THE DRUID TALIESAN

TOWARD sunset of a golden summer evening in a clearing in a dense oak forest five men and a woman sat beside a huge flat rock that lay half buried in the earth and tilted at an angle toward where the North Star would presently appear.

At the southern end of the clearing was a large house built of mud and wattle with a heavy thatched roof; it was surrounded by a fence of untrimmed branches, and within the enclosure there were about a dozen men and women attending a fire in the open air, cooking, and carrying water.

Across the clearing from a lane that led between enormous oaks, some cattle, driven by a few armed men clothed in little other than skins dawdled along a winding cow-path toward the opening in the fence. There was a smell of wood smoke and a hush that was entirely separate from the noise made by the cattle, the soft sigh of wind in the trees, the evensong of birds and the sound of voices. Expectancy was in the air.

The five men who sat by the rock were talking with interruptions, two of them being foreigners, who used

11

one of the dialects of southern Gaul; and that was intelligible to one of the Britons who was a druid, and to the woman, who seemed to understand it perfectly, but not to the other men, to whom the druid had to keep interpreting.

"Speak slowly, Tros, speak slowly," urged the druid; but the big man, although he spoke the Gaulish perfectly, had a way of pounding his left palm with his right fist and interjecting Greek phrases for added emphasis, making his meaning even more incomprehensible.

He looked a giant compared to the others although he was not much taller than they. His clothing was magnificent, but travel-stained. His black hair, hanging nearly to his shoulders, was bound by a heavy gold band across his forehead. A cloak of purple cloth, embroidered around the edges with gold thread, partly concealed a yellow tunic edged with gold and purple.

He wore a long sword with a purple scabbard, suspended from a leather belt that was heavily adorned with golden studs. His forearm was a Titan's, and the muscles on his calves were like the roots of trees; but it was his face that held attention: Force, under control with immense stores in reserve; youth unconquerable, yet peculiarly aged before its time; cunning of the sort that is entirely separate from cowardice; imagination undivorced from concrete fact; an iron will and great good humor, that looked capable of blazing into wrath—all were written in the contours of forehead, nose and jaw. His leonine, amberous eyes contained a hint of red, and the breadth between them accentuated the massive strength of the forehead; they were eyes that seemed afraid of nothing, and incredulous of much; not intolerant, but certainly not easy to persuade.

His jaw had been shaved recently, to permit attention to a wound that had now nearly healed, leaving a deep indentation in the chin, and the black re-growing beard, silky in texture, so darkened the bronze skin that except for his size, he might almost have passed for an Iberian.

"Conops will tell you," he said, laying a huge hand on the shoulder of the man beside him, "how well I know this Caius Julius Cæsar. Conops, too, has had a taste of him. I have seen Cæsar's butchery. I know how he behaves to druids and to kings and to women and to all who oppose him, if he once has power. To obtain power—hah!—he pretends sometimes to be magnanimous. To keep it—"

Tros made a gesture with his right fist, showed his teeth

in a grin of disgust and turned to the other Samothracian beside him.

"Is he or is he not cruel, Conops? Does he keep Rome's promises? Are Rome's or his worth that?" He snapped his fingers.

Conops grinned and laid a forefinger on the place where his right eye had been. Conops was a short man, of about the same age as Tros, possibly five-and-twenty, and of the same swarthy complexion; but he bore no other resemblance to his big companion. One bright-blue eye peered out from an impudent face, crowned with a knotted red kerchief. His nose was up-turned, as if it had been smashed in childhood. He had small brass earrings, similar in pattern to the heavy golden ones that Tros wore, and he was dressed in a smock of faded Tyrian blue, with a long knife tucked into a red sash at his waist. His thin, strong, bare legs looked as active as a cat's.

"Cæsar is as cruel as a fish!" he answered, nodding. "And he lies worse than a long-shore Alexandrian with a female slave for hire."

The druid had to interpret that remark, speaking in soft undertones from a habit of having his way without much argument. He was a broad-faced young man with a musical voice, a quiet smile and big brown eyes, dressed in a blue-dyed woolen robe that reached nearly to his heels—one of the bardic druids of the second rank.

It was the woman who spoke next, interrupting the druid's explanation, with her eyes on Tros. She seemed to gloat over his strength and yet to be more than half-suspicious of him, holding her husband by the arm and resting chin and elbow on her knee as she leaned forward to watch the big man's face. She was dressed in a marvelously worked tunic of soft leather, whose pricked-in, barbaric pattern had been stained with blue woad. Chestnut hair, beautifully cared for, hung to her waist; her brown eyes were as eager as a dog's; and though she was young and comely, and had not yet borne a child, she looked too pantherlike to be attractive to a man who had known gentler women.

"You say he is cruel, this Cæsar. Is that because he punished you for disobedience—or did you steal his woman?" she demanded.

Tros laughed—a heavy, scornful laugh from deep down near his stomach.

"No need to steal! Caius Julius Cæsar *gives* women away when he has amused himself," he answered. "He

13

cares for none unless some other man desires her; and when he has spoiled her, he uses her as a reward for his lieutenants. On the march his soldiers cry out to the rulers of the towns to hide their wives away, saying they bring the maker of cuckolds with them. Such is Cæsar; a self-worshiper, a brainy rascal, the meanest cynic and the boldest thief alive. But he is lucky as well as clever, have no doubt of that."

The druid interpreted, while the woman kept her eyes on Tros.

"Is he handsomer than you? Are you jealous of him? Did he steal *your* wife?" she asked; and Tros laughed again, meeting the woman's gaze with a calmness that seemed to irritate her.

"I have no wife, and no wife ever had me," he answered. "When I meet the woman who can turn my head, my heart shall be the judge of her, Gwenhwyfar."

"Are you a druid? Are you a priest of some sort?" the woman asked. Her glowing eyes examined the pattern of the gold embroidery that edged his cloak.

Tros smiled and looked straight at the druid instead of at her. Conops drew in his breath, as if he was aware of danger.

"He is from Samothrace," the druid remarked. "You do not know what that means, Gwenhwyfar. It is a mystery."

The woman looked dissatisfied and rather scornful. She lapsed into silence, laying both elbows on her knees and her chin in both hands to stare at Tros even more intently. Her husband took up the conversation. He was a middle-sized active-looking man with a long moustache, dressed in wolf-skin with the fur side outward over breeches and a smock of knitted wool.

An amber necklace and a beautifully worked gold bracelet on his right wrist signified chieftainship of some sort. He carried his head with an air of authority that was increased by the care with which his reddish hair had been arranged to fall over his shoulders; but there was a suggestion of cunning and of weakness and cupidity at the corners of his eyes and mouth. The skin of his body had been stained blue, and the color had faded until the natural weathered white showed through it; the resulting blend was barbarously beautiful.

"The Romans who come to our shore now and then have things they like to trade with us for other things that

14

we can easily supply. They are not good traders. We have much the best of it," he remarked.

Tros understood him without the druid's aid, laughed and thumped his right fist on his knee; but instead of speaking he paused and signed to them all to listen. There came one long howl, and then a wolf-pack chorus from the forest.

"This wolf smelt, and that wolf saw; then came the pack! What if ye let down the fence?" he said then. "It is good that ye have a sea around this island. I tell you, the wolves of the Tiber are less merciful than those, and more in number and more ingenious and more rapacious. *Those* wolves glut themselves; they steal a cow, maybe, but when they have a bellyful they go; and a full wolf falls prey to the hunter. But where Romans gain a foothold they remain, and there is no end to their devouring. I *saw* Cæsar cut off the right hands of thirty thousand Gauls because they disobeyed him. I say, I saw it."

"Perhaps they broke a promise," said the woman, tossing her head to throw the hair out of her eyes. "Commius the Gaul, whom Cæsar sent to talk with us, says the Romans bring peace and affluence and that they keep *their* promises."

"Affluence for *Commius,* aye, and for the Romans!" Tros answered. "Cæsar made Commius king of the Atrebates. But do you know what happened to the Atrebates first? How many men were crucified? How many women sold into slavery? How many girls dishonored? Aye, there is always peace where Rome keeps wolf's promises. Those are the only sort she ever keeps! Commius is king of a tribe that has no remaining fighting men nor virgins, and that toils from dawn to dark to pay the tribute money that Cæsar shall send to Rome—and for what? To bribe the Roman senators! And why? Because he plans to make himself the ruler of the world!"

"How do you know?" asked the woman, when the druid began to interpret that long speech. She motioned to the druid to be still—her ear was growing more accustomed to the Samothracian's strange pronunciation.

Tros paused, frowning, grinding his teeth with a forward movement of his iron jaw. Then he spoke, looking straight at the woman:

"I am from the isle of Samothrace, that never had a king, nor ever bowed to foreign yoke. My father is a prince of Samothrace, and *he* understands what that means." He glanced at the druid. "My father had a ship—a good ship, well manned with a crew of freemen—small, because there are no harbors in the isle of Samothrace and we must beach our ships, but seaworthy and built of Euxine timber, with fastenings of bronze. We had a purple sail; and that, the Romans said, was insolence.

"The Keepers of the Mysteries of Samothrace despatched my father in his ship to many lands, of which Gaul was one, for purposes which druids understand. Cæsar hates druids because the druids have secrets that they keep from him.

"He denounced my father as a pirate, although Pompey, the other tribune, who made war on pirates, paid my father homage and gave him a parchment with the Roman safe-conduct written on it. My name, as my father's son, was also on the parchment, as were the names of every member of the crew. I was second in command of that good ship. Conops was one of the crew; we two and my father are all who are left."

Tros paused, met Conops' one bright eye, nodded reminiscently, and waited while the druid translated what he had just said into the British tongue. The druid spoke carefully, avoiding further reference to the Mysteries. But the woman hardly listened to him; she had understood.

"Our business was wholly peaceful," Tros continued. "We carried succor to the Gauls, not in the form of weapons or appliances, but in the form of secret counsel to the druids whom Cæsar persecuted, giving them encouragement, advising them to bide their time and to depend on such resources as were no business of Cæsar's.

"And first, because Cæsar mistrusted us, he made us give up our weapons. Soon after, on a pretext, he sent for that parchment that Pompey had given my father; and he failed to return it. Then he sent men to burn our ship, for the sake of the bronze that was in her; and the excuse he gave was that our purple sail was a defiance of the Roman Eagles. Thereafter he made us all prisoners; and at that time Conops had two eyes."

Gwenhwyfar glanced sharply at Conops, made a half-contemptuous movement of her lips and threw the hair back on her shoulders.

"All of the crew, except myself and Conops, were flogged to death by Cæsar's orders in my father's presence," Tros went on. "They were accused of being spies. Cæsar himself affects to take no pleasure in such scenes, and he stayed in his tent until the cruelty was over. Nor did I witness it, for I also was in Cæsar's tent, he questioning me as to my father's secrets.

"But I pretended to know nothing of them. And Conops did not see the flogging, because they had put his eye out, by Cæsar's order, for a punishment, and for the time being they had forgotten him. When the last man was dead, my father was brought before Cæsar and the two beheld each other face to face, my father standing and Cæsar seated with his scarlet cloak over his shoulders, smiling with mean lips that look more cruel than a wolf's except when he is smiling at a compliment or flattering a woman. And because my father knows all these coasts, and Cæsar does not know them but, nevertheless, intends to invade this island—"

The druid interrupted.

"How does he know it is an island?" he asked. "Very few, except we and some of the chiefs, know that."

"My father, who has sailed around it, told him so in an unguarded moment."

"He should not have told," said the druid.

"True, he should not have told," Tros agreed. "But there are those who told Cæsar that Britain is a vast continent, rich in pearls and precious stones; he plans to get enough pearls to make a breastplate for the statue of the Venus Genetrix in Rome.

"So my father, hoping to discourage him, said that Britain is only an island, of no wealth at all, inhabited by useless people, whose women are ugly and whose men are for the most part deformed from starvation and sickness. But Cæsar did not believe him, having other information and being ambitious to possess pearls."

"We *have* pearls," said the woman, tossing her head again, pulling down the front of her garment to show a big pearl at her breast.

The druid frowned:

"Speak on, Tros. You were in the tent. Your father stood and confronted Cæsar. What then?"

"Cæsar, intending to invade this island of Britain, ordered that I should be flogged and crucified, saying: 'For your son looks strong, and he will die more painfully if he is flogged, because the flies will torture him. Let us see whether he will not talk, after they have tied him to the tree.'"

"What then?" asked the druid, with a strange expression in his eyes.

"Yes, what then?" said the woman, leaning farther

17

forward to watch Tros's face. There was a half smile on her lips.

"My father offered himself in place of me," said Tros.

"And you agreed to it!" said the woman, nodding, seeming to confirm her own suspicion, and yet dissatisfied.

Tros laughed at her.

"Gwenhwyfar, I am not thy lover!" he retorted, and the woman glared. "I said to Cæsar, I would die by any means rather than be the cause of my father's death; and I swore to him to his face, as I stood between the men who held me, that if my father should die first, at his hands, he must slay me, too, and swiftly.

"Cæsar understood that threat. He lapsed into thought awhile, crossing one knee over the other, in order to appear at ease. But he was not at ease, and I knew then that he did not wish to slay either my father or me, having another use for us. So I said nothing."

"Most men usually say too much," the druid commented.

"And presently Cæsar dismissed us, commanding that we should be confined in one hut together," Tros went on. "And for a long while my father and I said nothing, for fear the guard without might listen. But in the night we lay in the dirt floor with our heads together, whispering, and my father said:

"'Death is but a little matter and soon over with, for even torture must come to an end; but a man's life should be lived to its conclusion, and it may be we can yet serve the purpose for which we came to Gaul. Remember this, my son,' said he, 'that whereas force may not prevail, a man may gain his end by seeming to yield, as a ship yields to the sea. And that is good, provided the ship does not yield too much and be swamped.'

"Thereafter we whispered far into the night. And in the morning when Cæsar sent for us we stood before him in silence, he considering our faces and our strength. My father is a stronger man than I.

"There were the ropes on the floor of the tent, with which they were ready to bind us; and there were knotted cords for the flogging; and two executioners, who stood outside the tent—they were Numidians—black men with very evil faces. And when he had considered us a long time Cæsar said:

"'It is no pleasure to me to hand men of good birth over to the executioners.'

18

"He lied. There is nothing he loves better, for he craves the power of life and death, and the nobler his victim the more subtly he enjoys it. But we kept silence. Then he rearranged the wreath that he wears on his head to hide the baldness, and drew the ends of his scarlet cloak over his knees and smiled; for through the tent door he observed a woman they were bringing to him. He became in a hurry to have our business over with.

"It may be that the sight of the woman softened him, for she was very beautiful and very much afraid; or it may be that he knew all along what demand he would make. He made a gesture of magnanimity and said:

" 'I would that I might spare you; for you seem to me to be worthy men; but the affairs of the senate and the Roman people have precedence over my personal feelings, which all men will assure you are humane. If, out of respect for your good birth and courageous bearing—for I reckon courage chiefest of the virtues—I should not oblige you to reveal the druids' secrets, I would expect you in return to render Rome a service. Thereafter, you may both go free. What say you?'

"And my father answered: 'We would not reveal the druids' secrets, even if we knew them; nor are we afraid to die.'

"And Cæsar smiled. 'Brave men,' he said, 'are more likely than cowards to perform their promises. I am sending Caius Volusenus with a ship to the coast of Britain to discover harbors and the like, and to bring back information. If he can, he is to persuade the Britons not to oppose my landing; but if he can not, he is to discover the easiest place where troops can be disembarked. It would give me a very welcome opportunity to exercise my magnanimity, which I keep ever uppermost in mind, if both of you would give your promises to me to go with Caius Volusenus, to assist him with all your knowledge of navigation; and to return with him. Otherwise, I must not keep the executioners waiting any longer.'

"I looked into my father's eyes, and he into mine, and we nodded. My father said to Cæsar:

" 'We will go with Caius Volusenus and will return with him, on the condition of your guarantee that we may go free afterward. But we must be allowed to travel with proper dignity, as free men, with our weapons. Unless you will agree to that, you may as well command your executioners, for we will not yield.'

"And at that, Cæsar smiled again, for he appreciates

19

dignity—more especially if he can subtly submit it to an outrage.

" 'I have your promise then?' he asked; and we both said, 'Yes.'

"Whereat he answered: 'I am pleased. However, I will send but one of you. The other shall remain with me as hostage. You observe, I have not put you under oath, out of respect for your religion, which you have told me is very sacred and forbids the custom we Romans observe of swearing on the altar of the gods.'

"But he lied—he lied. Cæsar cares nothing for religion.

" 'The son shall make the journey and the father shall remain,' he said to us, 'since I perceive that each loves the other. Should the son not keep his promise, then the father shall be put to certain trying inconveniences in the infliction of which, I regret to say, my executioners have a large experience.'

"He would have dismissed us there and then, but I remembered Conops, who alone of all our crew was living, and I was minded to save Conops. Also I knew that my father would wish that, and at any cost, although we dared not speak to each other in Cæsar's presence. So I answered:

" 'So be it, Cæsar. But the promise on your part is that I shall go with dignity, and thereto I shall need a servant.'

" 'I will give you a Gaul,' said he.

" 'I have no use for Gauls,' I answered. 'They are treacherous.' And at that he nodded. 'But there is one of our men,' said I, 'who escaped your well-known clemency and still endures life. Mercifully, your lieutenants have deprived him of an eye, so he is not much use, but I prefer him, knowing he will not betray me to the Britons.'

"Cæsar was displeased with that speech, but he was eager they should bring the woman to him, so he gave assent. But he forbade me to speak with my father again until I should return from Britain, and they took my father away and placed him in close confinement.

"A little later they brought Conops to me, sick and starved; but the centurion who had charge of prisoners said to me that if I would promise to bring him back six fine pearls from Britain, he for his part would see to it that my father should be well treated in my absence. So I promised to do what might be done. I said neither yes nor no."

"We *have* pearls," said the woman, looking darkly at Tros, tossing her hair again.

"Nevertheless," Tros answered, "to give pearls to a Roman is to arouse greed less easy to assuage than fire!"

"You said Cæsar will make himself master of the world. What made you say that?" asked the woman.

"I will tell that presently, Gwenhwyfar—when Caswallon * and the other druids come," he answered.

CHAPTER II

"AND YE KNOW WHETHER CÆSAR LIES OR NOT"

Listen to me before ye fill your bellies in the places habit has accustomed you to think are safe. Aye, and while ye fill your bellies, ponder. Hospitality and generosity and peace, ye all agree are graces. Are they not your measures of a man's nobility? Ye measure well. But to ignorant men, to whom might is right, I tell you gentleness seems only an opportunity. If ye are slaves of things and places, appetites and habits, rather than masters of them, surely the despoiler shall inflict upon you a more degrading slavery. Your things and places he will seize. Your appetites and habits he will mock, asserting that they justify humiliation that his violence imposes on you. Be ye, each one, master of himself, or ye shall have worse masters.

FROM THE SAYINGS OF THE DRUID TALIESAN

THE long British twilight had deepened until the trees around the clearing were a whispering wall of gloom, and a few pale stars shone overhead. The wolves howled again, making the cattle shift restlessly within the fence, and a dozen dogs bayed angrily. But the five who sat by the rock in the midst of the clearing made no move, except to glance expectantly toward the end of the glade.

And presently there began to be a crimson glow behind the trees. A chant, barbaric, weird and wonderful, without drumbeat or accompaniment, repeating and repeating one refrain, swelled through the trees as the crimson glow grew nearer.

Tros rose to his feet, but the druid and the others

* By the Romans called Cassivelaunus.

remained seated, the woman watching Tros as if she contemplated springing at him, although whether for the purpose of killing him, or not, was not so evident. Conops watched *her* equally intently.

It looked as if the forest was on fire, until men bearing torches appeared in the mouth of the glade, and a long procession wound its way solemnly and slowly toward the rock. The others stood up then and grouped themselves behind Tros and the druid, the druid throwing back his head and chanting a response to the refrain, as if it were question and answer. The woman took her husband's hand, but he appeared hardly to notice it; he was more intent on watching the approaching druids, his expression a mixture of challenge and dissatisfaction. He began to look extremely dignified.

There were a dozen druids, clad in long robes, flanked and followed by torchbearers dressed in wolf-skin and knitted breeches. They were led by an old man whose white beard fell nearly to his waist. Five of the other druids were in white robes, and bearded, but the rest were clean-shaven and in blue; all wore their hair long and over their shoulders, and no druid had any weapon other than a sickle, tucked into a girdle at the waist. The torchbearers were armed with swords and spears; there were fifty of them, and nearly as many women, who joined in the refrain, but the old High Druid's voice boomed above all, mellow, resonant and musical.

The procession was solemn and the chant religious; yet there was hardly any ceremony when they came to a stand near the rock and the old druid strode out in front of the others, alone. The chant ceased then, and for a moment there was utter silence. Then the druid who had been acting as interpreter took Tros's right hand and led him toward the old man, moving so as to keep Tros's hand concealed from those behind. The old man held out his own right hand, the younger druid lifting the end of Tros's cloak so as to conceal what happened.

A moment later Tros stepped back and saluted with the graceful Mediterranean gesture of the hand palm outward, and there the ceremony ceased.

The old druid sat down on a stone beside the rock; his fellow druids found places near him in an irregular semi-circle; the crowd stood, shaking their torches at intervals to keep them burning, the glare and the smoke making splotches of crimson and black against the trees.

The younger druid spoke then in rapid undertones,

apparently rehearsing to the older man the conversation that had preceded his arrival. Then Tros, with his left hand at his back and his right thrown outward in a splendid gesture that made Gwenhwyfar's eyes blaze, broke silence, speaking very loud:

"My father, I know nothing of the stars, beyond such lore as seamen use; but they who do know say that Cæsar's star is in ascension, and that nightly in the sky there gleam the omens of increasing war."

The High Druid nodded gravely. The chief let go his wife's hand, irritated because she seemed able to understand all that was said, whereas he could not. The younger druid whispered to him. It was growing dark now, and scores of shadowy figures were gathering in the zone of torchlight from the direction of the forest. There was a low murmur, and an occasional clank of weapons. Tros, conscious of the increasing audience, raised his voice:

"They who sent me hither say this isle is sacred. Cæsar, whose camp-fires ye may see each night beyond the narrow sea that separates your cliffs from Gaul, is the relentless enemy of the druids and of all who keep the ancient secret.

"Ye have heard—ye *must* have heard—how Cæsar has stamped out the old religion from end to end of Gaul, as his armies have laid waste the corn and destroyed walled towns. Cæsar understands that where the Wisdom dwells, freedom persists and grows again, however many times its fields are reaped. Cæsar does not love freedom.

"In Gaul there is no druid now who dares to show himself. Where Cæsar found them, he has thrown their tortured carcasses to feed the dogs and crows. And for excuse, he says the druids make human sacrifice, averring that they burn their living victims in cages made of withes.

"Cæsar, who has slain his hecatombs, who mutilates and butchers men, women, children, openly in the name of Rome, but secretly for his own ambition; Cæsar, who has put to death more druids than ye have slain wolves in all Britain, *says* that the druids burn human sacrifices. Ye know whether Cæsar lies or not."

He paused. The ensuing silence was broken by the whispering of men and women who translated his words into the local dialect. Some of the druids moved among the crowd, assisting. Tros gave them time, watching the face of the chief and of his wife Gwenhwyfar, until the murmur died down into silence. Then he resumed:

"They who sent me into Gaul, are They who keep the

23

Seed from which your druids' wisdom springs. But he who sent me to this isle is Cæsar. They who sent me into Gaul are They who never bowed a knee to conqueror and never by stealth or violence subdued a nation to their will. But he who sent me hither knows no other law than violence; no other peace than that imposed by him; no other object than his own ambition.

"He has subdued the north of Gaul; he frets in idleness and plays with women, because there are no more Gauls to conquer before winter sets in. He has sent me hither to bid you let him land on your coast with an army. The excuse he offers you, is that he wishes to befriend you.

"The excuse he sends to Rome, where his nominal masters spend the extorted tribute money wrung by him from Gauls to buy his own preferment, is that you Britons have been sending assistance to the Gauls, wherefore he intends to punish you. And the excuse he gives to his army is, that here is plunder—here are virgins, cattle, clothing, precious metals and the pearls with which he hopes to make a breastplate for the Venus Genetrix.

"Cæsar holds my father hostage against my return. I came in Cæsar's ship, whose captain, Caius Volusenus, ordered me to show him harbors where a fleet of ships might anchor safely, threatening me that, unless I show them to him, he will swear away my father's life on my return; for Caius Volusenus hopes for Cæsar's good-will, and he knows the only way it may be had.

"But I told Caius Volusenus that I know no harbors. I persuaded him to beach his ship on the open shore, a two days' journey from this place. And there, where we landed with fifty men, we were attacked by Britons, of whom one wounded me, although I had not as much as drawn my sword.

"Your Britons drove the Romans back into the ship, which put to sea again, anchoring out of bowshot; but I, with my man Conops, remained prisoner in the Britons' hands—and a druid came, and staunched my wound.

"So I spoke with the druid—he is here—behold him— he will confirm my words. And a Roman was allowed to come from the ship and to take back a message to Caius Volusenus, that I am to be allowed to speak with certain chiefs and thereafter that I may return to the ship; but that none from the ship meanwhile may set foot on the shore.

"And in that message it was said that I am to have full opportunity to deliver to you Cæsar's words, and to obtain

24

your consent, if ye will give it, to his landing with an army before the winter storms set in.

"Thus Caius Volusenus waits. And yonder on the coast of Gaul waits Cæsar. My father waits with shackles on his wrists. And I, who bring you Cæsar's message, and who love my father, and who myself am young, with all my strength in me, so that death can not tempt, and life seems good and full of splendor—I say to you: Defy this Cæsar!"

He would have said more, but a horn sounded near the edge of the trees and another twenty men strode into the clearing, headed by a Gaul who rode beside a Briton in a British chariot. The horses were half frantic from the torchlight and fear of wolves, but their heads were held by men in wolf-skin who kept them to the track by main strength. Conops plucked at the skirt of Tros's tunic:

"Commius!" he whispered, and Tros growled an answer under his breath.

The two men in the chariot stood upright with the dignity of kings, and as they drew near, with the torch-light shining on their faces, Tros watched them narrowly. But Conops kept his one bright eye on Gwenhwyfar, for she, with strange, nervous twitching of the hands, was watching Tros as intently as he eyed the stranger. Her breast was heaving.

The man pointed out as Commius was a strongly built, black-bearded veteran, who stood half a head shorter than the Briton in the chariot beside him. He was dressed in a Roman toga, but with a tunic of unbleached Gaulish wool beneath. His eyes were bold and crafty, his head proud and erect, his smile assuring. Somewhere there was a trace of weakness in his face, but it was indefinable, suggestive of lack of honor rather than physical cowardice, and, at that, not superficial. His beard came up high on his cheek-bones and his black hair low on a broad and thoughtful forehead.

"Britomaris!" cried the driver of the chariot, and he was a chief beyond shadow of doubt, with his skin stained blue and his wolf-skins fastened by a golden brooch—a shaggy-headed, proud-eyed man with whipcord muscles and a bold smile half-hidden under a heavy brown moustache.

The husband of Gwenhwyfar stood up, dignified enough but irresolute, his smoldering eyes sulky and his right hand pushing at his wife to make her keep behind him. She stood staring over his shoulder, whispering between her teeth into his ear. The chief who drove the horses spoke

25

again, and the tone of his loud voice verged on the sarcastic:

"O Britomaris, this is Commius, who comes from Gaul to tell us about Cæsar. He brings gifts."

At the mention of gifts, Britomaris would have stepped up to the chariot, but his wife prevented, tugging at him, whispering; but none noticed that except Tros, Conops and the druids.

At a signal from the other chief a man in wolf-skins took up the presents from the chariot and brought them— a cloak of red cloth, a pair of Roman sandals and three strings of brass beads threaded on a copper wire.

It was cheap stuff of lower quality than the trade goods that occasional Roman merchants brought to British shores. Britomaris touched the gifts without any display of satisfaction. He hardly glanced at them, perhaps because his wife was whispering.

"Who is here?" asked Commius, looking straight at Tros.

At that Conops took a swift stride closer to his master, laying a hand on the hilt of his long knife. Gwenhwyfar laughed, and Britomaris nudged her angrily.

"I am one who knows Commius the Gaul!" said Tros, returning stare for stare. "I am another who runs Cæsar's errands, although Cæsar never offered me a puppet kingdom. Thou and I, O Commius, have eaten leavings from the same trough. Shall we try to persuade free men that it is a good thing to be slaves?"

The chief who had brought Commius laughed aloud, for he understood the Gaulish, and he also seemed to understand the meaning of Gwenhwyfar's glance at Britomaris. Commius, his grave eyes missing nothing of the scene, stepped down from the chariot and, followed by a dozen men with torches, walked straight up to Tros.

His face looked deathly white in the torch glare, but whether or not he was angry it was difficult to guess, because he smiled with thin lips and had his features wholly in control. Tros smiled back at him, good nature uppermost, but an immense suspicion in reserve.

Gwenhwyfar, clinging to her man's arm, listened with eager eyes and parted lips. Conops drew his knife clandestinely and hid it in a tunic fold.

"I know the terms on which Cæsar sent you. I know who is hostage for you in Cæsar's camp," said Commius; and Tros, looking down at him, for he was taller by a

26

full hand's breadth, laid a heavy right hand on his shoulder.

"Commius," he said, "it may be well to yield to Cæsar for the sake of temporary peace—to give a breathing spell to Gaul—to save thine own neck, that the Gauls may have a leader when the time comes. For this Cæsar, who seems invincible, will hardly live forever; and the Gauls in their day of defeat have need of you as surely as they will need your leadership when Cæsar's bolt is shot. That day will come. But is it the part of a man, to tempt these islanders to share your fate?"

"Tros, you are rash!" said Commius, speaking through his teeth. "I am the friend of Cæsar."

"I am the friend of all the world, and that is a higher friendship," Tros answered. "Though I were the friend of Cæsar, I would nonetheless hold Cæsar less than the whole world. But I speak of this isle and its people. Neither you nor I are Britons. Shall we play the man toward these folk, or shall we ruin them?"

The crowd was pressing closer, and the chief in his chariot urged the horses forward so that he might overhear; their white heads tossed in the torchlight like fierce apparitions from another world.

"If I dared trust you," Commius said, his black eyes searching Tros's face.

"Do the Gauls trust *you?*" asked Tros. "Are you a king among the Gauls? You may need *friends* from Britain when the day comes." *

"You intend to betray me to Cæsar!" said Commius, and at that Tros threw back his shock of hair and laughed, his eyes in the torchlight showing more red than amber.

"If that is all your wisdom, I waste breath," he answered.

Commius was about to speak when another voice broke on the stillness, and all eyes turned toward the rock. The old High Druid had climbed to its summit and stood leaning on a staff, his long beard whiter than stone against the darkness and ruffled in the faint wind—a splendid figure, dignity upholding age.

"O Caswallon, and you, O Britomaris, and ye sons of the isle, hear my words!" he began.

And as the crowd surged for a moment, turning to face

* Caesar made Commius king of the Atrebates, half of which tribe lived in Britain and half in Gaul. There is no historic record, however, of the British Atrebates having accepted Commius as king.

27

the rock and listen, Gwenhwyfar wife of Britomaris came and tugged at Tros's sleeve. He thought it was Conops, and waited, not moving his head, expecting a whispered warning; but the woman tugged again and he looked down into her glowing eyes. She pointed toward the house at the far end of the clearing.

"Thither I go," she whispered. "If you are as wise as you seem fearless, you will follow."

"I would hear this druid," Tros answered, smiling as he saw the point of Conops' knife within a half inch of the woman's ribs.

"He will talk until dawn!"

"Nonetheless, I will hear him."

"You will hear what is more important if you follow me," she answered; and at that, she left him, stepping back so quickly that the point of Conops' long knife pricked her and she struck him angrily, then vanished like a shadow.

Tros strode slowly after her, with Conops at his heels, but when he reached the gloom beyond the outskirts of the crowd he paused.

"Am I followed?" he asked.

"Nay, master. They are like the fish around a dead man. One could gather all of them within a net. Do we escape?"

"I know what the druid will say," Tros answered. "I could say it myself. What that woman has to say to me, I know not. Though it may be she has set an ambush."

Conops chuckled.

"Aye! The kind of ambush they set for sailormen on the wharfsides of Saguntum! A long drink, and then—"

He whistled a few bars of the love song of the Levantine ports:

> Oh, what is in the wind that fills
> The red sail straining at the mast?
> Oh, what beneath the purple hills
> That overlean the Cydnus, thrills
> The sailor seeing land at last?
> Oh, Chloe and—

"Be still!" commanded Tros. "If there were no more risk than that, my father would be free to-morrow! Which way went the woman?"

Conops pointed, speaking his mind as usual:

"That Briton who came in the chariot—Caswallon—fills

my eye. But I would not trust Commius the Gaul; he has a dark look."

"He is anxious for his Gauls, as I am anxious for my father," Tros answered. "He hates Cæsar, and he likes me; but for the sake of his Gauls he would stop at nothing. He would bring Cæsar to this island, just to give the Atrebates time to gather strength at Cæsar's rear. Nay, he may not be trusted."

"Master, will you trust these Britons?" Conops asked him, suddenly, from behind, as he followed close in his steps along a track that wound among half-rotted tree stumps toward the cattle fence. Tros turned and faced him.

"It is better that the Britons should trust *me,*" he answered.

"But to what end, master?"

"There are two ends to everything in this world, even to a ship," said Tros darkly; "two ends to Cæsar's trail, and two ways of living life: on land and water. Make sure we are not followed."

The dogs barked fiercely as they approached the fence, and Conops grew nervous, pulling at his master's cloak.

"Nay, it is a good sign," said Tros. "If it were a trap they would have quieted the dogs."

He turned again to make sure no one was following. The torchlight shone on the High Druid's long white robe and whiter beard, and on a sea of faces that watched him breathlessly. The old man was talking like a waterfall. They were too far away now for his words to reach them, but judging by his gestures he was very angry and was in no mood to be brief.

"On guard!" warned Conops suddenly as they started toward the fence again, but Tros made no move to reach for his sword.

It was the woman Gwenhwyfar, waiting in a shadow. She stepped out into the firelight that shone through a gap in the fence and signed to Tros to follow her, leading around to the rear of the house, where a door, sheltered by a rough porch, opened toward the forest.

She led the way in, and they found themselves in a room whose floor was made of mud and cow dung trampled hard. There was a fire in the midst, and a hole in the roof to let the smoke out. She spoke to a hag dressed in ragged skins, who stirred the fire to provide light and then vanished through an inner door.

29

The firelight shone on smooth mud walls, adzed beams, two benches and a table.

"Your home?" asked Tros, puzzled, and Gwenhwyfar laughed.

"I am a chief's wife; I am wife of Britomaris," she answered. "Our serfs, who mind the cattle, live in this place."

"Where then is your home?" asked Tros.

She pointed toward the north.

"When Caswallon comes, we leave home," she answered. "The power to use our house is his, but we are not his serfs."

Gwenhwyfar's attitude suggested secrecy. She seemed to wish Tros to speak first, as if she would prefer to answer questions rather than to force the conversation. She looked extremely beautiful in the firelight; the color had risen to her cheeks and her eyes shone like jewels, brighter than the gleaming ornaments on her hair and arms and breast.

"Why do you fear Caswallon?" Tros asked her suddenly.

"I? I am not afraid!" she answered. "Britomaris fears him, but not I! Why should I be afraid? Caswallon is a strong chief, a better man than Britomaris; and I hate him! He—how strong is Cæsar?" she demanded.

Tros studied her a moment. He gave her no answer. She sat down on one of the benches, signing to him and Conops to be seated on the other.

"You said Cæsar will make himself master of the world," she remarked after a minute, stretching her skin-clad legs toward the blaze. She was not looking at Tros now but at the fire. "Why did you say that?"

Suddenly she met his eyes, and glanced away again. Conops went and sat down on the floor on the far side of the fire.

CHAPTER III

GWENHWYFAR, WIFE OF BRITOMARIS

Beware the ambitious woman! All things and all men are her means to an end. All treacheries are hers. All reasons justify her. Though her end is ruin, shall that lighten your humiliation—ye whom she uses as means to that end that she contemptuously seeks?

FROM THE SAYINGS OF THE DRUID TALIESAN

TROS made no answer for a long time, but stared first at the fire and then at Gwenhwyfar.

"Send that man away," she suggested, nodding toward Conops; but Tros scratched his chin and smiled.

"I prefer to be well served," he answered. "How can he keep secrets unless he knows them? Nay, nay, Gwenhwyfar; two men with three eyes are as good again as one man with but two; and even so, the two are not too many when another's wife bears watching! Speak on."

Her eyes lighted up with challenge as she tossed her head. But she laughed and came to the point at once, looking straight and hard at him.

"Commius spoke to me of Cæsar. He said he is Cæsar's deputy. He urged me to go with him and visit Cæsar. Britomaris is a weak chief; he has no will; he hates Caswallon and yet bows to him. Cæsar is strong."

"I am *not* Cæsar's deputy, whatever Commius may be," said Tros. "But this I tell you, and you may as well remember it, Gwenhwyfar: A thousand women have listened to Cæsar's wooing, and I have been witness of the fate of some. There was a woman of the Gauls, a great chief's daughter, who offered herself to him to save her people. Cæsar passed her on to one of his lieutenants, and thereafter sold her into slavery."

"Perhaps she did not please him," Gwenhwyfar answered. And then, since Tros waited in silence, "I have pearls."

"You have also my advice regarding them," said Tros.

Gwenhwyfar waited a full minute, thinking, as if appraising him. She nodded, three times, slowly.

"You, who have lost all except your manhood and the clothes you wear!" she said at last, and her voice was bold and stirring, "what is *your* ambition?"

"To possess a ship," he answered, so promptly that he startled her.

"A ship? Is that all?"

"Aye, and enough. A man is master on his own poop. A swift ship, a crew well chosen, and a man may laugh at Cæsars."

"And yet—you say, you had a ship? And a crew well chosen?"

Tros did not answer. His brows fell heavily and half concealed eyes that shone red in the firelight.

31

"Better be Cæsar's ward, and rule a kingdom, than wife of a petty chief who dares not disobey Caswallon," Gwenhwyfar said, looking her proudest. "Caswallon might have had me to wife, but *he* chose Fflur. There was nothing left for me but Britomaris. If he were a strong man I could have loved him. He is weak.

"He likes to barter wolf-skins on the shore with the Roman and Tyrian traders. He pays tribute to Caswallon. He does not even dare to build a town and fortify it, least Caswallon should take offense.

"He obeys the druids, as a child obeys its nurse, in part because he is afraid of them, but also because it is the easiest thing to do. He is not a man, such as Caswallon might have been—such as *you* are."

She paused, with parted lips, looking full and straight at Tros. Conops tapped the dirt floor rhythmically with the handle of his knife. A man in the next room began singing about old mead and the new moon.

"It is a ship, not a woman that I seek," said Tros, and her expression hardened.

But she tried again:

"You might have a hundred ships."

"I will be better satisfied with one."

She began to look baffled; eyes and lips hinted anger that she found it difficult to hold in check.

"Is that your price?" she asked. "A ship?"

"Woman!" said Tros after a minute's silence, laying his great right fist on his knee, "you and I have no ground that we can meet on. You would sell your freedom. I would die for mine."

"Yet you live!" she retorted. "Did you come to Britain of your free will? Where is your freedom? You are Cæsar's messenger!"

She got up suddenly and sat down on the bench beside him, he not retreating an inch. Not even his expression changed, but his shoulders were rigid and his hands were pressing very firmly on his knees.

"Do you not understand?" she asked.

"I understand," he answered.

Suddenly she flared up, her eyes blazing and her voice trembling. She did not speak loud, but with a slow distinctness that made each word like an arrow speeding to the mark.

"Am I not fair?" she asked, and he nodded.

Her eyes softened for a moment, then she went on:

"Caswallon was the first and is the last who shall deny

me! I can be a good wife—a very god's wife to a man worth loving! Cæsar can conquer Caswallon, but not alone. He will need my help, and yours. Cæsar made Commius a king over the Atrebates; and what was Commius before that? Cæsar shall make me a queen where Caswallon lords it now! And you—?"

"And Britomaris?" asked Tros, watching her.

"And you?" she said again, answering stare for stare.

Her breast was heaving quickly, like a bird's.

"Oh, Tros!" she went on. "Are you a man, or are you timid? Here a kingdom waits for you! Yonder, in Gaul, is Cæsar, who can make and unmake kingdoms! Here am I! I am a woman, I am all a woman. I love manhood. I do not love Britomaris."

Conops stirred the fire.

"Do you not see that if you are all a woman you must oppose Cæsar?" Tros asked. "Then—let Cæsar outrage! Let him slay! He will have done nothing, because your spirit will go free, Gwenhwyfar. Cæsar plans an empire of men's bodies, with his own—his epileptic, foul, unchaste and hairless head crowned master of them all! Whoso submits to him is a slave—a living carcass. Hah! Defy him! Scorn him! Resist him to the last breath! The worst he can do then will be to torture a brave body till the braver soul goes free!"

His words thrilled her.

"Well enough," she answered promptly. "I am brave. I can defy Cæsar. But I need a braver chief to make the stand with me than Britomaris. If Caswallon had taken me to wife—but he chose Fflur—perhaps it was as well—you are nobler than Caswallon, and—"

"And what?" asked Tros.

She answered slowly:

"A bold man now could conquer Britain. The druids—I know them—the druids would support one who opposed the Romans. They fear for their own power should Cæsar gain a foothold. The druids trust you. Why? They do not trust me. Tros! Strike a bargain with the druids. Slay Caswallon. Seize the chieftainship, and raise an army against Cæsar!"

"And Britomaris?"

"Challenge him!" she answered. "He would run! I have the right according to our law, to leave a man who runs away."

"Gwenhwyfar!" Tros exclaimed, getting up and standing straight in front of her. "It is Cæsar, and not I who has

33

the falling sickness! You and I lack that excuse! Know this: I will neither steal a wife from Britomaris, nor a throne from Caswallon; nor will I impose my will on Britain."

She stood up, too, and faced him, very angry.

"Have you never loved?" she asked, and though her eyes were steady, the gold brooch on her breast was fluttering.

"Loved? Aye, like a man!" he answered. "I have loved the sea since I was old enough to scramble down the cliffs of Samothrace and stand knee deep to watch the waves come in! The sea is no man's master, nor a bed of idleness! The sea holds all adventure and the keys of all the doors of the unknown!

"The sea, Gwenhwyfar, is the image of a man's life. If he flinches, if he fails, it drowns him. Is he lazy, does he fail to mend his ship or steadfastly to be example to his crew, there are rocks, shoals, tides, the pirates, storms. But is he stanch, he sails, until he reaches unknown ports, where the gods trade honesty for the experience he brings! I seek but a ship, Gwenhwyfar. I will carve a destiny that suits me better than a stolen kingdom and a cheated husband's bed!"

She reached out a hand unconsciously and touched his arm:

"Tros," she answered, "Caswallon has some longships hidden in the marshes of the Thames. Take me—take a ship, and—"

"Nay," he answered. "Caswallon owes me nothing. He who owes me a good ship is Cæsar!"

"And you think that you can make Cæsar pay?" she asked. "Take me to Cæsar, Tros; between us we will cheat him of a ship! With you to teach me, I could learn to love the sea."

He stepped back a pace or two, would have stumbled backward against the clay hearth if Conops had not warned him.

"None learns to love," he answered. "Love is a man's nature. He is this, or he is that; none can change him. I am less than half a man, until I feel the deck heave under me and look into a rising gale. You, Gwenhwyfar, you are less than half a woman until you pit your wits against a man who loves to master you; and I find no amusement in such mastery. Make love to Britomaris."

She reddened in the firelight, stood up very proudly,

biting her lip. Her eyes glittered, but she managed to control herself; there were no tears.

"Shall I bear a coward's children?" she demanded.

"I know not," said Tros. "You shall not bear mine. I will save you, if I can, from Cæsar."

Tears were very near the surface now, but pride, and an emotion that she did her utmost to conceal, aided her to hold them back.

"Forgive me!" she said suddenly.

Her hands dropped, but she raised them again and folded them across her breast.

"Forgive me, Tros! I was mad for a short minute. It is maddening to be a coward's wife. I tempted you, to see how much a man you truly are."

Conops' knife hilt tapped the floor in slow staccato time.

"Kiss me, and say good-by," she coaxed, unclasping her hands again.

"Nay, no good-bys!" he answered, laughing. "We shall meet again. And as for kissing, a wise seaman takes no chances near the rocks, Gwenhwyfar!"

Stung—savage—silent, she gestured with her head toward the door, folding her arms on her breast, and Tros, bowing gravely, strode out into darkness. Conops shut the door swiftly behind them.

"If this isle were in *our* sea, she would have thrown a knife," said Conops, twitching his shoulder-blades. "Master, you have made an enemy."

"Not so," Tros answered. "I have found one. Better the rocks in sight than shoals unseen, my lad! Let us see now who our friends are."

He strode toward the torchlight, where the old High Druid was still holding forth, swaying back and forward on the summit of the rock as he leaned to hurl his emphasis. More chariots had come and horses' heads were nodding on the outskirts of the crowd—phantoms in the torch-smoke.

Tros kept to the deeper shadows, circling the crowd until he could approach Commius and Caswallon from the rear. He was stared at by new arrivals as he began to work his way toward them, but the Britons had too good manners and too much dignity to interfere with him or block his way.

The women in the crowd stared and smiled, standing on tiptoe, some of them, frankly curious, but neither impudent nor timid. Most of them were big-eyed women

35

with long eyelashes and well-combed braided hair hanging to the waist. Nearly all had golden ornaments; but there were slave women among them, who seemed to belong to another race, dressed in plain wool or even plainer skins.

It was a crowd that, on the whole, was more than vaguely conscious of the past it had sprung from.

Glances cast at Tros were less of admiration than expectancy, to see him exhibit manners less civilized than theirs—the inevitable attitude of islanders steeped in tradition and schooled in the spiritual mysticism of the druids; proud, and yet considerate of the stranger; warlike, because decadence had undermined material security, but chivalrous because chivalry never dies until the consciousness of noble ancestry is dead, and theirs was living.

Commius the Gaul, who, when he was not deliberately controlling his expression, had the hard face and the worried look of a financier, was seated beside Caswallon. The chief was standing in the chariot, his gold-and-amber shoulder-ornaments shining in the torchlight. He smiled when he caught sight of Tros, and with a nudge stirred Commius out of a brown study. Commius, adjusting his expression carefully, got down from the chariot, took Tros's arm, and led him to the chief.

"Tros, son of Perseus, Prince of Samothrace," he announced.

Caswallon stretched out a long, white, sleeveless arm, on which strange pagan designs had been drawn in light-blue woad. It was an immensely strong arm, with a heavy golden bracelet on the wrist.

They shook hands and, without letting go, the chieftain pulled Tros up into the chariot. Britomaris, from about a chariot's length away, watched thoughtfully, peering past a woman's shoulder.

The old High Druid was talking too fast for Tros to follow him; he was holding the rapt attention of the greater part of the crowd, and it was less than a minute before Tros was forgotten. The old druid had them by the ears, and their eyes became fixed on his face as if he hypnotized them.

But his eloquence by no means hypnotized himself. His bright old eyes scanned the faces in the torchlight as if he were judging the effect of what he said, and he turned at intervals to face another section of the crowd, signing to the torchmen to distribute their light where he needed it.

Moreover, he changed his tone of voice and his degree

36

of vehemence to suit whichever section of the crowd he happened to be facing. There were groups of dark-haired swarthy men and women, who looked consciously inferior to the taller, white-skinned, reddish-haired breed, or, if not consciously inferior, then aware that the others thought them so. He spoke to them in gentler, more persuasive cadences.

Caswallon watched the druid in silence for a long time; yet he hardly appeared to be listening; he seemed rather to be waiting for a signal. At last he lost patience and whispered to a man in a leather sleeveless tunic who leaned on a spear beside the chariot.

The man whispered to one of the younger druids, who approached the pulpit rock from a side that at the moment was in darkness. Climbing, he lay there in shadow, and, watching his opportunity when the old man paused for breath, spoke a dozen words.

The old druid nodded and dismissed him with a gesture. The younger druid worked his way back through the crowd to the chariot wheel and whispered to Caswallon.

The man with the spear received another whispered order from the chief, and he repeated it to the others. Without any appearance of concerted action, the torchmen began to edge themselves in both directions toward the far side of the rock, until the near side was almost in total darkness.

Then Caswallon took the reins without a word to Tros, and the man with the spear spoke to Commius the Gaul, who climbed into another chariot. The horses began to plunge, but Caswallon pulled them backward, edging the chariot gradually into deeper shadow.

Two other chariots followed suit; and in one there was a woman, who drove, and who had magnificent brown hair that reached below her waist. Conops jumped in and, curling on the floor, made ready to cling to Tros's knee in case of need; being a seaman, he had no love and less experience of chariots.

Suddenly Caswallon wheeled his team and sent it at full gallop toward the end of the lane that led into the forest. She who drove the second chariot wheeled after him; and a third, in which Commius the Gaul was clinging, bumped over the rotting tree-roots in the wake.

The pace, once the horses sprang into their stride, was furious. Tros, forever mindful of his dignity, clung nevertheless to the chariot side, setting his teeth as the wheels struck ruts and branches, feeling as if the dimly seen milk-white of the horses were foaming waves, and himself in a ship's bow on the lookout for unknown rocks.

They plunged into the forest, where the oaks met overhead. There was a sound, that might have been the sea, of wind in the upper branches—a sensation of tremendous speed—and nothing visible except the sudden-looming tree-trunks, which seemed to miss the wheel by hair's breadths.

There was a thudding of wheels and a thunder of pursuing hoofs, a splash now and then where shallow water lay in unseen hollows, a smell of horse-sweat, and of rotting leaves, and a whirring of unseen bats. One bat struck Tros in the face, and fell to the floor of the chariot, where Conops drew his knife and slew it—believing then, and forever afterwards, that he had killed a devil.

The horses appeared to be frantic and out of hand, and yet Caswallon managed them with art that concealed all method, standing with one foot resting on a sort of step, no more than feeling at the horses' mouths, balancing his weight as if by instinct in advance of sudden turns and low obstructions that the horses took in their stride, but that threw the chariot a yard in air.

Long—endless to Tros—darkness, and then moonlight silhouetting ghostly tree-trunks, a splash through a shadowy ford, then through a mile of stumps and seedlings at the forest's edge into a belt of fern and lush grass glistening with dew, and at last a rolling down, where patches of chalk gleamed milk-white under the moon and the track swung around a hillside under a scattering of fleecy clouds.

Then Caswallon glanced at Tros, and Tros forced a good-natured grin:

"O Chief," he said, "you are the first who has made me feel that kind of fear!"

Caswallon smiled, but the ends of his long moustache concealed what kind of smile it was. Instead of answering he glanced over his shoulder at the second chariot, not fifty yards behind. There was a woman driving it.

Then, with one swift look into Tros's eyes, he shook the reins and shouted to the team—a trumpet shout, that held a sort of note of laughter, but not of mockery to which a guest could take exception. He seemed pleased to have shown his prowess to a foreigner, that was all.

CHAPTER IV

FFLUR

Mark my words, ye who are deceived and undone and betrayed by women; ye who fight each other for a woman's favors; ye who value women by the numbers and strength of their sons, and by their labor at the loom. Lo, I tell you a secret. There is laughter in the eyes of some—aye, even within their anger, and beneath it. Those are the wise ones and the worthy. They are not ambitious. They know ambition is the yoke-mate of treachery. They will not betray themselves. How then can they betray another?

FROM THE SAYINGS OF THE DRUID TALIESAN

WOLVES worrying a kill yelped and vanished into shadow as the chariot thundered around a shoulder of the down and passed a cluster of low, flint-and-mud-built cottages with wooden roofs, surrounded by a wall, within which was bleating and the stifling smell of sheep.

Beyond that the moonlight shone on a big thatched house surrounded by a wooden paling. It was high and oblong, but of only one story with projecting eaves, built of wooden beams with flints and chalk packed into the interstices. Light shone through the chinks of the shutters. There were no trees near it.

They were expected, for a gate was flung wide at the sound of their approach and a dozen men with spears and shields formed up in line outside the entrance, raising their spears as Caswallon drove full-gallop past them.

Within the paling there was a smell of horses that stamped and whinnied at their pickets under a lean-to roof. The house door opened, showing a blazing fire on a hearth exactly facing it. Caswallon drew the team up on its haunches, and almost before their forefeet touched the ground again he let go the reins, jumped along the chariot pole, touched it lightly once with one foot, and seized their heads.*

Six women stood in the doorway, with three children clinging to their skirts.

Some one with dark, shaggy hair, who wore nothing but

* This was a favorite trick of the Britons in battle.

39

a wolf-skin, led away the horses just in time to avoid the second chariot that thundered through the gate and drew up as the first had done.

And, as the horses pawed the air, the woman who was driving dropped the reins and exactly repeated Caswallon's feat, springing along the pole to the ground to seize their heads. There was no sign yet of the third chariot and Commius. A man stepped out behind the chariot the woman had been driving and held the horses until another man dressed in skins came and led them away.

"O Tros, this is Fflur. She is my wife," said Caswallon, taking her by the hand.

She stepped forward and kissed Tros on both cheeks, then stepped back to her husband's side, and Tros wondered at her, for she was good to look at—strong, modest, matronly, gray-eyed, and dressed in embroidered woolen stuff, with a bodice of laced leather that showed the outlines of her graceful figure. There were pearls in her hair and in the big round brooches on her dress.

It was she who led the way into the house, scolding the dogs, throwing an arm about one of the women in the doorway, asking why the children were not asleep in bed—a very gracious lady, full of dignity and laughter and sincerity.

"This is not my house," said Caswallon, taking Tros by the arm. "I am the chief. They pay me tribute from the fen-land to the sea. It is a good kingdom. You shall tell me about Cæsar."

He did not wait for Commius' chariot but followed his wife into the house and shut the door behind him, pushing away the dogs, rolling one of them over playfully with his foot—then tasting a tankard of mead that his wife took from a woman's hand and brought to him.

He only sipped, then handed the tankard to Tros, who drank the half of it and passed it back. Caswallon swallowed the remainder, gave the empty tankard to a woman, wiped his wet moustache on a woolen towel that the woman passed to him, smiled and handed the towel to Tros.

"So one of us clove your chin? Was it a good blow?" he asked, laying a big white hand with rings on it on Tros's shoulder.

"No. A blow in haste," said Tros. "He was not strong."

"He is very strong. His name is Erbin. He can throw a

good-sized bullock by the horns. You broke his ribs," said Caswallon. "Can you break mine?"

"I *will* not," Tros answered.

Caswallon laughed, half-disappointed, wholly admiring Tros's strength, flexing his own great shoulder-muscles as he led to where two high-backed oaken seats faced each other on opposite sides of the hearth.

He threw himself on one, shoving the dogs away as he thrust his skin-clad legs toward the fire, signing to Tros to take the other.

Then he unbuckled his long sword, and Tros followed suit, each man setting his weapon against the wall. Conops sat down on the floor beside the hearth, within reach of Tros's legs, and a woman brought him a tankard of mead all to himself.

It was a high, oblong room, with great black beams overhead, from which hams and sides of bacon hung in the smoke that rose from the hearth and lost itself up in the shadows below the thatch. There was no light except from the fire, but one of the women prodded that to keep it blazing, and when she disappeared Conops assumed the duty.

Three sleepy children, two boys and a girl, came and clung to Caswallon's legs, begging him to tell them stories, but after he had tousled up their hair and rolled one of them on the floor among the dogs, he dismissed them, calling to one of the women to make them go to bed.

His wife Fflur was already busy with her women in another room; there was a clattering of dishes.

"And Cæsar?" said Caswallon. "I am told you know him? We can talk here."

He leaned against the back of the seat with his hands on his knees and looked at Tros confidently. His was the gift good breeding produces, of putting a guest mentally at ease. He spoke as to an equal, without any fuss of dignity.

"Has Commius not told you?" Tros asked, and Caswallon nodded.

"Commius also is a guest," he remarked. "But the chariot in which he rides will come more slowly. I ordered it."

"Commius," said Tros, "owes his life and his wealth to Cæsar. If I know anything of men, then Commius hates Cæsar, but is thinking of the Atrebates and the other Gauls. If Cæsar should invade this island, Commius might persuade

41

the Gauls to rise behind him. If that is not his plan, at least he thinks of it.

"He is a Gaul at heart, but afraid for his own skin and his own possessions. He does not dare speak openly, lest some one should betray his speech to Cæsar. Commius is a watchful and secretive man. He will stop at nothing to help the Gauls, provided he can save his own skin."

Caswallon nodded.

"And you?" he asked. "Did not Cæsar send you?"

"My father is a hostage in Cæsar's camp. I was to show the coast and the harbors to Caius Volusenus. I risk my own life and my father's; but I warn you to oppose Cæsar—to resist his landing in all ways possible."

"Why do you do that?" asked Caswallon. "If you were my own brother, or my wife's son, I could understand it. But you are neither a Briton nor a Gaul."

"Ask the druids," Tros answered. "They will tell you, if they see fit."

"You are a kind of druid?"

"No," said Tros.

"Perhaps you are a greater than a druid?"

"If you speak of my father—yes. As for me, I am young. Most of my life I have spent voyaging. In that way a man learns one thing, but not another. I am not deep in the Mysteries, but my father Perseus is a Prince of Samothrace."

Caswallon nodded again, but did not pretend to understand more than vaguely.

"I have heard of the Mysteries of Samothrace," he said respectfully. "I am a king. The druids say I am a good enough one. If Cæsar wants my kingdom, he must fight for it. I have said so to Commius."

"Have you quarreled with Commius?" asked Tros.

"No. He is my guest. He brought presents from Cæsar, a lot of trash that the women laughed at. I will send him back to Cæsar with some valuable gifts, to show him how a king is generous."

"Thus whetting Cæsar's appetite!" said Tros drily. "If you send a gift like that to Cæsar, lay your plans well, Caswallon. Good enough, if you bait an ambush for the Roman wolf. Be ready for him, that is all! Be sure what you are doing!"

The humorous, middle-aged-boyish face of Caswallon began to look puzzled. He was plainly meditating a blunt question, and yet too polite to ask it.

"Some men seek revenge, some fame, some riches,

some authority," he said at last, twisting at his long moustache. "All men whom I ever met sought something for themselves."

Whereat Tros grinned.

"I seek to keep my father's good opinion and to earn the praise of Those who sent me into Gaul," he answered.

"Nothing else?" asked Caswallon, watching his face steadily.

"I need a ship."

"I have ships."

"So has Cæsar. Big ones, that can out-fight yours."

Caswallon pushed a dog out of the way and stirred the fire with his foot.

"Do you propose to help me against Cæsar if I offer you a ship?" he asked, looking at Tros sideways, suddenly.

"No," said Tros. "I swear no oaths. I make no bargains. I will help you if I can, and freely. It is Cæsar who owes me a ship, having burnt mine. If a day comes when I think you owe mē anything, I will demand it of you."

"You will demand a ship of Cæsar?"

Tros laughed. "As well demand a fat lamb of a wolf! But you are not Cæsar. I would ask a debt of you, and you would pay it."

"If I thought I owed it, yes," said Caswallon. It was evident that he liked Tros finely. "I will give you a ship now, if you have need of it."

But Tros shook his head.

"What is the matter with my ships?" Caswallon asked him. There was challenge in his voice.

"You forget. My father is a hostage. I must set him free before I play my own hand."

"Yes. A man should do that. You want me to help you set your father free?" asked Caswallon, lowering his eyebrows. "How could I do that? My men would laugh at me, if I talked of invading Gaul! The druids would forbid it. Fflur would say no to it. Besides, I have never seen your father. Has he a claim on me?"

"No claim," Tros answered. "None. But Cæsar says he has a claim against you."

"He lies!" remarked Caswallon.

He himself did not look like a man who dealt in lies.

"And he will invade your island to levy tribute."

"It is I who levy tribute here!" Caswallon said slowly, scratching a dog's back with his foot.

He stared at the fire for about a minute, frowning.

43

"If you resolve to oppose Cæsar, will your men obey you?" wondered Tros.

"They have had to hitherto. I am the chief. There have been a few disputes, but I am more the chief than ever," he answered.

"Are you overconfident?" asked Tros. "Cæsar's method is to send his spies who promise big rewards and make atrocious threats, thus undermining a chief's authority."

"I have kept close watch on Commius."

"No doubt you have," said Tros. "Nevertheless, this night a woman offered me your kingdom if I would play Cæsar's game with her."

At that Caswallon suddenly threw off his thoughtful mood and laughed boisterously, hugely, spanking both knees with his hands so thunderously that the dogs yelped and Fflur came in with her wrists all white with meal to learn what the joke might be.

"Fflur—hah-hah-ho-ho-hoh!—yah-ha-ha-hah! Fflur, have you heard the latest? Britomaris' wife offers our kingdom to this man! What do you think of that?"

"I mentioned no name," said Tros.

"No! Hah-ha-ha-ho-hoh! That is a good one. Haw-haw-hah-hah-hoh! She hasn't a name *worth* mentioning! Hah-hah-hah! What say you, Fflur? Shall I put her in a sack and send her for a gift to Cæsar?"

"You know she is dangerous," his wife answered.

"She!" laughed Caswallon. "If she had a man like Tros here, she might be dangerous, but not with Britomaris! And if she were truly dangerous, she would have poisoned both of us—oh, years ago! I will let her try her blandishments on Cæsar."

"You are always overconfident," said Fflur, and left the room again, adding over her shoulder, "it is only thanks to me you are not poisoned."

Caswallon chuckled amiably to himself and shouted for some more mead. A woman brought two tankards full, and, as if it were a joke, he made her taste from both of them.

"She lives!" he laughed. "Tros, at the first sign of a bellyache call Fflur, who will give you stuff to make you vomit."

Tros laughed and drank quickly, for he was anxious to have more serious speech before Commius should arrive.

"Cæsar prepares a fleet and plans to sail for the coast of Britain before the equinox," he said abruptly.

Caswallon stiffened himself.

"How many men can he muster?"

"Many. But he has not ships enough for all, and he must also hold down the Gauls, who hate him. I think he will come with two legions, and perhaps five hundred cavalry."

"I laugh!" said Caswallon. "I will gather dogs enough to worry his two legions! Nay, the sheep shall chase him out of Britain!"

"Your lips laugh," said Tros, "but your eyes are thoughtful. My face is sober, but I laugh within. A deep plan pleases me. You have ships, but how big are they? And have you sailors for them?"

"I have three longships," said Caswallon, "that are rowed by twenty men, and each can carry fifty. Now and then they go a-fishing, so the crews are always ready. But do you think I will fight Cæsar on the sea? Not I! I went to sea once, as far as Gaul, and I vomited worse than Fflur makes me when she thinks I have been poisoned! I will fight Cæsar on dry land!"

"Where Cæsar will defeat you unless heaven intervenes!" said Tros grimly. "However, you could not fight Cæsar with three ships. Where are the ships?"

"In the river,* by the marsh edge, well hidden from the North Sea rovers."

"Could you send those ships, unknown to any one but you, around the coast, to a point that you and I will choose as the most dangerous landing place for Cæsar, and hide them near by at my disposal?"

Caswallon nodded, but the nod was noncommittal, not a promise.

"It is a long way by sea," he said slowly, as if he doubted that such a plan was feasible.

"Because, if you will do that," said Tros, "and if the crews of your three ships obey me, I believe I can wreck the whole of Cæsar's fleet and leave him at your mercy on the beach with his two legions. I can do it! I can do it! If I can only find a man who knows the tides."

"Ah!"

Caswallon sat bolt upright. Then he summoned his wife with a shout that made the dogs wake up and bark. She came and sat down on the seat beside him, her jewels gleaming in the firelight, but not more brilliantly than her eyes.

"I like this man. I like his speech," said Caswallon.

* The Thames—which was always *the* river.

"He is good," said Fflur, looking straight at Tros. "But he will not obey you. He has the eyes of a druid and a brow that is harder than bronze. He will never be a king, because none can serve themselves and make him take the blame. Nor will he ever be a slave, for none can tame him.

"He is like the wind that blows; if he blows your way, you may use him. He will tell no lies. He never thinks of treachery. But if he blows away from you, you can neither hold him nor call him back."

"So, Tros, now you know yourself," said Caswallon. "Fflur is always right."

Tros smiled, his lion's eyes half closing.

"I would like to know what she says of Commius," he answered.

"She says that he will surely betray me."

"If you let him," Fflur added.

"Mother of my sons, I will not let him!"

Tros smiled within himself and Fflur saw the change in his expression. She was very lovely when her gray eyes shone with hidden laughter. Suddenly, as if ashamed of a moment's mood, she put an arm around her husband's shoulder and nestled close to him.

"What is it I should hear?" she asked.

Tros repeated what he had said to Caswallon about the ships, and Fflur listened with her eyes closed. Her husband signaled to Tros to wait in silence for her answer. She sat quite still, with her head against the woodwork, hardly breathing.

"I see blood," she said at last, shuddering. She was not seeing with her eyes, for they were shut. "I see men slain—and doubts—and a disaster. But there is brightness at the farther side of it, and a year, or longer, but I think a year—and then more blood; and I do not quite see the end of that.

"There is another way than this one you propose, but it would lead to failure because of rivalry. This way is the best, because it gives the victor's crown to no man, yet it will succeed. But you—"

She opened her eyes slowly and looked straight at Tros.

"You will suffer. You will not return to Samothrace, although you will attempt it. In a way you will be a king, yet not a king, and not on land. More than one woman shall bless the day that you were born, and more than one woman shall hate you; and those that love you will come

46

very near to causing your destruction, whereas those who hate will serve your ends, though you will suffer much at their hands."

Conops stirred by the hearthside, prodding the fire with a charred stick, seeming to thrust at pictures that he saw within the embers. That was the only sound, until Caswallon spoke:

"I envy no man who shall have a kingdom, that is not a kingdom, on the sea. Fflur is always right. If you should suffer too much, Tros, Fflur shall find you a way of relief. I am your friend, and you are welcome."

"After a while he will go away, and he will not come back," said Fflur.

CHAPTER V

A PRINCE OF HOSTS

The Law is simple. There is nothing difficult about it. Why ask me to peer into your souls and say ye are good or evil? Judge ye for yourselves. Ye know your own hearts. Whoever could betray his host or his guest; whoever could misuse hospitality by treacherous betrayal of the secrets learned beneath a hospitable roof, that one is lower than any animal, he is capable of all treasons; he is vile, and virtue is not in him. He to whom hospitality is genuinely sacred, whom torture could not compel to yield the secrets learned by hearth and broken bread and mead, that one has manhood. He is capable of all the other virtues. He will be a god when his lives on the earth are finished.

FROM THE SAYINGS OF THE DRUID TALIESAN

THERE was a great shout at the gate and a thudding of hoofs on soft earth. The dogs awoke and barked with glaring eyes and their hair on end, as the other chariot brought Commius the Gaul. Some one struck the door three times with a sword-hilt and opened it.

In strode Commius with his cloak across the lower portion of his face, and paused a moment, blinking at the firelight. He seemed annoyed at the sight of Tros, but let his cloak fall and contrived to smile.

He was followed into the room by all the armed men who had been standing at the gate; they stacked their weapons in a corner after lifting their right hands one by one in salute to Caswallon.

"So this is your palace?" said Commius, glancing about him and assuming admiration.

Caswallon laughed.

"This is where we will eat and rest," he answered. "This belongs to Britomaris and Gwenhwyfar. Since they can not speak to me civilly, they pay me tribute nonetheless, they play the host from far off. They always go when I announce my coming. After I have gone, they say I stole the furniture! Yet they accept the gifts I leave. Be seated."

"Where *is* your palace?" Commius asked, taking the seat beside Tros after bowing with grave dignity.

"I have none," said Caswallon. "I have a home that Fflur keeps, where I give judgment."

"Where?" asked Commius, but Caswallon did not answer.

For excuse he found fault with the men, who were carrying in a long table and arranging it on trestles opposite the hearth. They worked clumsily, being evidently men of rank, not far below the chief himself in station, laughing when the women made fun of them.

When the table was set, and a heavy cloth laid on it, they dragged up a bench before the hearth and as many as could sat down on it, while the others sprawled on the floor between their legs.

Two of them were short and swarthy, but the others were tall, with long hair carefully combed and oiled; one man's hair was golden, and another's like spun flax. Not one but wore beautifully made brooches, and their arms were all covered with devices painted on with blue woad; they wore woolen breeches, and their legs were enclosed in leather stockings, cross-gartered to the thigh. Clean men, all of them, and courteously dignified, but thirsty and not at all retiring.

"Mead!" they shouted. "Where is the mead?"

And the women brought it in great brimming tankards.

They pledged the health of Fflur and of Caswallon; then, sending the tankards back to be refilled, they drank to Tros and to Commius, courteously wishing them a dozen sons apiece:

"Which will keep the good-wife busy," as one of them remarked.

"Aye," said another, "a childless woman is a restless
48

curse, so drink we to the midwife! If there were a son or two to this house, Britomaris would have more reason to call his wife his own! Hah-hah-hah-hah! Guest Tros, they saw thee track Gwenhwyfar to the herdsman's house—so says the charioteer who just brought Commius. Does he lie? Nay, out with it! All know her."

"They know more than I, then," Tros answered, and Fflur glanced approval. "My man Conops here attended that tryst. Let him answer for me."

"He has but one eye! Hah-hah-hah! A dozen pairs of eyes can watch Gwenhwyfar, and she will give them all the slip! Ho! Caswallon, what say you to it?"

"That you lack manners!" Caswallon answered. "I can throw the man who insults my guest as far as from here to the paling. This is Tros, who broke the ribs of Erbin. If I give him leave, he can break thine."

"Oh, well, I will save my ribs for another purpose. Let him have Gwenhwyfar! Whoever takes her from Britomaris does us all a service, for he will kill her very soon when he has found her out! And besides, without her Britomaris might become a man! Ho! I drink to the Lord Tros of the yellow eyes, who stole his shoulders from an oak tree, and who keeps a one-eyed servant lest the fellow see all that is happening in herdsmen's houses!"

"Ho-hah-hah-hah!" they chorused, and drank deep.

The women had to leave off loading food on to the table, to fill up their tankards, and they made so much noise that the children woke up and had to be bundled back to bed again behind a painted ox-hide curtain that cut off the far end of the room.

Then the meal was declared ready and they all fell to, Fflur sitting on the chief's right hand and Tros on his left hand, next to Commius, the other women serving and the dogs alert for bones or anything that anybody threw; for they cut the meat with their daggers, and tossed to the floor whatever they did not care to chew. There was a thunderstorm of growling underfoot and dog-fights most of the time, but no one took much notice, except to kick occasionally when the fighting was uncomfortably close.

There was bread, beef, mutton, pork, butter and cheese, onions, and a sort of cabbage boiled in milk, but no other vegetables. Conops received his food on a bench beside the hearth, and the women helped him to enough for three men. The Britons ate too steadfastly to do much talking, but Tros, possessing the Mediterranean temperament, had time for speech between the mouthfuls, and Commius had no appetite; so they exchanged words.

"Did Gwenhwyfar speak of me?" asked Commius.

"Aye, and of Cæsar."

A long pause, during which Tros listened to such sporadic conversation as passed between the Britons—mainly about horses and the scarcity of deer. One man, with his mouth full, urged Caswallon to summon all the able-bodied men to a wolf hunt.

"I will lead you to a wolf hunt soon enough," said Caswallon. "I will give you your bellyful of wolves."

Then:

"When do you return to Cæsar?" Commius asked.

"Soon," said Tros.

"You return with Caius Volusenus?"

"If he waits for me."

Caswallon did not appear to catch that conversation, but Fflur was watching Commius intently, and it may have been that second-sight involved the corollary of second-hearing. She glanced at her husband, making no remark, but he read some sort of warning in her eyes and nodded, looking then steadily during three slow breaths at Commius, slightly lowering his eyelids. Fflur appeared satisfied.

A moment later Caswallon left the table, muttering something about seeing whether the serfs were being fed. He strode outside and slammed the door behind him.

"He is forever thinking of the serfs," said Fflur. "That is why he is a great chief and none can overthrow him. Some of you think more of horses than of men and more of hunting than of other people's rights. And some of you are very clever"—she looked at Commius again—"but your chief is wiser than you all."

To please her, they began telling stories of Caswallon, pledging him in tankards full of mead as they recalled incident after incident, adding those imaginative touches that time lends to the deeds of heroes, until, if one had believed them, or even they had believed themselves, Caswallon would have seemed not much less than divine. He was a long time absent, and the glamour of him grew each minute.

Commius took advantage of the roars of laughter—as one man told how the chief had trapped a Norseman's ship that came a-raiding up the Thames, and how he had killed the pirate and enslaved the crew—to resume a conversation in low tones with Tros.

"I pledge you to keep this secret," he began.

But Tros was a man who made no rash pledges, so he held his peace.

"Do you hear me?" asked Commius. "Cæsar has a high opinion of me, and I of you. I trust you. I am minded to warn Cæsar that he will prod a wasps' nest if he sails for Britain. I have seen and heard enough. I will advise against invasion."

Tros's amber eyes observed the Gaul's face thoughtfully. He nodded, saying nothing, and helped himself to gravy, mopping it up with bread from the dish in front of him.

Commius waited for another roar of laughter, and resumed:

"I must go in haste to Cæsar. One of us should stay here. If I could say to Cæsar I have left you here to watch events and to spy out the strength and weakness, he would excuse the haste of my return. If you permit me to return with Caius Volusenus in your place, I will use my influence to set your father free."

Tros kept silence, munching steadily. After a minute Commius nudged him, and their eyes met.

"You agree?" he asked. "I pledge myself to set your father free, and to warn Cæsar not to invade Britain."

"If you heard a man warn the winter not to come; and if you heard him promise to pull Cæsar's teeth, how much of it would you believe?" asked Tros.

"Then you prefer not to trust me?"

"Oh, I trust you. A man is what he is. I trust you to work for Commius. But if I should trust you with my father's life, I should be a worse fool than even you suppose."

Commius' face darkened.

"I have influence with Cæsar," he said grimly.

"And I none," Tros answered. "Yet I will play a bolder hand than yours against him. Each to his own way, Commius!"

"Remember, I pledged you to secrecy!" the Gaul retorted.

"Hah! When you have my pledge, you may depend on me," said Tros. "My tongue is mine!"

Commius' eyes glittered coldly.

"I have seen men with their tongues torn out for saying less than you have said," he answered.

Caswallon entered, standing for a moment with the moonlight at his back, until they yelled to him to shut the door and keep the bats out. He strode to the fire and threw a faggot on. His eyes looked full of laughter.

"Commius," he said, "I go north in the morning. Will you come with me?"

"I have a boil," said Commius. "It irks me to ride in chariots; and I would as soon die now as try to sit a horse before the boil is healed."

Caswallon had to turn his back to hide some sort of emotion.

"You must be my guest then in my absence," he said over his shoulder.

"You are a prince of hosts," Commius answered, bowing and smiling leanly.

"Then when I return after two or three days, I will find you here?"

"By all means," said Commius.

There was a gleam of something like excitement in his eyes.

"You know this is Britomaris' house," Caswallon went on. "I have sent word to him that I shall leave at dawn. He and his wife Gwenhwyfar will be here soon after daybreak."

Commius was breathing very slowly. Almost the only sound came from a dog that cracked a bone under the table.

"Is my meaning clear to you?" Caswallon asked. "Britomaris pays tribute, but he is not my friend. You say you are my friend."

"Never doubt it. I am proud to be," said Commius.

"And you are my guest—here—wherever I may be. Britomaris will try to plot with you against me. Will you be for me, or for Britomaris—and Gwenhwyfar?"

"Over and above all laws is that of hospitality," said Commius without a moment's hesitation. "Even if my sympathy were not yours, as I think you know it is, I must nevertheless uphold you while I am your guest."

"Good," said Caswallon, turning with his back to the hearth and his hands behind him, legs well apart to avoid a dog that had taken sanctuary between his feet to gnaw a bone in safety. "I call you all to witness how I trust our friend, Lord Commius. I bid you all to trust him in like manner—exactly in like manner."

Commius stood up and bowed, and the men who sat at table murmured his name politely, raising their tankards to drink to him. But their eyes were on their chief, although no sign that a stranger could have noticed passed between them. Two or three times Commius looked as if about to speak, but he thought better of it, and it was Tros who spoke next:

"I am weary. Do the Britons never sleep?"

"I had forgotten that," said Caswallon. "Aye, we had better sleep. Do we? We are the soundest sleepers this side of the grave! But Lud pity those who sleep a minute later than I do in the morning, for I will prod them out o' blanket with a spear point! So away with all the kitchen-stuff, and one last drink!"

The women cleared away the dishes and the cloth, but left the table, for two men needed that to sleep on. The others laid their blankets on the floor, quarreling a little as to who had precedence.

Tros received two huge blankets and a pillow from Fflur, who led him and Conops to an inner room where she kissed him good night.

"Is your man with that one eye watchful?" she asked.

"Better than a dog!" said Tros.

"Bid him guard you against Commius. The Gaul will lie on the fireside seat in the outer room, but the others will sleep like dead men. I know murder when I see it in a man's eyes. Be sure he means to kill you one way or another. He believes you know too much about him."

"I fear no knife of his," said Tros.

"Yet you fear," she answered. "What is it?"

"I fear lest he will run to Caius Volusenus, and cross to Gaul, telling Cæsar I have joined with your husband. I fear for my father's life. Commius would sell me and my father, and another dozen like us, for a pat on the back from Cæsar."

"You need not fear," she answered. "Caswallon is awake. Commius will not return to Gaul—not yet. But be on guard against his knife, if he ever suspects that we suspect him."

She spread Tros's bed for him with her own hands, and called to one of the women to bring a pile of fleeces for Conops, bidding him spread them before the door as soon as it was shut.

"So you may both sleep," she said, smiling, "and if one tries to open in the night he must awaken Conops. Can you shout loud?" she asked.

"Aye, like a sailor!" Conops assured her with a nod.

"Shout then, and at the first alarm; and if the intruder takes flight, go to sleep again. Let there be no slaying in my house."

CHAPTER VI

CONCERNING A BOIL AND COMMIUS

It is wiser to take a liar at his word and oblige him to eat his lies, than to denounce him and too soon expose his enmity. It is wiser to seem to believe than to boast of your unbelief. Lies, like the moles, can burrow faster than ye dig. It is wiser to let them creep into the open.

FROM THE SAYINGS OF THE DRUID TALIESAN

ALMOST the next that Tros knew, day was breaking through the shutter chinks and there was a great row in the outer room—shouts, oaths and laughter. Caswallon was keeping his promise to rouse late sleepers with a spear point. Dog barks and the high-pitched laugh of children added to the din. The table upset with a crash. A dog yelped. Then there came a succession of grunts and thuds as one man after another was thrown, laughing and protesting, through the front door.

"Are we all awake?" cried Caswallon. "Come and wrestle with me, Tros! Let us see if your back is stronger than I can break!"

So Tros rubbed the sleep out of his eyes, and went and wrestled with him on the dew-soaked grass before the door, two dozen men admiring; for the horse-grooms and the herdsmen came and looked on, laughing like lunatics and offering to bet their freedom on the British chief.

But neither had the best of it, and they were locked in a grunting knot of arms and legs when Fflur came and summoned them to breakfast. Caswallon's oldest son, aged sixteen, promised on his honor to break Tros's neck the moment he was old enough.

"Gods! But he will have to fight a man!" laughed Caswallon, rubbing his woad-stained skin. "Yours is a neck worth breaking, Tros!"

They washed in tubs of water that the women set outside the door, combed their hair carefully, and went in to the business of eating, which was serious, devotional and too faithfully performed to allow much conversation. Commius, making notes on tablets, which he thrust cautiously into his bosom, was the last to the table and the first to use his mouth for anything but eating:

"You Britons," he said, "are you irreligious nowadays? In Gaul, our people all worship at sunrise. That is the first act of the day."

"Before strangers?" asked Caswallon. "No wonder the Romans have subdued you."

"What can the observance of religion have to do with that?" asked Commius.

"All," said Caswallon, "everything. If an enemy learns your thoughts, he is a fool if he can't throw you down and pin you under him. Religion not kept secret is weakness. Tell me *my* thoughts, Commius!"

Tros chuckled. Commius assumed the vaguely pained look of a financier who discovers that some one knows as much as he does. Caswallon studying him shrewdly between mouthfuls, which he washed down with beakers of warm milk, proceeded to amuse himself.

"You tell me you have a boil. Then I know where to kick you, don't I?"

"Would you kick your guest?" asked Commius.

"No," said Caswallon, "and I would kill the man who did. But let us suppose you were my secret enemy; for I have met such men, who spoke me fair and did me evil when my back was turned.

"Let us suppose *you* were my secret enemy. I know you have a boil. What would be easier than to lance that boil for you, and to put a little gangrene on the knife? You see, two can play at being secret enemies!

"It is just so with religion, which is why the druids keep it secret, and why we practise it in secret, and why Cæsar hates the druids, and why I like them. Cæsar never conquered Gaul until he slew the druids first. He will never conquer me, because he does not know my thoughts. Tell me my true thoughts, Commius!"

But before Commius could answer, Fflur put a word in:

"Ah! But what if the boil were feigned?"

She did not look at Commius; she was putting salt on an enormous skillet-full of fried eggs that one of the women had brought for her inspection.

"If the boil were feigned," said Caswallon. "Bah! What fool would pretend to have a boil? The truth would be too easy to discover. A dangerous man would pretend to have the toothache, or the bellyache. We risk offending the honorable Commius if we carry such a theme too far.

55

And by the way, Commius, shall I send for a druid to come and make you easier? They are very clever with their little knives."

"No," Commius answered. "It will burst soon of its own accord."

Followed boasting with excruciating details, by a man who claimed that he had ridden from Cair Lunden all the way to Pevensey, with boils so bad that, although he was weak with pain, a horse could not throw him because he had stuck to the saddle.

And that naturally led to rival reminiscences, including one by Tros, concerning a man who grew such calluses from friction on a rower's bench that when he was ashore, running away from King Ptolemy's press-gang, six arrows stuck into him like feathers in a bird's tail without his even knowing it.

So breakfast broke up in a storm of anecdotes, not all of them polite, and Commius was able to avoid attention to himself by simply keeping silence.

Then there was a clatter of hoofs and wheels outside, and a dozen serfs entered to carry out the bedding and other luggage, while Caswallon and his friends went outside to inspect the horses.

There were ten magnificent gray and white teams yoked to chariots, whose sides were built of wickerwork and wheels of bronze; and there were twelve more horses for the escort, mostly stallions, squealing and rearing with excitement.

Caswallon mounted a gray stallion and put him through his paces while the luggage chariots were being loaded, exhibiting such horsemanship as made the sea-wise Tros gasp, until the owner of the horse complained that there would be no strength left in the animal and Caswallon, jumping the horse over a chariot, vaulted to the ground beside him.

There was very little leave-taking from Commius, who stood in the door and bowed his pleasantest, pretending he was sorry not to make the journey with them. The only man he had much conversation with was Conops, to whom he gave a gold coin surreptitiously; but Conops, thanking him effusively, displayed it in his right palm so that Tros and the rest might see and draw their own conclusions.

Fflur did not kiss Commius, although from the hostess a kiss was customary. Caswallon shook him by the hand, signing to his wife and children and the other women to make haste into the chariots. His last remark sounded almost like a warning:

"Remember, Commius; you are my guest. Britomaris and Gwenhwyfar pay me tribute. They are not my friends."

Then they were off, with Tros up beside Caswallon and Conops on the floor, bracing his feet against the chariot's wicker sides that squeaked as Caswallon wheeled the team and sent it headlong at the open gate, with dogs barking, serfs shouting, the rattle and thump of the other chariots wheeling into column one by one, and then the thunder of the hoofs of the escort kicking up the dust a hundred yards behind.

For a long while Caswallon drove as if driving were life's one employment and speed the apex of desire, stooping to watch how the horses placed their feet. He never once glanced back at Fflur, who drove her own chariot with equal skill, her long hair flowing like a banner in the morning breeze and the heads of three children bobbing up and down beside her. At last he eased the pace a little and glanced at Tros sidewise, smiling:

"There will be fun with Commius," he remarked. "I like to see a fox caught in a trap. He will plot with Britomaris, who does exactly what Gwenhwyfar tells him, as long as she is there to make him do it. That will be treachery, he being my guest. Some men of mine, and a druid, will pick a quarrel with him. He having been my guest, they will spare his life. Alive, I can use him. He is no good dead. And they will spare Britomaris and Gwenhwyfar because I have so orderd it, for I can use them also.

"But they will fasten the fetters on Commius, and the druid will look for the boil, since it is his duty to attend to that. Finding none—the fool should have bethought him of a bellyache—the druid will denounce him as a liar. We have failings, but there is this about us Britons: When we have proved a man a liar, we disbelieve whatever else he says. Thus the harm that Commius has done by too much talking when he thought my back was turned will be undone."

"I see you work craftily," Tros observed.

"A man must, if he proposes to remain a king," said Caswallon. "Kingship is the first of all the crafts. This Cæsar who had conquered Gaul is bold and treacherous and fortunate and rather clever; but is he crafty?"

"Very," Tros answered. "If kinging is a craft, he is the master craftsman of them all."

57

"Has he a Fflur?"

"No. Women are his tools, or an amusement."

"Then I will beat him!" said Caswallon.

And at last he looked back at his wife, who laughed and waved a hand to him.

"You owe your life to Fflur," he remarked. "You sleep deep, friend Tros, and with the shutter off the thong—a compliment to me, no doubt, but dangerous! Commius stirred three times. Twice he was at your window. He carries poison with him, which he bought from a woman near the seashore where he landed when he first came. One drop on a man's lips in the night—"

"Who watched him?"

"Fflur heard him and she roused me. So it happened there were two kings at your window in the night—and twice!—each lying to the other as to how he came to be there! We agreed that from that spot there was the best view of the moon's eclipse, and that the cry of a strange night-bird had awakened both of us."

"There is no reason why Commius should fear me," said Tros. "I am not *his* enemy."

"There is no reason why Gwenhwyfar should fear me, and I am not *her* enemy," Caswallon answered. "But, man or woman, it is all one when they plan treachery. They are like a wolf then. None can say why they pursue this victim and not that one.

"But perhaps it would have suited Commius to have it said I poisoned you. You were sent by Cæsar, Tros. Thus Cæsar would have a plausible excuse for quarrel with me. But let us hear what the one-eyed fellow says."

Conops exhibited the gold coin, tossed it in air and missed it as the chariot bumped a hillock. They had to stop to let him recover it, and the escort galloped up full pelt to find out what was wrong.

"He said," Conops remarked when they were under way again, and he spat on the coin and polished it, "he said, if I should remember to tell him at the earliest moment all that is said and all that is done while my master is out of his sight, he for his part will remember to advance my cause with Cæsar, who has many lucrative employments in his gift."

Tros laughed. Caswallon glanced down at Conops half-a-dozen times.

"I will buy that man from you," he said at last. "How much in gold will you take for him? Or shall I swap you three for one?"

"He is a free man," Tros answered.

"Oh. Then I would kill him if he offered to change masters."

Caswallon lapsed into one of his silent moods, merely waving with his arm occasionally as they skirted mud-and-wattle hamlets, beautifully built, invariably fenced about with heavy tree-trunks, clean and prosperous, but containing no stone buildings and no roofs other than thatch.

There were sheep and cattle everywhere, and great numbers of horses, all carefully watched and guarded against wolves by herdsmen armed with spears; but there was surprisingly little grain, or stubble to show where grain had been, and such as there was, was fenced as heavily as the villages.

The main road seemed to avoid the hamlets purposely, but here and there the villagers seemed to have repaired it, and wherever there was much mud it was rendered passable by tree-trunks felled across it. There were no bridges whatever, but the fords were good and were evidently kept in order.

They changed horses at a village that Caswallon called a town, where a hundred armed men, very variously dressed, lined up to salute the chief in front of a big thatched house with painted mud walls. They saluted him more or less as an equal, calling him and Fflur by their names and gathering around the chariots when the formal shouting with their spears in air was finished.

The man who owned the house was a long, lean, fox-haired veteran with a naked breast covered with woad designs, whose wife was young enough to be his daughter. But she knew how to play the hostess and to command the village women, who brought out bread and meat and mead for every one, turning the half-hour wait into a picnic.

They all seemed much more impressed with Tros than with Caswallon and wanted to know whether he was one of Cæsar's generals or an ambassador.

But Caswallon warned Tros to keep silence, so he pretended not to understand their speech; instead of talking, he and Conops kissed the girls who carried mead to them, and that started a kissing riot that kept everybody busy, while Caswallon talked in undertones with the red-haired man and the group that stood about him leaning on their spears.

Then Caswallon mounted the rehorsed chariot and addressed the crowd, standing very splendidly and making his voice ring until even the giggling girls grew silent and the children gaped at him.

"Cæsar will not come yet; but he will surely come!" he told them. "Get ye to work and harvest all the corn. Make double store of dried meat. Increase the sheaves of arrows. Mend the chariots, and let no blacksmith put on fat in idleness!

"When the invader comes there shall be a sudden call to arms, but until then, he who wastes time leaning on his spear is a traitor to his wife and children! When Cæsar comes, he will lay waste the land, as he has laid all Gaul waste; he feeds his horses in the standing corn and burns what he does not need. So get ye the harvest in! It will be time enough to lean on spears when I send warning."

The man with red hair showed his teeth and leered with puckered eyes, but Caswallon beckoned him and clapped him on the back, pulling him up into the chariot beside him, bidding him make friends with Tros "who knows Cæsar well."

"Tros, this is Figol, whose grandfather came like you from over the sea, although from another quarter. He is a better man than Britomaris, for he looks like a lean fox but he acts like a fat Briton, whereas Britomaris looks like a Briton but acts like a fox. Figol pays me tribute of all between this forest and where Britomaris' land begins; and the old fox doesn't cheat me more than I permit for the sake of his young wife!"

With that he lifted Figol with one arm and hoisted him over the chariot-side into the crowd, waving him a merry good-by, and was off almost before Conops could scramble into the chariot. They plunged into a forest at the outskirts of the village and drove amid gloomy oaks for leagues on end, with clearings here and there, and well used tracks at intervals on either hand that evidently led to villages.

Caswallon had lapsed into silence again, for a long time studying the new team and then whistling to himself. He seemed to think he was alone, until suddenly he turned to Tros and grinned at him.

"Figol is a fox, but I out-fox him!" he remarked. "If I had let him keep a hundred men at hand, he would have dared me to come and fetch the tribute that is nine months in arrear! He would have talked to them against me, instead of making ready against Cæsar. But now they will get the harvest in, and when they have it I will have my share! We will deal with Cæsar when the time comes."

"When Cæsar does come, you will find he has made all ready in advance," said Tros.

"This is a good kingdom," said Caswallon. "Let Cæsar come, and he shall have a bellyful of fighting for it! But if I should raise an army too soon, they would grow tired of waiting; and first they would race the horses on the downs, and then they would drink all the mead, carousing through the night.

"And after that, because there was no more mead, they would say I was mistaken about Cæsar. Whereafter they would laugh a great deal, and they would all go home. I know my Britons. And when Cæsar came there would be no army.

"Some day you shall see my town, Caïr Lunden, and when you have stayed there awhile you will understand how crafty a king must be, if he is to earn—and also get—the tribute money."

"Crafty!" said Tros. "Are you crafty enough to trust me to tell Cæsar that if he comes soon, with a small force, he will find you unprepared?"

"Fflur trusts you. She knows," Caswallon answered. "I never knew her to be wrong in the matter of trusting a man."

CHAPTER VII

GOBHAN AND THE TIDES

Knowledge? Any fool can have it. But wisdom, with which to interpret knowledge and to use it, that is something that each one must learn for himself in the school of existence. It is a mark of the wise man that he can listen to fools and learn from them, although their speech is folly.

FROM THE SAYINGS OF THE DRUID TALIESAN

THE sun had crossed the meridian about two hours before, and they were still cantering through lush, green forest when Tros smelled tidewater and nudged Conops, who smelled it too and grinned. Four of the escort had been cantering behind them for an hour, screening the view down the track to the rear, and it was not until the horsemen maneuvered into single file to avoid a mud hole that Tros knew the other chariots were missing. When he asked where they had disappeared to, Caswallon merely motioned toward the northwest and said:

"Home. Cair Lunden."

"And we?"

"I will show you the longships."

But first they met Gobhan, in a house of logs and mud that overlooked long marshes where the snipe swarmed between the forest and the river Thames. In places the forest crept down almost to the water's edge; and there were creeks innumerable, crowded with wildfowl that filled the air with mournful longshore music. There was another huge forest on the far side, more than two miles away. The river rolled between the mud-flats, lonely and immense, with only one small boat in sight, working its way with oars and sail across the tide.

"Our weakness!" said Caswallon, pulling up the team where the trees ended and they could see the vast expanse of river. "If Cæsar only knew this river he could sail up with his hundred ships and have us at his mercy! The Northmen come now and then, which is why we hide our ships."

There they left the chariot, with the horses nibbling at the trees, and walked, all seven in single file with Caswallon leading, toward the mud-and-log house in the foreground, that stood with its front door almost in the marsh. There was smoke rising from a hole in the wooden roof, but no sign of an inhabitant until they reached the front by a narrow foot-path, and Caswallon shouted:

"Gobhan! Come out there, Gobhan!"

Almost instantly through the door showed a face that made Tros want to laugh, but that rather frightened the four members of the escort. It was comical, and yet immensely dignified, without a single feature that explained the dignity, old beyond calculation, toothless, nearly bald—there was a forehead that mounted so high it resembled a waxen skullcap with a gray-haired tassel on the top—and bearded, but with the beard enclosed in a leather bag and tied back behind the ears. The nose nearly met the chin. There were no eyebrows; a pair of lashless eyes as bright as a weasel's peeped alert and inquisitive from sunken sockets.

"What do you want?" the face asked, mumbling the words because of toothlessness.

Then a body followed the face; lean, scrawny, twisted, suffering apparently from ague caught from the marsh. He was dressed in a long brown smock with a leather apron over it and nothing to proclaim his rank in life except a plaited woolen girdle such as druids wore. He showed no respect for Caswallon, but stood and looked at him, his hands shaking, his hollow cheeks moving as he worked his gums.

"Such a host you are, Gobhan! Such welcome you offer us! Such courtesy!" said Caswallon, striking an attitude.

The ancient addressed as Gobhan grinned at last—if it was a grin that quaked among the wrinkles. He muttered something, shrugged his bony shoulders, turned, and led the way into the house. Caswallon strode in after him and Tros followed; Conops would have followed Tros through a furnace door, whatever his private feelings; but the escort withdrew toward the chariot, expressing strange emotions.

"Wizard!" was a word that one man used; and another one said something about "dirty magic and abominations."

The interior of the house—it had only one room—was almost as remarkable as its owner. There were two truckle-beds at one end, with a table between them and two stools, but the whole of the rest of the interior was given up to furnaces and clay retorts, instruments for measuring, benches piled with jars, mortars, ladles and a workbench down the middle of the room on which were appliances whose object Tros could not guess. The room was not exactly in confusion, but there was hardly standing room for the three who did not belong there.

Over in a corner a blind man clothed in skins plied an enormous bellows steadily, as if he did it in his sleep. There was the roar of a charcoal furnace and the stench of heated metal, but no sign of anything being made, although there were an anvil and great tongs and hammers near the door.

The owner of the place made no remark but simply waited in front of Caswallon, holding his apron to keep his hands from shaking and constantly moving his toothless gums. He seemed neither afraid, nor yet pleased to see his visitors.

"So now you see Gobhan," said Caswallon. "Look at him! My people wanted to roast him alive in his own furnace for wizardry; but I said no to it, for one reason and another. It cost me quite a quarrel with the younger druids, who proclaimed him an outlaw from their Mysteries, which I daresay is more or less true. And there is trouble now and then because the Northmen come to him, and he will not see the difference between a Briton and a foreigner, but teaches anything he knows to any one who asks him.

"If the druids know more than he does, I will say this: They conceal it! I never could have saved him, if I hadn't thought of using him to trap a longship full of Northmen, who sailed up the Thames to plunder Lunden.

"I sent a man to fall into their hands and tell them about Gobhan; so they turned aside to steal him, meaning to take him to their own country to teach the trick of metal to their shipwrights. And I caught them there, yonder where the creek flows through the rushes.

"We drew a chain across the creek behind them, and they burned their own ship rather than let us capture it, cattle and all; the forehold of the ship was full of bulls. It took three to kill the last man; never were such fighters! I would have saved him; I would have given him a wife and let him live in Lunden; but I could not reach his side before they ran a spear under his armpit and drowned him. He was fighting waist-deep when he fell.

"Northmen are thieves, and they come a-roving summer or winter, whenever they're least expected; but the fault I find with them is wearing armor, which is not the way a man should fight. We Britons fight nearly naked, not esteeming cowardice."

"You have brought me a long way to see Gobhan!" Tros interrupted drily.

"Aye, I was coming to that. You spoke of Cæsar's fleet, you remember. Now Gobhan owes his life to me. If you can understand that noise he makes between his gums, he shall tell you things that Cæsar does not know. Gobhan knows the Book of Domnu."*

"Does he understand the tides?" asked Tros, nudging Conops.

In Samothrace, where he came from, they knew more of "Domnu" and the inner meanings of the word than any druid did.

"Tides, full moons and the weather—he knows it all," said Caswallon. "Make shift to understand his yammerings, and I will send him south for you in one of the longships. He shall lie in wait at Hythe."

"There are strange tides around this island," said Tros, observing Gobhan closely.

* The very ancient sea-god of the Britons.

64

"Aye," said Caswallon. "Our tides puzzle the Northmen badly. And the worst of it is, that this old wizard teaches them as readily as he teaches us, when they can find him! He has no discretion. I have often wondered why I did not let my people burn him."

"Let me talk with him," said Tros, beckoning the old man.

Together they went and sat on logs up-ended near the furnace, where Tros could draw patterns with his finger in the charcoal-dust on the floor. Caswallon stood and watched them, with his legs astride and hands behind his back.

The only light in that corner came from the door and in a red glow from the charcoal furnace that the bellows-man was tending. Tros's eyes glowed like a lion's, but most of his bulk was lost in shadow, as his fingers roughly traced an outline of the shore of Kent and the coast of Gaul with the narrow sea between.

The old man wiped it out and drew a better one, and for a long while Tros studied that, until at last he laid a finger on the spot where he supposed the quicksands lay.* At that Gobhan nodded and looked strangely pleased. The ague left him. He began to grow excited.

Mumble-mumble— Tros could hardly understand a word of it, until Gobhan prodded the blind old bellows-man with a long stick. Then the purring roar of the furnace ceased, and the blind man sat beside them to interpret the toothless noises into more or less intelligible speech.

The blind man seemed to know as much as Gobhan did about the tides and winds and weather; as the two of them became aware of Tros's inborn understanding of the sea, they vied in their enthusiasm to explain to him, clutching him, striking each other's wrists, interrupting each other, croaking and squeaking like a pair of rusty-throated parrots, answering his questions both at once and abusing each other when he failed to understand exactly— Caswallon smiling all the while as if he watched a dog-fight.

Sun and moon—there was interminable talk about them. Gobhan suddenly wiped out the channel map and drew a diagram of sun and moon and earth, with circles to describe their courses.

But the blind man did not need the diagram to argue

* The Goodwins.

65

from; he used his two fists for earth and moon, and Gobhan's head to represent the sun, gesticulating with his foot to show the action of the tides as their positions changed.

Once in his excitement he would have burned himself by getting too close to the furnace, but Gobhan hurled him away, and the argument resumed with both men kneeling as if they were throwing dice, and Tros's heavy face, chin on hand, two feet from theirs as he leaned forward, studying first one and then the other, then the diagrams that Gobhan traced and the blind man kept on wiping out because he could not see, and did not need them.

At last Gobhan struck the blind man into silence and sat still with his eyes shut, counting days and hours, checking them off on his fingers; and by that time it was the blind man who appeared to have the ague, for he was sweating and trembling with irrepressible excitement. Gobhan on the other hand had grown as calm as if he were saying prayers.

"Mumble-mumble."

"Eight days," interpreted the blind man. Gobhan nodded.

Tros rose, facing Caswallon.

"What present shall I make?" he asked.

"None," said Caswallon. "If you give them money they will have no further use for you. And as for their needs, they eat at my cost. Have you learned what you came for?"

"Aye, and more," said Tros.

"I will send them both to Hythe to await you there, in the harbor with the three ships," said Caswallon.

And then Conops entered; he had slunk out to explore the marsh, and came back with slime up to his knees, resheathing the long knife in the red sash at his waist.

"Master, I have seen the ships. They are no good," he remarked in Greek. "They are too long for their beam, too high at bow and stern to steer in a breeze; and they would swallow a quartering sea and lie down under it as a Briton swallows mead, or my name isn't Conops!"

"That is their affair," said Tros.

"They are leaky," Conops insisted. "Their seams are as open as the gratings on a prison window. I vow I could stick my fingers in! I would as soon put to sea in an orange-basket. Some of the cordage is made of wool, and some of leather! Some of it is good flax, but you never saw such patchwork!"

66

The blind man returned to his bellows. Gobhan peered into a clay crucible that was set in the charcoal furnace, shaking again with ague and not pleased, because the crucible had cooled. Both of them appeared to have forgotten Tros, and they took no notice whatever of Caswallon who beckoned to Tros to come out and see the three longships.

They lay berthed in the mud up a creek well concealed from the river by a bank of rushes. There were branches fastened to their masts to render them invisible against the trees. They were very small, but not ill-built, and they were much more seaworthy than Conops made them out to be.

The woolen cordage Conops had described turned out to be the lashings that held in place the tent-cloth with which they were covered, but it was true they were moored with horse-hide warps made fast to the nearest trees. Nor were they very leaky; they were well tarred, and a day's work on their seams by half a dozen men would make them fit for sea.

"Where are the crews?" asked Tros.

"Doubtless carousing!" said Caswallon. "It needs a month to sober them when they have beaten off a North Sea rover. Three weeks gone, the three of them together sunk a longship down at Thames-mouth, and I paid them well for it."

"There is need for haste," said Tros.

"There shall be haste! I will promise them another big reward. And there will be Gobhan with them, whom they fear a great deal more than they fear me—for they who follow the sea are bigger fools than they who live on land!

"I will say that if they fail to reach Hythe and if they fail to obey you, Gobhan shall turn them all into fish. They will believe that, and they are too familiar with fish to wish to grow scales and fins! The rest is for you to contrive."

"Very well," said Tros. "Understand me: I do not know what the gods will have to say about all this. The gods prevent many things that men design; but I think the gods are not in league with Cæsar. Unless Cæsar's cold heart changes, I am likely to be pilot when he sets sail for the coasts of Britain.

"I will lead him to the high cliffs that are nearest to the coast of Gaul, and if it may be, I will wreck him on the quicksands in mid-channel. I will surely do that if I understand the tides aright and if the wind should favor.

"In that case, you and I will never meet again, because, of all the certainties the surest is, that if I set Cæsar on the quicksands he will slay me. And we may miss the quicksands; or Cæsar's men may see the water boiling over them and steer clear.

"So watch for his fleet, and be ready with an army to oppose his landing. And if he succeeds in landing, count on me nevertheless, provided you are sure that Gobhan and these three ships are safe in Hythe, and that the crews will obey me when I come."

"Tros!" said Caswallon, and seized him by the right hand.

Their eyes met for the space of seven breaths.

Then the Chief spoke again:

"You are a man. But I do not know yet why you do this."

"I have not yet done it!" Tros answered.

"Nevertheless, in my heart I know you will attempt it. Why? What am I to you? And what is Britain to you?"

"What is fire to water? Tros answered. "One stream serves as well as the next when it comes to checking forest fires. If you were invading Cæsar's rightful heritage, then I would side with him against you! I am a free man, Caswallon. A free man mocks himself, who sits in idleness while Cæsar burns up freedom!"

"I see you are not a man to whom I may offer a reward," said Caswallon, gripping his hand again. "But I am your friend, Tros; Fflur is also your friend."

"I am glad of it," Tros answered. "But be careful not to judge too hastily, for thus far we have only dealt in words. And next, I must trade words with Cæsar, who values nothing except deeds that glorify him. Remember: I will tell Cæsar that if he comes swiftly with a small force he will catch you unprepared. First then, prove me a false prophet and a liar! Then call me friend—if both of us deserve it—when we meet again!"

CHAPTER VIII

AN INTERVIEW NEAR A DRUID'S CAVE

Treason betrays itself. There was never a treachery yet that did not yield its secret. But not to the treacherous. He who is blinded by his own treacheries, how shall he read and understand the signs in others? In the presence of integrity treason must boast; it can not keep silence.

FROM THE SAYINGS OF THE DRUID TALIESAN

TROS drove back in the night, with a purse of gold at his waist that Caswallon gave him for expenses, in a chariot horsed with four of the finest stallions Britain could produce, driven by a long-haired charioteer whose pride was that no chariot had ever overtaken him since he had been made chief's messenger.

They were followed by a dozen riders, partly for protection from wolves that bayed in the forests all night long, but equally for the important business of compelling wayside autocrats to furnish fresh teams when required and to provide their best, instead of leading out old lame horses.

Even so, because of a bent bronze chariot-wheel, that caught between two sunken tree-trunks in a dark ford, and the time it took to find and awaken a blacksmith, and the time he took to get the wheel hot, straighten and replace it, the sun was up an hour before they came to Britomaris' house, where the charioteer shouted for a fresh team.

There was a rabble of men and women in the yard, and of all sorts, light- and dark-skinned, tall and stocky, some so dwarfish as to seem deformed. And they were not disposed to make way for the chariot, or to bring out horses at the charioteer's command.

Some one shouted for Britomaris; but it was Gwenhwyfar who came to the door and stood looking at Tros long and sullenly before she spoke.

"You? You dare to come here?" she said at last, curling her lip and glowering under lowered eyelids.

"Horses!" roared the charioteer, but she acted as if she had not heard him, and the mounted men rode off to the stables to help themselves.

"Look!" said Gwenhwyfar pointing. "These are my people. They have come to see the shame you brought on Britomaris and on me! Dog—that have slept in my house and betrayed me to Caswallon! Dog—that are servant of Cæsar and false to Cæsar, too! Insolent dog—with the eyes of a druid, the teeth of a wolf and the breath and the speech of a viper!"

There was none, now the escort were gone, except Conops, crouching in the chariot, to protect Tros from violence. Conops loosed his long knife, for the crowd

69

looked ugly, and the charioteer felt at the reins to get the stallions on their toes—ready to wheel them and charge through the crowd at a moment's warning.

"Draw your sword, master!" Conops whispered.

But Tros touched him on the back to calm him.

"Where is Commius?" he asked.

"Aye! Where is Commius! He was my guest. Who betrayed him?"

Gwenhwyfar sneered and tossed the hair out of her eyes.

"Commius, who was your friend! Commius, who ate at the same table with you in this, my house! Commius, who slept under my roof! Where is Commius, whom you betrayed?"

"I asked, where is he!" Tros had a voice like rolling thunder when the mood was on him.

Gwenhwyfar looked startled, but her eyes glared defiance.

"Go ask the druids! Go! You shall eat no more in my house! Drive him forth, men! Drive him!"

She threw out both arms in a gesture that condemned him to mob mercy, and the crowd hardly hesitated. Some one threw a javelin, that missed and stuck quivering in the house wall; and before the twang of that ceased, Tros was almost off his feet from the sudden jerk as the charioteer wheeled his team and sent it headlong at the crowd. There were no scythes in the sockets on the axles, or he would have mowed a dozen of them.

"Kill him!" screamed Gwenhwyfar.

But the words froze on her lips; for the escort arrived on the scene from behind the house, charging with lowered spears, riding fresh, corn-fed, frantic horses they had seized. No one was slain. The crowd scattered and ran, those who had weapons throwing them away; but many were knocked down, and some were soundly thumped with spear butts.

The charioteer laughed and wheeled the team around again to face the door, while four of the escort went to bring a fresh team for the chariot. They were laughing, and not in the least annoyed by the disturbance; two of the remaining escort chaffed Gwenhwyfar mercilessly, calling her "Caswallon's scornling," but she ignored them as if they were a mile away. Her whole hatred was aimed at Tros, concentrated on him, glaring, venomous.

"Do you love your father as you love your friends?" she asked.

But Tros, listening with both ears, pretended to be careful how they changed the team.

"Drive fast!" she mocked. "Aye, drive like the wind! You shall not reach Gaul before your father dies! Cæsar will avenge me! Cæsar will draw blood in exchange for Commius! Hurry, before the crows leave nothing you can recognize!"

Tros's face showed no emotion, but his grip on Conops' shoulder told another tale. The one-eyed sailor winced and tried to loosen the grip with cautious fingers.

"Who knows where Commius is? I will speak with him," said Tros; and one of the escort seized a man who tried to slink away around the corner of the house.

Backed against the wall and held there with a spear point at his throat, the man soon gave his information and was let go. The four fresh horses were yoked by that time.

And at last Tros spoke to Gwenhwyfar:

"Gwenhwyfar, wife of Britomaris, you will fall to Cæsar yet! Cæsar will treat you less kindly than I did. You may offer him ten kingdoms, and yourself thrown in, but I see you walking through the streets of Rome at Cæsar's chariot tail; and, if by then you are not too worn from weeping, and too sore-footed, and too thin, there will be an auction afterward.

"Rome stinks, Gwenhwyfar! You will miss the sweet earth smell of Britain, and the freedom, and the green oaks and the thick turf underfoot! Rome's streets are hard, and her heart is harder. But harder than all—aye, harder than that heart of yours—is Cæsar's! Farewell!"

He bowed to her as the chariot wheeled away, and the men of the escort paid her scurvy compliments; but she stood still, leaning back against the door-post with her head erect, glaring her anger until the chariot and its escort were lost to view.

"Lonely she looks, and I am sorry for her, for she will be lonelier still if ever she meets Cæsar," Tros said to Conops.

But she had friends; for as they galloped by the corner of the wall that shut the house from view, a stone hurled by an unseen hand missed Tros by so little that he almost felt the weight of it, and it broke the tough turf where it landed.

"But master—your father!" Conops was clenching and unclenching his fingers. "Has she sent a messenger to Cæsar? Had she betrayed us?" Conops clutched his knife

71

and spoke to Tros between thin, vindictive lips. "If your father is slain, my master, I will beg one favor of you: Let me live that I may bury this in her!"

He showed six inches of his knife-blade.

"I think she lied," said Tros.

But his voice betrayed him. He did not think that. He knew she spoke the truth; he knew some messenger had gone to inform Cæsar what had happened to Commius the Gaul, along with, doubtless, a long story about himself. His blood ran cold. He knew how much mercy his father would receive from Cæsar when that sort of tale should reach the Roman's ears.

"There is room for things to happen between here and Gaul," he said after a minute. "It is one thing to send a messenger; another for the man to reach his goal. Moreover, Caius Volusenus has a fairly swift ship. We may arrive there first."

There was delay, though, before they resumed the ride to where Caius Volusenus waited for them. The escort led into the forest and then wheeled out of the fairway down a lane that bore no tracks of wheels, where they had to stop a time or two to lift the chariot over fallen trees, and the bronze wheels cut deeply into moss.

At the end of a mile or two of winding between ancient oaks, where the deer fled suddenly in front of them and rabbits scampered for the undergrowth, they entered a wide clearing. There a dewy hillside faced them, scattered with enormous stones; and in the midst of the hill there was a considerable clump of very ancient yew trees, with a cave mouth just below that, its entrance arched with three adze-trimmed monoliths. Above the trees there was a cluster of neat, thatched dwellings.

Among the trees sat druids in their long robes, and one of them was the ancient who had held forth on the night when Tros first met Caswallon.

The druids, led by the old one, came solemnly down the hillside and surrounded Tros's chariot. He greeted them, and the escort jumped down from their horses to show respect, yet it was a peculiarly masked respect; they looked as little interested as they could, perhaps because Tros was a stranger.

"Is Commius here? May I have word with him?" asked Tros when the greeting was all done.

The old man sent two younger druids to the cave. They brought out Commius, with fetters on his wrists but not ill-treated otherwise. The Gaul's black-bearded face was set so as to mask emotion, and a lean smile hid whatever he might think of Tros. He nodded a curt greeting, holding the clasped hands in front of him to ease the bronze fetters' weight.

"Commius, I am on my way to Cæsar," said Tros.

The Gaul inclined his head slightly to signify that he understood, but he said nothing; nor did he glance at the druids, or make any sign except that unnoticeable nod.

It was only by imagining himself in the Gaul's position that Tros realized there would be no conversation while the druids listened. But the druids also realized it. Almost before Tros could face about to beg their indulgence the oldest of them made a signal and they walked away in silence and sat down at a sufficient distance to be out of earshot.

"Now!" said Tros. "What shall I say of you to Cæsar?"

Commius smiled thinly.

"You will say of me to Cæsar what you wish to say, if he permits," he answered. "*My* message has already gone."

"Have you a message for your Gauls?" asked Tros.

"Yes. Bid the Atrebates obey Cæsar. Cæsar will avenge me."

The voice was cleverly controlled, but the expression of his face masked contempt too studiously for Tros not to see through it.

"You think you have contrived my downfall, Commius," he answered. "I doubt it. A man is hard to kill until his time comes. For my own part I am not a dealer in men's lives. I have sought you out to see what I can do to help you."

"Can you set me free?" asked Commius, and the sneer in his voice was biting; it brought the fire into Tros's amber eyes.

"You could set yourself free very easily if you were not a traitor to your race," he answered. "Commius, we are two fools, I because I did not know how wholly you are Cæsar's slave—"

The word stung; Commius' black eyes blazed at last. He almost answered, but controlled himself.

"—and you, because you think to promote your own ambition before you do your duty to the Gauls. You have eaten from Cæsar's hand. You like the food! But he will treat you as he does the other dogs in due time."

"Dogs?" snarled Commius, losing his control at last. "The dogs shall tear your carcass before you are twelve hours older!"

"So that is it! I thank you for the warning, Commius!"

Tros laughed and turned away, having learned what he came to learn. The druids, observing that the conference was over, came forward in a group, and the two who had brought Commius from the cave took charge of him again. Tros spoke to the oldest druid, greeting him respectfully:

"Lord Druid, before Commius became your prisoner, he sent a messenger toward the coast. Where would such a messenger be likely to lie in wait to slay me before taking ship?"

The old druid glanced at the escort, who were munching bread in a group beside their horses, having washed their hands and faces in the dew.

"My son, those horsemen will take care of you," he answered.

"But a messenger did go?"

"Aye, a man went, with a letter to Etair, son of Etard. Gwenhwyfar, wife of Britomaris, wrote it. Etair is her half-brother, and his place lies near the seashore where you landed from the Roman ship. It was his men who attacked you when you landed."

Tros scratched his chin, grinning thoughtfully, and Conops went and stood where he could watch his master's face. Conops' only remedy for anything was that long knife he carried in his sash, but he knew that Tros despised fighting if a craftier way might be found out of a difficulty. Craftiness is much more nervous work than fighting, and Conops held his breath.

"If a druid might ride with me," said Tros at last, still scratching at his chin, "a druid who would lead me to a small seaworthy boat, whose owner would obey my orders—"

The old druid nodded and, turning his back on Tros, gave orders very swiftly in rumbling undertones. It was not clear why he did not wish Tros to hear what he said, unless it was the habit of keeping his own counsel and establishing a mystery whenever possible.

He had hardly finished speaking when the young druid, who had befriended Tros when he first landed, went and sat down in the chariot, tucking his long robe in under his feet.

Then the old High Druid dismissed Tros with one sentence:

74

"Caius Volusenus grows impatient because his ship lies close to a dangerous shore."

But he did not explain how he knew that. He held up his right hand in an act of invocation and boomed out words that sounded like a ritual, then gestured to Tros to be gone.

The escort mounted at once with an air of relief and began laughing and chattering; the charioteer preferred not to wait another second, but drove toward Tros, and the moment he and Conops had stepped in they were off at full gallop, returning down the same glade by which they had come.

"These druids," said Conops in Greek, thumbing his long knife for the scandalized druid's benefit, "are too much like specters from another world for me. They are not enough like honest men or criminals for me to trust them."

Tros smiled.

"Never mind," he answered. "I would trust you less if you should trust any man too much! Put your knife away!"

CHAPTER IX

TROS DISPLAYS HIS SEAMANSHIP AND A WAY OF HIS OWN OF MINDING HIS OWN BUSINESS

If it were true, as ye say, that to slay is to prevail, then why not kill me?

Ye could wear my robes and occupy my seat. But could ye know what I know? Could ye think what I think? Could ye do what I do? Could ye have my vision, and enjoy that, merely by proving that violence slays and that flesh becomes dust?

FROM THE SAYINGS OF THE DRUID TALIESAN

THE forest went down to the sea along the route that Tros took that morning; and because the druid ordered it they made a detour to the westward that brought them, near midday, to a swampy harbor hidden amid trees, not far from where the chalky downs begin that draw nearer to the shore southeastward until they form the white cliffs of Kent.

"Hythe," said the druid, pointing to where roofs over a

mud-and-wattle wall could be seen between wind-twisted branches.

The town was hidden from the sea; there were no signs of cultivation or of human dwellings that would be likely to tempt sea rovers into the reed-infested harbor mouth. There was not even an inhabitant in sight, although there were boats drawn up into the reeds, amid which narrow, winding paths led mazily toward the town wall. Gulls and other sea-fowl by the thousand filled the air with harsh music, under a bright sky flaked with fleecy clouds.

"Hythe, a high tide, and the wind in the southwest!" said Tros, meditating. "How often does the wind set thus?"

"More often than not," said the druid. "It is the winds from the west that save this land from pirates. Northwest, west, southwest—most days in the year. The Northmen set forth, but three times out of five storms blow them back again."*

"And a fair slant for Gaul, but a rising sea," said Tros. "Caius Volusenus will be fretting at his anchor, if he has not gone away and left me."

They went and stood on the shingle beach, where the rounded stones sang sharply of the weight behind the waves and they could see, amid the white-caps in the distance to the eastward, a galley that pitched at her anchor and rolled until her heavy fighting top looked like a plaything of the spray.

"The Romans are the worst seamen I have yet seen," Tros remarked, screwing up his eyes to stare along the waves. "They think weight is strength, and pit their strength against the sea. They hang on by brute force, when a seaman would employ a little strategy to use the sea against itself.

"If Caius Volusenus were a seaman, he would not be lying off a lee shore until his crew was weak from vomiting. If he were any kind of man except a Roman soldier, he would have explored this shore-line, instead of waiting for me to bring information.

"But that is the Roman method: Seize a hostage, threaten him, then send his son or his brother to save the hostage's life by betraying some one else! And because the world is what it is, and men are what they are, the plan succeeds too often!

"But I have seen the Romans lose a fleet of ninety ships

* Great Britain has always had the "weather-gage" of an invader.

76

on the coast of Sicily, because a land general ordered thus and so, and they knew no better than to obey the fool! What is that group of men along the beach a mile away?"

The druid, peering under the palm of his hand, looked anxious but said nothing. It was clear enough that the men were forcing a small boat into the sea, and at the first attempt it overturned in the surf. They had to haul it back on the beach and bail the water out.

"Now that is a strange state of affairs," said Tros. "They look to me like Britons."

"They *are* Britons," said the druid.

"Don't they know this harbor? Can't they take a boat from here?"

The druid nodded, putting two and two together, frowning:

"You are too late, Tros! That will be the messenger whom Commius sent to Cæsar. They who are helping him to launch the boat belong to Etair, son of Etard, who is against Caswallon, whereas the men of Hythe are for him. They plan to reach Caius Volusenus' ship ahead of you. They will succeed, because it will take us too long to procure a crew. The men of Hythe are doubtless on the hills behind us, tending cattle and watching Caius Volu—"

The druid coughed, for Tros clapped him on the back so suddenly that he bit a word off midway.

"Quick!" said Tros. "Show me a boat with a sail!"

"But a crew?" said the druid.

"I have one!"

"Those horsemen? They can hunt deer; they can drink and sing and fight, but—"

"I said, I have *one!* He is enough! Make haste, man!"

That druid never hurried faster in his life. They found a boat within a quarter of an hour, whose sail had not been carried ashore and hidden. They found oars and a pole in another boat, and from a third boat lifted a dozen yards of good hemp rope with which to repair the running gear.

Tros said good-by to the escort, gave them all the gold out of Caswallon's purse, and nearly broke the hand of one in his hurry to get the good-bys over and be gone. Then he kissed the druid on both cheeks, cried out to Conops to raise the sail and shoved the boat out from the reeds, jumping in as the keel slid free of the mud.

It was a strong boat, but awkward and as slow as a

77

drifting log, although they labored at the oars like Titans.

But at last they worked their way over the bar at the harbor mouth and caught the southwest wind that laid her over until the gunwale was awash. Then Tros took the steering oar and made experiments to discover the best point of sailing, but he found her a clumsy tub at best.

Her blunt bow checked her constantly, and he had hard work to keep from being swamped by the rising sea. Conops was bailing half the time.

They had made a drenching, wallowing mile of it, and Caius Volusenus' ship seemed farther off than ever, her hull down out of sight between the waves or rising over a big one with her nose toward the sky, when Conops shouted, pointing shoreward:

"They have launched that other! They are giving chase!"

It was a faster boat and a bigger one, manned by half a dozen men, who had forced her through the surf at last and were following in Tros's wake. Her big square lug-sail bellied in the wind and lifted her along a good three yards for his two.

Rolling dangerously as the helm changed, she began to work to windward, not more than a quarter of a mile astern, two men with bows and arrows standing in her bow and a very big man in a bearskin coat leaning his weight against the steering oar.

"He is reckless—they have promised him a fat reward for our two heads!" said Tros.

"Master, make for the shore!" urged Conops. "They are too fast and too many for us!"

But Tros headed farther out to sea, edging his boat craftily to keep the quartering waves from swamping her. He lost a little speed by doing that, and Caius Volusenus' ship was still a good six miles away.

"The tortoise who runs, and the hare who fights, are equal fools!" he growled in Conops' ear.

But Conops drew his long knife nervously, returned it to its sheath and then drew out Tros's sword, examined its keen edge and drove it home again into the scabbard.

"We two against seven—and no arrows!" he said in a discouraged voice.

But Tros, making no remark, continued his experiments, discovering a trick the awkward hull possessed of falling away from the wind stern-first whenever he relieved the pressure from the oar. Nothing saved her then

78

from swamping but the pressure of the wind that heeled her over and exposed more broadside to the waves—that, and instant skill at the helm.

As Tros eased her off from one of those experiments, an arrow hummed into the sail and stuck there. "Take cover below the weather gunwale," he ordered; so Conops knelt, begging leave to take the oar and run the risk himself.

"For if you die, master, and I live, can I save your father?"

Tros paid no attention to him. He was watching the approaching boat and her crew out of the corner of his eye and considering the flight of three more arrows that winged their way into the sail. The pursuing boat was to windward now, nearly abeam, changing her course so as gradually to reduce the distance between them.

"They shoot across the wind, yet all the arrows find their way into the sail," he said at last. "That is not bad shooting. That is done on purpose. They propose to make us prisoners. Let them see you throw up your hands!"

"Master! We have had enough of being prisoners!"

"Obey!" commanded Tros.

So Conops stood, throwing his hands up, while Tros edged his boat cautiously toward the other, which turned at once and came downwind toward him.

"They are seven," he growled between his teeth, for he did not want it seen that he was talking. "Return your knife to its sheath, Conops! Four of them will jump aboard us. See! They stand ready in the bow. That leaves three for us to tackle. When I give the word, jump! I like their boat better than this one. Leave the big man in the bearskin coat, and that other, to me. Take you the fellow with the bow and arrows who kneels by the mast. Are you ready?"

As he spoke, a big sea lifted both boats, and in the trough that followed the man in the bearskin shouted, shoving his helm hard over. They rose together, side by side and almost bumping on the crest of the next wave. Tros suddenly let go the sheet, exactly at the moment when the four men in the other boat's bow jumped.

They had calculated on his veering away from them, if anything; but it was his stern that fell to leeward; his bow came up into the wind. They missed, the pitch and roll assisting Tros as he plied the helm.

Three sprawled into the water and the fourth just grasped the gunwale, where he clung until the two boats crashed together and the force of the collision shook him off.

The man in the bearskin roared an order, leaning his whole strength against the steering oar, but he was too late; the collision spilled the wind out of his sail and he shipped the top of a wave over his stern that almost swamped him.

Tros, calculating to a hair's breadth, had timed the turn so that his bow struck the stranger amidships and, continuing the swing, he let the other boat bear down on him until for a second they lay parallel and bumping, facing opposite directions.

"Jump!" he shouted then. He and Conops sprang for the bigger boat, where the three men stood to receive them with drawn knives.

But each of them had to cling to something with one hand to preserve his balance because the boat was beam-on to the sea and wallowing, as the loose sail flapped and thundered.

Tros took his oar with him, and landed with the blade of it against a man's throat. That man went backward overboard, and Conops' knife went home to the hilt into the third man, striking upward from below the ribs.

The man in the bearskin thrust at Tros, but stumbled over the dead man, who flopped and slid to and fro, bleeding in knee-deep water. So the blow missed, but the butt of Tros's oar did not; it struck the out-thrust hand and spun the knife overside.

The fellow in the bearskin, shaking his hand because the blow had stung him, jumped in on Tros with a yell; but the boat lurched; Tros had the better sea legs. Roaring to Conops to keep his knife away, he seized his opponent by the neck and slowly forced him backward overboard.

"Haul on the sheet!" he shouted then, jumping for the steering oar that swung and banged in its iron bracket. In a moment they were paying off before the wind, and the boat they had left was down between the waves a hundred yeards behind, half-full of water and sinking.

"Take that bucket and bail for your life!" Tros shouted, conning the rising sea as he headed up a bit toward the wind; for the tide set inshore; they had made a lot of leeway while the short fight lasted.

For a long time after that he made no remark, until Conops had bailed most of the water overside.

Then Conops, with his back toward Tros, searched his victim carefully and, finding nothing worth appropriating, picked him up and threw him into the sea to leeward When he had seen the body sink he came and sat down by his master.

"Clean up the blood!" Tros commanded.

Conops went to work again, using a piece of sail-cloth that he found in a box under a coil of rope. Presently he returned, and resumed the seat.

"So now you have a dead man to account for," was all Tros said, sparing him one swift glance as they rose over a big wave.

Conops looked surprised, indignant, irritated. He had expected praise.

"It was him or me," he answered after a moment's pause.

"Well—you killed him. Can you give him back his life?"

"But, master, *you* killed two men!"

"Not I! I gave them leave to swim!" said Tros.

"They could not swim. They are all drowned, master."

"That is their affair. I never forbade them to learn to swim."

"But that fellow clad in a bearskin—how could he have swum? His coat drowned him."

"He never asked my leave to wear that coat," said Tros. "I could have slain him with my sword as easily as you slew your man. But I spared him. I gave them leave to swim. No enemy of mine can hold me answerable for the bearskin coat he wears!"

"I am glad I slew," said Conops, glaring fiercely through his one eye.

"Laugh, if you wish," said Tros. "But a man should mind his own business. At some time or another, you will have that fellow's life to answer for, which should have been his business and not yours."

Conops was silent for a long time.

"Well. At least you have a stolen boat," he said at last.

"So?" said Tros. "When, then? One I borrowed, by a druid's leave. This one I exchanged for that one; and who started the exchange? I tell you, Conops, you have nearly as much as Cæsar has to learn about the art of living! It is a coward's act to kill, if there is any other way."

"Then you call me a coward, master?"

"Yes," said Tros, "but not as bad a one as Cæsar; which, if you were, I would contrive to get along without

81

you, instead of trying to teach you wisdom. Ease off the sheet a little—so—plenty. Now get forward and see whether Caius Volusenus signals us."

CHAPTER X

CAIUS JULIUS CÆSAR

Ye invite me to blame the conqueror. But I find fault with the conquered. If ye were men, who would truly rather die than eat the bread of slavery or bow the knee to arrogance, none could conquer you. Nay, none I tell you. If ye were steadfastly unwilling to enslave others, none could enslave you. Be ye your own masters. If ye are the slaves of envy, malice, greed and vanity, the vainest, greediest, most malicious and most envious man is far greater than you. His ambition will impel him to prove it. Your meanness will enable him to prove it.

FROM THE SAYINGS OF THE DRUID TALIESAN

TROS went about between two waves as he came nearly abreast of the plunging galley and, falling away before the wind as close to her side as he dared, shouted for a rope. But none was thrown to him. He had to work like fury at the steering oar, bump the galley's side and jump for it, thanking the clumsy shipwrights who had left good toe- and finger-hold.

For that galley had been thrown together by unwilling Gauls at Cæsar's order, very roughly in the Roman fashion under the eyes of Roman overseers, and had been rendered fit for sea by laying strips of wood to hold the caulking in the seams.

Tros and Conops clambered aboard and let the small boat drift away. There were seasick Romans lying everywhere—they all but stepped on two of them—but not a sign of Caius Volusenus.

Lemon-countenanced and weak from vomiting, a legionary summoned him at last. He came out of his cabin below the after fighting deck and dropped himself weakly against the bulkhead—a middle-aged man, dignified and handsome even in that predicament, with his toga nearly blown off in the wind and his bare knees trembling. His eyes were a bit too close together to create instant confidence.

"How dare you keep me waiting all this while?" he

grumbled, trying to make a weary voice vibrate with anger. "We might have lost the ship, plunging in this welter at a cable's end!"

"You will lose her yet!" said Tros; but his eye was up-wind, and he knew the wind was falling. "Have you a spar to make fast to the cable? You had better let the anchor go and make sail as she turns before the wind."

Caius Volusenus doubted that advice, but Tros was in haste now to return to Cæsar, so he talked glibly of a lee shore and a gale, and pointed to the rocks where the tide would carry them.

One thing was certain—that the crew was much too weak and discouraged to haul the anchor up; so while Caius Volusenus and two young decurions aroused and bullied the crew into a semblance of activity, Tros and Conops lashed a spar to the cable-end and tossed it overboard.

Then, when Caius Volusenus gave the signal, they slipped the cable and the galley swung away before the wind with three reefs in her great square-sail.

Tros took the helm and no man questioned him. It was not until they reached mid-channel and the wind fell almost to a calm that Caius Volusenus climbed up to the after-deck and leaned there, yellow and weak-kneed, resuming the command.

"Not for Cæsar—not even for Cæsar," he grumbled, "will I take charge of a ship again on this thrice cursed sea! He would not trust a crew of Gauls. He said they would overpower us Romans if a gale should make us seasick. Well, I would rather fight Gauls than vomit like a fool in Neptune's bosom. What news have you?"

"News for Cæsar," Tros answered.

"Speak!" commanded Caius Volusenus.

"No," said Tros. "You are a faithful soldier, I don't doubt; but you are not Cæsar."

Caius Volusenus scowled, but Tros knew better than to let his information reach Cæsar at second-hand, for then Caius Volusenus would receive the credit for it. He, Tros, needed all the credit he could get with Cæsar, and on more counts than one.

"Well, there are two of you," said Caius Volusenus. "I will have them flog that man of yours, and see what he can tell me."

He stepped toward the break of the deck to give the order to a legionary who was standing watch beside the weather sheet.

"Better order them to row," said Tros. "There is not enough wind now to fill the sail. Flog Conops, and you injure me. Injure me, and I will fashion a tale for Cæsar that shall make you sorry for it. Hasten to Cæsar, and I will say what may be said in your behalf."

Caius Volusenus turned and faced him, his skin no longer quite so yellow since the wind had ceased.

There was an avaricious, hard look in his eyes, not quite accounted for by the ship's rolling over the ground-swell.

"Did you find pearls?" he demanded.

"Plenty," said Tros after a moment's thought.

"Have you any?"

"No. But I know how to come by them."

He thought another moment and then added:

"If I should return as Cæsar's pilot, and you, let us say, were to lend me a small boat in which to slip away by night, I could lay my hands on a good sized potful of pearls, and I would give you half of them."

Caius Volusenus ordered out the oars and watched until the rowing was in full swing, beating time for the discouraged men until the oars all moved in unison. Then he turned on Tros suddenly:

"Why should I trust you?" he demanded.

"Why not? By the gods, why not?" Tros answered. "Have I played you false? I might have stayed in Britain. I might have wrecked this ship. For the rest, you shall hear me speak in praise of you to Cæsar's face. What do you find untrustworthy about me?"

"You are a Greek!" said Caius Volusenus.

"Nay, not I! I am a Samothracian," said Tros.

Caius Volusenus did not care to know the difference. He snorted. Then he ordered the idle sail brailed up to the spar; and for a while after that he beat time for the rowers, who were making hardly any headway against the tide that was setting strongly now the other way.

At last he turned again to Tros, standing squarely with his hands behind him, for the ship was reasonably steady; and except for those too narrowly spaced eyes he looked like a gallant Roman in his fine bronze armor; but he spoke like a tradesman:

"If you will swear to me on your father's honor, and if you will agree to leave your father in Gaul as a hostage for fulfilment of your oath, I will see what can be done about a small boat—in the matter of the pearls. You would have to give me two thirds of the pearls."

"Two thirds if you like," said Tros, "but not my father!

He knows these waters better than I do. He is a better pilot and a wiser seaman. Unless Cæsar sets him free on my return, Cæsar may rot for a pilot—and all his ships and crews—and you along with him!"

Caius Volusenus faced about again and cursed the rowers volubly. Then, after a while, he ordered wine brought out for them and served in brass cups. That seemed to revive their spirits and the rowing resumed steadily.

After a long time Caius Volusenus, with his hands behind him, came within a pace of Tros and thrust his eagle nose within a hand's length of his face.

"Where are these pearls?" he demanded.

"In a woman's keeping."

"Why did you bring none with you?"

"Because, although the woman loved me nicely, there was scant time, and she has a husband, who is something of a chief. She begged me to take her with me. But I did not see why Cæsar should have those pearls, and I had thought of you and what a confederate you might be."

Conops, squatting on the steps that led to the after-deck, was listening, admiring, wondering. Greek to the backbone, he loved an artful lie. His face rose slowly above the level of the deck; his one eye winked, and then he ducked again.

"Well, let us leave your father out of it," said Caius Volusenus. "He is Cæsar's prisoner; let Cæsar free, keep, or kill him. That is nothing to me. I have a wife in Rome. Strike the bargain, Tros—"

Tros nodded.

"—and remember this: I hold no Greek's oath worth a drachma, but I hold my own inviolable. If you fail me, I swear by the immortal gods that I will never rest until you, and your father both, have been flogged to death. Bear that well in mind. I have the confidence of Cæsar."

"You are a hard man," Tros answered, looking mildly at him; he could make those amber eyes of his look melting when he chose.

"I am a very hard man. I am a Roman of the old school."

Caius Volusenus called for wine, and his own slave brought it to him in a silver goblet. He drank two gobletsful and then, as an afterthought, offered some to Tros. It was thin, sour stuff.

There was no more conversation. Caius Volusenus went below into his cabin, to sleep and regain strength after the long seasickness. The rowers just kept steering way, and

Tros plied the helm until the tide turned; but even with the changing tide no wind came and they made but slow progress until moonlight showed the coast of Gaul and Caritia* sands still ten or twelve miles in the offing.

Then Caius Volusenus came on deck again and fumed because the anchor had been left behind. He feared those sand-banks, having seen too many galleys go to pieces on them and he did not want to do the same thing under Cæsar's eyes.

Beyond the banks the masts of half a hundred ships stood out like etchings in the haze, and the glow of Cæsar's camp-fires was like rubies in the night. The sea was dead, flat calm, but Caius Volusenus would not risk the narrow channel in darkness, and the rowers had to dawdle at the oars all night long, while Conops took the helm and Tros slept.

As day was breaking, with the tide behind him and a puff of wind enough to fill the sail, Tros took the helm again and worked his way into a berth between galleys that lay with their noses lined along the shore.

There all was bustle and a sort of orderly confusion, with the ringing of the shipwrights' anvils and the roar of bellows, the squeaking of loaded ox-wains and the tramping of the squads of slaves who carried down munitions and the provender to put aboard the ships.

At the rear was a fortified, rectangular camp, enclosed within a deep ditch and an earth wall, along which sentries paced at intervals.

Within the camp the soldiers' tents were pitched in perfectly even rows, with streets between, and in the center, on one side of an open space, where four streets met, was Cæsar's, no better and no larger than the rest, but with the eagles planted in the earth in front of it and sentries standing by.

The huts, where prisoners and supplies were guarded, were at the rear end of the camp, enclosed within a secondary ditch-and-wall. The horse lines, where the stamping stallions squealed for breakfast, were along one side, but Cæsar's special war-horse had a tent all to himself behind his master's.

In a line with Cæsar's sleeping tent there was a bigger, square one, with a table set in it and an awning spread in front; it was there, in a chair of oak and ivory, beside the

* The modern Calais.

table at which his secretary sat, that Cæsar attended to business.

He was up betimes and being shaved by a Spanish barber, when Caius Volusenus marched up and answered the challenge of the sentries, swaggering with the stately Roman military stride and followed by Tros and Conops, who made no effort to disguise their deep-sea roll, although it made the sentries laugh.

There were a dozen officers in waiting underneath the awning, but they made way for Caius Volusenus; he passed through, nodding to them, leaving Tros and Conops to wait until they were summoned.

But they were not without entertainment, although no man spoke to them; for in the middle of the open space exactly in front of the eagles,* a naked Gaul, held down by four legionaries, was being flogged by two others for stealing, each stroke of the cords laying open the flesh.

And there was a row of prisoners to be considered, women among them, lined up under guard awaiting Cæsar's will concerning them.

It was a long time before Cæsar sent for Tros. The Gaul was very nearly flogged to death, and the earth was purple with his blood when Caius Volusenus thrust his way between the other officers and beckoned.

Having satisfied his dignity to that extent, he came forward a stride or two to be out of earshot of the others, and whispered as Tros fell into stride beside him.

"Cæsar is in a good mood. I have spoken for you. Make your news brief and satisfactory, and all will be well. Remember: Cæsar has decided to invade Britain. Speak accordingly, and offer no discouragement. I have told him you are a splendid pilot. Let him know that you and I explored the coast together."

Tros, smothering a smile, followed him between the officers and stood before the table where the Lombard secretary eyed him insolently.

Cæsar sat with a rug over his knees and his scarlet cloak hung on the back of the chair behind him. He was hardly forty-five, but he looked very bald and very old, because the barber was not yet through with him and had not yet bound on the wreath he usually wore. His cheeks looked hollow, as if the molars were all missing, and the wrinkles

* Standards bearing the insignia of the different legions and the letters S.P.Q.R.

at the corners of his mouth twitched slightly, as if he were not perfectly at ease.

Nevertheless, he was alert and handsome from self-consciousness of power and intelligence. He sat bolt up-right like a soldier; his pale smile was suave, and his eyes were as bold and calculating as a Forum money-lender's. Handsome, very handsome in a cold and studied way—he seemed to know exactly how he looked—dishonest, intel-lectual, extravagant, a liar, capable of any cruelty and almost any generosity at other men's expense; above all, mischievous and vicious, pouched below the eyes and lecherously lipped, but handsome—not a doubt of it.

"So Tros, you return to us?"

His voice was cultured, calm, containing just the least suggestion of a challenge. He crossed one knee over the other underneath the rug and laid his head back for the barber to adjust the golden laurel wreath. It made him look ten years younger.

"I claim my father," Tros answered.

Cæsar frowned. Caius Volusenus coughed behind his hand.

"Tell me your news," said Cæsar in a dry voice; the note of challenge was much more perceptible, and his eyes all but closed, as if he could see straight through Tros to the British coast beyond him.

"I landed. I was wounded. I was rescued by a druid. I met Caswallon and his wife Fflur. I was shown an army of a hundred men, and I saw it dismissed for the harvesting. I heard dissensions. There was some talk of an invasion, but none ready to repel it. I saw Commius, and he is held a prisoner in chains. I stole a boat and came back."

"Examining the coast with me," put in Caius Volusenus.

"Saving the interruption, that is a very proper way to turn in a report," said Cæsar.

"You may withdraw." He glanced at Caius Volusenus sharply, once, and took no further notice of him as he backed away under the awning.

"Harbors?" asked Cæsar.

"None," said Tros. "There is a good beach for the ships, good camping ground, and standing corn not far away."

"And the equinox?" asked Cæsar, glancing at the blue sky.

"I spoke about that with the druids. Yesterday's gale will be the last until the equinox arrives; that period is accurately known but none knows how soon thereafter the storms will begin, since they vary from year to year. But for the next few days there is sure to be calm weather."

"Why do they hold Commius prisoner?"

"Because he urged them to permit your army to land on the shore of Britain."

"Do they not know my reputation? Do they not know that I punish insults? Do they not know Commius is my ambassador?"

"They say he brought trashy presents that the women laughed at. They say he is a spy, not an ambassador," Tros answered.

Cæsar's face colored slightly.

"Barbarians!" he sneered, and then smiled condescendingly. "What kind of man is Caswallon?"

"He fights nearly naked," said Tros. "He thinks armor is a coward's clothing."

Cæsar looked amused.

"Has he ships?" he asked.

"I heard him boast of three."

Cæsar drummed his lean, strong fingers on the chair-arm.

"Well—I will wait until after the equinox," he said after a moment. "I have some small experience of druids. They are sly and untrustworthy. I am afraid these storms might catch me in mid-channel and scatter the fleet. I have only one strong ship; the rest were built in haste by inexperienced Gauls, good enough for calm weather, dangerous in heavy storms. And now of course, you wish to see your father?"

Tros nodded and smiled. For a moment he was off guard—almost ready to believe that sometimes Cæsar's word was worth face value.

"A splendid, dignified and noble looking man, your father. All the fault I find with him is his affection for the druids; a strange affection, not becoming to him. A great sailor, I am told. You say he knows these waters around Britain as well as you do?"

Tros nodded again, but the smile was gone. He forefelt trickery now.

"I will speak with him first," said Cæsar. "You shall see him afterward."

"Is he well?" asked Tros nervously. "Has he been treated properly, or—"

"I always treat people properly," said Cæsar in a suave

voice. "There is nothing done in this camp except by my orders. You may retire."

He said the last words in a louder voice, and an officer marched in, who took Tros by the arm and led him out under the awning. Another officer was summoned.

Tros heard Cæsar's voice speaking in undertones, and less than a minute later he was marching between two officers toward the far end of the camp, where the prisoners were confined within the inner ditch and wall. There, in the gap that served as gate, he recognized the centurion who had promised to treat his father kindly, but he had no opportunity to speak with him.

He first knew that Conops was dogging his steps when the centurion on guard demanded weapons, and Conops swore in Greek because they took away his knife with scant ceremony.

"Unbuckle my sword. Hand it to them," he ordered, and Conops obeyed.

A moment later they were both shut into a low shed that had no window; a door was locked on them, and for fifteen minutes they listened to the steady tramp of a sentry, and the clank of his weapons as he turned at each end of a twenty-yard beat, before either of them spoke.

Then Conops broke the silence:

"Master," he whispered, "I can work my way out of this place. Look, where the wall is broken at the top. Lift me, and I can crawl out between wall and thatch. Let me find your father."

Tros hesitated for a moment, looking troubled.

"If they catch you, they will flog or kill you, Conops."

"I am a free man," Conops answered. "I may do what I will with my own life."

"Look like a slave, and speak like one. They will take less notice of you. Strip yourself," said Tros.

So Conops pulled off everything except a sort of kilt that he had on under the smock. Tros lifted him, and he crawled into the narrow gap where the top of the mud wall had crumbled because rain leaked through the thatch.

He had to force his way through carefully to make no noise, and he was delayed by having to wait until a sentry on the outer rampart passed on his regular beat. Then he dropped to the ground outside, and Tros heard him whisper:

"I may be a long time. Don't despair of me."

Tros picked up Conops' clothes and stowed them under

90

his own, then paced the hut restlessly, for there was nothing to sit down on but the damp earth floor, and nothing to do but worry. At the end of an hour the door opened, and a slave in charge of a centurion brought in a bowl of boiled wheat.

"Weren't there two in here?" asked the centurion.

"I don't know," said Tros. "The hut was empty when they put me in."

The centurion shrugged his shoulders, slammed the door again and passed on. Tros heard him ask another officer whether any record had been kept of the beheadings since a week ago, but he could not catch the reply.

There began to be a lot of trumpeting, the clang of arms and the tramp of horses. A voice that spoke in stirring cadences appeared to be addressing Roman troops, but the voice was not Cæsar's. Trumpets again, and then the sound of cavalry moving off in regular formation. Half an hour after that a Latin slave-dealer, with his secretary slave and tablets, looked in while a legionary held the door open.

"I tell you, this one is not for sale," said the legionary. "Cæsar has another use for him. There was another, a one-eyed man, but I suppose he has been executed."

"Extravagance!" said the slave-dealer. "You soldiers kill off all the best ones. What with the beheadings and the draft for gladiators, males are worth a premium and females are a glut. I could bid a price for this one. He looks good."

"Save yourself trouble," said the legionary. "I tell you, Cæsar needs him."

And he slammed the door.

An hour after that came Conops, scrambling through the hole under the eaves and knocking down dry mud in handfuls. They picked it all up carefully and tossed it through the opening. Then Conops resumed his clothes.

"Master, your father was in a round hut at the other end of this prison yard."

"Was?" asked Tros.

"Was. He has gone. There is a window to that hut, with wooden bars set in the opening; and the window is toward the rampart, so I stood in shadow and had word with him. He has not been harmed, but he suffers from confinement. He was very grateful for the news of you.

"While I hid below the window, between the back of the hut and the rampart, an officer came who led him away to Cæsar. Then a sentry on the rampart spied me; so

91

I pretended to be one of the slaves who clean the camp of rubbish.

"I picked up trash and climbed the rampart to throw the stuff into the ditch, as the others do; and so I saw them take your father into Cæsar's tent. Then I kept gathering more rubbish, and kept on climbing the rampart to throw the stuff away; so I saw them bring your father out and set him on horseback.

"The cavalry was lined up then—five hundred of them—and when they went away your father rode with them between two soldiers."

"Was he wearing his sword?" asked Tros.

"Yes."

"Which way went the cavalry?"

"Alongshore to the eastward."

"Did my father send me any message?"

"Yes, master. He said this: That after you started for Britain, Cæsar sent for him and told him he must pilot one portion of the fleet to Britain when the time comes, if he hopes ever again to see you alive.

"And your father added this: That that fleet will not reach Britain if he can prevent it.

" 'Tell him,' he said, 'it is better to die obstructing Cæsar than to live assisting him to work more havoc.'

"Then he told me to bid you not to be deceived by anything Cæsar may say, but pretend to serve Cæsar for your own life's sake, obstructing him in all ways possible, for the sake of Those who sent you forth from Samothrace."

"That will I!" said Tros, scowling.

"Then I hid awhile and watched them change the guard at this end of the prison yard. None saw me, although the sentry on the rampart passed me twice as I was making shift to climb in, setting a forked stick against the wall to set my foot on, and kicking it away afterward."

Tros paced the floor like a caged animal, his hands behind him and his chin down on his breast.

"What if Cæsar should leave me here!" he exploded at last. "He can find other pilots than me."

But Caius Volusenus was too eager for imaginary pearls to let that happen. He came striding to the hut and gained admittance after the officer on duty had sent him back, fuming and indignant, to obtain a pass from some superior.

"Now Cæsar would have left you here in chains and have used your father only, for he trusts neither of you," he began, when he was sure the door was shut and none was listening. "But I spoke up for you, and I told Cæsar you are a man whose instincts compel you to navigate safely.

"I suggested he should send your father as a pilot for the cavalry, who are embarking a few miles down the coast. He agreed because that will keep the two of you apart. It is no use arguing with Cæsar."

"No use whatever," said Tros. "What then?"

"Pluto paralyze him! He began to wonder why I set such store by you! Cæsar would suspect his mother if she brought him milk!

"He decided you are not to go with me on my ship, but with him on his, where he can keep an eye on you. And he has told me off to bring up the rear of the expedition."

Tros had not ceased to pace the floor all the while the Roman was speaking. Suddenly now he turned and faced him where a stream of sunlight shone through a crack beside the door-post.

"How much of this is true?" he demanded. "Cæsar told me he will not start until after the equinox."

"All of it is true," said the Roman, showing his decayed front teeth in something between a smile and a snarl. "Shall Cæsar tell his real plans to every prisoner he questions? Listen to me now, Tros: You would never dare to play a trick on Cæsar; but perhaps you think because I am only Caius Volusenus I am easier to trifle with.

"I remind you of my oath! At the first chance I will take care to provide you with a small boat. That is my part of it. Thereafter you bring pearls, and the woman with them, if you see fit. You may keep the woman; but two thirds of the pearls are mine, according to agreement. And if the pearls are not enough, or if you fail me"—he showed his teeth again—"remember my oath, that is all!"

"Do your part," said Tros. "I will do mine."

Caius Volusenus nodded drily and shouted to the sentry to unlock the door and let him out. When he was gone, Tros took Conops by the shoulders.

"Little man, little man!" he exclaimed, "that Roman's avarice will thwart a worse rascal than himself! Cæsar, for this once at least, shall fail!"

CHAPTER XI

THE EXPEDITION SAILS

Ye have heard, ye have seen the sea and all its waves come
thundering against the cliffs. Lo, it fails; it is hurled back upon
itself. But does the sea cease? Neither shall envy and all its
armies cease. It shall thunder and roar and suck and under-
mine, until ye learn, at some time in this Eternity, that Motion
is Law. But ye think of the motion of chariots, whereas I
speak of the growth of Wisdom.

FROM THE SAYINGS OF THE DRUID TALIESAN

NOTHING further happened until midnight. Then the trumpets sounded. There began the steady tramp of armed
men and the sharp, staccato orders of centurions. After
that, Cæsar's voice, hard, brilliant, not saying much, but
saying it with vigor. Then a shuddering clang as two whole
legions raised their shields—a pause, two deep breaths
long—and a roar like the bursting of a wave on fanged
rocks—

"Ave!"

Short, sharp commands and the clang of shields, as
cohort after cohort tramped away in fours toward the
harbor. Silence at the end of half an hour, and then a dog
howling and screams from a woman prisoner. At last
gruff voices and a heavy tread at Tros's door, a glare of
torchlight through the crack, a clang as a bronze shield
touched another one—and the door opened slowly.

"Come!" said a pleasant voice. Tros, whispering to
Conops to keep close behind him, strode out into the
torch-glare. The red light shone on the bronze body-armor
of a veteran-officer, who beckoned and turned at once,
leading through the opening in the prison-yard wall, where
half a dozen legionaries sprang to the salute. The two men
who had held the torches stayed behind to search the hut
for anything worth appropriating.

The officer led toward mid-camp, where Cæsar sat on
horseback, erect and splendid in his scarlet cloak, surrounded by a dozen torches and about two-score officers
on foot, who were crowding in to listen to his last instruc-
tions.

No finer horseman ever lived than Cæsar; he looked like

a god in the glare of the sputtering firelight, and the helmeted faces peering up at him shone with enthusiasm. His voice was calm, confident, unforced, and it vibrated with authority.

"Who is that?" he demanded, as Tros stepped into the zone of light. Tros bulked bigger than any Roman near him, standing like a monarch in his gold-edged purple cloak. Sea-water stains and the dirt of travel did not show at midnight.

"Tros the pilot, General."

"What? Has he been put to an indignity? Where is his sword?"

Cæsar frowned, glaring at the faces all around him, but omitting Tros. Some one ran away into the darkness, shouting as he ran. Cæsar leaned forward and spoke to a slave who stood near him with tablet and stylus.

"Write," he commanded: " 'Cæsar will ascertain who submitted Tros to indignity and will punish the offender.' Pilot," he went on, meeting Tros's eyes at last, with a smile that would have mollified an angry woman, "not all of Cæsar's men are as thoughtful for Rome's friends as Cæsar is. On the eve of great events mistakes occur. You will understand that this indignity was not inflicted by my order. The offender shall be called to strict account for it."

The man who had deprived Tros of his sword was standing in the torchlight almost straight in front of Cæsar; he turned his head and looked at Tros brazenly, unblinking, with a faint, sarcastic smile. Some one came running through the darkness and thrust Tros's sword into his hands. The same man gave Conops his knife.

"That is better," said Cæsar. "I don't doubt that now you feel better."

He surveyed the sea of faces.

"Officers," he went on, "learn from this that there is nothing Cæsar overlooks."

With that he pressed his greave against the horse's flank and rode away at a walk, the torchmen marching to his right and left hand and the officers following in a group, their helmets gleaming, Cæsar's scarlet cloak like a symbol of Rome's majesty looming above them.

Tros was not left alone; two officers marched with him, one on either hand, and he knew himself, as they intended that he should, as much a prisoner as ever. Conops was no more noticed than a dog that follows a marching regiment.

All was in darkness along the harbor side, but Tros noticed that the usual beacon fires around the camp were burning as brightly as if the troops were still there.

A nearly full moon shone on rows of ships that had been pushed off from the shore and anchored; only one ship, and that the highest pooped and longest of them all, lay broadside to a wooden wharf, from which a heavy gangplank with handrails reached to her deck amidships.

Most of the officers stepped into small boats and were rowed off to their separate commands, but Cæsar, followed by five of them, rode straight to the wharf and urged his horse across the gangplank, laughing cheerfully when the animal objected.

Two legionaries started forward along the plank to seize the horse's head, but he ordered them back sharply and compelled the horse to do his bidding.

"A good omen!" he shouted, as the horse reached deck. "The gods, as ever, befriend Cæsar!"

"Ave!" roared the legionaries, packed so closely in the ship's waist they could hardly raise their shields; and the soldiers in the other ships took up the roar, until across the moonlit water in the distance came the last dull din of the salute.

An officer nudged Tros, motioning toward the gangplank, so he walked aboard, followed by Conops, and neither man dreamed of going anywhere except to the high poop, swinging themselves up the ladder as if the ship belonged to them. Then men on the dark wharf pulled the gangplank clear, and some one lighted a beacon in the ship's bow.

A man on the poop roared an order at once. Rowers, ready on the benches, thrust their long oars through the port-holes and shoved the ship clear of the wharf.

Then another sharp order, and they swung together in the short, quick starting-stroke, their heads in line resembling the remorseless to-and-fro beat of a battering ram. That illusion was heightened by the thumping in the oarlocks and the hollow clang of metal striking on a shield as some one marked the time.

Cæsar stood gazing astern, with his scarlet cloak wrapped tightly, and a shawl over his shoulders, watching the other ships haul their anchors and follow one by one. There were a dozen biremes, clumsy with engines for hurling stones and shooting volleys of arrows, their great

96

iron dolphins swinging from heavy yardarms and their midship sections looking like a fortress.

But the remainder—nearly a hundred ships—were for the most part unarmed transports and high-sided, heavy-laden merchantships with corn, oil, wine, munitions and supplies.

The harbor became noisy with the thumping of oars, but there was no shouting, and no light on any of the ships but Cæsar's, where half a dozen men stood by the beacon with sand and water, ready to extinguish sparks.

There was no wind outside the harbor. Cæsar's ship worked out beyond the shoals and waited until nearly all the fleet was clear and had taken station in four lines behind him. Then, in keeping with Cæsar's usual luck, a light south wind began to fill the sails. He turned at once to Tros:

"Pilot," he said, "make haste now and show me that anchorage on the shore of Britain. I will show you how Cæsar leads Roman soldiers."

Tros went and stood beside the helmsman, a Roman making way for him. There was a great deal of low-voiced talking on the poop, where a dozen officers were gathered; it annoyed him, he was trying to recall what Gobhan had explained about the tides, and to remember where the quicksands lay. He ordered the ship headed up a point or two to eastward, and Cæsar noticed it.

"Pilot," he said, "this is a Roman fleet. Each ship will follow me exactly. Carry that in mind."

Then he turned to laugh and talk with his staff officers. There was excitement in his voice. He was like a boy setting out on a great adventure, although the moonlight shining on the back of his bald head considerably weakened that illusion.

He was the only Roman on the poop who wore no helmet and one of the officers warned him of the night air, so he tied the shawl over his head, and he looked like a hooded vulture then.

"For two years I have longed for this!" he exclaimed with a conceited laugh. "It will interest the Roman crowd, won't it, to see Britons walking in my triumph! They paint themselves blue. We will have to take some of their blue paint along with us to redecorate them before we enter Rome.

"I want it understood that any pearls taken in the loot are for me; I need them for the Venus Genetrix. I will be generous with everything else—you may tell that to the men."

Tros changed the course another point or two to eastward. Cæsar noticed it again. He came and stood beside him, staring toward the coast of Britain, where two or three enormous fires were burning on the cliffs that would have resembled dark clouds except for those dots of crimson.

"Druids at their beastly practices!" said Cæsar.

For a moment he looked piercingly at Tros.

"Some one may have told them I am coming; they are probably burning human sacrifices to ward off the Roman eagles! However, they will find the eagles take their sacrifices in another way!"

Suddenly his mood changed, and the tone of his voice with it; he became even more conceited as he toyed with condescension—he would probably have called it mercy.

"I hope for their own sakes the British will not be foolish. The Gauls have shown them what must happen if they oppose Romans under Cæsar's leadership! Is there any wisdom outside Rome, I wonder? Sometimes I am forced to think not. I trust that you are wise, Tros. I reward as richly as I punish."

He returned to the group of officers and chatted with them for a while, Tros seizing the opportunity to head the ship a trifle more to eastward. But Cæsar noticed it. He came and stood by the helm again.

"Show me the place for which we are sailing," he commanded; and Tros pointed out the highest cliffs that overlook the channel from the British shore.

"Why not sail straight for them, as a Roman road goes straight over hill and valley?" asked Cæsar.

Tros dissertated about tides and currents, that would carry the fleet too far to westward unless they made good their easting before the ebb; and for a moment after that as he watched Cæsar's face he trembled for the whole of his plan and for his friend Caswallon.

"Why not westward?" Cæsar asked. "Those cliffs frown gloomily. To me they look ill-omened—an inhospitable shore. Yonder to the westward, there are no cliffs."

And, as Tros well knew, there were harbors to the westward, where a fleet might anchor safely through autumn storms.

"Swamps!" he answered curtly. "Mud, where ships stick firm until the high tides fill them! Unseen quicksands! Rocks! However—it is your business."

He made as if to change the helm, but Cæsar checked him:

"No, I hold you responsible. You are the pilot. It will be my pleasure to reward or punish."

The wind increased, and the following fleet began to lose formation, the heavily loaded provision ships falling behind and the others scattering according to their speed. Cæsar's ship was fastest of all and was a long way first to reach the "chops," where wind and tide met and the sea boiled like a caldron.

Most of the legionaries, crowded in the waist, groaned and vomited, and Cæsar's war-horse had to be thrown and tied to prevent him from injuring himself.

Then Tros swore fervidly between his teeth, and Conops came to him to find out what was wrong, leaning on the rail behind him, tugging his cloak to call attention.

"Wrong?" groaned Tros. "I am! I have missed the quicksands!"

"Then we live!" laughed Conops. "I see nothing wrong with that!"

But Tros swore again.

"I misjudged the tide. An hour earlier, and all this fleet had—"

Cæsar returned to find out what the talking was about; his sharp ears possibly had caught a word or two of Greek. He stood and stared eastward, swaying, watching where the current boiled around shoals. The moonlight gleamed on the projecting spur of an island that was hardly above sea level.* There was white water within an arrow-shot of the ship's side.

Cæsar stared at Tros coldly and then looked southward for a glimpse of following sails; the nearest ones were sweeping westward; tide, wind and current all combining to carry them clear of the shoals. Tros felt the goose-flesh creeping up his spine.

"You Romans are no sailors," he remarked. "If Rome were an island, you would be a vassal nation. Do you see those shoals? A Roman pilot would have wrecked this whole fleet on them. As it is—"

Cæsar nodded; he could hardly keep his feet on the heaving deck; a cloud of stinging spray burst overside and drenched him; he clung to the rail.

* There was an island at one end of the Goodwin Sands until comparatively recently.

"Let me not doubt you again, Tros," he answered grimly. Tros laughed.

"Cæsar," he answered, "do you let your troops doubt you? When danger seems imminent, do you let them doubt you?"

"You are a bold rogue," Cæsar answered.

"Yet you live—and I could drown you easily," said Tros, "as easily as any of your men could kill you with a javelin in battle. Yonder is Britain, Cæsar. There are no more shoals."

Cæsar did not answer, but kept glancing from the ship's bow, where a long stream of sparks from the beacon flew downwind, toward the fleet, that had been forbidden to show lights. The rowing had ceased long ago; all sails were spread and glistening like wan ghosts in the moonlight.

Suddenly a ship a mile astern lighted a warning beacon and changed course westward. Fifty ships answered, and a blare of trumpets, like the bleating of terrified monsters, came fitfully downwind.

"Romans! Romans!" Tros exclaimed. "The Britons sleep deep, eh? Will you blame me if they know now how many ships are coming?" he asked Cæsar, jerking his head in the direction of the crimson flares that dotted the dancing sea for miles around.

Cæsar walked away to leeward and sat on a camp-stool where his staff, most of them seasick, were sprawling on the wet deck.

"He suspected you," Conops whispered. "Master, he was nearer death that minute than ever you brought him. My knife was ready."

Tros made a sound between his teeth.

"Any fool can slay a Cæsar," he remarked.

"What would you have done to him?" Conops asked resentfully. "Was it accident that—"

"I would have given him a true emergency in which to play the Cæsar."

Conops was puzzled.

"Then—then you favor him, master?"

"If I ever should, may my guiding star forget me."

"Then—"

"I gave the gods an opportunity to do their part," Tros went on. "It may be there are honest men on these ships, for whom the gods have other uses than to drown them. Or it may be that the gods prefer a second opportunity; the gods are like men, Conops; they delight in choosing. I will offer the gods a second choice. Bid that Roman

100

yonder to set his crew of duffers hauling on the main sheet, if they are not all seasick. Up helm a little. So."

CHAPTER XII

THE BATTLE ON THE BEACH

It is better to die in battle than to emerge victorious. Is the victor not convinced that violence prevails? How seldom he perceives, until too late, that what he has gained at another's cost is nothing—aye, and less than nothing. But he who dies in battle may have learned that nothingness. When he returns to earth for another existence, he may be wiser. He will at least be no more foolish. Whereas the victorious, convinced by violence, proceed from one stupidity to worse.

But battles happen. They are a consequence of cowardice, not of courage; of deceit and treachery, not of truth and high ideals; of contemptible lies, not of honor and virtue. But they happen, because ye are liars and worse. So face the consequences of your own self-slavery to treasons such as animals believe are necessary. Eat the consequences. Die. And in death ye may advance one step at least, toward the manhood that ye claim.

FROM THE SAYINGS OF THE DRUID TALIESAN

THE wind grew flukey toward morning, and at dawn it died away. The white cliffs of Britain loomed out of a gray mist as Cæsar's men unlashed the coverings of the war-engines and set basketsful of arrows in position.

A doctor moved about among the men reminding them how to apply first aid, and two or three veterans inspected the armor of the younger men. The standard-bearer and his chosen inner-guards stood erect and splendid in the bow, and beside each rower two men stood ready to protect him with their shields and two more to fight for him.

But there was no sign of the fleet. A few lone trumpets bleated through the mist in proof that the ships were not entirely scattered, and the sound stirred the gulls; thousands of them swooped and circled alongside, filling the air with melancholy.

One of Cæsar's staff officers approached him on the poop and, in a voice that every man on the ship could hear, announced:

"Cæsar, we Romans are ready!"

But Cæsar ordered a delay until at least a few more ships should come within hail; so the rowers dipped lazily, just keeping steering way, and the men in charge of the commissariat served coarse dry bread in basketsful.

At the end of an hour's drifting a light breeze scattered the jeweled mist and Britain's cliffs shone dazzling in the sun, hardly a bowshot distant. To seaward the fleet lay spread over a dozen miles of steel-blue water, the supply ships almost out of sight and only eight or ten of the lighter galleys near enough to come within hail in less than an hour; but among those, and almost the nearest of them, Tros recognized the small ship with the heavy fighting top commanded by Caius Volusenus.

Cæsar ordered the trumpets sounded; and almost before the blast reechoed from the cliffs an arrow plunked into the water fifty feet away; whoever had shot it was invisible, but along the summit of the cliff, beyond the range even of the war-machines, there had appeared a swarm of men, who looked like dots against the sky-line.

"There is no beach to land an army on," Cæsar remarked, looking sternly at Tros.

Tros glanced eastward to where, several miles away, the beach was wider and the cliffs gave way to lower and more rounded hills that seemed to offer an opening inland.

"Have you a Roman who could have brought you thus near in the night?" he retorted, pointing. "Yonder you can land—or nowhere. And you had better make a landing this day, for I warn you, I can smell the weather breeding. To-morrow, or the next day, or the next, the wind will scatter all your ships."

As the nearest galleys came within a mile Cæsar ordered the officers' assembly sounded. There was a race to obey the summons, and the first to arrive was Caius Volusenus, stepping out of a rowboat manned by Gauls; he stepped on to the poop and saluted Cæsar.

"I commanded you to bring up the rear with your ship," said Cæsar.

"General, where is the rear?" he retorted, sweeping his arm toward where the fleet lay spread on the horizon.

As he turned his head he spared a swift, wrinkled glance for Tros.

Other small boats arrived, and other ships' commanders climbed up to the poop, eager-faced and looking splendid in their armor, but some of them deathly white from seasickness.

Cæsar, making a great show of consultation, nodding as each man made his swift report, ordered them to signal as many fighting ships as could be gathered in a hurry and to follow him along the coast toward that break in the cliffs that Tros had pointed out.

And meanwhile, Caius Volusenus, working his way gradually out from the group of officers, had opportunity for a hundred words with Tros.

"This is a farce. It will be a failure," he said grimly. "Cæsar will force a landing, because he is Cæsar. I smell defeat. We shall be driven back into our ships. Now, about those pearls."

Tros smiled.

"You left an anchor down there to the westward. Conops and I could recover it," he answered.

"Good. It was a good, new, heavy one. It were a shame to lose it."

Caius Volusenus slipped back into the group of officers and presently returned to his own ship.

Then ten or twelve ships, Cæsar's leading, rowed in double line along the coast in search of a practicable landing place; and Tros noticed that the Britons on the summit of the cliffs had vanished.

They rowed slowly, observing the beach, and before they reached that gap between the hills, where the shingle sloped into the sea at an angle that looked as if beaching might be fairly easy, a small, fast galley overtook them, bringing word that the ships conveying cavalry had become scattered in the night and, finding themselves too near the quicksands with a rising wind and rough water, had put back to Gaul to save disaster.

Cæsar glanced sharply at Tros, who overheard the news and very nearly let a smile escape him. He could not altogether keep the laughter from his eyes. Cæsar beckoned him.

"Your father piloted the cavalry," he said.

Tros nodded.

"If I heard aright, he would seem to have preserved them from the shoals."

"And me from victory," said Cæsar, scowling. Then suddenly he laughed. "Whether or not you and your father are to be given to the executioners, shall depend on the outcome. Pray for my victory, Tros."

But he had grown thoughtful, and when they drew abreast of the chosen landing place he waited until nearly three in the afternoon for the heavier fighting ships to

103

overtake him. That gave the Britons ample time to gather in hundreds to oppose him, waiting for the time being out of bowshot, chariots, horse and foot all massed together, the men nearly naked and armed to the teeth, the stallions neighing and the war-horns braying as party after party arrived from inland.

"Barbarians," said Cæsar in a loud voice. "They will be no match for Romans."

And the legionaries laughed; but Cæsar continued to wait for more ships to arrive, until at last the whole of his two thousand infantry lay rolling within a bowshot of the shore.

But by that time it had been discovered that none except the very lightest ships could approach the shore close enough for the men to jump overboard without the certainty of being drowned in their heavy armor.

The lightest ships were ordered forward, but the Britons charged into the sea on horseback and in chariots and met them with such showers of javelins and arrows that the Romans had to lock shields.

One centurion leaped over the bow, shouting to his men to follow, and twenty of them did, but the Britons rode them down and drowned them, managing their horses in the sea as skillfully as on dry land.

Meanwhile, a score more men had been killed on board ship by arrow fire and javelins, in spite of locked shields. Cæsar ordered the ships back out of range, and the Britons yelled defiance from the beach, showing off, wheeling their chariots like whirlwinds.

But Cæsar ordered the ten heaviest warships into position on his right flank, as close as they could get to shore without grounding, and a hail of rocks and arrows from their engines swept the beach and then the rising ground beyond the beach, scattering the chariots and spreading death.

The Britons scampered out of range, leaving a writhing swath behind them, and Cæsar ordered the lighter ships inshore again.

The Britons wheeled, yelled, trumpeted and charged through the hail of stones and arrows into the sea once more to meet them. Fifty of them boarded one ship by the bow, leaping from the chariot poles and from horseback, and the warships could do nothing to aid in that emergency, for fear of killing their own men. The Britons were all slain, but they wrought red havoc first.

Roman after Roman plunged into the sea, only to be

ridden down and killed; for they jumped in shoulder deep and the weight of their armor made them helpless, whereas the Britons seemed to know the very underwater holes and were as active as their horses.

But when a Briton was slain, he floated with the water crimsoning around him, whereas the legionaries with their heavy armor sank; so that at the end of an hour's fighting there were scores of British corpses floating, and some horses, but no Roman dead in sight; and that fact encouraged Cæsar's men.

Moreover, the hail of arrow fire from the warships' engines had had its effect on the British reserves drawn up at the back of the beach to await their turn in the crowded fighting line—for the British method was to rush in and fight until they had a stomachful and then to retire and give fresh men a chance to prove their mettle.

"These Romans are cowards and Cæsar is a fool," said Conops in Tros's ear. "Two thousand Greeks would have landed an hour ago, against twice that number. Watch Cæsar's face. I wager we return to Gaul tonight."

But Tros had hardly taken his eyes off Cæsar, even when the great war-engines twanged and whirred and almost any other man would have been fascinated by the grim, mechanical precision of the gangs who worked them.

But it was Cæsar himself who fascinated Tros. Cæsar in his scarlet cloak was looking ten years younger. His cold eyes were glittering. He stood in one place, motionless, except that his head turned swiftly now and then. His men were flinching and discouraged, but not he.

"Bring me the standard-bearer of the Tenth!" he ordered suddenly.

A small boat went to bring the man, who left his "eagle" in another's hands and came and saluted Cæsar on the poop.

"Who can die better than in Rome's behalf?" asked Cæsar, looking straight at him.

It was a calculating, cold look, but the man smiled proudly.

"None," he answered. "I will gladly die for Rome."

"Lead the Tenth to the shore!" commanded Cæsar. "I will watch you."

The man grinned and saluted, Cæsar merely nodding. Nothing more was said, no other order given; but, as if the eyes of all the fleet had watched that incident, there was a sudden stiffening and an expectancy that could be felt.

The man was rowed back to his ship, and in another moment he was standing in the bow with his standard raised.

In all that din of twanging engines, clatter of the javelins on shields, grinding of sea on the beach and the creaking of cordage, the man's words were inaudible, but his gesture as he courted death was histrionic, dignified, superb.

He made a short speech, raised the standard high above his head, and plunged into the sea, neck deep, working his way toward the nearest Britons, daring the immortal Tenth to let their standard fall into enemy hands.

With a roar and a clanging of shields they plunged in after him, many drowning instantly because the ship had backed off into slightly deeper water and the Britons were there in hundreds, leaping from horseback to swim and meet them where armor was a disadvantage.

The standard-bearer fell, but the eagle passed to another soldier of the Tenth, who carried it farther inshore before he went down and yet another soldier raised it; and by that time shipload after shipload of Romans had leaped into the sea and men were trying to lock shields, neck deep, around whatever standard happened to be near them.

As they worked their way shoreward they had to meet the British chariots that charged in, hubs awash, six fighting men in each, who leaped along the pole between the horses and over the heads of the front-rank Romans, turning then to break up the formation from the rear.

Twice the legionaries quailed and fell back toward deeper water, but Cæsar withdrew the ships behind them, forcing them to stand and fight, or drown. And in the end it was that, and the British system of rushing forward to engage and retreating to give a fresher man a chance, that decided the battle.

The engines of destruction on the warships swept the beach, making it more and more difficult to reënforce the fighting line, smashing chariots with catapulted rocks and cutting down the horses with volleys of low-flying arrows.

And the legionaries knew their Cæsar; knew that he would let them drown unless they gained the day for him.

So the standards swayed forever nearer to the shore;

and in the shallower water they could hold their close formation, although the chariots, with scythes set in the wheel-hubs, mowed them again and again. But they learned the trick of slashing at the horses before they could wheel to bring the scythes in play.

And at last a standard reached the shore, with twenty men around it, and the standard-bearer raised it high to plant it in British earth. The catapults and arrow-engines had to cease fire then, as one standard after another gained the margin of the shore and paused an instant for the men to lock their shields in solid lines behind it.

The legions sang then—they were ever noisy winners— roaring to the British chiefs to lock their wives away because they brought Rome's common husband with them, who would leave a trail of Cæsarlings to improve the breed.

They sang of Cæsar; and they warmed themselves pursuing Britons up the beach. For after a few more chariot charges the Britons withdrew toward the forests inland, carrying off most of their dead and wounded, not exactly beaten, but in no mood to continue the battle.

"Barbarians," said Cæsar blandly on the high poop. "Such people rarely care for fighting when the sun goes down. We will anchor here. Put provisions ashore."

A centurion came rowing out to say that there was good ground for a camp within a furlong of the shore, so Cæsar ordered the picks and shovels overside. Then he jumped his horse into the water very splendidly in sight of the men of the Tenth, who cheered him to the echo, and rode ashore to hear the roll called and to weep and moan over the list of slain—for he was very good indeed at that.

"Anchor here for the night?" said Tros in Greek to Conops. "Cæsar is mad. The gods—"

"Aye, anchor!" said a Roman voice beside him. "Can you pick up an anchor in darkness, Tros?"

Tros turned and looked into the eyes of Caius Volusenus. A small boat rocked alongside.

"Come," said Caius Volusenus with a sidewise gesture of the head.

But Cæsar habitually did not overlook much, even in the hour of victory. A centurion stepped up, who announced that by Cæsar's order Tros and his servant must remain on board ship. Caius Volusenus cursed the fellow's impudence, but there was nothing to be gained by that.

107

"He who obeys Cæsar can afford to be impudent," said the centurion, leaning back against the rail and spitting overside. "What nice dry feet has Caius Volusenus!"

His own were wet, and he had a slight wound in the shoulder.

So Caius Volusenus, cursing savagely, climbed into his boat and had himself rowed ashore, while Tros watched the bustle of unloading and studied the sunset thoughtfully. He observed that no ship had more than one anchor out, nor much scope to her cable.

"Cæsar is quite mad," he remarked to Conops pleasantly. "If Caswallon is not so mad, and if he happens to be sober, and remembers, I can see the end of this."

An hour or so later in the deepening twilight, leaning over the stern, he saw three shadowy ships that ghosted westward, three miles out to sea.

They were smaller than the smallest Cæsar had with him, and the silhouettes were nearly crescent-moon shaped, so high they were at prow and stern. His seaman's eye observed how clumsily they yawed over the ground-swell, and how different the oar stroke was from Roman pratice.

The centurion also observed them.

"Gauls," he suggested. "Barbarous looking craft—how I would hate to put to sea in them. I suppose Cæsar ordered them to follow the fleet and guide the stragglers, or perhaps to scout, in case the Britons should have a ship or two. But I wonder that he trusts such fishy looking rabble."

"So do I," said Tros, noticing that the three dim ships had picked up a light wind that carried them westward finely.

He said nothing more until a slave came to call the centurion down to the surgeon, who had established a rough dressing station in the ship's waist. Then he turned to Conops.

"Caswallon is not mad. He is not drunk. He has not forgotten," he remarked. "Those three ships were his."

Inland, camp-fires began glowing on the earthwork that the legionaries raised with pick and shovel—they had brought the firewood for the purpose with them on the ships. From the camp to the shore there was a line of sentries posted, but they were invisible; only the clank of their shields sounded as they moved occasionally, and a rising and falling murmur as they called their numbers, each man to the next one.

108

It was pitch dark, and the full moon not yet due for an hour, when Caius Volusenus came with an order from Cæsar in writing.

"I am to take my ship and pick that anchor up," he said to Tros. "You and your servant are to come and help me find it."

The centurion, with a bandage on his shoulder and his bronze waist-armor laid aside, objected. It appeared that the surgeon had hurt him, for he spoke between his teeth.

"Bite that!" said Caius Volusenus, thrusting the written order under his nose. "He who obeys Cæsar has the last word!"

But the centurion called for a torch and demanded to see what was written, and it was he who had the last word after all:

"Be careful. I am sure that Cæsar would be sorry if you should wet your feet or get hurt!" he sneered, and turned his back before the other man could answer.

CHAPTER XIII

HYTHE AND CASWALLON

Though I have condemned you for brawling, never have I counseled peace at any price. I know but one man meaner than the coward so self-loving that he will not face the consequences of the common treasons against manhood. He is too mean to be worthy of death by ordeal; let him run; let him hide; let him live and be humiliated by his meanness. But he is a paragon of manhood in comparison to him who might have fought, and should have fought, but dared not fight, and who afterwards sneers at the vanquished.

There is nothing wholesome, nothing good in war except the willingness of each to face the consequences of the mischiefs ye have all wrought and condoned. It is your war and ye made it. Face it like men. There is no peace other than an earned peace worth the having.

FROM THE SAYINGS OF THE DRUID TALIESAN

CAIUS VOLUSENUS' galley picked up the same wind that had wafted the three ghost-ships on their way, but it began to blow considerably harder, and Tros, with his eyes toward the weather, chuckled to himself; for a nearly full moon rose astern with a double halo, and was presently so overcast with clouds that Cæsar's camp-fires seemed to grow doubly bright.

There were no lights on the ships that pitched and rolled at anchor, nor any on that of Caius Volusenus; but great fires burned in forest clearings and along the cliffs in proof the Britons were awake and stirring.

Caius Volusenus fretted on his poop, anticipating sea-sickness and fearing it as some men dread an evil conscience.

"Is this that cursed equinox?" he asked, squinting at the wan moon as it showed for a moment through a bank of clouds.

"A foretaste," Tros answered.

But he was not so sure. He was afraid old Gobhan had miscalculated, for the gale blew fresher every minute and, with a rising sea behind, the galley pitched and yawed like a barrel adrift.

"Keep a lookout for the bearings," he ordered Conops. "Remember that bleak headland and the level land to westward of it."

Conops waited until Caius Volusenus went and lay to leeward vomiting. Then:

"Master," he said in a low voice, "neither you nor I can find a spar tied to an anchor on a night like this. Why not run into the port of Hythe, if we can find the entrance, and seize this ship with the aid of those Britons, and—"

"Because we would have to fight for the ship, and there would be men slain, of whom you and I would be the first, and we have work to do."

"Then what? Are we to wait until the morning, and quarter the sea until we find that spar?"

"I am a liar on occasion," Tros answered. "If I lie like a Greek this night, and you lie like a Trojan; and if Caius Volusenus' brains are all aswim from vomiting; and if his crew is not much better off, who shall know we lie, except we two?

"Look out, then, for the bearings of that spar; for I hate to lie like a Roman, without appearance of excuse. Pick them up soon, Conops, pick them up soon. For if I am ever to bring this wallowing hulk into the wind I must do it presently, before the gale grows worse."

So when they bore down by the great grim headland near where the galley had pitched at anchor while Tros was in Britain, Conops cried out suddenly and pointed to where the moon shone for a moment between black waves.

Tros roared out to the crew and wore the ship around, at a risk of swamping, dousing the sail then and letting her high poop serve the purpose of a sail to keep her head to the waves.

Then Conops tied an oil-soaked bundle of corn sacks to the ship's bow, and in the smooth, slick wake of that he launched a small boat, forcing four of the crew to help him by pretending he had orders straight from Caius Volusenus.

But the Roman commander was in no condition to give orders. Dimly, in between the throes of vomiting, he understood that they had reached the place where the anchor had been buoyed; it certainly never occurred to him that, even if the dancing spar should have been seen, the ship had drifted from it downwind long since, and that no small boat could hope to work to windward.

He groaned and wished whoever came to question him .across the Styx.

Had he given orders, it is likely they had come too late; for Tros held the boat while Conops jumped in—then followed in the darkness, pushing off before a man could interfere, and the last they saw of Caius Volusenus was his pale face over the ship's stern—whether vomiting, or watching to see them drown, they never knew.

They had no sail. Their oars were short, and the boat was made for harbor work—an unsafe, rickety, flat-bottomed thing that steered like a dinner dish.

"To the shore!" yelled Tros, pulling stroke, "and when she upsets, cling to your oar and swim for it."

But when a man and a loyal mate give thought to nothing except speed and are perfectly willing to upset if that is written in their destiny, they upset not so easily. It is the men who hesitate and calculate who lose out on a dark night in a stormy sea. Strength, and a vision of what is beyond, work wonders.

So it happened that the breakers pounding on the shingle beach that guards the marshes to the east of Hythe threw up a boat and two men clinging to it, who stood still, shivering in the wind awhile and watched by the light of the moon a ship a mile away that rolled her beam ends under while her crew struggled to make sail and run before the storm.

"May they drown," remarked Conops bitterly, perhaps because his teeth were chattering.

"They will not," said Tros, half closing his eyes as he peered into the wind. "There is no real weight to this. It is

111

a foretaste. It will die before daylight. Old Gobhan was right after all—I was a fool to doubt him. The equinox will come after the full moon. Cæsar's men will ride this out successfully and think they can repeat it when the full gales come. Now—best foot forward and be warm."

Tros wrung the salt water from his cloak and led the way, keeping to the beach where the going was difficult, but the direction sure, swinging his sword as he went along, until he found dry sand into which to plunge the blade.

There was no sound to break the solitude except the pounding of waves on shingles; no light except the wan moon breaking through the clouds; no sight of Caius Volusenus' ship. They could no longer see the lights of Cæsar's camp behind them, but on the hills to the right the Britons had huge fires burning, that made the wind-swept beach seem all the lonelier.

Hungry and utterly tired, they reached the swamp beside Hythe harbor three hours before dawn, and chanced on one of the narrow tracks that wound among the reeds, between which, once, they caught a glimpse of four shadowy ships at anchor, one much smaller than the other three.

But though they hailed, crying, "Gobhan! Oh, Gobhan!" there was no answer; their voices echoed over empty wastes of water, and the track they were following came to an end at a place where a boat had been hidden in the rushes. But the boat was gone.

"Shall we swim for it?" asked Conops.

Tros had had enough of swimming for one night. He roared again for Gobhan and, disgusted with failure, turned to retrace his steps and find another track, jerking his heels out of the soggy mud and stumbling, until suddenly he heard a voice among the reeds ten yards away, and crouched, sword forward. Then he heard three Britons talking, and one voice he thought he recognized.

"I am Tros," he shouted, louder than he knew. A laugh he could have picked out of a hundred answered him:

"Why not call for me? As well cry out for the Sea-God as for Gobhan."

Caswallon broke through the reeds, seized Tros by the hand and dragged him on to firmer ground, where two other Britons, one of them wounded, leaned on spears.

"Gobhan died, say I. The sailors say the Sea-God called him. If you should tell me that the sailors threw him overboard, I would think three times before giving you the

112

lie," said Caswallon. "I knew you would come, Tros. My chariot is yonder. I heard you shouting."

He led the way with long, sure-footed strides to where his chariot waited with at least a dozen mounted men who wore wolf-skin cloaks over their nearly naked bodies.

"I left Fflur with the army, because she can hold them as none else can," he explained. "What do you think now of us Britons? Did we fight well?"

"Not so well as Cæsar," Tros answered.

Caswallon laughed, a shade grimly.

"Two thirds of my men were late. They are not here yet," he added. "If Cæsar's cavalry should come—"

But it was Tros's turn to laugh. He knew the cavalry would not come.

"My father is the pilot for the cavalry," he answered. "He is a wiser man than I—a better sailor. If he has not wrecked them on the quicksands—"

"Yonder with my three ships is a little one from Gaul," said Caswallon. "The Gaul brings word that Cæsar's cavalry have put back into port."

"They will never reach Britain, if my father lives," said Tros; to which Caswallon answered two words:

"Gobhan died."

He seemed to think that was an evil omen.

There was no more talk until they reached a long, low building just outside the town of Hythe, where women were serving mead and meat by torchlight to a score of men who had evidently not been near the fighting.

Caswallon was in a grim mood, with an overlying smile that rather heightened than concealed it, hardly nodding when the new men greeted him, refusing mead, refusing to be seated, saying nothing until silence fell.

But Tros ate and drank; the chieftainship was none of his affair.

"We are beaten," said Caswallon at last, "and for lack of a thousand men to answer their chief's summons. Cæsar has landed and has already fortified his camp. It is your fault—yours and the others' who have not come. I am ashamed."

There was murmuring, particularly in the darker corners where the torchlight hardly reached.

"We defend Hythe. Cæsar fears us, or he would have brought his fleet to Hythe," a man remarked. "He does not fear you, because he knows you are a weak chief. Was he wrong? Has he not defeated you?"

Caswallon made a gesture of contempt, then folded

both arms on his breast—and it was naked, as he had exposed it to the enemy.

"Hold Hythe then," he answered. "Ye are not worth coaxing. The men who fought to-day are my friends, and I know them. Ye are not my friends, and I will never know you. But I bid you hold Hythe for your own sakes.

For if Cæsar learns of the harbor and brings his fleet in here, he will stay all winter; and then, forever ye are Cæsar's slaves. But it may be, ye would sooner be the slaves of Cæsar than free men under Caswallon."

They murmured again, but he dismissed them with a splendid gesture.

"Get ye gone into the darkness, where your souls live!" he commanded.

But a dozen stayed and swore to follow him, and when he had repudiated them a time or two he accepted their promises, although without much cordiality.

"They who fought to-day, have fought. I know them. Ye who have not fought, have to prove yourselves."

And presently, one by one, the others who had gone out at his bidding into darkness began to slink back, until the room was full again. The women brought in mead, and Caswallon consented to drink when they begged him two or three times, but he only tasted and then set the stuff aside.

"And now, Lord Tros—my brother Tros," he said, smiling gratefully at last, "so your father is safe? I am not in debt to you for that life yet?"

"I am a free man and you owe me nothing," Tros answered. "My father is a free man, and his life is his, to give or to withhold until his time comes. And I told you that I drive no bargains, for I never knew the bargain that was fair to both sides; so I give or I withhold, I accept or I reject, as I see right, and let Them judge my acts whose business that is.

"But I warn you: If I live, and if my father lives and is a prisoner in Gaul, I will invite you to help me rescue him. As to what your answer will be, that is your affair."

"I am your friend and your father's friend," said Caswallon. "I have spoken before witnesses."

There was a pause, a long, deep breathing silence, until Caswallon glanced around the room, and said:

"I would be alone with Lord Tros."

They filed out into darkness one by one; but Conops stayed, and Caswallon nodded to him.

"What said Gobhan of the tides?" he asked, and sat down on a roughly carved chair, leaning his head against the back of it. He seemed tired out. "I can wear out Cæsar and his little army. But if more ships come, and cavalry, and more supplies—"

He shrugged his shoulders.

"The full moon, and the high tide, and the equinox," said Tros grimly. "Three more days, and then the storm will burst. For my part, I would rather that the gods should kill men than that I should be the butcher. How many were slain to-day?"

"Of my side? Three hundred and nine. And of Cæsar's?"

"More than four hundred," said Tros. "That is death enough for the sake of one man's glory and a helmet full of pearls. Are you a crafty liar? Can you lie to Cæsar and delay him while I loose his ships for the storm to play with?"

"How shall I convince him?" asked Caswallon.

"Give him Commius. Promise to give other hostages and to pay him tribute. Promise him pearls."

Caswallon nodded.

"Aye—he is welcome to Commius the Gaul."

"A lie well told is worth a thousand men," said Tros. "Truth is good, and pride is good. But Cæsar measures truth by bucketsful, and he is prouder, with a meaner pride, than you or I could be if we should live forever. Therefore, swallow pride and lie to him."

"That is what Fflur advised," said Caswallon.

"She has vision. Her advice is good."

"And the longships?"

"Will the crews obey me?" asked Tros. "If they slew Gobhan, what will they do to me?"

"You are a man after their own heart. Gobhan was a wizard and they feared him," said Caswallon. "They will stand by you, for I have promised each man coin enough to buy mead for a year."

Tros thought a minute.

"Hide two ships among the reeds," he answered then, "and put all three crews on the third ship. Select the worst ship for me, for you will lose it. See that the men have knives or axes. Then leave me here; fetch Commius the Gaul, and send him to Cæsar with a man you trust, to offer hostages and tributes.

115

"But don't trust yourself within Cæsar's reach, because he is a craftier liar than ever you can hope to be. He will speak you fair, but he will hold you prisoner if you approach him near enough; and he will march you in his triumph through the Roman streets, if he has to lose a thousand of his men in order to accomplish it.

"Thereafter they will cut your head off in a stinking dungeon and toss your carcass to the city dogs and crows —they keep a dunghill for the purpose."

They talked for an hour after that, and then went and routed out the ships' crews, who had come ashore to drink in Hythe. Half drunk already, wholly mutinous, they challenged Tros, telling him they had no use for autumn storms and still less use for lee shores where Roman fleets were anchored. They had seen enough of Cæsar on their way down.

But Tros smote a captain with his fist and flung the mate crashing through a shutter. Thereafter, disdaining to draw his sword on fishermen, he seized a wooden bench and cracked a skull or two with that, until the bench broke and the Britons began to admire him.

Caswallon looked on grimly, offering no aid.

"For if I help you, Tros, they will say I helped you. It is better that they learn to fear you on your own account," he remarked.

They also learned a quite peculiar respect for Conops. He knew all the tricks the longshore press-gangs used in the Levant for crimping sailors. He could use the handle of his knife more deftly than those Britons used a blade, and it was hardly dawn when all three crews decided they had met their masters, piled, swearing but completely satisfied, into small boats and rowed themselves to one ship, ready to continue to obey their new commander.

CHAPTER XIV

"IF CÆSAR COULD ONLY KNOW"

Ye call youselves the heirs of this or that one who begat you. I say, ye are heirs of Eternity. What does it matter who saw your triumph? Whose praise seek ye? And whose hatred stirs your pride? Eternity is Life. Life knows. And as ye do, it shall be done unto you. No matter what your generosity, I tell

116

you malice is a mean man's comfort and begets its own
humiliation.

FROM THE SAYINGS OF THE DRUID TALIESAN

THAT ship, with sixty men aboard, was something worse
than Tros had ever known in all his sea experience. It
would have been bad enough, if he could have put to sea
at once, with hard labor at the oars to keep the three
crews busy; but a three-day wait, with all provisions short
and Hythe in sight, full of mead and women, and no
news—but a mystery—and fires along the hills at night
was invitation to the Britons to display the whole of their
inborn and accumulated zeal for doing just the opposite of
what they should.

They knew a thousand reasons why they ought to go
ashore; not one for staying where they were. They wanted
to revisit the two other ships and make sure all was well
with them in the mud berths where they lay concealed.

They demanded money, mead, more food and better;
they insisted on new cordage; they proposed to go a-
fishing; they fought with one another, with the new knives
Caswallon had provided; they refused to make repairs,
and pointed out whatever needed doing as a good enough
excuse for going ashore forever.

They listened to Tros's promises with leering grins that
told of disbelief; and when he scuttled the small boats, to
keep them aboard ship, eleven of them swam ashore and
yelled from a place of safety amid the reeds to all the
others to swim and join them.

That same night the eleven swam back again, reporting
that the men of Hythe were a scurvy gang, and the
women worse; they proposed to storm the town and burn
it in revenge for having been refused free food and drink,
and they promised Tros full obedience thereafter, if he
would only lead them to the night assault.

And Tros suffered another anxiety, even greater than
they could provide. The weather held calm and gray, with
varying light winds that might have tempted Cæsar's ships
to look for safer anchorage—or might have tempted the
cavalry to sail again from Gaul.

He had no means of knowing whether the cavalry had
come at last, nor where his father might be; and all that
held him from setting sail for Gaul to find his father, was
the knowledge that his father would despise him for having left a promise unkept and a duty unattempted.

Thirty times in three days his determination nearly

117

failed him, only to return because he had to show himself a man to Conops, and a master on his own poop to the Britons.

But at last the night of full moon, and an offshore wind that blew the reeds flat. That afternoon there was a tide so low that a man could have walked knee-deep across the harbor mouth. The gulls flocked close inshore, and by evening the sky was black with racing clouds.

By night, when the raging wind kicked up steep waves against the tide, the crew swore to a man that they would never put to sea in that storm even if Tros should carry out his threat to burn the ship beneath them by way of penalty.

Yet he had his way, and even he could hardly have told afterwards how he contrived it. It was Conops who slipped the cable, so that the ship drifted toward the harbor mouth.

Tros steered her for the boiling bar, guessing by the milk-white foam that gleamed against the darkness and the thunder of the waves; and when the ship pitched and rolled, beam-on, the crew took to the oars to save themselves.

Once clear of the bar, in darkness and a howling sea, there was nothing left for them but to hoist a three-reefed sail and pray to all the gods they had ever heard of.

There was no risk of Cæsar's men seeing them too soon, nor any other problem than to keep the ship afloat and close inshore. If the wind should blow them offshore, there would be no hope of beating back; and the oars were useless, with the waves boiling black and hungry and irregular.

The one hope was to hug the beach until they should work under the lee of the high cliffs, where Cæsar's fleet had more or less protection as long as the wind held in the north-northwest; and to that end Tros took all the chances, judging his distance from shore by the roar of the surf on the beach—for he could not see a ship's length overside.

Once he sailed so close inshore and the crew were so afraid, that six men rushed him at the helm, meaning to beach the ship and jump for it; but Conops fought them off, and Tros held his course—in good deep water within thirty feet of shore.*

* A modern battleship can approach the shore between Hythe and Sandgate close enough for a stone to be thrown on her deck from the beach.

118

And presently the crew began to wonder at him and to think him an immortal. When the moon broke through the racing clouds he looked enormous at the helm, with his cloak and his black hair streaming in the wind, one leg against the bulwark and his full weight strained against the long oar.

Then the rain came, and the lightning gleamed on the gold band on his forehead. And when he laughed they knew he was a god and he knew something else—that Cæsar's fleet was at his mercy.

For the lightning flashes shone on high white cliffs with foam below them, tossing Cæsar's anchored ships; and he knew old Gobhan had been right about the high tide and the full moon; knew that he, too, had been right when he declared that Cæsar and his men were mad.

For they had beached the lighter ships, and as they lay careened the high tide had reached and filled them. Flash after flash of lightning showed the Romans laboring at cable-ends to haul them higher out of water, while the surf stove in their sterns and rolled them beam-on, while a cable-length from shore the bigger ships plunged madly at short anchor-ropes, without a crew on board to man them if they broke adrift.

So Tros laughed aloud and sang, and Conops chanted with him. And because they reached the lee of the high cliffs it grew a little calmer; but the Britons thought that Tros, being superhuman, had so ordered it, so when he roared to them to shake out all the reefs and man the sheets and stand by, they obeyed him, knowing there would be a miracle.

They hauled the yard up high and let the full force of the wind into the sail, all sixty of them working with a will. Then Tros put the helm up and turned square before the storm, for he had picked out Cæsar's galley, with the high poop, plunging closer inshore than the rest.

"Belay the sheets! Stand by to grapple!" he commanded, bellowing bull-throated downwind.

Conops leaped into the waist to hammer men's ribs with his knife-hilt and drive them aft along the bulwark ready for the crash.

They struck the galley head-on, crashing in their own bows on the Roman's beak. No need then to tell those Britons what to do; they had fought too many Northmen at close quarters. The galley's cable parted at the shock. The sail bore both ships seaward, grinding as they plunged, until the sail split into ribbons and Tros let go the helm at last.

"Jump!" he roared.

There was no need. He was the last man overside, scrambling up the galley's bows as the British longship heeled and filled and sank under the grinding iron beak.

He was at the helm of Cæsar's ship more swiftly than she swung her broadside to the wind. Before Conops could compel the Britons to make sail—they were bent on looting, and the knife-hilt had to go to work—he got control enough, by straining at the helm, to drift across a warship's bows and break her cable, sending her loose into the next one.

Then, wallowing in the trough of steep waves, clumsily and fumbling in the dark with Conops jumping here and there among them, the Britons hoisted sail. And Tros, caring nothing whether the sail held or parted, nor whether he sank the galley and himself too, broke cable after cable down the line until the whole of Cæsar's anchored fleet was drifting in confusion, galley crashing galley, timbers splintering, and here and there the cry of a Roman watchman for help from nobody knew where.

Black night and sudden lightning shimmering on the white cliffs. Darkness again and the crimson of Cæsar's camp-fires streaming down the wind. Thunder of the hollow warships dueling together in the trough between the waves.

Cracking of spars and masts—shouts—panic—trumpet blowing on the beach—and then a roar from Tros as he brought the galley head to wind:

"Three reefs!"

He had drifted too far seaward. There was another line of forty ships he hoped to smash. But though Conops, laboring like Hercules and cursing himself hoarse, did make the Britons reef the thundering sail, he found he could not work the galley back to windward.

So he kept her wallowing shoulder to the sea and watched the havoc on the beach, where men were drowning as they tried to save the smaller vessels.

"Master, for what do we wait?" asked Conops, climbing to the poop to stand beside him.

"For Cæsar!" Tros answered. "I must see him! He must see me!"

But the lightning flashes were too short, and the fires the Romans lighted on the beach too dim and wet and smoky for that perfect climax to a perfect night.

120

"If only he might know who did this to him," Tros grumbled. "I could die then."

"And your father?" asked Conops. "If we knew that your father was safe," he shouted, with his mouth to Tros's ear. "But if he is Cæsar's prisoner—"

"Ready about!" roared Tros. "All hands on the sheets!"

Conops sprang into the waist, translating that command with the aid of fists and knife-hilt, bullying but one third of the crew because the rest were searching like a wolf pack for the loot, ripping open sacks and using axes on the chests of stores. The twenty wore the ship around, and Tros headed her south by east.

"Where to, then, now?" asked Conops, climbing to the poop again, breathless and exhausted. "Caritia?" *

"In Cæsar's ship? With such a crew? To fight ashore with one or two of Cæsar's legions?" Tros answered. "Nay. I am not so mad as that."

"What then?" asked Conops.

"I think we have given Cæsar all his bellyful. I think he will return to Gaul, if he can gather ships enough—for if he doesn't, Caswallon will destroy him.

"Then I will claim that Caswallon owes a debt to me. I think that he will pay it. He is worth ten Cæsars. He will help me free my father. Find me one of those British captains. Shake him from the loot and bring him here before they ax the ship's bottom loose!"

Conops returned with two of them.

"Gold!" one Briton exclaimed, gasping. "Chests of gold coin!"

"Can you find the way up Thames-mouth to Lunden?" Tros roared, making them stand downwind where they could hear him plainly. For the wind shrieked in the rigging.

They nodded.

"Do you dare it in this weather?"

They nodded again, hugging armsful of plunder beneath stolen Roman cloaks. All they craved now was to take the plunder home, and time to broach the wine-casks in the ship's waist.

They were afraid of nothing any longer, except Tros; he had not quite lost his superhuman aspect. But he knew the end of that would come as soon as they should broach the wine-casks.

"With a different crew and a south wind I would dare it

* Calais.

121

too," said Tros. "You Britons will never become sailors if you live a thousand years, but I must make the best of you. Do you think, if you were dead, that you could work this ship to windward?"

They shook their heads as if they had not understood him.

"You can do it better with your life in you? Well then, throw all that wine overboard—all hands to it! You have your choice of dying two ways. I will kill the man who dares to broach a cask. And if you think you can kill me and then drink Cæsar's wine, you will all die of a burning bellyache!

"You doubt it? Hah! That wine was meant for Cæsar's gift to Caswallon. He poisoned it with gangrened adders' blood and hemlock! Drink it, will you? Heave it overboard, if you hope to live and see Thames River!"

They doubted him, and yet—he had done wonders; it was hardly safe to doubt him. It was difficult to rig a tackle in that sea. They were very weary.

"Die if you wish," said Tros. "Or make Thames-mouth if we can; for I am ready to attempt it. Choose!"

They elected to obey him and, to save hard labor, broached the wine into the ship's bilge, where not even a rat would care to drink it.

"How did you know that Cæsar poisoned it?" asked Conops, as the empty casks went overside one by one.

"I didn't," Tros answered. "But I knew we could never make Thames-mouth with a crew of drunken Britons. And a lie, my little man, well told, on suitable occasions, sounds as good in the gods' ears as a morning hymn—as good as the crash of the breaking of Cæsar's ships!

"Set ten men in the bows on watch. Bring those fisher captains back to me to help me find the way. Then turn in, and be ready to relieve me at the helm."

He turned and shook his fist at Cæsar's camp-fires.

"Ye gods! Ye great and holy gods! This were a perfect night if only Cæsar could know who smashed his ships! Who has his pay-chests!"

too," said Tros. "You fellows will never become sailors if you live a thousand years; but I must make the best of you. He can think if you were dead that you could work then—"

CHAPTER XV

EARLY AUTUMN: 55 B.C.

It is not victory, which either side may win by chance, but what ye do with victory that weighs for or against you in the eternal scales.

FROM THE SAYINGS OF THE DRUID TALIESAN

TROS found the Thames. His stolen bireme with a long slit in her sail and half of her cordage hanging overside, lolled on the incoming tide up Thames-mouth. The shore, far away on either hand, was mud with dense forest behind it. Thousands of sea-birds flocked and screamed over the mussel beds, and hundreds followed the ship's wake; but the five and sixty men on board had had no rations for two days, so there was no waste for the gulls to get excited over. The crew was even short of water.

Tros sat on the only water-cask on the high poop, beside Conops who held the steering oar. There were half a dozen sullen Britons in the bow. The remainder sat, chin on knees, in the ship's waist, abaft the low, square citadel.

Tros's amber eyes were heavy from lack of sleep. The gold band across his forehead that held his heavy black hair in place, was awry, giving him a drunken look. His purple cloak, creased and sea-stained, was torn; one slit looked as if it might have been done by some one's knife. The knuckles of his left hand were bruised and bleeding.

One Briton in the ship's waist kept feeling at his teeth, as if to count those that remained.

Forward, on the ship's bow, there were two machines for shooting flights of arrows. There were two more on a kind of citadel amidships and two on the poop. But all except those on the poop had been put out of commission by removing the gut strings. The Britons had no knives nor any other weapons and looked sullenly aware of it.

Conops, after hauling at the long steering oar half a dozen times to keep the ship from drifting beam-on to the tide, cocked his one bloodshot eye at Tros.

"Master, they have not drunk since yesterday."

123

"Nor I. Nor you," Tros answered.

"Better give them a drink now, master, else I think they will come at us again. They look ugly. They are close to home."

"Aye, too close." Tros hitched his long purple scabbard so that the sword hilt lay readier to hand.

"When a man has been paid off he is no more use until he has spent the money. When a thirsty Briton has had drink—back there!" he roared, striding toward the ladder that led down into the ship's waist.

His hand was on the ship's sword hilt. The Britons retreated and sat down again. But an iron bolt thrown from forward of the citadel missed Tros by the thickness of the whiskers on his dark, determined jaw. He squared his shoulders.

"Bring me that man!" he commanded.

For a moment or two there was no response. Conops let go the steering oar, fitted the iron crank to one of the after arrow-machines and, laying twelve long arrows in the grooves, wound the bow taut. Four of the Britons went then and fetched a man who was hiding forward of the citadel, hustling him aft, toward the poop ladder. He climbed up alone and stood glaring at Tros—dark-skinned, dark-eyed, nearly a head shorter and not so broad as he, but lithe and active looking, with a week's growth of straight black hair on his face and a desperate stare in his eyes.

"What have you to say?" Tros asked him.

"I threw. I missed. If I loved you, I would not have thrown. If I were not parched and hungry, I would not have missed."

Tros laughed, with his hands on his hips and his head thrown back. His was a volcanic "Ho-ho-hoh!" that shook his shoulders.

"That is a man's answer! Hah! I like it. So you love me not? Let us see whether the sea-gods or the gods of Britain love you."

Suddenly he tripped the man, seized him as he fell and, lifting him by arm and leg, hurled him down among the others in the ship's waist, where a dozen of them broke his fall because they could not get out of the way in time. Tros stood, arms akimbo, and laughed again.

"I am a better shot than he was," he remarked. "How many have I hit with one bolt? Six—seven. And the bolt still good for a day's work. Man the oars now, every mother's son of you, before I—"

He made a gesture with his thumb toward the arrow-engine, but his eyes were scanning the northern riverbank. One Briton dived off the bow and began swimming like a seal toward a drifting log.

"Down off that bow, the rest of you!" roared Tros, and Conops took aim.

They had more sense than to wait for a flight of arrows that could hardly miss one of them. They might have hidden forward of the ship's citadel, but panic is uncalculating stuff. They went to the oars instead. Thirty oars on each side went out through the ports and the steady thump and swing began, Tros beating time with his sword hilt on a Roman soldier's bronze shield—Cæsar's own, for aught he knew; it was a work of art, embossed with figures of Alexander of Macedon and his generals, in high relief.

"Now!" he shouted. "Two hours' strong rowing, and I broach the water barrel. You shall drink as you shall row—enough or not enough. My word on it."

Conops no longer had to strain at the steering oar. The galley steered easily with all that way on her. He and Tros watched the swimmer, who was steadily pushing the log in front of him across the tide toward where three crowded, unsafe looking craft had put out from a creek two miles away.

"Better shoot him, master. Of twelve arrows, one would surely hit."

"Aye, but what use, Conops? If he drowns, that is the gods' affair, and his. The men in those boats have already seen us. If they think we are some new kind of northern rover, I like their spunk. If they recognize this for a Roman galley, I admire their spunk still more. It is no child's play, Conops, to put out in skin-covered baskets and offer fight to a warship! And I think these Britons of ours may help us fight them off—plunder being plunder."

"It looks to me as if there are at least thirty or forty of them in each of those boats," Conops answered. "Look! Three more boats. Spunk? They will come close and throw fire into us."

"Not they," said Tros. "What plunder is there from a burned ship? They will follow until the tide turns, or our rowers tire, or until we stick our beak into a mud bank. Then they will try to fight their way aboard, as wolves attack a cornered stag. And it would be no use ramming them," he mused. "That basket-work they build with wouldn't crush; they would simply climb over our beak."

"That swimmer will tell them we are only two, and our crew against us. Turn, master! Put to sea again," Conops urged, making ready to throw his weight against the steering oar.

"Without water enough for a day!"

"But look! There come three more of them."

"Four more, making eight. There will be others as we go up-river. We have but a netted fish's chance, Conops, unless we get a slant of wind. They are all pirates along the riverbank. Unless we reach Lunden and find Caswallon this will be our last journey in this world, little man. Keep her more in midstream; we need the full force of the tide."

Tros went and stood by the poop ladder, watching the rowers. One of them drew his oar back through the port and offered argument:

"What is the use? Our friends come. Wait."

"Out with that oar and row!" Tros thundered. "If you don't, you shall sizzle like eggs on a skillet, for I'll burn the ship before one Briton comes aboard without my leave."

Eight days of thrashing to and fro in storms, from Kent to the coast of Belgium and half way to Germany before they made Thames-mouth at last, had taught them that he did everything he said he would, including the breaking of heads.

They rowed steadily for half an hour, but the galley was heavy; two feet of solid water flopped in her bilge. The pursuing Britons gained, as the rowers could see from time to time, when their heads swung by the oar ports and the galley turned at a bend in the river. He who had been a captain, and was still one in his own opinion, gave tongue again, but this time did not slacken at the oar:

"You are a fool, Tros. You make us work for nothing. They gain on us all the time, and now the river narrows. We have no anchor. When the tide turns we shall drift into the mud, and there they will have their will of us, unless we come to terms. For how can we fight? You made us all throw our new knives overboard."

"Aye, a fool, and none can argue with a fool," said Tros. "I am like the tide, that has not yet turned. Row, you sons of fish-wives! Row! Row harder!"

He resumed his beating on the shield, and then, because the crew was obviously weakening, he broached the water-barrel and, taking the helm himself, sent Conops down to give them drink one by one—Conops with a two-edged knife in one hand and a copper bowl in the other, ready to jump and fight his way back to the poop. The Britons were less afraid of him than of his lion-eyed master.

The drink did the rowers good. But even so the pursuers gained. A rather futile and ill-shapen arrow plunked at the planking of the poop deck and stuck there quivering within a yard of Tros's foot. He called Conops back to the helm, swung the arrow-engine around on its swivel and fired it.

Twelve arrows swept into the crowded boat that had ventured closest. There was an answering yell, but six or seven men dropped out of view below the gunwale and, at once, all the pursuers fell back out of range, presently dividing themselves into two columns that began again to overtake the galley, four long, crowded boats on either hand, with withes erected all around them now, cross-plaited into a sort of screen to protect the crews. They had set up the withe screens incredibly swiftly.

They were unsafe, unseaworthy looking craft, too narrow for the length and having to be bailed incessantly. The men who manned the paddles were inconvenienced by the screen erection around the sides, but nevertheless comparatively safe at anything but very close range, because an arrow would have to be marvelously aimed to strike straight between the withes except by sheer luck. In the bow and the stern of each boat there were skin-clad men who brandished shields and yelled to the paddlers, exposing themselves recklessly and dancing to attract attention.

"They have fought many Northmen," Tros remarked to Conops. "They know how to draw a longship's fire and to protect the paddlers."

"Master, let them have the ship," Conops answered nervously. "While they loot this galley you and I can swim ashore, and then find our way along the bank to Lunden. Our own Britons will cease rowing presently and then—"

"Little man, all Cæsar's pay-chests lie under the hatch in the cabin below us."

"What is gold to a dead man, master?"

"Or death to a live one. Nay, I think we are not far from Lunden."

"But I see more boats," urged Conops. "Look—by the bend in the river ahead of us."

Arrows began humming into the galley. One rower fell

off his bench, shot through the eye. The other rowers stopped work and began shouting to the Britons in the boats, who answered with yells and drew closer. Conops let go the helm and jumped for the arrow-engine, twisting at the crank and shouting to Tros to lay arrows in the grooves.

But Tros took a torch from a box beside the water barrel, lighted it at an earthen firepot and brandished it around his head to make it blaze.

"Now," he roared down at the rowers. "Tell those pirates I'll burn the ship unless they haul off!"

He jumped into the ship's waist and stood with his back to the cabin door, just as Conops sent a flight of arrows twanging from the engine. If the ship were burned and beached there would still be one chance in a thousand of recovering the gold, and at any rate he was determined not to let longshore pirates have it. The best place to fire the ship would be in the cabin under the poop, where there was plenty of stuff that was inflammable.

There began to be a lot of shouting back and forth as the galley swung beam to the tide. Some of the rowers jumped overboard and swam for the already overcrowded boats; some stood on the benches to show they had no weapons and would not fight even if they had. Another flight of arrows twanged and whistled from Conops' engine, but the galley's crew yelled to the attacking parties not to answer it.

"There are two men—only two men!" they kept shouting. "Keep away, or they will burn the ship!"

Five or six more plunged overboard, and Tros decided to let them all go; he would be better off without them, better able to make terms. He swung himself up onto the poop, still brandishing the torch, and a spear thrown from alongside slit his cloak. He caught the spear and raised it as whalers hold a harpoon, leaning overside to hurl it through the bottom of the nearest boat, and paused, rigid, in that attitude.

"They run," remarked Conops from over by the arrow-engine. In some way he had jammed the mechanism and was jerking at it nervously. "Likewise, we drift into the mud."

He jumped for the helm and began straining his whole strength against it, with one foot on the bulwark rail, but Tros saw it was too late to keep the galley off the mud bank.

128

"Let her take it as she drifts," he ordered. "If she buries her beak she will lie here forever."

The galley's oars sprawled this and that way like the legs of a drunken water beetle as she swung round on the tide and settled herself comfortably on the mud.

The hide-and-wattle boats were scurrying away as fast as the paddles could drive them, but fourteen other boats, all wooden, rowed with oars and crowded with armed men, were coming on, downriver, against the tide, and in the stern of one of them, that had a gilded figurehead carved like a swan, there sat a woman, whose fair hair streamed over her shoulders.

"Fflur!"

Tros waved the torch and flung it overboard. There were still about thirty Britons in a cluster in the galley's waist, and Tros had promised that every member of the crew who should stand by faithfully until the journey's end should have a fair share of the loot. Not one of them had been what he considered faithful, and they were not at Lunden yet.

"Whoever fears Fflur, swim for it!" he shouted.

Nine or ten men heeded that suggestion.

Tros counted the remaining men and made the count nineteen, including all three captains of the three crews he had started with.

"Little man, we have the lion's share," he remarked to Conops.

"I would sell mine for one drachma in hand," said Conops.

Then Fflur came, jumping up the galley's side as actively as if she had been born to sailoring, not taking Tros's outstretched hand, until her leather-stockinged feet were on the poop deck. She kissed him on both cheeks, laughing and friendly.

In less than a minute after that the galley was a-swarm with Britons of the white-skinned, fair-haired type, some in peaked iron caps and all dressed handsomely, with their legs in dyed woolen trousers and their long shirts embroidered in three colors. They examined and laughed at everything, ignoring the crew as if they were some sort of inferior animals.

"Keep them out of the cabin below this poop," said Tros. Fflur nodded.

She had been a chief's wife long enough to take hints swiftly. She gave an order in low tones. Four men did her bidding, standing by the cabin door in the attitude of

129

bored alertness that the British climate breeds in gentlemen. They said nothing, did nothing, drew no weapon; but none offered to encroach on their preserve.

Fflur's gray eyes appeared to take in everything, including the slits in Tros's cloak.

"Caswallon will be in Lunden to-night," she said quietly. "Cæsar has left Britain will all his troops, after two battles and some skirmishing. He ordered us to send him hostages to Gaul, but Caswallon has been trying to prevent the men of Kent from doing that. Is this ship stuck fast? The beacon warned us of a Northman in the Thames, and when Caswallon is away that is my business."

Tros answered that the tide would probably lift them off the mud before long, but that he had no anchor. Then he whispered what lay under the cabin floor.

"It is yours," she said promptly, but Tros laughed.

He had a way of smiling, when the laugh was finished, that was irresistible, holding his great head a little to one side and half closing his eyes.

"Life and money are his who can keep them," he answered.

She nodded again.

"Yes. And Britain is his who can keep it. Caswallon is a king still. You helped us, Tros. I will help you."

She went down the poop ladder before Tros could offer her a hand, and into the cabin, he after her. There was hardly more than head room underneath the beams, and the place was crowded with Cæsar's personal belongings—his bed, tent, chests of clothes, toilet articles and a chest full of memoranda written by his secretary, not yet annotated.

Tros stirred among the tablets and parchments, with his cloak in Fflur's way. Then together they moved the chest from off the hatch and discovered gold in bags beneath it, bags that even Tros found heavy.

There were ten, and Fflur's eyes glistened in the dim light through the partly opened door; but not so keenly as Tros's eyes had blazed at the sight of Cæsar's seal in the box with the memoranda. While she looked at the gold he took the seal and hid it in a pocket in his cloak. Fflur called to her iron-capped gentlemen:

"Put these ten bags into my boat. Guard them."

They obeyed without comment, summoning the inferiors to do the portering, two men to a bag, themselves surveying the proceedings leisurely, arranging among

130

themselves which three should guard the gold when it was safely overside, and which one should wait with Fflur.

He looked like the most casual cockerel who ever lived—a youngish man with a very long, tawny moustache, which he twisted whenever anybody looked at him. He wore a cloak of yellow dyed linen trimmed with beaver fur, and a golden-hilted sword in a scabbard inlaid with gold. There had been a big dent in his iron cap, but it had been hammered out again until only a vague shadow of it showed.

"Anything else?" he asked in a bored voice, that was hardly insolent and yet contained no hint of deference.

Tros gestured toward the chest of memoranda. The Briton ignored him, absolutely, seemed unaware of his existence.

"Take that too," Fflur ordered, pointing at the chest, and the Briton strolled to the door to summon a sailor, who carried the chest overside.

Fflur examined Cæsar's bed and all the other odds and ends that filled the cabin.

"Is Cæsar a woman?" she asked scornfully, opening a small chest of cosmetics that reeked of eastern scents.

"I have heard strange tales of him," Tros answered. "But it may be all that stuff is for the women he meets in his wanderings."

"And this?" she asked, holding up a bowl, in which lay a strange four-bladed knife.

"He has the falling-sickness,* and at such times they bleed him with that," Tros answered. "He has them use a silver bowl because, he says, his blood is Cæsar's, which is blood of the gods, since he claims descent from Venus Genetrix. The blood is laid before her altar afterwards, and then burned with great ceremony."

The Briton in the iron cap returned and was at pains to appear disinterested, stroking his moustache and leaning his back against the door-post. Fflur introduced him at last:

"This is Orwic, son of my husband's cousin. Orwic, this is Tros, my husband's friend, a son of a Prince of Samothrace."

Orwic bowed almost imperceptibly; it was only his eyes that betrayed any real emotion.

"Oh, are you Tros? I saw you smash Cæsar's fleet off the beach eight days ago. I am glad to meet you."

* Epilepsy.

His manner altered. He looked more cordial.

"Were you in that fight on the beach?" Tros asked him.

"Oh, yes."

Fflur added details:

"His chariot was the first into the water. He was the first to slay a Roman hand to hand. It was he who slew the Roman standard-bearer of the Tenth, and he who led the boarding of a Roman galley. He was the last in retreat when the Romans won their landing on the beach. Caswallon sent him with me, in my chariot, to Lunden as a mark of honor."

"I liked the ride with you, of course," said Orwic, looking miserably self-conscious. "Fflur, do we wait here forever, or—"

"Choose twenty of the safest men and put them in charge of this ship, responsible to me," Fflur answered. "I will take Tros and his man to Lunden in my boat. Order all the captains of the other boats to fasten ropes to this ship and tow it to Lunden as soon as the tide lifts it off the mud. Tell them to be sure that the men who came with Tros have food and drink, and say that if a thing is stolen or a man harmed, Caswallon will do the punishing."

"And I?" asked Orwic.

"Come with me in my boat."

Orwic heaved a deep sigh of relief and strolled out on the deck to issue orders, pulling his moustache and looking languid, as if the mere suggestion of having anything to do bored him to the verge of death.

"A man?" Tros asked, raising his heavy eyebrows.

Fflur met his gaze and nodded, nodded twice.

CHAPTER XVI

LUNDEN TOWN

None can lie concerning nothing. Never hath lived the liar who did not hear, or see, or imagine a truth, that he might betray it. Truth is necessary to a lie as bones are necessary to a man. But concerning any truth whatever, a resourceful, or a reckless, or a stupid man can tell as many lies as there are stars on the face of heaven. Look ye, therefore, for the truth amid the lies that men tell for one sake or another.

FROM THE SAYINGS OF THE DRUID TALIESAN

LUNDEN lay amid the marshes in a forest so dense that the nearness of a town was unsuspected until one came on it around a river bend.

Then there was a gray mist on the river and the wooden buildings were wreathed in that and in smoke that rose straight up and hung like a veil between earth and sky. The sunset glowed through the haze as if all earth to westward were on fire, silhouetting the masts and spars of nearly a dozen ships, at which Tros wondered.

He had dozed away a time or two on the long row up the Thames—Conops snored shamelessly, with his head on one of Cæsar's bags of gold—and now, between sleeping and waking, he was not sure at first whether he was awake or dreaming.

"How came such ships to be here?" he demanded, speaking first in Greek, because that was his native tongue, and not remembering to talk Gaulish until Fflur laughed.

Eight storm-thrashed days and nights he and Conops had stood watch and watch over a mutinously superstitious crew, who would have sacrificed them to the sea-gods if they could have managed it.

Now to Tros, with his weary frame relaxed and the rhythmic oar thump in his ears, his head on a seat beside Fflur's knees and good cool mead under his sword belt, it almost seemed as if he had died and were in another world. There was nothing in focus, nothing as he had supposed it should be. However, Fflur's quiet voice enlightened him:

"Those are all merchant-ships from Gaul, and from the lowlands where the Belgae live, and from the cold lands to the northward."

He began to remember, as in a dream, how the longshore Britons had hunted him up Thames-mouth.

"How get they here?"

"None harms a merchant-ship," she answered. "It is only when the longships come in quest of slaves and tribute that there is any fighting, except when the merchant crews get drunk in Lunden and a little blood flows."

"I have been told, and I told Cæsar, that there is no such place as Lunden," Tros said sleepily. "I was told it is a myth place, like the land-locked sea to northward of which a man named Pytheas told two centuries ago on his return from many wanderings."

"Three of yonder ships are from that land-locked sea," Fflur answered.

Tros felt all the blood go tingling through his veins anew, for he would rather journey into unknown lands than be the emperor of all the known ones. Fflur felt, or saw the change in him and ceased smoothing his hair—he had hardly felt it.

"If the Romans knew of this river and this town," he said, musing.

"Too many know," Fflur answered. "Never a year but we must fight a dozen times to keep the Northmen from laying Lunden waste. And that is strange, because we like the Northmen, and they like us. Some we have made prisoners and have given wives to, and they have settled down among us, some even becoming lesser chiefs, and helping to fight their own folk when the longships come.

"In the spring of the year they come, and in the autumn now and then, when their own harvests have been scant and they dread the long dark winter without corn enough to keep their bellies easy, and no seed in the spring.

"And in the spring, if they have eaten all the seed that winter, they come in twos and threes and dozens, fighting one another for the right to enter Thames-mouth first. Then there is red war that lasts sometimes for weeks, and we have been hard put to it at times to drive them forth, but sometimes we burn their ships behind them.

"Once, when Caswallon had been chief not more than a few months, they sacked Lunden and burned it. But he rallied his men, and burned one ship, and sank another and made Thordsen the Northman prisoner—him and all his men.

"So Thordsen rebuilt Lunden for us, using wood and teaching us the trick of chimneys and adze-hewn timber. Caswallon gave Thordsen his own sister to wife, and she lives where the nights and days are half a year long, or so I have been told, but the Northmen are great liars.

"None of us has seen the girl since then, although we hear of her at times. It was after that Caswallon married me. My folk are the Iceni, who breed the best horses in Britain and have fought the Northmen since the world began."

Orwic, who steered the boat, and the three other young bloods, who guarded the bags of gold without appearing to admit, even to themselves, that they were doing anything unusual, betrayed interest in nothing except the

134

wild-fowl that swarmed among the reeds on either bank, commenting on those and naming them, as grebe, duck, mallard, geese, snipe and half a dozen other sorts appeared and vanished.

To listen to their conversation, nothing was wrong with Britain but the vermin that destroyed the game. Twelve rowers labored at the oars, and nodded when game was discussed, but they seemed to disapprove of Fflur's remarks about the Northmen.

They skirted the swamps around Lunden and brought the boat alongside a tiny pier that jutted out into the river where a shallow brook* flowed out between the bulrushes. To their right a low hill rose jeweled in the setting sun, enormous oaks and the roofs of painted wooden houses glowing in a mystery of mist and smoke.

There was a wall of mud and wattle, reenforced at intervals with oaken beams, that curved around the hill and out of sight; and there were thatch-roofed houses close to the wall, with their backs toward it.

Chariot tracks, some rutted deep into the clay, crisscrossed in every direction toward other houses half-invisible among the trees, but there seemed to be only one regular street, that ran between two rows of solemn and tremendous oaks toward the summit of the hill, where the red roof of a mansion bulked above ancient yews against the skyline.†

There were not many people in evidence, although a number of swarthy-skinned, dark-eyed serfs, men and women, were filling water bags and buckets at the brook and carrying them uphill with an air of having done the same thing since the world began.

But wood smoke came from a thousand chimneys and from holes in thatch roofs, suggesting supper time and plenty. The air was full of the cawing of rooks that wheeled over the trees in thousands, and the lowing of home-coming cattle, with the occasional bay of a hound or the neigh of a horse who heard the corn bin being opened.

"Lunden is a good town," said Fflur, springing out of the boat and waiting for the chariot that came galloping downhill toward them. "The druids say Lunden was a town a thousand years ago, and will be a town forever

* In later years known as the Fleet; nowadays a sewer under Fleet Street, not far from Ludgate Hill.
† Where St. Paul's Cathedral now stands.

135

until Britain disappears under the sea, because the gods know no dearer place and will preserve it."

"The gods will have to show you how to build a better wall," said Tros, eyeing the defenses sleepily.

He had seen walls twenty times a man's height, of solid stone and thicker than a house, go down before the Roman battering rams. But Orwic betrayed interest at last:

"That wall keeps the serfs at home, and the knee-high children within call," he said. "We have the forests and the swamps to fight behind. Time and again we have caught the Northmen in the swamps by felling trees around them. As long as we can hunt the wolf and stag and fox, and know the forest better than the beasts do, it seems to me likely that our wall will serve its purpose well enough. Besides, as Fflur just said, the gods love Lunden."

Tros laughed.

"I have heard them say the gods love Rome," he answered, "and I know Cæsar."

"Cæsar is beaten," Orwic answered.

He spoke with an air of calm, assured finality. One might as well have argued with the sunset—better, because the sunset could not have looked bored.

The bags of gold were heaped on the chariot floor. Fflur drove the impatient stallions with Tros beside her, and Conops asleep again beside the charioteer.

But Orwic and the other Britons waited for their horses to be brought, their youth and strength apparently too precious to be squandered on a mile's walk, or perhaps it was contrary to their religion. At any rate, walking was something a man did not argue about, but did not do.

The chariot galloped past a hundred houses that looked as if their roots were in the very soul of Britain, each in its own oak-fenced garden, with flower-beds, bee-hives, stables, cow-sheds, and a great front door of oak six inches thick.

The window openings were screened with linen, loosely woven, grayed and yellowed by the wood smoke. The soft, mouse color of the woodwork was relieved by beautifully weathered paint on doors and shutters, blue, yellow, red—the earth colors that blend with autumn leaves and dew and lush green grass.

The great house on the hill-top was surrounded by an oak fence half a foot thick, but not so high that a tall man could not see over it.

Within the compound there were giant yews clipped into fantastic patterns and almost a village of stables, cow-sheds, quarters for the serfs and barns for the storage of corn and what-not else.

The great door, with the deep, roofed porch in front of it, resembled nothing Tros had ever seen, although in some vague, indefinable way it recalled to memory the prow of a longship manned by reddish-haired, bearded strangers, that he had once seen ostensibly whaling off the western coast of Spain.

"This is the house that Thordsen built," said Fflur, as serfs ran forward to seize the stallions' heads and she tossed the reins to them. "There is none other like it in Britain, although Thordsen told us that in his land all the kings are housed thus. The Northmen are great liars when they speak of their own land—good friends, bitter enemies. We never believe them unless they swear on their great swords, and even so they lie, if they are made to swear too often. But somewhere Thordsen must have learned to build like this."

Women of all ages, from dried-apple-cheeked old hags to young girls with rosy cheeks and skin like white rose petals in the dew, came out to the porch to greet Fflur and to stare at Tros.

Fflur sent them running to prepare a bed for the distinguished guest, and he stared for a while at the great oak-paneled hall, with its gallery at one end and a fireplace big enough to roast an ox whole, with a chair like a throne under the gallery, and spears and shields hung on the walls, and rich, embroidered hangings.

Then they all came back and kissed him one by one, until Fflur took him by the hand and led him to a small room off the great one, with no door between, but a leather curtain dyed and figured, and showed him a huge wooden bed all heaped with furs and woolen blankets.

"Here you are safe among friends, Tros, and you may sleep to your heart's content."

Fflur watched while the women pulled his outer garments off, taking the stained, slit cloak away, and brought him meat and mead, watched them lay a mattress on the floor for Conops, ordered the women away and watched, standing by the curtain, while a great, gray, shaggy hound went to the bedside, sniffed Tros cautiously and then lay down beside him.

Then she nodded, as if the hound's behavior had confirmed her own opinion.

"Sleep until Caswallon comes," she said. "He drives fast. He will be here at midnight."

Food, strong mead and the knowledge that he lay with friends, combined with sheer exhaustion to make Tros almost instantly lose consciousness. But he was first and last a seaman, with a seaman's habit of responsibility. An eight-day battle with the wind and waves had fixed in that portion of the consciousness that never sleeps an impulse to arouse the senses suddenly, all nervous and alert.

He could sleep deep, awaken, and be conscious of his whole surroundings in an instant; then fall off to sleep again when he discovered all was well, his senses swaying as if a ship still labored under him.

The first thought that roused him was the gold. He remembered Fflur's eyes when she first beheld it in the hole beneath the floor of Cæsar's cabin. But he dismissed that, knowing he was helpless if Fflur should see fit to deprive him of it. The gold seemed relatively unimportant with a mattress underneath him stuffed with goose-breast feathers.

Then he awakened suddenly to think of the galley being towed up-Thames by rowboats, to wonder how they would manage when the tide turned, whether they would not moor her out of sight among the marshes and then plunder her, sink her, perhaps, or burn her to destroy the proofs of pilfering.

He desired that galley above all things except one, and even more than all that gold. She was much too heavy and unwieldy, and steered like a house in a gale of wind, but she was strong, with any amount of bronze in her, and there were changes he knew he could make that would render her almost un-Roman, by which he meant almost seaworthy.

However, he remembered that the galley, like the gold, was in the hands of people who presumably were friends.

The next he knew it was very dark and only a faint suggestion of crimson firelight gleamed between the curtain and the wall, making the darkness move a little as the low flames danced on the hearth. There was a coming and going of cloth-shod feet, with occasional clatter of dishes, as if women were spreading tables in the great hall.

There was considerable noise in what he supposed must be the kitchen, several rooms away. But the arresting sounds, that held attention, were the voices of two men beside the curtain.

He had a mental vision of them seated on a low bench

138

with their backs against the wall, and after a minute or two he recognized one voice as Orwic's. Orwic sounded rather bored, as usual, and spoke, when he did speak, as if he were yawning between every other sentence. It was the other man who carried the brunt of the conversation.

"No, Orwic"—Tros heard the words distinctly—"I was not in the fighting on the beach, because a man cannot be in two places. I was at Hythe when Caswallon came to turn out every able-bodied man. He made a fine speech, but all they promised was to hold Hythe, and very few went back with him to fight the Romans.

"I would have gone with him, but I thought of a better idea. You remember what a storm there was three or four days later?

"Well, there was a man named Tros in Hythe, a Syrian or a Greek or a Phœnician, I am sure I don't know which, a big fellow, but a fool, with lots of pluck, who helped me drive three of Caswallon's crews aboard two ships.

"He took one ship, I the other, and we stormed along the coast ahead of the gale until we came on Cæsar's fleet at anchor and crashed into them, breaking the cables.

"Tros was afraid at first, but I led the way and that encouraged him. And he was a pirate born, take my word for it, that fellow Tros was a pirate if ever there was one—hah!"

He had a heavy, sonorous voice that carried distinctly, although he seemed to be trying not to speak loud. Tros, as wide awake now as he had ever been in his life, proposed that Conops should hear too, and reached out with his foot, but Conops was already awake and crouching by the curtain.

"Master," he whispered, creeping to the bedside, "there is a fellow out there claiming to have done what you did!"

Tros laid a hand on his mouth and pressed him to the floor.

"Pirate, you say?" said the voice of Orwic.

"Aye, a pirate! I wish you had been there to see him. He was no sooner alongside a Roman ship than he boarded it and put out to sea. He did not wait to finish the work we had begun—not he!

"He had what must have seemed to him a good ship after that leaky old trap he had smashed on the Roman's bows, and no doubt he knew there was loot in the hold. Anyhow, he put to sea and left me to do the rest of it alone."

"You mean you were all alone?"

"Not quite, but the crew wasn't much good. They were afraid. I did all the work at the helm. You see, it was simply a matter of seamanship and steering straight before the wind.

"Seamanship is in my bones. I was brought up on the South Coast, near Pevensey. I have crossed to Gaul a hundred times, in every kind of weather; and you know my father was a Northman. I sailed downwind and smashed those galleys, wondering why Caswallon had never thought of it. However, I did think; and I live to remind him of it. Caswallon owes me a turn now."

"What became of Tros?" asked Orwic.

"Ask the sea-gods! But I wager he was drowned, and I know those channel waters. The gale shifted and I was driven back toward Vectis,* where my rotten ship went to pieces under me. I crawled out on the beach near by the place where they trade tin to the Phœnicians. But it was a long time before I could find a boat to bring me back to Pevensey, and then I had a hard time getting horses. However, here I am."

"Yes," said Orwic. "And you look well preserved for a man who has done all that storming, and galley-smashing and swimming and what-not else. You look to me, Skell, more like a man who has sunned himself on benches of an afternoon."

"Aye, I have a strong frame and a great endurance," said the gruff voice.

"Orwic!" It was the voice of Fflur now, just a shade excited. "Summon our guest. Caswallon comes."

CHAPTER XVII

A HOME-COMING

Listen to me, ye who judge a horse's value by his paces, I will tell you a man's paces.

He who seeks a violent revenge upon one who has wronged him, trust ye that man never. That one is a coward; he is untrustworthy; he is afraid to trust the Law that in his act of vengeance he pretends to serve. Boasting of right, he does

* Probably the Isle of Wight.

140

wrong; and he will do you a wrong when opportunity permits.

But beware, and behave justly to the man who, seeing wrong done to himself, is neither humble nor yet vengeful but abides the time that Law shall choose to force the doer of the wrong to make such restitution as is meet. That man's wisdom is like a wheel and its circumference is greater than the earth's rim that ye see around you; whereas vengeance is only a sharp spear that a shield can turn aside and that a turning wheel can smash into a thousand pieces.

FROM THE SAYINGS OF THE DRUID TALIESAN

CASWALLON came by torchlight, standing in a four-horse chariot, with fifty chariots behind him and a hundred mounted men in single file on either side of the procession.

Lunden, man, woman and child, turned out to greet him, though it was midnight, and the windows glowed red behind shadowy trees that seemed afire in torch-smoke. They had Julius Cæsar in effigy hanging from an arch of boughs under which Caswallon must pass—a thing with a long nose made of beeswax and a wreath on its head.

The mist, that deadened voices, spread the light in moving whirlpools that made men seem like specters and Caswallon himself a great god in a golden chariot drawn by monsters.

"The Lunden fog! The Lunden fog!" Fflur exclaimed. "I can't see his face!"

The crowd, on the whole, was silent. Now and then a horn blew. Here and there a woman cried half hysterically, as they lighted the bonfires and the smoky glare increased. Three times a cheer went in waves up-street and volleyed down again, the long, deep-throated, sobbing "Aa-a-a-a-a-h" of men who are too pleased with another man to care to say exactly what they think, a good, back-straightening, gutful sound.

There was a bigger crowd than Lunden had any right to. Men had come from all the countryside, and even from the grassland beyond the forest to the north, where the Iceni raised horses. The Iceni had come south in scores, in the hope of selling remounts to the men who fought the Romans on the Kentish shore, and a group of them, by right of blood relationship, was standing not far from Fflur, all big men, fair complexioned, wearing sleeveless embroidered tunics over their long-sleeved shirts and woolen trousers—friends, in a sense, but not henchmen, and sarcastic when they spoke at all.

Tros, clad in a new cloak that Fflur's women had brought him, stood beside a lean Phœnician, a black-bearded man with a long, hooked nose, wrapped and wrapped again in shawls of camel-hair against the chill of the night, his black eyes red-rimmed, his whole body shaking as he coughed.

He owned the lateen-rigged ship that lay with her nose among the rushes half a mile away and was a prince by British reckoning—no mean man by his own.

Around Fflur there were druids, trousered philosophers in long robes whom Orwic treated with courteous con-tempt, ordering stools brought for them "lest they should tire out all their righteousness before the time for blessings came."

And behind the druids were the women, nearly fifty of them, fluttering with excitement, some fussing because Fflur had refused to wear hood or cloak.

Fflur's three young children stood beside her, sleepy and wrapped in woolen shawls, but her sixteen-year-old son was with his father in the second chariot behind him, driving his own team and laughing as if it were he alone who had sent Cæsar sneaking back to Gaul.

Fflur's jewelry and her fair hair, beaded with the mist, shone in the flickering torchlight; but when she turned her head a moment it seemed to Tros that her eyes outshone them all and that her face was lighted from within.

"If I should ever find her equal, I would marry," he said quietly to Conops.

But Conops demurred to that: "Master, you would be the slave of such a wife. Freedom is good—the world is full of easy women."

"Aye, and of whoring seamen," Tros answered testily.

Then he saw Orwic, plucked him by the cloak and asked who Skell might be. Orwic, now apparently not bored at all, grew tersely communicative.

The cheering increased in volume as the procession came slowly uphill* to where Fflur waited in the open gateway. There was much more torchlight there, for all the notables of Lunden were on the green common in front of the gate to see Caswallon greet his wife, without missing the burning of the effigy of Cæsar afterwards and all the dancing around bonfires that was sure to take place.

* Nowadays Ludgate Hill.

They had their serfs with them—two or three serfs to each man and woman—and some of Fflur's own domestics were having hard work to keep the space clear. Serf to serf was simple enough, but Lunden's citizenry took it ill when they were smitten on the shins with holly cudgels.

There was quite a little shouting about freemen's rights, and a couple of dark-skinned serving-men were roughly handled, until Orwic took five other stalwarts like himself and swaggered blandly around the circle a time or two. There was no argument with Orwic. He was roundly cheered and most abominably bored by the ovation.

Then, into the torch smoke and the glare, Caswallon came, holding back the four dun stallions to a plunging walk, until he wheeled them in front of where Fflur stood, threw the reins to the man beside him, and reached over and lifted her in his arms. No fool for ceremony was he, simply a shock-headed gentleman who loved his wife and did not even greet the druids until he had hugged her and kissed his children.

Then the druids crowned him with oak leaves as he stepped down from the chariot. Horns blew a blare that split the ear-drums—for every Briton had a hunting horn—and the crowd called him king!

"King Caswallon! King!"

He turned and faced them in the gateway, laughing, holding Fflur's hand, with the children clinging to his knees, signing to the other chariots to open up to right and left. And then, because the crowd still could not see him, he shook off the children and the great hound that sprang at his shoulders whimpering affection, and, leaping on the gate-post, stood there, upright as a graven image, with his right hand raised until they all grew still.

"Not bad," Tros muttered. "Nay, not bad. That man is fit to rule."

"Men of Lunden," Caswallon said, "and men of the Iceni—for I see a number of you—ye are pleased to call me king, and I am proud to answer you that this our land is free. No living Roman rests on it. Our own dead and the Roman dead lie buried where the sea sings dirges. And I listened to the dirges. And the sea said: 'Again—and again—and again!' And I listened, and the wind blew. And the wind said: 'I blow sails over the waters.' And the rain fell and I listened. And the rain said: 'He who owns this shall defend it.'

"Then the sea gulls mewed above the surf, and I could

143

see the cliffs of Gaul and the short seas between, and I listened. And the gulls cried: 'Gaul was set against Gaul—Ohê—Gaul is Cæsar's!'

"So I think not many new moons shall look down on us before we fight once more. For the Romans come as the springtide rolls up Thames—little by little at first, and then in full flood, with the eagles screaming overhead.

"Now ye are free, and ye have called me king. I am king. But ye shall choose between me and Cæsar before long. Cæsar shall not rule me, for I will die first. I will lie beside those men whose widows mourn them on the shore of Kent. I know a thousand who will die with me, aye, more than a thousand, rather than submit to Cæsar.

"Bear ye in mind: That if ye let a thousand of us die, lacking your aid, in defense of this good land we all call ours, they will have died in vain; and ye who value life more than you do your friends shall learn what a mean and melancholy thing is life under Cæsar's heel.

"Ye men of Lunden, whose chief I am—ye men of the Iceni, whose friend I am, whose chief I am not—I have spoken."

He jumped down from the gate-post, hugged his wife again and led the way into the house, followed by his sixteen-year-old son, and all the owners of the other chariots, many of whom bore Roman shields in proof that they had stood their ground against the invading legions.

He did not see Tros. He was too busy talking with Fflur and his three children and laughing at the antics of the hound that wriggled and yelped in front of him.

At the threshold a young girl gave a golden cup to Fflur, and he accepted it from Fflur's hands, drinking deep and murmuring a few words of ritual before striding into the hall.

There all was horse-play and pandemonium in a minute, as the servants lighted the torches in the sconces and the guests swarmed in to jockey for the best seats at the two long, laden tables, some shoving each other backward off the benches and wrestling on the floor, laughing as they held each other's wrists to keep the little daggers out of play, until a master of ceremonies pulled them apart and placed them at table arbitrarily, threatening to feed them on the floor with the dogs unless they acted seemly.

"Ye are not drunken yet—not yet," he scolded.

The hall was splendid with woven hangings and stags' antlers. Great gold pitchers, marvelously chased, stood at

144

the chief's end of the table. There were silver and golden goblets, and many of the trenchers on which meat and cakes were piled were of solid gold. When they had dragged the throne chair to the table-end Caswallon led Fflur to a smaller chair beside it, everybody standing while the women poured mead into the goblets and every man raised his goblet high, waiting for the chief to give the word to a High Druid to pronounce the blessing.

It was then that Caswallon saw Tros, ten places down the table on his right hand, and paused, almost setting down his golden cup. But Tros shook his head and raised a hand, smiling, requesting silence, catching Orwic's eye next. And Orwic nodded to the chief.

So the sonorous chant of the druids began, and none drooped his head, but raised it because the hymn was of Mother Earth, who uplifts, from whom all human life emerges and to whom full reverence and loyalty and love is due.

There was chant, and response led by Caswallon, until the great beams rang to the refrain and they tossed the cups high, drinking deep to Mother Earth and to the gods who had sent the Romans sneaking back to sea at midnight.

"For let none doubt," Caswallon said, thumping down his golden goblet on the table and following that with a blow of his fist that made the rafters ring, "that the gods sent a man to preserve us! I pay honor to the men who died. I swear fellowship with them who fought and did not die.

"I say that but for the gods who sent a storm, and a true man in the midst of it to harry Cæsar's fleet and break it, we were all dead men this day, or worse, with our wives at the Romans' mercy and our homes destroyed."

He sat down, and there was a little murmuring, because the men who had not fought were at least as proud of British heart and muscle as those who had. Let the druids praise the gods. Themselves were there to toast the men who fought, to eat beef and venison and to drink themselves drunker than the drunkest Roman who ever coveted in vain a good land fit to stay at home in.

Piety—good in its proper place, of course—struck a flat note at a banquet table, and a few men at the far end began a song about the stout hearts of Cair Lunden and the Northmen they had vanquished in the Thames.

Then the women took away the goblets—for they were

precious—and put beakers in their place, made of a dull metal that the Britons knew how to blend of tin and iron, and the feasting began in earnest, each man's mouth too full of meat and mead and cakes, and anything else he could reach, to talk at all.

For a while there was no other sound but munching, and the laughing of the girls who poured the mead and took fresh trenchers of hot food from the serfs to the table—for no serf touched the tablecloth or poured a drink. It was Orwic who was first to speak above a murmur, three places down the table on Caswallon's right hand with two rosy-cheeked maids in very close attendance on him.

"We have thanked the gods, who are no doubt gratified," he remarked. "Shall we forget the man?"

Caswallon glanced at Tros and raised his fist to beat on the table for silence, but something in Orwic's eye restrained him. The chief stroked his long moustache instead, caught Fflur's eyes beside him, and waited.

"Skell of Pevensey," Orwic went on, nodding with a dry smile toward a heavy-shouldered man, red-bearded and rather white-skinned, who sat exactly facing Tros, "has been telling me how he destroyed Cæsar's fleet with the aid of a man, who, says Skell, was a pirate. Should Skell not tell that tale to all of us?"

Skell's mouth at the moment was too full for speech, and, it might be, there was a lump in his throat beside; when he tried to wash the stuff down with a draught of mead it made him cough so that the man beside him had to thump him lustily between the shoulder-blades.

There was plenty of time for Caswallon to meet Tros's eyes again. Tros laid a finger on his lips. But Conops, acting serving-man behind his master—to the annoyance of the girls, who would have enjoyed the sport of serving both of them since any foreigner was good to giggle at—leaned over his shoulder, pretending to reach the meat, and whispered:

"Look to yourself now, master, before the mead brews madness. Flout that liar to his teeth before they are all too drunk to understand."

But Tros thumped him in the belly with his elbow, being minded not to let a servant do his thinking for him and aware of how much mead he could drink safely. By that time Skell had finished coughing.

"Skell shall tell us," said Caswallon.

So Skell squared his shoulders and stood, after quarrel-

146

ing a moment with the men on either side, who did not want to let him push the bench back—it caught him in the knees, and a man can't boast to advantage with his knees bent forward between bench and table.

And the tale he told was an amazing one of storm and daring, better by far than what he had told Orwic, because he now had a gallon of mead beneath his belt.

He spoke of himself standing in a British ship's bow— he had stood at the helm when he told it to Orwic the first time—sword-slashing at the cables of the plunging Roman ships; but he said nothing of Cæsar's camp-fires streaming in the gale, or of the shouts of the Roman legionaries drowning in the surf as they tried to haul the smaller ships up-beach, as really happened.

He spoke only of himself, and once or twice of Tros, the lees of a neglected intuition keeping him from some liberties he might have taken with the name of the man who really had done the work.

His egotism stirred by mead, but not yet to the point of actual drunkenness, he told his tale well, when no facts hampered him and he reached the account of his swim from a broken ship to the rock-bound shore of Vectis, in a gale that he had already described as the worst that ever rocked the cliffs of Britain. He described the swimming stroke he used, and how the crew of his broken ship cried out to him to save them:

"But sailors never can swim," he went on, "so the fish had their revenge. But I was sorry for them. When I reached the shore at last, and lay exhausted, I bethought me of that fellow Tros, and for a while I prayed for him to the gods who loose the winds and hurl the lightnings, that I might meet him again and shake him by the hand."

"By Nodens,"* said Caswallon drily, "your prayer was granted. Tros—"

But Tros had already made excuse to leave the room and was standing in the porch outside the great front door, filling his lungs with the clean night mist, and watching the yelling crowd downhill burn Cæsar's effigy in chains.

It was not usual for a host to leave his place at table before all the courses had been tasted, but Caswallon called his oldest son, Tasciovanus, to take his place and followed Tros out to the porch.

* A sea-god of the Britons, later confused with Neptune by the Romans.

147

And first he embraced him silently, then looked him in the eyes in the light of the horn lantern that hung from the porch beams.

"Tros," he said, "my brother Tros, if it had not been that Fflur received you and made you free of this, my house, I would not have sat still. I would have had you at the table end beside me, next where Fflur sits. But Fflur whispered of the gold, and it lies in her bed, where none but I dares go.

"She spoke of Cæsar's galley. My men shall bring that ship and all that it contains to Lunden. She whispered of what she had heard Skell say to Orwic. And you know Fflur, but you do not know Skell. Her gift I know. She has a second-sight, that forever leads me wisely when I heed her, but I find it strange that you should have sat so still while Skell stole for himself the glory that is rightly yours."

"How is it strange?" Tros answered. "There is nothing for nothing in this world, and I am in dire need. If Skell desires that glory, he shall pay for it, unless you beg me to release the debt, for I am your friend, and I will not make trouble for you."

Caswallon laughed.

"Brother Tros, if you lack anything," he answered, "you have me to look to. But I would rather see Skell put to honest use than receive three favors from the gods."

"Then leave him to me," Tros said, stroking at his black beard, grinning like an ogre.

Caswallon grinned, too, pulling at his long moustache. Like all Britons, he admired guile, as long as it observed unwritten rules.

"He is yours—as the gold is yours—and the galley is yours," he answered. "But I warn you: Skell has a dark spirit that is too much even for the druids. He is a doer of evil, a thief of reputations, a crafty coward, whose lies are as bold as his deeds are treacherous. And yet, by promises and what-not else he always has enough friends to keep him out of danger from the druids or from me.

"Four months ago he made believe to uncover a plot to poison me. He struck the goblet fom my lips and slew the serf who brought it. I think he poisoned the mead with his own hand, but now he boasts of having saved my life and how can I deny it?

"I sent him to Gaul on an embassy, hoping Cæsar would pack him off to Rome, perhaps. But Cæsar gave him presents, and now Skell boasts he has more influence with

Cæsar than an army of a thousand men. If I had killed him for acting as Cæsar's spy, there are plenty who would rebel against me—for Cæsar sends money now and then, some of which Skell distributes.

"Skell was in Hythe when I went there to raise men, and when you put to sea in the storm to break up Cæsar's fleet; but he did not see you, because he did not want me to see him. There was a doubt in his mind then as to whether the Romans might not make good their foothold. No doubt he saw what happened, from the cliffs, and doubtless he believed you drowned, as I did, as we all did, until the beacon told of another Northman in the Thames and Fflur set out to fight an enemy and found you.

"Skell knows I can not swear he didn't put to sea in one of those ships from Hythe, for the one you took, you smashed, and another is missing. It is likely Skell sunk that other one to lend truth to his boast that it was he who did the work that night. It will be hard to prove, for he covers his tracks well sometimes. But what can you want, Tros, with such a fanged louse as this Skell is? He will fasten to you like a limpet to a rock. He will suck you dry."

"He seems even a worse rascal than I hoped," Tros answered. "My father, who is Cæsar's prisoner in Gaul, might not like to come free, if a good man were the victim in his place."

"I had forgotten your father," Caswallon said awkwardly.

"My father may be in chains, and I must make haste," Tros replied. "If Cæsar should learn it was I who smashed his fleet, my father would be made to pay the penalty. Skell seems sent by the very gods."

"You shall speak with Skell."

Caswallon clapped Tros on the shoulder and returned into the house. Tros stood watching the bonfires that had been heaped in midstreet at fifty-yard intervals all the way up the hill. Wild figures like demons danced around them, yelling, with long hair streaming, some waving torches, some holding hands. The mist was crimson with the bonfire glare, distorting things, making men and trees seem nearer than they were, but the din seemed very far away, because the mist refused to carry it.

Tros watched until Skell came out alone and, closing the heavy door with a thud behind him, stood eyeing him in silence.

Very slowly indeed, almost inch by inch, Tros faced

149

him, conscious of his sword-hilt but avoiding any semblance of a move toward it.

"You touch your dagger. Why?" he asked.

Skell blinked at him. His eyes, perhaps, were not yet quite accustomed to the fog-dimmed lantern light. But his throat moved too. He had a face that looked strong rather than crafty, except that the mouth was thin-lipped and a bit irregular. His red moustache was bushy, instead of drooping as most Britons wore theirs. His hair was shorter than the ordinary, and his neck was like a bull's.

"Speak!" he commanded, still clutching at the dagger-hilt. "Why did you not name yourself to me? I am a dangerous man on whom to play such tricks."

The snarl and the sneer in his voice were icy cold. He was a calculator of men's fears, but not so Tros, who liked to turn strength to his own use.

"So I tricked you?" Tros answered.

His voice was almost friendly. There was a laugh in it. He even turned a little sidewise, as if off guard, being able to afford that because he could see the blade of Conops' knife.

Conops had found another way out of the house, a good man-servant being better than the best dog, and was crouching in the shadow where the honeysuckle had been blown through the open porch side by a recent wind.

Skell sneered again, his thin lip curling until one side of his moustache pointed almost at the corner of his eye. He said something in a low voice and had to repeat it, because a salvo of applause and laughter in the hall echoed under the porch and drowned his words:

"Do you think you can make a fool of me?"

Tros's amber eyes grew narrow as he judged his man.

"I have heard men lie for many reasons," he said, smiling, and again his voice was almost friendly. "When I tell a lie, it is to save my skin, or possibly some other man's. Boasting gives me no amusement, because I have found I must pay for it sooner or later. Do you pay like a man, or do you bilk your creditors?"

Skell's hand was on his dagger hilt, but he relaxed and leaned against the door, with his head to one side, trying to read Tros's eyes by the lantern rays.

"I supposed you were drowned," he said at last. "There was no harm in taking a dead man's credit. You should have made yourself known if you wanted—"

"Ah-h-h!"

Tros interrupted, with a sudden gesture of his right hand that made Skell almost draw the dagger.

"Does a trader want the skins he sells? Because he does not want them, does he give them without price?"

"Money?" Skell asked him, sneering.

"My price—at my convenience," Tros answered.

And at last he stood square up to Skell, and drew his long sword six inches from the scabbard. Skell did not move, because Conops came out of the shadow then and slapped a blade on the palm of his left hand.

"I am able to care for myself," said Skell, "but I will listen to your proposal."

His heel struck the door behind him twice.

"A third time, and when they open they shall carry you in feet first!" said Tros. "For if I should run a sword point into you, none could blame Caswallon for that. If I should say that I did it, is there a Briton who would blame me?"

"Speak your proposal," Skell answered, "and make haste."

He spoke on the intake of breath, for Tros had drawn the long sword, taking one step backward. Skell's angry eyes recognized a man who knew his own mind on land as well as sea, and knew how not to tell his mind, which is a sign of great strength.

"I have spoken it," Tros answered. "There was no price named when you took my credit for your own gain. Now the credit is yours, for I have no use for spoiled goods. But the price of it is mine. Do I deal with a thief, or with a man who pays willingly?"

"I pay," said Skell, "if you are reasonable."

"Skell," said Tros, "I am so reasonable, I would not give a drachma for your promise, at sword's point or before a thousand witnesses. You shall plight a pledge. Thereto I will add persuasions, since a thrashed horse runs slowly unless fed."

"Pledge? I have neither money nor jewels by me."

"I have money and I have jewels. I would let both go for a friend's sake," Tros retorted. "You would forfeit yours to vent your spleen. Nay, Skell, you shall give a pledge that you will risk all to redeem."

"I think they will come for us soon," said Skell.

He was growing nervous. He could no more stand his ground against a strong will and uncertainty than a bull can face the whip.

"I am cornered; I yield," he said, trying to say it proudly.

"You shall come with me into the hall," said Tros, "and you shall say this: that you have wagered you can bring my father safely out of Gaul, or wherever else he is Cæsar's prisoner. And the stake is your life against Cæsar's galley that they are now towing up the Thames."

Skell made a gesture of ridicule, but Tros continued, speaking slowly:

"They will ask why you made such a wager, for they know you, Skell, and they will doubt your word. You will answer, in terms of what you have already said without my leave, that you and I did a venture together against Cæsar, whereby we are pledged to mutual esteem, but that I seized plunder, and you none, concerning which an argument arose between us, you claiming a share in what I seized, but I dissenting.

"They will believe that tale readily enough. So you will tell them that, you, knowing Cæsar and being fond of daring exploits, proposed this wager to me, and I agreed. Thereafter, Skell, I think it would be dangerous for you to play me an act of treachery, for these Britons are strict about wagers and bargains and the treatment of a guest— I being their guest, remember.

"They will watch me, and they will watch you, so the temptation will be very small to stick a knife into my back, which if you should do, or if another should do, they would instantly suspect you of having done."

"I neither know your father nor where to look for him," Skell answered. "The thing is impossible."

"Skell, so was your story about smashing Cæsar's fleet impossible, since it was I who did that, and you were not there. You will say what I bid you to say, or I will march you now into the hall and name you liar before all the company.

"I see you understand what that would mean, Skell. Your sword against mine, in the fog, before a hundred witnesses. Choose then. I have offered you a chance to win a Roman galley and all the power that should go with owning such a ship, or a swifter chance to prove your manhood with your sword against mine this night."

He did not give Skell long to think, but ordered Conops to open the front door wide, and there they stood, the three of them together with the firelight in their faces, Tros with a naked sword in his right hand, Conops with a naked knife and only Skell with his weapon sheathed.

152

A roar went up as a hundred voices asked the meaning of drawn weapons, and a bench upset as the feasters faced about. Caswallon rose from his great chair at the table end, and Skell had only time to draw three breaths before he had to answer, for Tros kept still and some one had to speak.

"It seems, in Samothrace men bind a wager by an oath made on a sword blade," Skell said, with a catch in his throat.

Then, because he had gone too far to withdraw, he continued in a loud voice, laying his hand on Tros's broad shoulder:

"This is Tros, who aided me in smashing Cæsar's ships. I did not recognize him until now, but he knew me on the instant. Tros will tell you of the wager we have made."

But Tros was not to be caught so easily. When they had done drinking to him and shouting his name until the rafters rang with it, he stood—his toes beyond the threshold still, because he had not sheathed his sword—and, showing his strong teeth in a grin such as men do not learn the use of without earning the right to it, let loose a "Ho-ha-hah!" that shook his shoulders.

"Nay," he answered. "For you all know Skell, so you shall have Skell's word on what has passed between us."

And he smote Skell such a slap between the shoulder-blades as made him take a quick step forward. Whereat Caswallon, bending his head to catch Fflur's whisper, sat down and called on Skell to speak, and all the company roared to Tros to shut the door to keep the fog outside.

But Tros continued standing at the threshold, and did not sheathe his sword until Skell stood thoroughly committed by his own lips and had vowed before all that company that he would rescue Tros's father, Perseus, Prince of Samothrace, from Cæsar's camp in Gaul or from wherever else Cæsar might have sent him, or die in the attempt. Skell made the best of a bad bargain, boasting with his chin high and with an easy, reckless motion of the shoulders.

"And for my part," Tros said then, "I will gladly give Cæsar's galley to a man so shrewd and brave as can accomplish that."

He sheathed his sword then, and strode in, shutting the great door.

And from then until nearly dawn, while the company, growing more and more uproarious, wove Skell into a net of lies of his own spinning, Caswallon remained very

sober, not summoning Tros to sit beside him lest Skell
should appear slighted, and he did not care to have Skell
sit at the table end.

Skell also remained sober, because the strong mead
could not bite a brain that had so much embarrassment to
think of. And Tros, who was the son of Initiate of Samothrace, never drank more than comforted the stomach
without touching the brain at all, because "drink that dulls
the senses," say the Ancients, "is an insult to the Soul, and
to refuse the hospitality of strangers is an insult to their
kindness; wherefore, wisely observe temperance in all
things."

CHAPTER XVIII

THE PHŒNICIAN TIN TRADER

As the wind blows pollen, so are the bolder spirits blown
forth by their own necessities and by their own desire and by
their courage.

FROM THE SAYINGS OF THE DRUID TALIESAN

At dawn, when the company was mostly drunk and Fflur
had sent away the women—but she stayed, since none
dared offer her indignity—Caswallon strode out to fill his
lungs with air and to watch the watery sun rise over the
swamps to eastward.

There was a bank of white mist where the Thames
flowed, and the tops of oak trees loomed like phantoms
through a cloud that blew before the morning breeze.
Downstreet, above the smoky embers of abandoned bonfires, was the blackened shred of Cæsar's effigy still swinging from its chain, stretched from tree to tree. In lamplit
darkness by the waterside was singing, where sailors from
the foreign ships held revelry of their own. And here and
there a house light made a pale halo in the fog.

"No need for Northmen to burn Lunden," Caswallon
said, yawning and stretching himself. "One of these drunk-
en nights we will do it for them, and that were worse than
a defeat. Oh, Lunden is a good town."

Tros, kneeling to wet his hands and face in the dew on
the grass before the gate, looked up and laughed at him.

"If Cæsar had known of Lunden, he would be here

154

now," he answered. "In war he is unconquerable if he knows of a point to drive at. Now the boasting is over, how did he really leave Britain?"

"Oh, he used the metal of some broken ships to repair the others, and a few more small ships came from Gaul. And while we made ready to storm his camp he slipped away at midnight, leaving the camp-fires burning."

"He would not have gone," said Tros, "if he had known of Lunden. I know Cæsar. He will write to Rome of a victory, but defeat will rankle in him. It will eat his heart. I will wager you, this minute he is laying plans to try again, and his spies are on the way. The spies will tell him you eat off golden dishes, and that your wife—Cæsar would rather steal a king's wife and enjoy her shame than play at any other sport the world holds."

"You are as black-haired as a raven, and you croak like one," Caswallon answered.

"I am your friend."

Tros stood up, his beard all wet with dew. Caswallon looked him in the eyes and nodded, then wetted his hands at a yew tree and laved his face in the dew until his long moustache dropped in untidy strands below his chin.

Fflur came then, all new-dressed and smiling, wearing amber jewelry, and twisted the moustache until it hung respectably, then kissed him and called him some absurd name in an undertone.

Two girls and Orwic were in attendance on her, but Orwic was so drunk he could hardly walk straight although he used a spear to lean on, and the girls were pushing him surreptitiously, giggling at his attempts to appear dignified. The only remark Orwic made was that druids were more trouble than they were worth.

"If they drank more and preached less, a gentleman could have more patience with them," he concluded.

Caswallon, with an arm around Fflur, led the way toward a grove of yews within a wooden paling. In a clearing in the midst six druids stood before an unhewn rock, whose highest point faced the rising sun. A druid knelt, peering along the rock and down a vista between the yews, toward where the sun's rim was beginning to appear above the mist.

There were rock seats spaced at intervals around the clearing, with a bank of grass-grown earth behind for less important folk. Caswallon sat on the seat that faced the altar and the others took places on either hand, the women to the left.

"The sun has been up for an hour," said Orwic, hiccoughing. "It's all nonsense waiting for it to touch the top of that old rock. Who cares anyhow?"

But he bowed his head when the kneeling druid raised both hands and those who were standing chanted the orison, each in turn advancing as he sang to lay flowers, corn, honey, earth and water on the altar stone. Then the old High Druid turned with his back to the sun, the others facing him, and blessed them sonorously. That was all.

"Doubtless you do these things better in Samothrace," Caswallon remarked at they filed out.

He seemed in a mood to find fault with anything at all.

"I know nothing better than the best a man can do," Tros answered, "and no hour better than the dawn."

Fflur smiled at that and stroked Caswallon's hand that was on her shoulder, but he turned and faced Tros as they reached the gate in the paling.

"I like that you accepted Fflur's word that the galley and the gold are yours. That you promised the galley to Skell, I do not like," he said abruptly.

"Is it yet Skell's? Has he earned it?" Tros replied.

"Skell never did earn the cost of a horse's bellyful, but he has made me more trouble than I can count," Caswallon said grimly. "You have set the mischief working in his mind. You have forced him to be up and doing. It had entered my thought to kill him for his lies about Cæsar's ships; now I can not kill him, because you have given him the right to make good his pledge before any other man may call him to account. That is our law."

"It is a good law," Tros replied.

"Now Skell will go to Cæsar. And I must let him go, or else discredit you, who have been my friend."

Tros grinned craftily. "The man who claims he wrecked all Cæsar's ships will go to Cæsar."

Caswallon shook his head. Fflur glanced from one man to the other, and Orwic poked with his spear at the tip of Tros's sword.

"You should have gutted Skell last night with that thing," he remarked.

But Fflur was pleased that there had been no murder done. There was seldom a drunken feast without bloodshed afterwards, and she had the name of being too tight with the purse-strings, because she opposed feasting whenever she could make her voice heard.

She suggested it was time to sleep and led her grum-

156

bling lord and master by the hand, making the girls laugh by the way she tugged at him as if he were a stubborn horse being led to the chariot pole.

They entered the hall—it reeked of mead and wood smoke and the after-stench of food—where most of the men were snoring on the floor, or on benches against the wall, and the dogs were cracking bones under the table.

Caswallon strode off to his own room, but Fflur went first with Tros to the guest chamber and stood by while he threw out two Iceni who had made themselves free of the bed. Then she kissed him and said:

"Tros, you did well, because you must certainly set your father free by some means. And Cæsar will try again, so you did doubly well, for you are more dangerous to him and a stronger friend to us as long as Cæsar does not know you broke his ships. But he will know it, if Skell should reach him; I suppose you understand that and are counting on Skell's treachery. Sleep well, and at noon Caswallon will have changed his mind."

But Tros did not sleep for a long time. First he sent Conops to find Skell and watch him.

"If Skell goes, I wish to know where he goes, and what reason he gives. Let him not see you are watching him, but make talk with the maids and serving-men and grooms," he commanded.

Then, very shortly after that, there came the old Phœnician trader, still wrapped in his camel-hair, greeting Tros, between bouts of coughing, with courteous eastern phrases, sitting cross-legged on the bed when Tros invited him, and naming himself Hiram-bin-Ahab.

He had gold rings, chased with strange designs, on all his fingers, and a gold band on his forehead very much like the one that Tros wore. They exchanged peculiar signs, and then strange passwords in a said-to-be-forgotten tongue that sounded like challenge and answer or some sort of magic ritual.

After which they shook hands, taking a long time about it, looking straight into each other's eyes. Thereafter they conversed in Greek.

"My son, I am sure now you are not mad," said the Phœnician. "Why did you act like a madman? The Britons keep their secrets well, but even I know Skell lied and that it was you who wrecked Cæsar's fleet. The very maids who wait on table know it. Why did you let Skell take the credit to himself?"

157

"I take what the gods send my way," Tros answered. "Skell is a mean fish, but I have him in my net."

"Son, you are a stranger in a strange land. I foresmell difficulties. Skell is an older man than you, and I am older than the two of you together. I warn you, such men as he is are the same the wide world over. Skell—"

"—will run to Cæsar," Tros interrupted. "What else can he do? He fears to fight me. The good gods know it is not in him to keep faith. He has no more thought of rescuing my father than of loving me. Yet he can not lie idle here with that wager on his hands or the Britons will mock him, and he will have no rights whatever—and no peace.

"He must pretend to keep faith. And how can he do that unless he leaves Britain for Gaul? I wish I knew a captain who was sailing for Caritia* presently, and who would take Skell with him."

"Son," said the old man, screwing up his face and rubbing the end of his nose with a lean forefinger, "I would not go near Cæsar for all Cæsar's gold—*keh-keh-keh-khaah,* these fogs!—because Cæsar would take my cargo of tin and would give me for it an order on Rome for money—*phaagh!*"

"Did you obtain tin here in Lunden?" Tros asked him.

"Nay, at Ictis,† where they make it into ingots like sheeps' knuckles. I traded my Tyrian dye and my silken stuff for tin and did well, for the Britons are a reasonable people when they want a thing badly enough.

"Then I came here to hide, because I heard of Roman galleys off the coast of Gaul. You know, if those over-bearing rogues catch sight of you they send their liburni-ans‡ in chase and ask for all sorts of documents until they chance on one you haven't. After which, if they want your cargo, they just take it. It is all very legal, I don't doubt. They say the Romans are great law-makers."

"And you count on the Roman ships being laid up for the winter now?"

"Surely," he answered. "You know the Romans are no sailors. I have stepped a new mast. My men have made

* Calais.
† Some authorities say Thanet, which was really an island in those days.
‡ Liburnians: small, fast boats, very lightly built.

158

and rove new cordage. The British women have sewed me a sail out of linen that I think will stand the storms off the west coast of Hispania.* It is a small sail, very stout, with good, wide strapping on all the seams and with a stout cord all around the edge of it. My crew have scoured the hull and payed the seams.

"We have food aboard, good dry venison and apples. Those are very good against the scurvy, Tros, and they keep better than our Mediterranean fruit. Water for four months in new oaken casks that have been well soaked to kill the bitter taste. I have raised the freeboard more than half a cubit from bow to stern, using oaken planks."

"Better a big sea on an open deck than a lesser one caught between bulwarks where it can't escape," Tros cautioned him.

"Ah! But I have hinged the planking from above, and the waves can pour off as the ship rolls. You had better come with me, Tros," he said, red-eyed from another bout of coughing. "I have lost three of my men in a drunken brawl by the riverside. I bought three Britons to replace them, but—I will pay you, I will pay you a percentage if you come. I grow old, too old for storming the Gates of Hercules† in winter. This is my last journey. Come with me to Alexandria, you and that one-eyed fellow, Conops, and when I have sold my tin to Esias the Jew, the ship is yours, Tros."

Tros shook his head, grinning kindly.

"I must go to Caritia," he answered. "My father was the pilot who had charge of Cæsar's cavalry. The cavalry never reached Britain. Caius Julius Cæsar will blame my father for that, and justly. My father Perseus is a Prince of Samothrace; he will not lend himself to such purposes as Cæsar's.

"I don't doubt he led the cavalry astray, even as I tried to wreck all the rest of the fleet in the quicksands—I being no Initiate and therefore not wholly averse to drowning a few thousand Romans."

"Your father must be dead long since," said the Phœnician. "Cæsar will have had him beaten to death."

"I think not," Tros answered. "My father is wise in the Mysteries. He would know how to speak with Cæsar. Cæsar might torture him; I have seen him torture others,

* Spain.
† The Straits of Gibraltar.

with fire and ropes and wedges and all manner of cruelty; it was Cæsar who ordered Conops' eye put out in return for a saucy answer. But Cæsar is not such fool as to kill whom he hopes to use. I expect to find my father living."

"He were better dead."

The Phœnician coughed until every sinew of his frame was wrenched and he lay back gasping.

"So you and I might think, Hiram-bin-Ahab. But such men as my father, by the oath of their Initiation, must live as long as life can be spun out, enduring all things. That is a charge imposed on them when they are chosen for the Inner Secrets."

"God spare me from such initiation," said Hiram, coughing again with his face among the shawls. "*Kuff-kuff*—this one last voyage and—*heyh-yeyh*—then I am ready if my time has come."

Tros sat thinking, cudgeling his brain.

"It is early yet for the Roman ships to be laid up for the winter," he said after a while.

"But I will die if I stay here. I *must* go, I *must* go," said the Phœnician, breathing through his nose.

"Then you need a safe-conduct that Romans will recognize," said Tros, slapping his thigh, for a bold idea had dawned on him. "The liburnians might put to sea in any moderate gale and overhaul you. What if I escort you with a Roman bireme all the way to the farthest western limit of the coast of Gaul? If I promise to do that, will you give Skell a passage to Caritia first?"

The Phœnician propped himself against the wall and stared through red-rimmed eyes. The shutter was closed tight, but a dim light filtered past the edges of the leather curtain that hung in the doorway and they could see each other's faces well enough.

"Your eyes are the color of gold, and you do not look mad," said the old man.

"Nay," Tros answered. "And I will pass you by the Romans as far as the corner of Gaul, if you will first pass Skell into Caritia."

Hiram-bin-Ahab turned that over in his mind. His cargo of tin was as good as lost if the Romans should learn of it. They claimed a monopoly of all commerce in tin, because of their own tin mines in Spain and their own need of tin for making bronze for military purposes.

Even if he should succeed in passing the Gates of Hercules undetected, he would still risk being caught in the Mediterranean, in which case he would be made to hand over his tin against Roman promises to pay, promises which he would have to discount with the Roman money-lenders if he ever hoped to cash them.

And all of that Tros understood so well that he could almost read the thoughts passing in the old man's mind. Almost, but not quite. Hiram-bin-Ahab was fifty years older than Tros and could see four sides to everything, plus a fifth that included unpredictable contingencies.

"I see what you intend, Tros," he said, at last, after another long bout of coughing. "You will take that galley and keep far enough to sea to escape detection. But that will not help me if I should run in close to Caritia. They would ask for documents."

"Easy. You shall have them!" Tros exploded.

Hiram-bin-Ahab stared.

"I will give you an order in Latin with Cæsar's seal on it."

Tros's ribs began to shake with silent laughter, for the idea was growing in his mind.

"Silly! A child's notion," said the Phœnician. "Talk sensibly. Skell would tell the Romans all about the bireme in the offing. What then?"

"He will not," Tros answered, "for he will not know."

And he laughed again, because his humor reveled in far-seeing subtleties.

"We have a perfect instrument in Skell. If I say one thing to Skell, and you say another—wait! Your ship is loaded? Water and stores aboard? The crew drunk half the time?"

"Aye, forever drunk, and I can't prevent. They earn money caulking boats and mending cordage for the Britons, and they spend it like madmen along the waterside. They will be fit for nothing until we have been a week at sea."

"Why spend that week at sea?" Tros answered. "The ship can lie at anchor down Thames, with the crew all snug aboard and sobering up. Have you a good mate, or shall I lend you my man Conops? We can trust Conops to keep Skell safe aboard, even if the ship lies at anchor a month.

"Moreover, maybe I can frighten Skell so that he'll be willing enough to hide down Thames on shipboard. Then, when I have made the galley ready, you row down to your ship and wait one more day, making the tide the excuse, or the wind, or whatever you please.

161

"And I will take the galley on the tide, being careful to pass you in the night-time, so that Skell shall not see the galley, but I will make a signal in passing that you will recognize."

"Madness! Madness!" said the old Phœnician.

But his eyes were brighter than they had been, and his thin lips twitched with the beginnings of a smile.

"And at sea," said Tros, "when you have left the cliffs of Britain on your starboard quarter and are headed toward Gaul, I will put about, discover you, and hoist a challenge in the name of the Senate and the Roman People.

"You douse your sail. You lower a boat and send Conops to me, with two other men. I do as any Roman commander would and keep Conops on my ship as hostage for your obedience; but I send the other two men back with permission to you to land Skell in Caritia.

"Thus Skell will not know I am not a Roman, and you will have a good excuse for landing him in a small boat as swiftly as possible."

"But suppose, then, that the Romans put out from Caritia and search me?" the Phœnician objected. "And they will," he added. "And they will! I know the Romans."

"The officers who put out in liburnians to search ships are not important people who will dare to question Cæsar's seal or act high-handedly with the commander of a bireme looking on," Tros answered. "And now I have thought of a better idea.

"You will wait, tacking to and fro outside the bar until the liburnians do come out, since that will look more regular, and one of the documents that I shall give you will be an authority to proceed to Ostia with tin, under my escort.

"They will see my bireme waiting for you in the offing. And we will take care to persuade Skell thoroughly in advance that you really are sailing for the Roman port, not Alexandria. Thus, if they should ask Skell anything, he is likely to confirm what you say."

"Maybe, and maybe not," said the Phœnician. "Skell would be more likely to tell the truth by accident, if one should depend on him for a lie. He has an evil spirit."

"I can cover that point, too," said Tros. "The man is vain. I can suggest to him that, since you are on your way to Ostia, he should write a letter to the Roman Senate, for you to deliver, recounting his own services to Cæsar. Let

162

him ask for a minor appointment of some sort. He will be so full of that notion, once the thought is in his head, that he will never suspect you of not intending to sail to Ostia."

Hiram-bin-Ahab folded and unfolded his hands in sudden jerks, sucked his yellow teeth and shook his head.

"It is a grave risk. It is a foolish risk, as if the sea and the storms were not enough."

"I have gold," said Tros, and for a moment the old man's eyes looked brighter, but he shook his head again.

"I would not take gold or any payment for a service to a Prince of Samothrace," he answered. "Nay, nay! I am no Roman to put a price on such things."

"But if you should lose your cargo at the Romans' hands, would it be unseemly of me to reimburse you for it with Cæsar's gold?" asked Tros. "I guarantee your cargo, as far as the corner of Gaul, subject to your service in this matter. Moreover, the letter I shall give you bearing Cæsar's seal should pass you through the Gates of Hercules, if there are any triremes thereabout, and should make you free of any port you happen to put into for supplies and water, or repairs. I will forge it skillfully, using good sheep's parchment, of which there is plenty in Cæsar's chest."

"Well, I will have to see those documents before I strike a bargain with you."

Hiram-bin-Ahab frowned pessimistically, but without effect on Tros, who understood Phœnicians as well as he knew Greeks. If the Phœnician had smiled, he might have been in doubt as to the outcome. As it was, he was sure the old man was considering the proposal in all its bearings.

Craftily then, he struck his master stroke, judging his man, giving him full scope without the prejudice of bargaining.

"Hiram-bin-Ahab," he said, "you are old, and you say this is your last voyage. I will forge that document and give it to you, whether you see fit to help me or not. You shall have it freely to help you pass the Roman ports. Now feel free to say yes or no concerning Skell, because I will do what I can for you in any case."

CHAPTER XIX

A SITTING OF THE COURT OF ADMIRALITY: 55 B.C.

There is nothing beautiful or valuable under heaven but that some one wishes to destroy it in the name of virtue. Sons of darkness! Ye believe triumph is a virtue. Ye believe revenge is a virtue. Ye believe it proves your prowess if ye burn the product of another's labor. Ye believe ye burn up evil. Ye are like the dogs—I say the dogs, who bite the stick that smites them. And why are ye smitten? Because ye are blind, who need not be; because ye are proud without reason; because ye forget ye are sons of Light and dig into the darkness lest the Light should burn the shadows that ye love.

FROM THE SAYINGS OF THE DRUID TALIESAN

AT noon, when as many as had slept away the fumes of mead had eaten, and Fflur had set some women to making a new purple cloak for Tros after the pattern of the torn one he was wearing when he came, Tros asked for the box containing Cæsar's memoranda and went through the documents carefully, whistling to himself.

Now and then he laughed. Now and then he rolled a parchment thoughtfully and stowed it in a small, square wicker basket he had begged from Fflur, and when he had finished he entrusted that basket to her to keep for him.

"There is better in that than a mint," he said darkly.

But as Fflur could not read the Roman script, and especially not the shorthand notes of Cæsar's secretary, she had to take his word for it.

Then Caswallon came, in a great good humor because he had been to the stables, where the sight of new horses had pleased him mightily.

As Fflur had prophesied, he had changed his mind already. He sat on the porch rail, where Tros was listening to Conops' account of how Skell slept at last after whispering with a man who afterward went away toward the riverside.

"Sleeps with one eye open, I wager," Caswallon interrupted, scratching on the porch with the point of a throwing spear. Then, as if the news were unimportant:

"They have rowed that galley of yours to the pool below the ford.* They ask my leave to burn it when night

* Just below where London Bridge now stands.

164

comes. They say there are Cæsar's clothes on board; they want to make a new effigy of Cæsar wrapped in his own scarlet cloak and burn it, galley and all, in mid-Thames. They love a bonfire. What say you?"

"I say what Fflur said, that the ship is mine," Tros answered, trying not to betray alarm.

But Caswallon detected and enjoyed it thoroughly. His blue-stained white skin, his trousers and the spear almost suggested a barbarian, but his easy manner and the quiet smile under the long moustache belonged to a man of many parts, and he could play them all well.

"But you wagered the galley with Skell. Why not dress up Skell in Cæsar's clothes and burn the lot?" he suggested. He looked deadly serious. "Skell would fancy himself in Cæsar's second-best scarlet cloak. We could trick him aboard with the promise of that, and the rest could be recorded as an accident."

"Skell must not even *see* that galley," Tros exclaimed excitedly. "God of fogs and foolishness! Can you think of no better use for a well-found ship than to burn her for fools to shout at?"

Caswallon pulled at his moustache and did not let his hand drop until his face was fixed in an expression of boiled stupidity. He was enjoying himself thoroughly, and so was Orwic, who had got down off a squealing horse to discover what his chief's and Tros's talk was about.

"Use for a galley?" said Caswallon. "If she lay here in the Thames my men would never rest until they had put to sea in her and drowned themselves. They would all be captains and the ship would have to go a dozen ways at once to suit them!

"As for my using her, I crossed to Gaul once in a fair-sized ship, and I suppose I returned, since here I am. I remember I lay on my back to stop the vomiting, but the sea went on pitching victuals out of me.

"When I stood, clinging to the mast, I acted like an eel up-ended, so weak-kneed I was, with the world going round and round and the ship spinning in the opposite direction. It was a rotten waste of good food, Tros, to make no other argument about it. The sea was intended for fish, but I am no fish. For me, not one foot farther than I can ride a horse into the surf. What say you, Orwic?"

"She would make a fine sight burning with her sail set.

165

There hasn't been such a sight since the Northmen burned Cair Lunden," Orwic drawled.

"Well, come and let's look at her, before they burn her anyhow," Caswallon suggested, adding, as Orwic whistled to the grooms to bring a chariot:

"Wake Skell. Tell him the word he sent that they should burn the galley has reached my ears. Warn him I am angry that he should try to creep out of a wager made at my board by causing the stake at issue to be burned! Bid him keep out of my sight. And then set men to watch him, or he will run before Tros is ready, for Lud knows what.

"Tell the men to mock him for a shirkbet if he shows his face outdoors. Tell the girls to mock him. Tell the grooms he is not to have chariot or horse and let them steal his own two horses from the stable behind his house. Tell him his only chance of being reckoned a man is to take ship very soon for Gaul."

He jumped into the chariot and drove away almost before Tros could swing up beside him, sending the horses headlong over the rear of the hill toward the river, watching their forefeet, taking more delight in them, apparently, than in all the other details of a kingdom.

"For a horse is a horse and you know where his feet will land," he said presently, continuing his thoughts aloud. "But Skell is neither horse nor herring. None knows what Skell will do, except that he will do a mean thing and in some way filch men's praise for it.

"I spoke with Fflur, and she said let him go to Gaul, where if Cæsar whips him none can blame me. Fflur is always right, although I know Skell will offer himself to Cæsar, because there is nothing else left for him to do. I hope Cæsar flogs him and flays him!"

He double-cracked the driving whip over the horses' heads until they galloped madly.

"I hate to own that I dare not throw Skell's carcass to the crows, but that is truth, Tros. He has few friends, if any, but he has bought the loyalty of men who look for more at his hands, and it is not wise just now to stir their anger."

It was no road they took, but a track deep-rutted in the clay where ten-horse teams had dragged sledloads of cord wood and charcoal, and it ended at a ford.

"Where I will some day build a bridge," Caswallon said.

The galley lay in midpool, made fast to an oaken pile

that bent like a bow under the weight of ship and tide, and she was in worse shape than when Tros left her, because the twenty men in charge had seen fit to carry all the loot on deck, and there had been some fighting with the crew, who claimed sole right to all of it.

Caswallon drove into the ford until the horses were almost swimming, then roared at the top of his lungs to know whether Lunden had no boats, that a king must get his feet wet. So they brought him a boat and rowed him and Tros to the galley, where the twenty men in charge were all sulky because they had missed the feasting of the night before.

"And not drunk yet," as one of them complained, "although the men who did the towing are ashore and drunker than bees already."

Liquor they had, however. There was an earthen jar of *curmi** on the poop and they were dipping it out with their little peaked helmets.† They pledged Caswallon in the stuff, and then Tros, after which they staged a dance in all the Roman costumes they had found aboard, putting Cæsar's scarlet cloak and a golden laurel wreath on Caswallon and dressing Orwic in the bed sheets to represent the King of Bithynia, of whom even Britain had heard. There were some very improper interludes at that stage of the game, of which the druids and Fflur, for instance, would have disapproved.

Caswallon did a very excellent imitation of the falling sickness, much more realistic than the real thing, because he had never seen an actual case of it and only knew Cæsar's reputation, which had naturally been exaggerated.

They pretended to bleed him in the silver bowl, using *curmi* for the blood, and the ceremony following would almost have shocked Cæsar himself, because they had only heard vague stories about Roman Gods, and the Venus Genetrix had been represented to them as a most improper lady.

They had fired away all the arrows from the two poop arrow-engines at ducks on their way up Thames and,

---

* A sort of beer, made without hops—for there were none in Britain in those days—producing, according to the Roman writer Posidonius, "pain in the head and injury to the nerves."
† Just like modern jockey-caps, only made of iron. They may have been the origin of the modern jockey-cap, since the Britons were a race of horsemen, and Britain is a country in which scores of traditional customs, the wearing of trousers included, have survived until to-day.

having hit nothing, were of opinion that mechanical contrivances were no good, having already forgotten the dreadful work those engines did in the fighting off the Kentish beach.

And they thought the iron dolphin swinging from the yardarm was some kind of Roman deity hung there to pacify the waves, until one of them cut the halyard—"to introduce the foreign godlet to the good god Lud who keeps the Thames"—and it crashed through the bottom of a boat alongside, sinking it instantly.

Tros did not recover the dolphin until next day, when Conops dived and found the halyard, after which it took a dozen men two hours to haul the murderous contrivance from the mud.

It was only little by little that Caswallon, at Tros's urging, persuaded them to lay all the loot in heaps on the main deck, after which he announced that Tros had promised full and fair division among such seamen as remained of the sixty who had first set out with him.

But Tros and Caswallon had done some whispering, and Caswallon claimed the ship as lawful prize by right of capture, Fflur and his own men having saved it from the river pirates. He declared that was the law of Britain and, since there was no higher court than himself, it did not do the seamen any good to grumble, albeit they did grumble noisily, until some of the gentlemen in peaked iron caps struck them for improper language to their betters.

Then Caswallon held an auction, Orwic acting auctioneer, and Tros did all the bidding, naming what he considered fair prices in view of the state of the market.

The Britons had spent all their money on horse flesh and, except the seamen, who, of course, never had any money, were mostly in debt to the Iceni in the bargain. It was distinctly a falling market, but Tros was generous. The total came to a bigger sum than those seamen had ever dreamed of owning.

Caswallon, after eight or nine attempts, succeeded in dividing the total equally and—what was much more difficult—in persuading them that the calculation was correct. Then he ordered Tros to pay them in gold pieces out of Cæsar's treasure, undertaking himself to change the money into honest British coin from his own mint at Verulam, whereby the seamen learned for the first time what they had missed by failing to kill Tros and throw him overboard at Thames-mouth. And being seamen, they

168

changed their opinion of Tros and began to consider him a right good captain.

By that time it was dusk, and women and children had flocked aboard to laugh at everything, especially at Cæsar's underwear. The women were set to carrying everything that could be carried to Caswallon's house, shields, armor and swords included, and when a new guard had been set over the ship they sent for chariots and all drove home to supper.

But first Tros went alone to the house where Skell lay sulking, a small house, very well built and thatched with wheat straw, two hundred yards away from Caswallon's paling. Some said that he owned the house, and some that he did not, but he lived in it, which was the main thing.

And the seamen, who had followed Tros to get their money, joined with the children and grooms outside, who were pointing fingers at the house and singing a sort of nursery-rhyme about a man who boasted and ran away. It seemed to delight them hugely that Skell's name fitted in the rhyme, and to Tros's ears it sounded something like:

Skell, Skell the Northman's son
Told a lie and away he run!

The sailors would have burned the thatch and pelted Skell as he ran from cover if Tros had let them, not that they knew anything about the facts, but they made common cause with the children on general principles.

Tros found Skell on a frame bed strung with deer-sinews before a good oak fire, at which an old woman was stirring a stew in an earthen pot. He had a cloak over him, and shivered as if he were suffering from ague, but he sat up when Tros entered, offered Tros a stool and threw off his fit of depression along with the cloak.

He was still wearing the dagger, as Tros noticed, and he touched it, which was not good manners; but he sent the old woman for mead and two beakers, bidding her warm it at the fireside when it came, and he had the good sense to make no reference to the caterwauling and insulting song outside.

Tros kept an eye on the hag and on the mead beside the fire, for he knew Skell's reputation and yet did not wish to refuse to drink with him.

"I am ill," said Skell, "and I wish you would cry this bargain off that we have made between us. I am willing to

169

do whatever you say, provided I *can* do it. Name me another tryst that I should keep instead."

But Tros had expected that.

"You are too late, Skell," he answered. "They have brought that galley up the river. Caswallon has claimed it, to hold it in trust until he shall decide the outcome of the wager."

"But I can not cross to Gaul. No ship will take me," Skell objected. "At this season of the year they lay up all the ships in mud berths. Now if you would let me take that galley, Caswallon might consent to that, then perhaps I could get a crew together and—"

But Tros had thought of that, too. He interrupted:

"The galley is unfit for sea, Skell. She needs alterations and repairs, which I will make in good time. But I know a man who will take you to Gaul. He is Hiram-bin-Ahab, the Phœnician, whose ship sails soon."

And then, with both eyes on the hag who warmed the mead, for he knew Skell could not spring at him to use the dagger without the string bed squeaking a warning, he baited a trap into which he felt sure Skell must walk.

"I have a plan, Skell, to make it easy for you to get my father out of Gaul. There is a river called the Seine that flows northwestward into the channel between Gaul and Britain, reaching the sea a good long journey to the westward of Caritia.

"I will take a ship, and there, in the mouth of that river, I will wait for you, so you can deliver my father alive to me without much difficulty, making your way across country in the night-time until you reach the river-mouth."

"But how shall I find your ship?" asked Skell.

The mead was warm enough and would be too warm in a minute, so he signed to the hag to pour it. Tros took the beaker that was farthest from him and held it while the hag poured, withdrawing it suddenly before it was full so that the hag spilled quite a little, after which he watched Skell's face in the firelight.

Skell said the lip of the other beaker was dirty and bade the hag go and wash it, then went on talking in a hurry.

"How shall I find your ship?" he repeated. There was a thin smile somewhere in the midst of his foxy beard. "You will be in hiding, I suppose?"

"Among the reeds and with my mast down, yes," Tros answered. "But ashore, near where I hide, I will set up a

170

cairn of white stones, and if you shout my name three times from there, I will come for you."

Skell's eyes betrayed that he was tempted by the bait, but Tros proposed to tempt a bigger fox than Skell. The man he wanted out of winter camp was Cæsar, the restless aspirant for fame who spent all winter editing a secretary's summer notes.

"I said I would make it easy for you, Skell. Now listen: I have Cæsar's memoranda and his seal, to recover which, Cæsar would set all his prisoners free, to say nothing of my father. I, on the other hand, value my father higher than Cæsar's secret papers, although I have read some of them and there are documents that I daresay Cæsar would be glad to have. What if I should bury that box of documents and seals under the cairn of white stones? Knowing that was there, would you not find it easier then to bargain for my father's freedom?"

"How do I know you would do that?" Skell demanded, trying to look indifferent, but his eyes betrayed him.

"I must trust you, and you must trust me, Skell."

"Yes, we must more or less trust each other."

Tros played his favorite trick then, of raw, cold frankness:

"You see, Skell, I do not pretend to like you. You are a man who did me an ill service. I am compelling you to pay the price for that, and I do not think you like me any better than I like you. I am offering to help you carry out your bargain, because I know that you are not to be trusted otherwise. For my part, you shall have the seal and documents, and the galley, if you deliver my father alive into my hands at the mouth of the Seine within a month from now."

Skell stroked his red beard. He could hear the singing outside, as the fox hears hounds in the covert.

"All right," he said. "Cæsar knows me. He will listen. But I must have money for my expenses."

But again, Tros was not to be caught. He hoped it was true that Skell needed money.

"I will settle with the Phœnician for your passage to Caritia," he answered. "Nothing more than that."

"Then I must have a pledge from you that you will really wait for me at Seine-mouth."

"My father is in Cæsar's hands," Tros answered. "I could not give a more compelling pledge."

"Nevertheless, as you said just now, you and I are not

171

friends. Something of value is needed, to make your word good to me," Skell objected.

The glint of avarice was in his eyes, and a vague look, as if he were hopeful still of finding an excuse to back out. But Tros laughed, kicking his sword-point to the rear and drawing the blade six inches.

"Very well," he said. "You shall have this sword, the best sword in the world, a sword that once was Philip of Macedon's. You shall have it through the middle of your heart, Skell, if you fail to deliver my father at Seine-mouth and I ever set eyes on you again! Is that a pledge you value? Would you like to test it? If so, arm yourself and come outside."

"I can not fight. I have the ague," Skell answered. "When does the Phœnician sail?"

"In a few days. If you go aboard his ship to-night, or to-morrow night, you will be rid of all this annoyance."

Tros jerked his head toward the door, against which clods of earth were thumping.

"They are likely to burn your thatch if you delay," he added. "Shall I tell the Phœnician to send his seamen for your baggage?"

Skell agreed, with a mean, exasperated glare in his eyes, scratching his teeth with his thumb nail, grinning as Tros turned his back to go. But Tros turned again suddenly, because of that dagger and its possibilities, and caught the grin before Skell could cover it, which put him in a marvelous good humor, because he was sure then that Skell was contemplating exactly such treachery as would fit in with his own plans.

So as he left the house he caught a clod of earth intended for Skell's door and pelted one of the children with it. Then, because that frightened some of them— since they knew Tros was Caswallon's friend—he found a lump of chalk and drew a caricature of Skell, beard, moustache and all, on the oaken door and left them pelting rocks, earth, acorns and all manner of dirt at that.

Later, on the grass before Caswallon's porch, he paid the seamen and, as their eyes glinted at the gold coin, he made them a proposal:

"Ye have found me a hard captain but a profitable man to serve. If ye had served me with less knife throwing and with more good-will, ye should have had the double of all that money."

He picked up handfuls of gold from one of Cæsar's bags and let the coins dribble through his fingers.

"What now if I promise you two for one of what you have received, for one more short voyage before winter sets in? Think of it. Money enough to buy a farm apiece and to live the rest of your lives ashore like gentlemen!"

They agreed, for never sailor lived who did not covet a farm, until he had one. But Caswallon laughed.

"Buy farms? They will buy drink and the caresses of the womenfolk who gut fish by Ludgate wharf!"

"Maybe," Tros answered. "They are no doubt better at that than at seamanship. But they don't spew their victuals overside whenever a ship rolls, and I shall need them when some of your peak-capped cockerels are lying belly upward on that galley's deck praying to the mast and sky to stand still!"

"You will find my cockerels crave money too," Caswallon answered.

"For a venture against Cæsar?"

"Oh! No, perhaps not, not, that is, if Cæsar can be made to foot the reckoning!"

CHAPTER XX

HIRAM-BIN-AHAB STIPULATES

Bargains! Bargains! Listen to me: Who but the highest bidder names the price of that which can be bought and sold? And does Eternity make bargains? Unbidden, unbought, unpaid for, all the affluence of all Eternity is poured upon you, aye, unceasing. And ye bargain? I will tell you a secret. Though I tell it, it remaineth secret, saving only to the wise; and the wise are they whom Wisdom guideth through the maze of other men's illusions. That which is freely given without thought of recompense, and without stipulation or pity or blame, but given simply from the storehouse of the giver's affluence, whether it be goods or deeds or good-will—that is a free gift. It setteth the giver free and him to whom the gift is given. Because it is a free gift, it is free to go forth as the sunshine and the wind, unlimited by ignorance, envy, greed, ambition and the bonds that ye impose on one another. And I tell you, in all this universe there is nothing as good as freedom. But ye seek to burden to-morrow with the harness of to-day's necessities; and your necessities, I say, are nothing but the shadows of your fear of that very freedom ye pretend to seek.

FROM THE SAYINGS OF THE DRUID TALIESAN

Tros sat by the hearth in Caswallon's hall, staring with leonine eyes at the fire, reading pictures in it. Caswallon sat beside Fflur, his long legs stretched toward the blaze, his skin, where it showed at neck and breast, looking whiter than ever because the firelight threw it into contrast with the fading blue designs that were drawn on it with woad.

Three hounds slept on the warm tiles. Red apples simmered in the warming mead. Orwic faced the fire with knees clasped in his hands and his back against an upset table.

A dozen men snored on the benches that lined three walls. Wind whined under the eaves, rattling the shutters, and now and then a gust of smoke was blown down chimney, followed by soot and enough rain drops to make a splutter.

"Of what are you thinking?" asked Fflur.

She had been watching Tros, marveling at his strength and at his brow under the black hair, that was as splendid as the carving of an ancient king's.

"Of Skell, of Cæsar, of you," Tros answered.

"What of Skell? You named him first."

"He will go to Cæsar, saying that I, Tros, son of Perseus, am the man who wrecked that fleet off the shore of Kent. That I, Tros, have bribed him with the promise of Cæsar's own galley, to go to Cæsar and make terms for my father's freedom.

"That I, Tros, will be waiting at Seine-mouth for my father to be delivered to me, having with me Cæsar's own seal and Cæsar's chest containing all his private memoranda.

"He will say to Cæsar, 'Make haste! Set an ambush at Seine-mouth! Thus you will recover your seal and documents, and will have two prisoners instead of one—one of whom knows much about Caswallon and the Britons!' Thereafter, Skell will say, 'Reward me commensurately with the dignity and sense of justice of a Roman Imperator to whom important service has been done.' Thus Skell will speak to Cæsar."

"And Cæsar?" asked Fflur.

"He will listen, and smile. He will see through Skell as readily as you see through a serf who comes telling tales about the kitchen wenches. He will ask whether Skell has seen the seal and documents; and he will not be sure whether to believe Skell when that foxy-haired liar says Yes.

174

"But Cæsar is a restless man, and by that time he will have grown tired of a woman, that being his habit; and maybe there will be no other woman there just then who pleases him. He likes them educated, entertaining. He grows difficult to please. He will bethink him that the Gauls along the coast might be caught brewing mischief if he should pay them an unexpected visit, for he knows the Gauls squirm under his heel. It will occur to him that life in camp is stupid, more particularly to a man of scholarly mind who has lost his secretary's notes.

"And he will remember that among those notes are some that would be very dangerous to him, if they should happen to reach Rome or fall into the hands of one of his own lieutenants, who might have brains enough to use them. So he will not dare to send a subordinate to Seine-mouth; he will go in person, with a cohort or perhaps two cohorts of cavalry, moving secretly and very swiftly, as his habit is. At Seine-mouth he will lie in wait for me."

"And me?" asked Fflur.

"Skell will tell Cæsar of you. To suck himself into Cæsar's good grace, he will fill Cæsar's mind so full of you that Cæsar will never rest until he shall have made you prisoner. And that is why I need Orwic and as many other young blades as will endure the sea a while and pledge themselves to obey me. If my good fortune holds, Fflur shall have Cæsar and hold him to ransom!"

"By Lud of Lunden, nay!" Caswallon swore. "If Cæsar again sets foot in Britain, he shall die here. I will give him his choice of weapons, and he shall fight me, without armor, before all my men."

"He will choose scent bottles and powder puffs," said Orwic, glancing at Cæsar's neat case of cosmetics that Tros had bestowed on Fflur. "I like this venture against Cæsar, though I hate the sea. Say more about it."

"Is not all said, except what the gods shall say to it?" Tros answered. "We have the galley. We must fit her like a well-found Roman warship straight from Ostia with a despatch for Cæsar from the Roman Senate. The despatch, you understand, calls for delivery of my father, Perseus, Prince of Samothrace, who is to be taken to Rome for trial on charges of conspiracy against the Senate and the Roman People, which is how all those robbers refer to themselves.

"First we set Skell ashore, and he talks. When we return, Cæsar will not be there, because he will have gone to wait for me at Seine-mouth, hoping to catch me. I,

175

commander of the bireme, deliver the despatch by Hiram-bin-Ahab, the Phœnician, and will not wait, but order it to be opened by whoever is in command in Caritia, declaring I am in great haste to return to Rome because of winter storms."

"If I were a Roman in Caritia," said Orwic, "I would ask why you had not delivered that demand for Perseus when you came the first time. The Romans will think it strange that you should return with a message which you might just as easily have sent ashore with Skell."

"You don't know the Romans," Tros answered. "In the first place, they will never dream that one of their biremes might fall into the hands of an enemy who could use it. They think Cæsar's galley was sunk when his fleet was destroyed off Kent.

"In the second place, Hiram-bin-Ahab shall say the omens were unfavorable when I came the first time. Romans are mad on the subject of omens. Furthermore, Hiram-bin-Ahab shall say that I did not, nor do I, care to bring my crew too near the shore, for fear of desertions, they having grown discontented because of contrary winds, much labor at the oars and scurvy.

"Omens, tides, contrary winds, scurvy, they know those well. That list will satisfy their curiosity."

"It wouldn't mine," said Orwic. "But perhaps we Britons are less stupid than the Romans. Lud knows, they were stupid enough in the fighting at Kent. They won the first battle by being too stupid to know they were beaten! What if their liburnians, as you call them, should come out to investigate you?"

Tros, who was an opportunist first and last and liked to fit his plans to each emergency as it arose, began to wish he had worked out the details thoroughly before taking Britons into his confidence. They were good friends, and generous enthusiasts, but so full of their own superiority to foreigners of any kind that a man needed all his wit to manage them.

Orwic began suggesting wild plans of his own, that included loading horses on the galley, sailing to Caritia and setting fire to Cæsar's camp.

"And if we do that at night, we can ride 'em down in darkness as they run downwind in a panic!"

"I have it!" Tros slapped his thigh so suddenly he woke the dogs. "The first time Hiram-bin-Ahab puts in to Caritia, he lands Skell and says I wait offshore because I suspect my crew of sickening with smallpox.

"My name for the occasion, let us say, is Caius Marius Poseidonius. The Phœnician shows an order signed by Caius Marius Poseidonius, commander of the bireme, authorizing him to land Skell in Caritia. And he, also, prefers not to stay in port because his men who visited my galley may have caught the sickness."

"Good," Caswallon nodded. "That should satisfy them. The worst plague we ever had was caught from a ship. We burned the ship and slew the crew, kindly and with dignity. The druids saw to that; but the sickness spread all over Britain, because the Iceni carried it north on their way home from selling horses. The Romans will want none of that stuff."

"And Cæsar," said Tros, "will have another good excuse to leave Caritia. He is afraid of smallpox. He will think Hiram-bin-Ahab may have brought it into port. He will certainly go that same night, very likely throwing Skell into a pest-house under observation of the surgeons, who will set fire to the hut and say it was an accident. Cæsar will go that very day to Seine-mouth to investigate Skell's story."

Fflur nodded, and nodded, and nodded, her gray eyes watching Tros. Caswallon held a finger up for silence; he knew that mood of hers. But all she said was, "You are right now, Tros."

"And when I appear the second time," said Tros, "Hiram-bin-Ahab shall say I have seen Cæsar at a place along the coast. He shall add, it is true about smallpox. They will understand that Cæsar wishes to kill my father Perseus without risk of being blamed for it. They will put him aboard Hiram-bin-Ahab's ship and order Hiram-bin-Ahab out of harbor with all speed."

"If the druids had more sense and less sanctity," said Orwic, "they might visit some real smallpox on the Romans. Why can't they do an honest day's work against Britain's enemies, instead of pulling long faces at the sunrise? I believe in results. By Lud's ill-smelling mud," he went on impiously, "I'd sooner sail with Tros, vomit or not, than be blessed by all the druids between here and Mona."*

"Don't blaspheme the druids," Tros retorted. "As for me, I would rather have their blessing than all Cæsar's gold."

"Well, you have both, you have both!" said Orwic

* Anglesea, a very sacred place.

pleasantly. "The druids like you, and the gold rings genuine. What have you to worry about?"

"This," Tros answered: "that a number of you young horse-performers"—Caswallon and Orwic laughed delightedly at that—"must be on that galley and obedient to me. That is worry enough. Everything aboard a ship is just so, with one man giving orders and the rest obeying, or the ship sinks."

"What of it?" Orwic asked.

Caswallon held a finger up again for silence. Fflur's eyes were looking dreamy. A great gust of wind blew down the chimney, sending a cloud of smoke into the room. The wind howled, and a log fell suddenly sending up an explosion of sparks. Fflur's voice, when she spoke at last, was far-away and colorless, pitched in a middle monotone.

"Whatever you do, or whatever you do not, Cæsar will come again, but not yet. He will cross the Thames; but I see Lunden standing after Cæsar has gone, taking many with him—prisoners, hostages, slaves, women.

"Do what you will, you can not prevent Cæsar from coming. Do what he will, he can not win Britain, although Gaul is his, and so are the lands of the Belgæ. Tros shall injure him, but not much, and again a little, and that time more severely, only to befriend him in the end.

"Tros shall do Cæsar a service that neither he nor Cæsar will value at the moment; but it will place the world at Cæsar's feet, and kill him before he can grasp it. Tros and a woman, whom he shall serve to her own undoing."

She ceased, coughing in the sharp smoke, and Caswallon sent a serf outside to climb on the roof and fix a slab of wood against the chimney top. When that was done, he drank heavily of mead with apples in it, and, wiping his mouth on his sleeve, pronounced judgment.

"I never knew Fflur wrong when she is in that mood. So I think it is a good thing to launch this venture against Cæsar, because Tros, she says, shall injure him. What of the Phœnician? Is he willing?"

Tros admitted with a gruff laugh that the Phœnician had not yet given his consent.

"But I have gone the right way to persuade him. I have promised him my help to get past the Romans on his way home, whether he helps me or not. He will do more in that way, than if I bargained with him."

At which Caswallon roared with laughter.

"Try that trick on the Iceni!" he shouted. "Eh, Orwic?

178

Let him try to buy a horse or two on such terms. Lud! Oh, Lud of Lunden Town! Hey there! Send for the Phœnician."

He threw a lump of wood at one of the sleepers on the benches and sent him to bring Hiram-bin-Ahab "shawls and all."

"Bring him in a basket if he won't walk."

Tros urged that the Phœnician was a brave old sailor who should be treated with the courtesy due to a blood relation. But that was because he and Hiram-bin-Ahab were members of the same secret fraternity, although of different chapters of it.

"I know these blood relations," said Caswallon. "Aye, he is a very bloody one. Eh, Fflur? Eh, Orwic? He underpaid us for the tin and overcharged us for the dyes. He has lived at our expense, and his crew have robbed our townsmen, mending boats that the lazy rascals should have mended for themselves, demanding twice what the work is worth, and saving money for their master, who pays them nothing while they are in port. Drunken, knife-throwing thieves! What's worse, there will be a lot of little half-Phœnician bastards for us to try and make good Britons of!"

However, he was courteous when the old Phœnician came, coughing and shivering in his camel-hair shawls. He had a great chair set for him before the fire and woke up the dogs to make room for him, offering him warm mead, saying that Fflur knew how to cure all kinds of coughs.

"Only she will purge you worse than druids do," he added reminiscently. "The last time she cured me of a headache I had belly burning for a week."

"She's better than the druids, though," said Orwic. "Druids put you on rations of dry bread and carrots, and make you drink water like a horse. When you're properly famished they preach about your latter end and being born again into another body, until you feel like burning all the undesirables, so that it won't be into one of their bodies anyhow. I'd rather be purged by Fflur than preached at by a druid."

"None can cure me," Hiram-bin-Ahab answered, coughing. "This is my last journey."

"Hah!" remarked Caswallon. "Then make it one to be remembered. On a man's last journey he should play a man's part."

The old Phœnician glanced from face to face, his fingers twitching nervously.

179

"You will reach home," Fflur assured him.

Hiram-bin-Ahab coughed, perhaps to hide a grin, or so at least thought Tros.

"If I knew surely I would reach home, I would put into no port on the way," he answered.

"Fflur is always right," Caswallon retorted, almost angrily. "So it is certain you will reach home. Therefore you can afford to do your friends a service on the way."

"I have done you many services," said the Phœnician. "I taught your women how to use the dye so that it would not wash out. I taught your sailors how to make boats water-tight; how to make a proper rope by twisting seven sets of linen strands; how to bind the edges of a sail, and how to cut the sail so that it will catch more wind. What more do you want of me?"

"No more than you shall do," Caswallon answered, laying a great blue-and-white fist on his knee and leaning forward. "You wish to go before the winter storms. But unless you will do what I propose, you shall not sail until spring comes."

The Phœnician coughed, perhaps to hide embarrassment, but it racked his frame for all that.

"What could you profit by keeping me here all winter?" he asked.

"I am thinking of you," Caswallon answered. "If you will do what I wish, I will send an escort with you, a great bireme, as far as the end of the coast of Gaul to protect you against Romans and Northmen and pirates. But if not, then I could not spare the escort. And I should be a mean host to let you go away alone before the spring in that case. There might be fewer pirates in the spring, and fewer storms and possibly no Romans. Name a price if you will; but you shall do what I demand."

"There is nothing I could ask," said the Phœnician, "except, perhaps, a pair of pretty slave girls for the court of Ptolemy."

But he knew Caswallon would not grant that favor, because he had tried before and Fflur had vetoed it.

"I have sold you three rowers," said Caswallon. "I will give you back the price of them, if that will satisfy you."

Hiram-bin-Ahab coughed again and spat into the fire. The expression of his face might have been due to physical agony, but Tros thought not.

"I am a trader," he said at last, and his words were arresting because he spoke slowly in a foreign accent, with harsh gutturals and none of the soft, swift, liquid sounds the Britons used.

"I fill a ship. I buy men or I hire them, and I drive them to the world's end. Some die; some live; all suffer. I trade and I fill my ship again and go home, I suffering more than any, because it is my ship, my risk. You understand me?

"Sickness, mutiny, Romans, pirates, rocks, tides, quicksands, storms, all these and more I struggle with, day and night, month after month. Ever I swear each journey is the last. Ever I set forth again, because two spirits in me urge. One beckons and the other drives.

"Trade I must, because I am a trader and I itch for trade. Adventure I must have, because I am an adventurer; it is in my blood, my bones, my dreams. It frets me when I count the profits of a journey and men say to me, 'Hiram-bin-Ahab, you are rich at last. Go not again. Remember the pot that went too often to the well.'

"And yet I go again, because I love adventure and I love trade, being wedded to them as to two wives, each of whom is jealous of the other and I striving to serve both equally, giving each her turn, yet living, as it were, in one house with the two."

The howling wind blew away the board from the chimney top, sending it clattering along the roof. A great cloud of smoke filled the room and the old Phœnician coughed until it seemed as if his lungs would burst under the strain.

Caswallon scolded the serf and sent him to fix the board in place again, threatening to make him stand and hold it there all night unless he should fasten it properly. Then when the smoke had thinned a little and they had thrown fresh oak knots on the fire, Hiram-bin-Ahab cleared his throat with warm mead and, biting an apple, went on talking:

"Trade and adventure, two jealous wives, helping, hindering each other. *Hey-hey!* I have been a good husband to both of them—*keh-keh-keh*—and I am old. A too good husband ages sooner than a bad one.

"Trade and adventure—the same and not the same. For when I trade"—he thrust his hands forward, palms upward, and moved the fingers in a "hither! come ye hither!" gesture—"I look to profit. That wife is a thrifty one, you understand me? Eh? *Keh-keh-keh-ka-a-gh*—these fogs! These fogs!

"And when I go adventuring—*eh-h-h,* but I have seen

strange sights in my day: mountains of ice in the sea, and whales around them, and the big fish warring with the whales until the sea was blood-red; land where you could see the sun at midnight, where fir trees taller than British elms came to the sea's edge and the men wore bearskin and ate fish; black stone that burns—"

"We have that," said Caswallon. "Our fishermen bring it from the country north of the Iceni. We have burned it on this hearth."

"Have you seen fish fly?" asked the Phœnician.

"No," said Caswallon, "but I have listened to a lot of lies in my day."

"Oh, well. When I go adventuring, it is for love of the adventure. That wife is a mistress, teases, coaxes, is extravagant"—he threw his hand outward, and smiled as if he were pouring a fortune into a woman's lap, a lovely, lucky woman to be wooed by that tough old master of experience—"but I never forget that I have *two* wives.

"I have carried the stone that burns, all the way from an island where it snows at midsummer and the sun shines at midnight* to Alexandria, where I sold it to King Ptolemy the Piper† for its weight in corn, which I took to Ostia in four ships and sold to the Romans for silver. *Hey-yey!*

"And Ptolemy burned the black stone all in one night, when he was drunk, to entertain a Roman money-lender; made a circle of it in the execution place and burned I don't know how many convicted criminals, throwing in more and more until the fire was finished. But he would have killed them anyhow, so that is not on my head. Let Ptolemy answer for that.

"Of all the men who set sail with me on my first voyage—I was younger than Tros then; that is fifty years ago—not one man lives but I. Storms, sickness, strife: I have enough to answer for."

"You haven't answered me," said Caswallon firmly. "Tros spoke to you of what I require. Will you do it, or no?"

Hiram-bin-Ahab took a drink of mead. Then he looked at Fflur a long time. Then he met Caswallon's eyes.

"If it is for Tros and his father Perseus, I will do it gladly and for nothing," he said, drawing up his legs and

* Spitzbergen?
† Father of Cleopatra.

folding them under him, as if he were sitting on his own poop. "But if it is for you, you pay."

Fflur nodded. She understood him perfectly, but Caswallon looked piqued and Orwic swore under his breath.

"Have I not been your good host?" Caswallon asked.

"Aye, and I have been your good guest. As to that there is no account awaiting settlement. But Tros, who might have made a bargain, and a hard one—for I will need that permit he can sign with Cæsar's seal—Tros chose to make none, but promised, as a young man to an old one—"

Caswallon stood up suddenly. He was a giant, and he looked like the god of battles when he tossed his head to throw back the long, fair hair.

"By the Blood of Lud!" he thundered, "I am not behind Tros in this my kingdom! Take what you will! Help yourself to anything your old eyes covet, and go free. For I think as you say, this is to be your last journey. I ask nothing of you."

"Then I must do the best I can," said the Phœnician, sipping at the mead again and glancing at Tros slyly. "Hey-yey! When a man has two wives, it is not always the thrifty one whose counsel guides him."

Later, when the men-at-arms were very fast asleep, Caswallon went and fetched a druid, who had lived in Gaul and learned great skill with the pen. Then they brought out Cæsar's chest, and after much confabulation between Tros and Hiram-bin-Ahab the druid copied Roman documents on parchment, making changes at Tros's dictation, and forging Cæsar's signature so perfectly that not even Fflur's keen eyes could tell the difference when she compared copy and original.

At last, with a great laugh of contentment, Tros affixed Cæsar's seal, and went out with his arm around the shivering Phœnician, to greet the golden dawn.

CHAPTER XXI

IN WHICH THE WOMEN LEND A HAND

Ye think obedience is indignity; and so it is, if ye obey your baser selves, or if ye serve another's avarice. But will ye all be kings and captains? It is neither freedom nor love of freedom

that makes you disobedient, but envy, and fear lest a leader
should prove what muddleheads ye are.

FROM THE SAYINGS OF THE DRUID TALIESAN

THE Britons called it fun, until the third, or maybe the
fourth day, when even Orwic tired of it. The women had
enough to do to copy Roman costumes, and all the blacksmiths on the countryside were set to making Roman
shields and swords in imitation of those captured on the
Kentish beach.

The helmets were the greatest difficulty, until they
found a way of imitating them with basketwork, at which
Britons were experts. They stretched skin over that and
painted it, making plumes of horse-hair.

Conops had a hard time keeping the Britons from
making their own improvements. They wanted to make
the plumes three times the size and to lengthen the
swords, and to paint the shields blue because that was the
color that always brought them luck.

Tros saw to the galley, which needed such an overhaul
as was next to impossible to make in haste in that undisci-
plined community. They had a Celtic kind of individuality
that fused them into one mercurial mass in opposition to
authority, but made them units in deciding what to do and
when to do it.

When all other excuses for not working had been tried,
they discovered that the day was sacred to some god or
other and decamped to the woods to listen to a sermon
from the druids.

So the druids had to be won over, and Tros did that by
letting them into the secret that he hoped to capture
Cæsar, enemy of their religion. Their forest dwellings were
a-hum with fugitives from Gaul, who had brought details
of the tortures Cæsar used in his efforts to learn druidic
secrets.

So the druids came down in procession from forest to
waterside and blessed the bireme, with dew and earth and
mistletoe, proclaiming the ship sacred and whoever should
lend a hand to recondition her, or whoever should sail in
her under Tros's command, thrice blessed.

"You'll find we'll have to fight for what we want
though," Orwic commented.

The galley had been built in Gaul, from a Roman
model but by unaccustomed shipwrights, and in haste,
because Cæsar did everything in half the time that other
people liked to squander. So, to a practised eye, she would

have been an obvious fraud if she had appeared off Caritia pretending to have come from a Roman port through the Gates of Hercules.

She was too small, too clumsily built, and undersparred. It called for a very great deal of crafty reconstruction to make up for the lack of size, and, even so, pitch and linen-covered wickerwork had to masquerade in many instances as heavy timber, not that timber was lacking, but time. And the Britons were nimble with their favorite withes.

Tros built a whole new bow and stern of wickerwork on light oak frames, and covered that with painted cloth to make the ship look larger, praying to all the gods he had ever heard of, and they were many, not to send even such a half-gale as should break it all away.

In all that, he was ably helped by Hiram-bin-Ahab, who had sent his own tight ship downriver, with Skell on board, to lie up in a creek and wait for him. Thus they lost the services of the Phœnician's crew, but prevented Skell from seeing the galley or learning of what was taking place.

They mended the great arrow-engines and crammed the baskets full of new-made arrows nearly a yard long, Tros stowing those below deck to keep the Britons from firing them at marks across the river—they claiming they must have pratice; he swearing he would have ammunition. They filled the water casks. That was a prodigious business, because the Britons swore that any sort of water was a miserable substitute for mead; but Tros made them clean the cask with charcoal and then haul water from a dozen miles away, having seen too many crews die of the stuff they put into ships from longshore wells. And by that time the Britons voted him a despot, although, and perhaps because, he had only used up ten days for the entire business.

But it was not until the ship was ready and the crew had to be broken in that his real trouble began.

Fflur, Caswallon and Orwic had chosen a hundred of the brassiest young coxcombs Britain could produce. Most of them had ridden into the waves in the teeth of Cæsar's legions and had slain their Romans, hand-to-hand, but were chosen chiefly for their horsemanship. That was not so foolish as at first appeared, because the men with the highest courage and the strongest sense of manhood took the trouble to excel at that. But they were coxcombs.

Orwic himself would have challenged Tros a hundred

185

times if the other ninety-nine had not been so continually challenging him that he had to stand by the commander to uphold his own lieutenancy.

Their theory was that they should stand around the deck in imitation Roman armor and look handsome until they came in sight of Gaul, when they would land by some unexplained stratagem by night and rape the lair of Cæsar.

The twenty paid seamen who had brought the galley up the Thames with Tros, and perhaps a few more pressed for the occasion, were to do the work; and they were perfectly willing to help Tros lick those seamen into absolute obedience.

Tros stood on the poop with arms akimbo and laughed gaily at them, because if he had shown his real feelings there would have been no chance that he could handle them at all.

"Why not have *me* do all the work, and you all be the captains?" he suggested amiably.

He bulked big in a Roman's armor that the blacksmiths had enlarged to fit him, and he wore his own long sword as well as a short Roman one, which made him look dangerous. An imitation Roman helmet—none of the captured ones was big enough—cocked at a bit of an angle suggested an indifference to consequences. The toga thrown back over his shoulder gave him dignity.

And there were always those leonine eyes, that a man could not see without knowing there was a volcano not exactly slumbering behind them, but under control until needed.

"You!"

He singled out the most opinionated of them all, a youth of twenty, whose wife had painted new blue pictures on his white skin, and whose moustache was like a fox's, about ten reddish hairs on either side.

"Come up here on the poop and show me how to set that sail! Stand by, the rest of you, to take his orders!"

The coxcomb had the good sense to refuse, but that did not save him from being laughed at, and when the laugh had died and they had all done imitating what they thought were deep-sea orders—such as they had heard along the riverbank when the fisher-crews put out for herring in the North Sea—Tros dealt out information. He was growing very fluent in the Gaulish dialect they used.

"Ye know the feel of a horse's backbone, when ye ride

186

ten leagues without a saddle. Ye know soreness of the hams and how the spine can tremble like a stick with a weight of pain atop. Those are beginnings. I deal now in middle matters. And the end is not yet.

"Ye shall learn now what hard corns feel like on the hams; and how red hot the blisters grow on hands that have pulled on an oar a day or two. Ache? Ye have never ached as ye shall before this journey ends.

"Ye need now spines like oak trees, sinews like new ropes, belly muscles like a bear's. Ye need guts such as go into a wild boar's constitution, and a lot more courage than ye showed there on the beach when ye stood off Cæsar's men!

"I saw that fight. I watched it from this poop. I saw each turn of it, and perceived how Cæsar won. That day, ye fought by fits and starts. Ye charged into the sea, and out again to let the rear ranks have a turn, resting yourselves behind the fighting line, to come at it again; whereas Cæsar's men stuck to it until they won the beach.

"And now ye are trigged like Romans, ye must do as Romans! There is no pausing between encounters with the wind and sea. The tides don't cease because your hams smart with the salt in open blisters. Ye may cry, but the storm shrieks louder, and the only answer to the storm is work.

"Ye can get off your horses and walk home if your buttocks are on fire and your shoulders feel like a sack of wheat on a knitting needle. Not so at sea! Ye must sit and row until the oar-handle bucks back and lifts you by the chin, and the oar-end of the man behind you takes you in the shoulder-blades.

"With the ship rolling and the wind howling and the water squirting through the oar-port, ye must keep on rowing, while the blisters burn and your bones ache as if chariots had driven over them. This sea game is a calling that needs guts.

"So I will think no worse of any man who cries off now. I will cry good bed to him and good mead and a fireside. I need the daring men on this adventure, the bold spirits who would rather die than quit, the men who can endure pain and the cold and vomiting, and still row until I bid them cease. Ashore then now, every man who thinks himself unfit for this adventure!"

They howled at him to show them something he could do and they could not, mocking the sea and all its tantrums, as any young cockerel can who hasn't tried it and

187

who has a quart or two of *curmi* or some other potent liquor under his sword-belt. So he changed his strategy then and promised, by the great North Light that never failed a mariner, that he would leave behind whoever should disobey one order or shirk one trick of training before the start.

"Ye have stood up to the big bear and the lean wolf and the gray boar. But I will make you fit to face the sea! May the gods, who laugh, forgive me!" he added in an undertone to the old Phœnician. "Can a man turn Britons into mariners?"

Caswallon kept away.

"They will appeal to me and I might have to side with them," he said when Tros invited him to come and watch proceedings.

But he took care to learn how Tros had handled them and laughed until the tears ran down his cheeks.

For one of the things that Tros did was to moor the galley by the stern to the oak pile in mid-river, and to set those free and fearless horsemen rowing against that, with the paid seamen placed at intervals along the benches to set the pace and show them an example. And that, as Orwic swore, was no amusement for a British gentleman.

For a while they made sport of it, trying to break the warp or else the oaken pile, but all they succeeded in doing was to stir up Thames mud until the stink offended them, and to crack one another in the back with oar-ends until hot words led to fighting, and Tros had to get down among them with a mop to swab their indignant faces and get them all laughing again.

Conops' services were lost then, when most needed. He was used to teaching men to row. He could have run along the plank beside the benches, singling out this man and that, showing exactly how to hold an oar and how to throw the head back when the blade struck water.

But word came up-river, brought by Hiram-bin-Ahab's second mate in a small boat, that Skell was growing restless and threatening to leave the Phœnician's ship unless something happened before nightfall. So Conops had to be sent back with him to manage Skell. Tros's parting words were careful.

"Understand me—he mustn't be tied. He mustn't think he is a prisoner, or he may see through the whole trick. Also, I want him alive and fit for treachery in Gaul. So, first, try lying to him. Say Hiram-bin-Ahab will come to-morrow, then the next day, and so on. When that fails, pick a quarrel with him.

"He will call you a liar, no doubt. Be offended by that and lay him out with a belaying pin or with your knife-hilt. But mind, no overdoing it. A sore head may stir the venom in him, which I need. But a knife wound might let the impudence out, and he will need all his impudence this journey."

Conops winked his only eye, bowed with a movement like a curtsey until his weather-stained blue kirtle nearly touched the deck, holding his right hand up, palm outward, and departed overside. He would have gone to Gaul, to try and kidnap Cæsar single-handed, if Tros had ordered it.

Thereafter, Tros was in a quandary, because the girls came down to the riverbank and crowded into boats, to laugh at the oarsmen's antics and at the oar blades spraddling this and that way like the legs of a drunken centipede.

They screamed idiotically when the galley lurched toward them, and asked, when it lurched away again, whether Tros had his crew chained by the foot, the way the Northmen chained slaves to the benches.

When Orwic leaned over the side to order them away in his haughtiest manner, they called him "sailor-man Orwic" and asked how much a basket were the fish.

So the first day's practice at the oars broke up in rowdy repartee and ended by the girls all being chased home, screaming, Orwic vowing that women were the curse of the human race.

"That's one thing I concede the druids," he said scornfully. "They are born of women, like the rest of us, but they know enough to keep away from them when they once take vows. What puzzles me is, why a man can't do that without pulling a long face and singing hymns at sunrise. I was through with women long ago. They spoil everything."

But Tros went straight to a woman, Fflur, by her fireside, where she knitted the first trousers of her youngest son and listened to the calf-love story of her eldest, who had seen a girl who suited him "by Verulam, where Merlin son of Merlin keeps the mill. Aye, Mother, Merlin's daughter."

When she had said her say concerning Merlin's daughter—and there was much she said that was pointed, but without a barb, and much more that was understood she

189

might have said, had it not been better that Caswallon should say that for her—she listened to Tros, seeming to listen with those gray eyes rather than with her ears, which were hidden under the gray-shot golden hair.

And that night Fflur gave a party to the women, at which no men were present, although the men made bonfires all around the house and caterwauled and burned a witch in effigy, pretending they thought the women were conspiring to sell Lunden to the Romans and submit themselves to Roman husbands. They even made a Roman out of a pig's bladder and some meal bags, and pushed it through the window on a stick.

But what happened at that party did not leak out, because Fflur knew how secrets are told in such a way that women keep them. The girls had a great air of importance when they let the men lead them home at last, but no amount of cajoling or teasing made them talk.

And next day, when most of his hundred—as Tros had expected they would—refused downrightly to return to rowing and be made ridiculous, the girls joined hands and danced around them, mocking them, singing a new song Fflur had set to an old tune. It was about the men of Lunden, who were such babies that they could only ride horseback and were afraid to hurt their lily-white hands by pulling at ash oars.

So the hundred went back to the rowing, because the girls declared they wouldn't kiss a man who hadn't blisters on his hands and couldn't make an ash oar keep time as it smote the water. In fact, there were more than a hundred who offered themselves in place of the mutineers, and several heads were broken as the original hundred defended their claim to be the first gentlemen rowers in all Britain, a kind of brand-new aristocracy with first claim on the admiration of the women.

Orwic had two girls in attendance on him when he sauntered back to duty. He contrived to look bored, but the appearance was unconvincing.

CHAPTER XXII

MUTINY AND MAL DE MER

Ye speak to me with deference, and in my presence ye behave with reverence for the Wisdom that I worship. But why do ye not slay me? I will tell you. Ye fear those underlings, for whom I insist on such small justice as your law permits. And they fear you. But I fear neither them, nor you, nor death.

FROM THE SAYINGS OF THE DRUID TALIESAN

THEN came, after a series of gales, one of those clear October nights when Britain is hushed, as if she heard the winter coming and were waiting in her bridal robes. The very animals were still. The river sucked by the wharf-piles with a hint of bell notes in the splash, and the stars shone as if wet with dew.

That was the night Tros started. He had sent Hiram-bin-Ahab downriver in the afternoon, the rowboat keeping close inshore to avoid the incoming tide. There were no farewell feasts or mead drinkings, because the old man protested he could not sit through another such ordeal.

Caswallon permitted him to vanish like a specter of the past, wrapped in his camel-hair shawls and seated in the stern of Fflur's swan-carved barge.

But twenty of the young girls kissed him first, lest Britain be disgraced, and hung three garlands around his neck, filling the boat so full of flowers that the rowers had hard work to take their seats.

And Tros would have no feasting because he wanted his crew sober. If they had sat down in Caswallon's hall to meat and mead there would have been no hope of getting them on board before morning.

But he could not keep Fflur and Caswallon off the ship, and although Caswallon, at Tros's request, gave out that the galley would leave on the following day, all Lunden was there, nevertheless, two hours after sunset, when the tide changed, and the girls so flocked around the ship in punts and rowboats that when Tros ordered the warp cast off and struck the first beat on the bull-hide drum to time the oarsmen, there were upsets, screams, girls in the river, and it needed Tros's voice, roaring louder than the drum, to keep the oars at work.

Even so, as the tide took hold of the galley, she almost buried her beak in the mud below the pool.

But Caswallon had brought along three druids to forfend ill luck. There was mistletoe at the masthead. The moon was just exactly right, a crescent with the points so oriented as to gather fortune from the sky and pour it on the undertaking.

So nobody was drowned, as Orwic, leaning out from the

191

fighting top at the masthead, where he was supposed to be conning the course, reported.

Orwic said he knew those reaches of the Thames. So Tros had sent him up there, chiefly to flatter him, but he sent a seaman up there too, and Caswallon made Orwic his admiral afterwards, he was so impressed by the way the ship was piloted in darkness.

They rowed downstream to drumbeat, towing Caswallon's barge, filling the night with throbbing until the ducks awoke and scuttered into deeper reed beds, until the singing of the girls by Lunden Pool grew faint and died away in a murmur, until mud appeared, as the tide receded, and Tros held the galley in mid-river, not trusting even Orwic's skilled assistant to know short cuts in the gloom.

And at last they saw a dim light in the marshes, which was Hiram-bin-Ahab's riding light, and there Fflur, Caswallon and the druids were put overside to wait for the tide to change again and bear them back, upstream, to Lunden Town.

But first Caswallon made a speech to the gentlemen adventurers who leaned on the white-ash oars to listen, each man with an imitation Roman helmet, sword and armor under his rowing bench.

"Sons of good British mothers! Let none return to Britain less a man than he set forth! Into Tros's hands I have given you, charging him that he shall lead you nobly. Do ye obey him. Trust him. I hold him answerable. If he brings you back with honor, I will honor him; and I think he will lead you craftily to great deeds, the which I would that I might share in.

"But I am the king, whose foot should not leave Britain, save in extremity. Smite, each of you, a blow for me! For lo! I am a king who strikes at Cæsar with a hundred sword hands, with the cunning of a hundred brains. So be ye valiant!"

They did not cheer, lest Skell should hear them on the old Phœnician's ship. Caswallon, Fflur and the druids went overside into the lapping darkness and were rowed into the reeds to await the coming tide.

Then Tros called to Orwic to light a masthead flare, and when that had burned for the space of a hundred heart-beats the pitch-dipped branch was cast into the river like a plunging meteor and Tros set the drumbeat going, low, slow, regular, muting the drum with his knee, lest

Skell should catch the rhythm and add two and two together later on.

Then, when they had cleared the mouth of Medway and at dawn the river broadened out of view on either hand, he set the drum to thundering and made the oarsmen grunt and sweat until they felt the long swell under them and, as the tide was near the slack, an off-shore breeze awoke.

"This Lud of Lunden is a god with brains," Tros shouted then. "Tide he gives us, and then a wind exactly in the quarter whence we need it!"

He laughed when the hirelings manned the halyards and the wind filled the bellying sail, for he had those young cockerels at his mercy now. Soon he could hear Orwic's groan and vomit from the fighting top, for the tide had turned against the wind.

There was a lively motion in the dark, uplifting rollers and a drift of white scud splashing through the oar-ports. Now was not much need to bid the rowing cease; good half the oars were idle before the order came.

And as Tros leaned on the helm to make the utmost of the wind to gain an offing before he should turn, with tide abeam, southward along the coast of Kent, he chuckled— first at the silence in the ship's waist, then at the noise of resurrected mead and venison that gurgled overside or in between the benches, anywhere at all!

The twenty sea-wise hirelings, who had fought him all the way from Gaul to Lunden not so long ago, gave him no trouble at all on this adventure, since he had them too, at disadvantage.

As surely as they were none too many to man the sheets and braces, they were all too few to offer disobedience, with a hundred of Caswallon's blooded cockerels, seasick though those were, at hand to put them in their place. The scorn was mutual and thorough.

The more sick the aristocracy became, the less they admired such human cattle as could thrive in a box on a heaving sea and, by the same compelling instinct, the less pleased it made them to be patronized.

One seaman, who dared to grin between decks when sent below to wedge a shifting water cask in place, was almost killed, which set Tros thinking.

He put a seaman at the helm and went below, discovering more than twenty oarsmen who were only sick enough to fell ill-tempered, chilly and ashamed. He gathered them in the ship's waist, abaft the citadel.

193

"Choose," he ordered gruffly. "Take mops and clean up all that mess of vomiting, or stand a watch on deck and let the seamen swab."

They chose the deck, and Tros, in no hurry at all, since he must let the Phœnician overtake him after the next tide, spilled the wind out of the sail repeatedly until they learned the use of brace and sheet. There being no such cure for seasickness as work aboard a plunging ship, he quartered the sea in every possible direction to keep them busy at the ropes and to accustom them to every kind of belly-empty motion, until they grew new sea legs under them and were aware of appetite.

When they had eaten of the sacked dry venison and bread, such sleepiness came over them as only sea produces, sleepiness of bone and brain and muscle, eyes, skin, all the senses, until an oak deck felt like a feather bed and any kind of wind-break was a haven of dreamless bliss.

So he let them sleep wherever they lay down to it, and the seamen stood watch and watch that night, but later, when the storm came, Tros had a score of proud men he could call on, half of them in either watch, not expert, but enthusiastic. Thus he was able to rest ten tired-out real seamen at a time.

And that worked wonders. For the aristocracy discovered they were not so far behind the seamen after all, stronger than they when their muscle counted, lacking only knowledge of what to do, and how to do it with the least exertion.

That led to rivalry, even to blows, until Orwic, green-cheeked, swaying and self-conscious, crawled down from the fighting top at last, compelled himself to eat, and took charge of his friends.

Then Tros rearranged the watches, keeping gentlemen and seamen to themselves, and matched one against the other. By the afternoon of the first day out the men who had lain groaning in the scuppers began appearing one by one on deck, and some of them added themselves to Orwic's watch, getting in one another's way, but learning rapidly.

So all went increasingly well until Tros hove the ship to in fine weather, the second day out from Lunden, with the Kentish cliffs in sight on one hand and the cliffs of Gaul just visible through a haze to southward.

Being hove to was another kind of motion. There were prompt defections from the ranks of Orwic's men. But Tros was more concerned about the blue haze masking the cliffs of Gaul and a change of weather in the northwest where a bank of gray cold-looking clouds looked full of wind.

Watching that cloudbank and the line of white across the sea beneath it, his eye detected two specks that he liked still less, for they followed a third, which was certainly the three-reefed mainsail of Hiram-bin-Ahab's ship. He knew that Phœnician curved spar as he knew the cliffs of Samothrace, and, though he had only seen the spar and lug-sail of a Northman once, he did not need Orwic's voice from the fighting top to warn him that Hiram-bin-Ahab was running from a pair of North Sea pirates.

The Britons began roaring for a battle on the deep, and even the seasick oarsmen crawled on deck, recovering their strength from sheer excitement, some of them demanding food, that they might gain strength for the fighting. But Tros stood scratching at his beard, perplexed.

The gods—and he was a whole-souled pantheist, who saw the hand of one god or another in every splash of spray and change of circumstances—were staging a conundrum for him that demanded wit.

He felt reasonably sure he could beat those Northmen off, for he knew his Britons and the dreadful havoc he could wreak with six great arrow-engines. Too, if he could trust his oarsmen, by a deft maneuver he might wreck one Northman, catching her in a following sea—it was boiling white now under the racing clouds, and the following sea would swamp her as her slim bows crumpled on the galley's oak-and-iron ram. That would leave but one Northman to deal with, and six arrow-engines for the work: one slim-waisted longship, that had run too long before the rising sea to dare to turn about.

He smiled at the nerve of the old Phœnician, who had dared to reef down snugly even though the Northmen gained on him and he had no fighting crew. He supposed old Hiram-bin-Ahab had counted on the sight of a Roman bireme to send the pirates scurrying for shelter, calculating speed and distance with the accuracy that a man learns in fifty years at sea.

But what if the Northmen did not know the bireme's possibilities? Had Rome ever sent a ship up their way? They might mistake her for some freakish foreign thing hove to and helpless, as she surely would be presently, unless he should go about in time. The storm would burst

195

on him as the galley lay a-rolling with her yard braced nearly fore and aft.

Tros felt at the helm, watching all three ships, and there was hardly a mile between them, or more than three miles between them and himself. The Northmen seemed not far behind the old Phœnician in seamanship.

If he should fail to put the galley about before the thundering northwester hurled high seas on him—and it would be too late then—they would simply storm along past him and pursue the old Phœnician until they could close with him at their own discretion, perhaps in the lee of Vectis or wherever the wind and sea should offer opportunity.

But if he should go about in time, ahead of that tumbling sea, and run, he was afraid the Northmen might think he ran from them, and that involved a second problem: that his own Britons might believe the same thing and be mutinous.

Then, though he had improved her, the galley still steered like a house when a following sea lumped under her high stern. There was the risk, amounting almost to a certainty, that a high sea under that stern would break away the wicker false end he had erected at such pains to increase the ship's apparent size.

However, he went about, and squared away under a three-reefed mainsail before the storm struck him, boiling along beam to beam with Hiram-bin-Ahab three-quarters of a mile to starboard and one of the Northmen half a mile astern. The other lurched and pitched off the Phœnician's quarter like a lean wolf keeping a stag in view.

Then Tros began to curse the day when Romans ever left dry land and built themselves floating islands that they fondly thought were ships. Hiram-bin-Ahab's sweet-lined little merchant-ship, with her great eye painted in the bow, deep-laden though she was, sailed faster than he could follow without spreading more sail than he dared.

The Northmen raced along like hungry fish, their beautifully molded bows preventing them from plunging. It was going to be a hopeless stern chase, with all the ever-widening channel in which to scatter, and small hope of coming to the Phœnician's aid in time.

Tros made up his mind swiftly when he realized that, for the waves were thundering under his stern and loosening the wicker dummy work with every plunge. Already the cloth covering was washed away and there was nothing to be gained by maneuvering to save what seemed already doomed.

He changed his helm and ordered two reefs shaken out, turning the reeling galley's broadside almost square to the waves, and bore down on the nearest Northman.

It was then that he cursed himself for letting Conops go to the Phœnician. There was no one he could trust to rush below and make sure of the closing of the oar-ports; no one to stand below the poop and enforce his orders on the instant that he roared them; no one to see that the arrow baskets did not lurch overside while the Britons wrestled with one another for the right to serve the engines; no one to see that the gut was sheltered from the spray.

Some fool loosened the dolphin from its lashings and the great iron horror began swinging from the yardarm like Fate's pendulum, threatening to chafe its halyard and go crashing through the deck, striking the shrouds when the ship lurched, swinging the yard and spilling wind out of the sail.

Nor had he a seaman fit to send aloft to throw a rope around the thing and make it fast. He *had* to let the helm go then. He gave it to Orwic, jumped to the main deck and up on to the citadel. Thence he sprang into the shrouds with drawn sword, slashing at the halyard as it swung, and the dolphin grazed the ship's side as it plunged through the crest of a wave, forever harmless.

Orwic, laughing happily when Tros took the helm again, cuffed another Briton away from one of the poop arrow-engines. He had feared he might miss something by having to stand there hauling at a steering oar, and in another minute he would have let the helm go anyhow.

The heads of the Northmen showed plainly now between the shields erected all along the longship's bulwark. Orwic began laying arrows in the grooves, while half a dozen young enthusiasts got in one another's way to turn the crank and strain the bows taut.

But it was the bow engines that fired first, ignoring the galley's roll and shoulder plunge, that were increased by the weight of the fighting top, where no man could have clung and kept his senses.

One volley of arrows plunked into the sea like a flight of hurrying fish, three waves away. The other went rocketing so high over the Northmen's mast that the pirates did not even guess of its existence.

What the Northmen did see was a row of tousled heads along the galley's bulwark, and a galley plunging down on

197

them under a weight of sail that looked like carrying the mast away and bore her down until the keel showed in the trough between two waves.

They could see the boiling ram, and they were smart of helm enough to miss that easily. But they could not see much, in the way of men or weapons, that alarmed them, until Orwic, steadying himself with a foot against the poop rail, loosed his trial shot exactly at the moment when the galley's stern paused swaying on a wave. It was the sway that did the spreading. It was luck, or Lud of Lunden, maybe, that sent twelve arrows screaming straight into the gaps between the Northmen's shields.

The Northmen did not wait for any more of that.

Their helm went over instantly. A big man, whose long, fair hair streamed out from under a peaked helmet, shook his fist as the crew hauled on the braces and the longship changed her course toward the coast of Britain.

Tros's cockerels sent flight after flight of arrows after her, and one chance volley of a dozen plunked through the crimson sail, but most of them went wide by half a dozen ships' lengths, and there was no hope of pursuit.

But the other Northman, who had been edging his way gradually closer to Hiram-bin-Ahab's flank, turned tail too, because Northmen were easily scared when they did not understand just what was happening, and both longships shook down a reef in a hurry to reach shelter under the cliffs of Kent. So Tros, too, changed his helm, to follow the Phœnician, hoping the Northmen would suppose he had chased them from their quarry in order to capture it himself.

But the instant he changed his course he had to deal with mutiny. The Britons, Orwic leading, swore they would not sail another yard with him unless he should follow the Northmen and force them to give battle.

They called him coward, traitor, a purse-loving Samothracian. They struck the helm away from him and tried to sail the galley for themselves, laying her over until even Tros cried out in terror and half of the water casks broke adrift below, thundering and crashing as if the ship were falling apart.

But the sail did not split, because Tros had jumped to the deck and let the sheets go. So when they all discovered they were helpless—and that was only after they had tried to row with heavy water squirting through the oar-ports and a dozen or more knocked senseless as the oar-ends caught them in the jaw—they let Tros take the helm again, threatening to hang him where the dolphin used to swing unless he should pursue the Northmen.

"Then hang me and have done with it!" Tros answered.

He laughed at them. At which they also laughed, because they understood that he had them at his mercy just then. What should happen later was another matter!

The sail thundered and snapped in the wind and none had a notion how to get it sheeted down again, while the galley rolled and every third or fourth wave swept her from stem to stern.

It was more than Tros knew how to do, although he did have twenty men who could go aloft and lay their bellies on the spar, once he could get that braced and steady, but in some way he had to save that sail. So he sent the twenty men aloft to tie a stout line to its corner and then to cut it loose to blow downwind. When it had flopped into the sea he towed it, to help keep his stern to the waves, wondering what Conops might be thinking, for he knew Conops had missed none of that performance. Conops would be watching with one eye as good as half a dozen from the old Phœnician's poop.

The Britons grew seasick again, the excitement having died. There were some who said the expedition was a failure; they demanded that Tros should put back to Lunden as soon as the storm might permit.

"Where the women will laugh at you, and I will bid them laugh, whether you hang me for it or not," Tros answered.

He had only one dread now. The galley would survive the storm, but Hiram-bin-Ahab might run out of his bargain. The Phœnician's ship was out of sight, hidden by spume and rain that made a howling twilight of high noon.

A sudden shift of wind made even the direction doubtful, since without a glimpse of sun or coastline, tide across the current and the wind kicking both into a three-way mess of wallowing confusion, there was nothing to set a course by. At dawn old Hiram-bin-Ahab might be a hundred miles ahead.

Tros laughed at himself bitterly. His whole ingenious plan had gone downwind, and, what was nearly as bad, he had lost his good man Conops. He would not have willingly exchanged him for all the Britons, Orwic included. He knew Conops could take care of himself; but he laughed again, and not so bitterly, to think of Skell's predicament, without friends in some foreign port, and with plenty of press gangs on the prowl for a likely oarsman.

There was no one to consult with. Orwic was indignant because he had refused to chase the Northmen.

"Who will be burning Hythe or Pevensey to-morrow as surely as we've lost the way!" he yelled against the wind when Tros said something flattering about his marksmanship with the arrow-engine.

Nothing after that to do but pace the poop and watch the sea.

Orwic went below. Even the seaman, who relieved Tros at the helm so that he might sleep in snatches, was impudent and made a suggestive motion of finger to throat, prophetic of what might happen when Orwic had done talking to the crew.

However, they were still afloat and likely to survive the storm. The wickerwork structures built at bow and stern were almost undamaged. The pitched cloth covering was gone, but the marvelously twisted basketwork had offered no resistance to the waves, which washed through the interstices, even breaking their force without being torn loose, and keeping many a wave from bursting on the deck.

Tros fell asleep considering that contraption, dreaming of the sweet ship he would some day build—he had her half-designed already in his head—and calculating on a basketwork construction all around her above the water-line, perhaps covered with well-pitched sail-cloth, wondering whether that might not serve better than the metal plates he had always had in mind. He could see the possibilities.

He set himself to try to dream of something better than the sail-cloth for a covering, and dreamed, instead, of deep-sea monsters that came overside and threatened him with death.

When he awoke, both his own long sword and the shorter Roman one were gone. He was not tied, but Orwic and a dozen other Britons were on the poop, eyeing him with guarded curiosity. They were leaning against the poop rail, an obvious committee of mutineers.

It lacked an hour of sundown, and the storm had died, but a tremendous swell was running. The sun was an angry red ball above a welter of gray water, and the coast of Gaul was like a pencil line behind a curtain of haze on the left hand. The twenty seamen were all clustered in the bow, as panicky as sheep that smell wolf.

"We propose to go home," Orwic announced drily, definitely.

"Very well," Tros answered, standing up, arms akimbo, facing them. "Set me ashore on the coast of Gaul."

But Orwic laughed.

"You take us home," he answered.

Tros studied the drift awhile, for there was hardly any wind, although the waves were running too high for that crew of horsemen to manage the oars. It was difficult to judge direction in the gray haze, but at the end of a minute he was nearly sure he could hear surf pounding on a beach.

"Let us see whither we go," he answered, facing them again.

"Home!" repeated Orwic, gesturing rather vaguely to the northward.

But Tros realized that Orwic was ashamed beneath that air of well-bred calm, and that, though he spoke for the committee, he was not its instigator. He had seen a many deep-sea mutinies. He made a gesture to his sword-belt, saying nothing. Orwic actually blushed, which made him look ridiculous, with his hair all blown and tousled and a two days' growth of yellow beard.

"Give me my sword and I will fight the lot of you," said Tros, turning his back again.

He put both hands behind him, listening. He was sure now he could hear surf pounding on a beach, equally sure that it didn't much matter what happened unless he could control the crew. The mutineers consulted in whispers, which is no way to conduct a mutiny. Out of the corner of his eye Tros could see all the rest of the men clustered around the citadel, most of them chin on knee, squatting on the deck, watching the outcome. And that is not the spirit in which mutinies succeed. It was too bad to have to make a fool of Orwic, but even nephews of Caswallons have to learn.

Tros leaned overside and noticed that the basketwork was still in place. He was careful to display his interest in that, watching the suck and movement of it as the galley rolled and the sea swirled in and out through the interstices, as if the mutiny were unimportant.

"We will give you your sword if you will agree to take us home," said Orwic.

"No!" Tros answered, facing them again. "If I have my sword I will be captain, and you will obey me. Without my sword I am not captain."

"Then you must obey us," said Orwic.

"No," Tros answered. "I gave no undertaking to obey you."

"But you shall!" said Orwic.

Tros laughed, for he saw the boy was desperate—between the devil and the deep sea—obliged either to take command of a ship he could not handle or to yield and lose prestige with his own people. There was only one thing that a man of Orwic's breeding could do in that predicament.

"You shall give the undertaking now," he said grimly. But he could not challenge an unarmed man to fight. "Give Tros his sword!" he added, snapping out the four words to a man beside him.

He was pale now, almost gray-white. He could fight on horseback, but he had never tackled a trained swordsman on a swaying deck, and it was growing dark. The sun's red rim was disappearing in a smear of angry haze.

The brought Tros's sword out of the cabin, and Orwic gave it to him, stepping back at once and stripping his own breast bare. For it was against a Briton's code of honor to fight hand to hand unless the opponent could see the naked skin over throat and heart.

Tros threw his own cloak off and unbuckled the heavy Roman breast-plate, letting it fall with a clank on deck. Then he tore his shirt to lay bare the huge, hairy breast beneath it, and kicked off his high-laced Roman sandals, for he knew how slippery a swaying deck could be.

He was glad then that the sun went down, being minded to spare Orwic what distress he could. He liked him, liked him well enough to take a chance.

"Clear the poop!" he snarled, drawing the long blade.

He took three steps forward, straight at the committee, who were leaning with their backs against the rail. They had to go or else resist him. Orwic said nothing, so they went, one by one, down the ladder. All the other Britons swarmed up on the midship citadel to watch. But even as they were swaying shadows in the gloom, so were Tros and Orwic no more than dim specters. Nobody could see much. There was a catching of deep breaths, no shouting, no other sound than the creaking of cordage and the splosh of the waves against the rolling galley's bilge.

"Are you ready?" asked Tros.

Orwic came at him with a leap, whirling a long sword that made the darkness whistle. Tros met him point first, meaning to stand his ground, but the sparks flew and the

202

blows rained on his blade with a din like a blacksmith's anvil and two hammers going.

He had to sidestep and let Orwic flounder away to leeward down the slippery deck, where he could have skewered him as easily against the poop rail as a butcher sticks a sheep. There was a gasp from the midship citadel, followed by a dozen shouts to Orwic to use the point and not the edge, then silence, broken by a cry from the night and the waves:

"Master! Oh, Master!"

The words were Greek. They sounded to the Britons like the voice of a spirit howling in a wilderness of dark sea. Tros heard them draw their breaths, could almost feel them shudder. He knew the voice, and his heart leaped as he laughed. The old Phœnician had kept faith! Conops! But he had to keep his eyes on Orwic, who was crouching in shadow, watching his chance to spring.

The voice cried again as Orwic drove with the point at Tros's throat, slipping on the wet deck as he lunged. Tros caught the point under his own hilt, jerking with a sudden movement of the wrist that snapped the Briton's blade. Then, swift as a loosed bowstring, before Orwic could recover he struck upward at the Briton's hilt. The broken sword spun overside, humming, and Tros's point touched the naked skin of Orwic's throat.

"Now cry 'Enough!' Say it! Speak!" Tros ordered.

"Kill!" said Orwic, swallowing and breathing through his nose.

He even pressed his throat against the point until Tros lowered it.

"Will you have another sword?" asked Tros, "and fight me till I slay you? Or will you cry 'Enough!' and take my hand? It seems to me no shame that you should yield. Caswallon gave a hundred of you into my hands—"

"Master! Oh, Master!" cried a hollow voice across the waves.

This time the words were in Gaulish, as if Conops had despaired of his native Greek.

"Lo, the sea answers for me," laughed Orwic. "Did you offer your right hand?"

Tros passed his sword into his left, and waited. Orwic stepped closer, and Tros hugged him as a father hugs his son, though he was barely four years older than the Briton. It is experience that makes age.

Then suddenly out of darkness Conops climbed the ship's side, springing for the poop, crying:

"Master! Get the anchor down! Rocks! You're drifting on rocks!"

The Britons all surged aft off the citadel to find out what was happening, but Tros drew his sword again at the head of the poop-ladder.

"Back!" he thundered. "Every mother's son! I'll brain the first who disobeys me! To your oars! Out oars!"

There was no chance that they could row. He gave them something to divert attention. He could hear the sea a-wash among half-hidden rocks. The pounding of waves on a beach had swelled into one continued roar.

"To the oars and save the ship!" he shouted, pounding the sodden drum.

As they fell back, doubting whether to obey him, Conops went scampering between them through the gloom toward the ship's bow. In another second there were thumps and protests as his knife-hilt struck the ribs of seamen, then the splash of the anchor and the hum of a hawser reeling overside.

"She holds!" he roared between his hands a moment later, then charged back to the poop.

"Where is Hiram-bin-Ahab?" Tros asked him.

"A scant mile away, sir, anchored in a cove to leeward of the rocks you came near splitting on!" Conops glanced about him, baring his teeth at Orwic. "Any fighting before we work her out of here? She's riding in twice her depth within a ship's length of the reef. We'd better move."

But Tros could trust that hawser and knew, too, what a frenzied panic the Britons would make of oar work unless he should wait for the sea to die down a bit. There was no top on the sea, but it rolled along, high backed and heavy ahead of the tide.

"Get into your boat and get the sail first, if there's any of it left!" he answered. Then, standing by the poop-ladder: "Man the benches!"

Half of the crew was still doubting whether to obey him.

"What does she look like?" he asked, turning his back to the crew to give them a chance to obey him without feeling they were being driven.

"Fine in the dark," said Conops. "She looks twice her size. I didn't know the cloth was all ripped off the wicker-work until I lay alongside in the boat. If we show up off Caritia Sands at dusk, the Romans'll never doubt us."

He went overside with three of the British seamen and spent half an hour disentangling the sail to spill the water out of it before he shouted: "All clear!"

Then Tros stood over the rest of the twenty and made them haul the sail on deck. Meanwhile, the mist had shifted, gathering itself into a dense bank and following the tide. He could see the reef now and the white line of breakers on the beach beyond it.

"Lud of Lunden Town!" he muttered. "Britons, not being sailors, haven't yet spent their sea-luck!"

He shivered. The reef was almost near enough to spit on.

"Out oars!" he shouted, and this time they obeyed him.

Conops ran to the bow to use his knife-hilt on the seamen's ribs again, forcing them to man the hawser and haul in the slack. Tros pounded slowly on the sodden bull-skin drum, ready to roar to Conops to let go if the rowers should come to grief and lose the steering way.

The oars dipped deep when the galley rolled and scudded on the wave tops when she hove her side skyward, but the anchor came home foot by foot, and Conops let it swing until there was half a mile between them and the reef.

Then, after taking a sounding or two, he let it go and they rolled to it in safety until dawn, with Hiram-bin-Ahab's small boat dancing astern at a long painter's end.

The two men who had come with Conops were a godsend then, for there was the sail to bend on and they had it done before the light wind came that blew away the mist banks and showed Hiram-bin-Ahab's ship rolling easily at anchor, like a living thing that laughed. The great eyes painted on her bow—so that she might see the way home—seemed to wink when the waves half covered them.

"And Skell?" asked Tros, when Conops came up to the poop for a moment's rest.

"First, when the Northmen hove in sight off Thamesmouth, Skell swore he knew them and could make terms," said Conops. "He proposed to show the Northmen the way to Lunden, saying Northmen would not harm a merchant ship * but would be generous in return for such aid as that. He said the Northmen's harvest must have failed and they were coming to seize foothold in Britain.

"But Hiram-bin-Ahab agreed with me there would be a

---

* This seems to have been the unwritten rule. A merchant ship was not molested by the North Sea rovers.

storm before long, and he determined to save Lunden from those pirates if it might be done. So, being sure he had the faster ship, he shortened sail a bit to let them come within arrow range. Then he fired a volley at the nearest one, and shook out reefs, and ran, they giving chase since he had forfeited his rights.

"So he decoyed them until the storm broke and, what with wind and tide, it was too late for them to turn into the river-mouth for shelter. Hey! But he knows how to handle his crew, that old Phœnician! And he handles a ship as if she were a king's mistress!

"When he changed the helm a bit, so that the sea took us under the quarter, Skell was seasick, and riding at anchor hasn't helped him to recover. When I came away he was lying like a dead man on a coil of rope on top of the cargo."

"Is he hurt? You haven't—"

"No sir. He did call me a liar, as you said he might perhaps. He spoke truth: I changed the lie so often, that he could not do less than turn on me at last.

"No, sir, not the blade, although he tried to use his; no, sir, I didn't tie him; he didn't need it. Those heavy men fall hard. There's a world of chin sticks out under that red beard of his. For a minute or two I feared I'd broken it adrift, and he carries a lump there now as big as a Joppa orange, but the bone's in one piece.

"What troubles him most is his belly. He vomits more than you'd believe a man could hold. Now he thinks he's dead, and now he fears he isn't, but he'll be fit enough for mischief when you land him."

"Good," said Tros. "Get back to the Phœnician and tell him, if we both live and ever meet again, there's nothing he mayn't ask of me and see it done! Then come and tell me what this galley looks like from a distance. Try to imagine yourself a Roman in Caritia at dusk.

"If we show up at dusk, we'll have another good excuse for not putting in—shoals, tide, wind. But I want to know whether that basketwork looks like the real thing from a mile or two away. If it does, tell Hiram-bin-Ahab to sail the minute there's a fair wind for Caritia, but make sure he understands we're to turn up there at dusk. Wait! Has Skell seen this galley yet?"

"No, sir. He's lain below ever since seasickness took him."

"Tell Hiram-bin-Ahab to use every ruse he can think of to make Skell *sure* this is a Roman galley straight from

Ostia. Let him begin talking smallpox now. Let him ask Skell whether he knows a remedy against it."

CHAPTER XXIII

TROS MAKES A PROMISE

Have I spoken of your folly? Aye, times out of number. But ye are wizards, ye are paragons of judgment and wisdom compared to the braggart who pretendeth to wisdom that he hath not. Again, and again, and again I have said: if brawl ye must, because of follies ye have not outgrown, then brawl like men. I brawl not, because I hate not. Ye who hate, shall ye avoid the pains of hatred by pretending to a virtue that ye have not? It is better, I say, to die in battle than to do lip-service to the Wisdom whose outer threshold ye have not the strength of character to cross.

FROM THE SAYINGS OF THE DRUID TALIESAN

ALL that day and most of the night following, they lay at anchor while Conops spread pitch liberally on the bows and stern and Tros coaxed his Britons back into a friendly frame of mind. First he had to reëstablish Orwic in their estimation. Orwic had plainly mishandled the mutiny, and some of them were disposed to think he had deliberately lost that hand-to-hand fight in the dark.

So he began by asking whether they thought they had a better man than Orwic. He offered to fight any ten of their own choosing, two at a time, which was sheer guile, because he knew their code of honor did not permit of two men fighting one. They cat-called at him from the benches, but none offered to match swords, and they listened when he uttered his great rolling laugh and spoke his mind.

"Orwic is blood of your blood. I am not. He had to listen to you, because you are all his equals more or less. But not I! I am the master of this ship. Who gainsays that?"

There was no answer until after a long pause; Tros was not avoiding issues, he was forcing one.

A bow oarsman shouted the word "coward" at him.

"Since when?" Tros asked, and waited.

But that man did not answer. It was another who shouted: "You ran from two Northmen's ships!"

"As I have eyes, it was the Northmen who ran," Tros answered. "As I have eyes, it was Orwic's work that put

207

them both to flight! As I am a sailor and ye are horsemen, it was impossible to follow. But for my hand at the helm, ye would all be among the fish this minute, belly upward, with the sea-birds pecking at your dead eyes!"

"This minute the Northmen are burning our villages!" another voice retorted, and at that there was a murmur of assent.

A heavy man with brown hair down to his shoulders, who pulled the stroke oar on the port side, shouted: "Sail in search of the Northmen now, and we will catch them at Hythe or Pevensey."

"Since when have ye so loved the men of Hythe?" Tros answered. "I was there when Caswallon came to summon them to join him against Cæsar, but not a man from Hythe would go. They said they would hold Hythe, and no more. If they were so sure they could hold it then against the Romans who had beaten such gallant lads as you are, can't they hold it now against mere North Sea rovers? What are two ships when Cæsar had more than a hundred ships full of well-armed Roman infantry?"

He had struck the right note, and he knew it. There was no love lost between Lunden and Hythe and Pevensey since the men of Lunden and a handful from eastern Kent had to stand off Cæsar's legions without assistance.

"Now listen to me!" he thundered. His hairy breast was naked, which was intimation that he stood there ready to fight whoever challenged him.

"Caswallon gave you into my charge, holding me answerable, bidding you obey me and be valiant. I will neither flinch nor turn aside. Ye shall obey me, or I will fight you one by one! It is not Hythe ye love, or Pevensey. It is your own town and the honor of your women and the fun of burning the Northmen's ships behind them."

There was a cheer, but he raised his hand for silence.

"And now ye help me rescue my father, in which there shall be no fighting if I can help it, since he loves fighting no more than the druids do. But does any man accuse me of not paying what I owe? Has my word ever failed you? I think not. Then hear ye this."

He paused dramatically, but the histrionics were a ruse. He was scanning faces, making sure that the moment was ripe for the master argument.

"Ye shall obey me first, and I will do my business. Then ye shall have your bellyful of Northmen, for I will lead you on such a raid as ye have never imagined. No matter whether we catch those two ships, or whether they escape us, or whether they have wrecked themselves along the coast, or whether the men of Hythe* have slain them all. I will take this ship, or another, and as many of you as dare come with me, and we will raid the Northmen in their own roosts in midwinter when they least expect us. We will let them feel for a change what burned homes mean! Now—?"

He had them. They roared him an ovation, knowing he did what he said he would do. None doubted that promise, except Tros, who made it; it was far too prophetic for him to believe; but it served a purpose. They wanted to get the oars out then and hurry through the business of catching Cæsar, who was unimportant in their minds compared to the hereditary enemies who had ravaged their coasts and villages since, according to legend, Britain first rose from the sea.·

The Roman was an incident. Northmen were a habit, like wolf hunting and marrying and feasting. Besides, the Northmen fought according to accepted and unwritten rules, which made a sport of it, whereas Cæsar was no gentleman; he fought in armor, and used cosmetics, and wore skirts, and—from what they had heard of him— couldn't even carry liquor handsomely.

There was no more trouble after that, not even need for Conops to keep watch while Tros slept. Tros forbade it, rather than let the Britons think he doubted them. And, two hours after midnight, came the favoring wind, a light air that hardly filled the sail, so that they had to row to keep Hiram-bin-Ahab's curved spar in sight, that could ghost along two ships' lengths to their one.

The wind failed by morning, but they were out in mid-channel then, so that it was an easy matter to time their arrival off Caritia, dawdling along as if they had picked up the Phœnician at sea and were adjusting their speed to his. Hiram-bin-Ahab kept a good three miles away. There was no risk of Skell detecting anything wrong.

Three miles to the windward of Caritia sands Tros backed the oars and dropped anchor, hoisting, as agreed, a white cloth signal at the yardarm, which meant that the Phœnician should proceed.

Hiram-bin-Ahab had all the necessary documents.

---

* The crypt of Hythe Church is full of bones of Northmen killed on the beach. Historians have set a much later—post-Roman—date to the unrecorded battle in which they are presumed to have been killed; but, like many another date "determined" by those same historians, this one is at least doubtful. It is certain that the Northmen regularly raided Britain long before the Romans came.

Tros's father's chance depended solely now on whether the Phœnician should act his part artfully or make some unforeseen mistake.

Tros had a strange, impersonal respect for his old father mixed of many contradictions. As a seaman, who understood strange seas better than most priests know human nature, he almost worshiped him. As an obedient emissary of the Hierophants of Samothrace, he thought him an impractical old visionary.

In theory Tros was willing to admire the mystery-teaching of non-resistance and no vengeance. But in practice he had hung back from initiation beyond the novice's degree—which imposed few obligations—and he forever chafed at his father's prohibitions against taking life. Besides, he knew that his father had been a storming swordsman in his youth.

"Conops," he said, watching the Phœnician's ship through a light mist that dimmed its outline, "that old mariner knows his own mind. He keeps a promise, Romans or no Romans. You know yours. You are a faithful man. I know mine. I will snatch my father out of Cæsar's hands by any means. But who shall know my father's mind? I think he may blame us all because our method is unethical, as if ethics could influence Cæsar."

Conops was not quite sure what ethics were, but he knew Tros's father, having sailed under him since Tros and he were old enough to learn to splice ropes.

"Master, a Prince of Samothrace must be a dreadful thing to be," he answered. "He is not meek, for you and I have quailed under his wrath when we displeased him. So it is not that he does not feel anger or suffer when Cæsar orders the crew beaten to death before his eyes.

"Hey! What a crew that was! Will we ever find such another? No drink; no women in the ports; no knifing, no neglect, never an order disobeyed. And seamanly! Hey! Master!

"And yet your father, who had trained them, saw them flogged, saw them flogged to death—*hey-yeh—tstchah!* And do you suppose, if we gave him a knife, and showed him Cæsar, he would kill?"

"Not he," Tros answered. "But, as I said, I know my own mind. I am not one to balk at killing in extremity. Mind you, I said in extremity. I will have no brawling. I have a father, and I choose to rescue him, whether he approves my way or not."

It was very nearly sundown. The Phœnician's sail was a

splurge of red on golden water, blurred a trifle by a mauve mist. The galley rolled gently on the swell and all the Britons were leaning overside, their helmets tilted back as they had seen the Roman legionaries wear them.

But there was very little to be seen except shed roofs ashore, the lines of Cæsar's tent tops and the masts of fifty or sixty ships that lay hauled out on balks of timber under the protection of the camp earthwork.

The town itself, such as it was—shops, booths, drinking-dens, and brothels—was invisible beyond the camp. Cæsar kept the front door clean.

"You see," said Tros, watching Hiram-bin-Ahab's slow, cautious dip and drift toward the port, "in a sense I am the cause of my father's difficulty. He married, and as long as my mother lived he was not eligible for the higher offices.* So they sent him to sea as Legate of the Mysteries. My mother died, but she died giving birth to me.

"So there he was with a son; whereas, if I had not been born, they would have ceased to reckon him a married man and he might have stayed ashore in Samothrace to attain who knows what eminence in the Inner Shrine. Therefore, but for me, he should never have been Cæsar's prisoner. And that, since it makes me responsible, confers on me the right to rescue him."

"Aye, and in your own way," Conops answered. He would have agreed with Tros if he had said that the world was round and not flat. "Zeus! But I would like to burn that camp! Look, Master. If the wind blew from the westward, and a man should creep—"

Silence. Then a murmur all along the ship-side. A liburnian, low in the water and rowed at high speed by a dozen oars, put out from the harbor-mouth and headed straight for Hiram-bin-Ahab's ship. Before the Phœnician could back his sail, the sun went down, leaving the galley no more than a creaking black shadow, invisible from shore. Tros ordered lights out; for he did not want that liburnian to come and hail him.

"To the benches! Out oars!"

He sent Conops to the masthead. Then, muffling the drum, he moved the galley slowly to a new position about three miles to the westward, and waited again, the men resting on the oars. It was a long time before his ears caught the sound of a splash and the creak of cordage.

---

* Marriage was not held to be a crime, but it stood in the way of advancement, being a concession to materiality and lust, according to that doctrine.

211

"Who comes?" he demanded.

"Both!" Conops leaned from the masthead, trying to make himself heard without shouting. "Hiram-bin-Ahab and the liburnian!"

"Man that arrow-engine, Orwic!"

Followed a clicking and squeak as Orwic wound the crank—the rattle of arrows laid in the grooves in a hurry. Then, dimly, Hiram-bin-Ahab's spar loomed out of the dark and a hail came over the water from the liburnian, invisible astern of the Phœnician.

"Oh, Poseidonius!"

Tros prayed to the gods for a Roman accent. A hoarse voice was his best subterfuge, and his heart in his throat rendered that trick simple. But he waited for the man in the liburnian to repeat the hail; and then, when it came, he almost laughed aloud.

The man was no Roman. By his accent he was from Macedonia or Thrace, one of those adventurers who sold their swords to Rome and often rendered much more faithful service than the Romans did. Tros could talk Latin twice as well!

"Keep away!" he roared. "Smallpox! Half the crew sickening! They'll try to jump aboard you if you come close!"

The liburnian backed away. He could hear the hurried oars splash. Then Hiram-bin-Ahab's voice, between coughs, croaking from the poop. Tros could not hear what he said. Then Skell, unmistakable, from the liburnian, in Gaulish, abusing the Phœnician in a voice weak from exhaustion. It appeared he had left money on the ship, and wanted it.

Tros bellowed through cupped hands, omitting verbs because of distance, trusting to the hollow sound to hide discrepancies of accent. The rowers in the liburnian might be Romans, although they probably were not.

"Despatch—Roman Senate—for Cæsar! To-morrow—or next day! Fair wind—tide—"

"Have you food and water?" he in the liburnian called back.

"Yes, for a few days."

"Keep away then! Anchor outside! Send in your despatch by the Phœnician. If you want stores, they can be put aboard his ship for you."

"All right," Tros answered. Then, as he heard the liburnian's oars go thumping off into the darkness: "Now, you friends of the god of pestilence! Let Cæsar only be afraid of catching your complaint from Skell, and I think we have him! Row!"

He beat the drum unmuffled, rolling out the strokes triumphantly, setting a course westward along the coast for the Phœnician to follow. Neither ship showed any lights, so there was no chance of the troops in Caritia knowing which way they had gone.

And because it seemed the gods were blessing the adventure, a light wind blew and wafted them along the coast of Gaul until Hiram-bin-Ahab changed his helm and led the way into a cove he knew. And there they anchored, side by side, a little before dawn. Tros did not dare to leave his Britons so he sent a boat for Hiram-bin-Ahab, who came and sat beside him on the poop.

"There is a village here," said the Phœnician. "But they will run away inland. They will fear we need rowers."

"Skell?" Tros asked him.

The Phœnician laughed, and paid for it, coughed for nearly a minute.

"*Ahkh*—Skell! Sick, yes; but not so very. All the while listening. So he is very sure you are from Ostia; very sure you have a pestilence aboard. He asked whether Tros had gone to Seine-mouth, and in what ship? *Hey-yeh!* I told him—dung to a dog—lies to a liar!

"He offered me money if I would persuade the commander of this galley to put into Seine-mouth and prevent Tros from escaping before Cæsar could come! *Hey-yey!* I let my sailors take the money. They took it from him just before they dropped him into the liburnian. *Yarrh!* But he is angry, angry! He is full of spite."

"Cæsar?" asked Tros.

"The men in the liburnian said Cæsar drills his troops too much because there is nothing else to do. The ships, he said, are all laid up for the winter—hauled out. He was surprised when I said I thought you had despatches from the Senate. He said Cæsar receives despatches overland.

"But I said it was none of my business, only that I was glad to have an escort all the way back to Ostia, and I showed him my permit, signed by you. He could read, but not readily. The seal impressed him."

"And the pestilence?"

"He dreaded it! He did not want to take Skell, fearing my ship might have caught infection. But I said, unless he would take Skell I would sail into the harbor and put him ashore, having your authority to do that.

"Then I told him Skell had information for Cæsar,

213

concerning the Britons, and after that he did not dare to refuse to take him. He laughed, and said, 'Let us hope Cæsar will fear the pestilence, and go away for a while, and give the troops a rest. But I don't envy Skell,' said he, 'because Cæsar will order him to the pest-house, which is no good place.'

"But Skell did not hear that, nor would he have understood, because we conversed in Greek. That fellow is a Macedonian from Pontus, a long way from home. He would have liked to sail with me, although he fears the winter storms."

"Did he ask many questions?"

"Very few. But he said Cæsar would doubtless like to talk with me about the Britons. So I said that Skell, being born in Britain, knew more of them than I did, I being merely a trader in tin, conveying my tin to Ostia for the bronze founders.

"He understood that well enough, but he was puzzled to know why you should risk your galley down the coast of Hispania in winter-time, until I told him Rome was in dire straits for tin and you had been sent to look for me and bring me in spite of winter and storms and everything."

"Good!" exclaimed Tros. "You are a man after my own heart, a friend, a lordly liar in emergency!"

"We run a great risk yet," the Phœnician answered. "It may be, Cæsar will not believe Skell. It may be, he will not fear pestilence. It may be, he will be there when we go back to Caritia. What then?"

"We will go soon," Tros answered. "They have hauled out their ships, you say? They can't condition a ship for fighting in less than three or four days. So, if Cæsar smells a rat and sends out the liburnians to seize you, I will rub my Britons' noses into a fight that'll do the rogues good.

"Understand me, Hiram-bin-Ahab: *I* am no Prince of Samothrace. If I don't get my father, I will do such damage to the Romans as shall make them remember me."

CHAPTER XXIV

ROME'S CENTURION

He who is loyal and faithful to false gods, and who beareth himself manfully in a false cause—aye, and though that cause mean ruin for all who obey him, and all who oppose him— that one, in the scales of the Eternal weigheth well. Aye, he is

214

infinitely greater than the fool who serveth Wisdom with his lips, but in his heart serveth malice, greed, ambition, fame or any other of the weaknesses that strength despiseth and that Wisdom no more knoweth than the Light knoweth darkness. Hold ye fast to faith and loyalty; and though ye slay me for a false cause, ye shall stand forgiven.

FROM THE SAYINGS OF THE DRUID TALIESAN

THOUGH Tros was not a Prince of Samothrace, he had lived in much too close association with his father, who was one, not to be influenced by the occult philosophy that governed every detail of his father's life.

The secrets of the Inner Mysteries Tros did not know; the power that Samothracian Hierarchs could wield, should they decide to do so, over circumstances and events he thoroughly believed in. He simply was unwilling to pay the price, in abstinence and selflessness, required of aspirants to Initiation, and it was against the drastically administered law of the Mysteries for his father to oblige, persuade or even to invite him to make that effort.

Necessarily, however, he was influenced by his father's views. He habitually ascribed to an Unseen Force things which to other people appeared as mere coincidence.

Tros was less superstitious, more devout, and a vastly more intelligent believer in the Unseen, than most men of his generation. He acknowledged a whole pantheon of gods, but never prayed to them, believing them to be innumerable aspects of a First Cause, whose formless Being was unthinkable, and whose name—supposing anybody knew it—it was blasphemy to utter.

Hiram-bin-Ahab, steeped in strange monotheism tinged by Jewish teaching, was a member of a minor Mystery to which Tros, too, belonged. The world was full of such secret brotherhoods, some based on the Jewish Cabala, some on eastern lore, and all intended to preserve the idea of Brotherhood in the face of cruel superstitions and a growing atheism.

So Tros and Hiram-bin-Ahab—good pious opportunists —were of one mind at dawn, or a little after, when Conops returned from a scouting venture ashore and announced that Cæsar had already passed through a near-by village.

"The gods," said Tros, "have been instructed to make this easy for us."

He did not believe that any gods did more than that; the rest was left to human energy.

"Certainly," Hiram-bin-Ahab agreed. "Your noble fa-

215

ther must have seen with his third eye* what we are doing. He has summoned the gods† to our aid. We can not fail."

Conops had his own opinion.

"Master, you have more brains than a shipload of kings' uncles! Cæsar left Caritia at once. I found one fisherman ashore there, and he lame. He said a chariot came summoning all hands to a place a three hours' journey inland to repair a road, Cæsar having passed along it in the night and complained of its bad condition."‡

"The tide serves. No storm—no storm!" Tros warned the weather-gods, his eyes on the horizon. "Up anchor, Conops!"

So with oars and flapping sails, for the wind only came in capful, they dawdled back toward Caritia, keeping well off-shore and timing themselves to arrive again at dusk.

Tros dropped anchor five miles out, but this time he left Conops in charge of the galley and, divesting himself of Roman clothes and armor, wrapping his head in a knotted handkerchief, had himself rowed to Hiram-bin-Ahab's ship, where one of the crew curled his beard for him in the Phœnician style.

"Sail in as close as you dare," he said, pacing the Phœnician's poop.

But as the masts of Cæsar's ships and the tent tops began to appear in detail through the haze—and that was nearly half an hour before the sun went down—two liburnians came rowing at top speed from the harbor mouth, a man in the leading one signaling with a red cloth to the Phœnician to come no farther.

The crews of both liburnians stopped rowing when they came within hail. The man with the red cloth stood up in the stern, bellowing through a speaking trumpet:

"Cæsar's orders! You are not to put in to Caritia! Smallpox! Stores—water—elsewhere! Away with you! Proceed at once to Ostia."

It was Tros who answered, giving a rich Greek accent rein:

* A synonym for occult vision.
† The gods were the various aspects of natural forces, obedient to such men as knew how to command them. Hiram-bin-Ahab's near-monotheism did not preclude his use of the expression "gods."
‡ Cæsar habitually traveled at the rate of one hundred miles a day, and was, consequently, very particular about the condition of the roads on which mobility depended. They were built and repaired by forced labor.

216

"We know Cæsar is not in Caritia! We have Cæsar's command in writing to bring away a prisoner named Perseus, who is to be taken to Rome for trial on charges of conspiracy."

"Who are you?" demanded he in the liburnian, bringing his boat a few lengths closer. It was growing very dark.

"Mate of this ship."

"Why doesn't the captain speak?"

"His voice fails. He coughs," Tros answered, signing to Hiram-bin-Ahab to stand up and be seen.

"When did you receive Cæsar's order?"

"Last night, when Cæsar visited a cove in which we dropped anchor."

"Did the commander of the bireme deliver Cæsar's writing to *you?*"

"Yes. Smallpox. Five of his crew are down with it. He hopes to reach Vectis, where he may land the crew for a while without risk of desertions or of spreading the sickness among Roman troops. Thereafter, if the winds permit, he will proceed to Ostia."

There was a conference between the captains of the two liburnians. They appeared to be men of the centurion type—the non-commissioned backbone of Rome's army—men used to emergency in every corner of the empire, not supposed or encouraged to be original, but marvelous disciplinarians, obedient unto death.

"Cæsar's orders are: 'No communication with you!'" one of them shouted at last.

"Our order, in Cæsar's writing, supersedes that," Tros retorted.

There was another conference. Then:

"The prisoner you seek is dead or dying."

Tros swore under his breath. There was a long pause before he could get his voice under control. His only chance of success was to seem utterly indifferent. His impulse was to sink the two liburnians and drown their crews.

"Torture!" he growled under his breath, and Hiram-bin-Ahab nodded.

"Maybe Cæsar hopes the pestilence may finish him!" he roared at last, for the liburnians had backed away. "Put him aboard. The outcome is none of your affair!"

The liburnians came closer again.

"Put Cæsar's writing into something that will float, and throw it at us," shouted a centurion.

"No!" roared Tros. "Poseidonius the Roman, who com-

217

mands the bireme, spoke thus: 'Give them the writing in exchange for the prisoner. Not otherwise!' Poseidonius must answer to the Senate. Shall he give you his authority and whistle to the wide seas for his man? What kind of officers are you, to try that trick? Bring out the prisoner! There may be a wind before morning, and we want to make the tide."

There was another conference, and then the liburnians rowed away. Tros shouted after them:

"Poseidonius says this: 'Unless you deliver the prisoner promptly, he will sail into the harbor at dawn, and you must take your chance with the pestilence. Having Cæsar's writing, he will not be delayed. He is in haste to proceed to Vectis.' "

Hiram-bin-Ahab gestured and croaked from out of his doubled and redoubled shawls:

"A mistake! A mistake! They will not believe a bireme dares to land a crew on Vectis. A trader, yes. A warship, no."

Tros clicked his teeth irritably.

"I had to tell them some place! Maybe they will think you told me of Vectis. You are a trader. They may suppose I don't know the people of Vectis are warlike."

But Hiram-bin-Ahab shook his head. He looked like an old vulture of ill omen. Then worse happened—and worse again!

Over the water from the galley came the noise of singing and a row of dots of light gleaming through the cabin ports.

"They have broached the mead!"

Tros thrust a paper into the Phœnician's hands.

"Don't part with that until they hand my father over. Hoist him aboard with the halyard. Satisfy yourself that he really is Perseus, Prince of Samothrace. Then throw them the document. If I don't quiet those idiots they'll—"

He went overside into a small boat like a squall out of a dark sky, and the British rowers nearly broke their backs to try to please him. Ten minutes later he leaped up the galley's side, and the first thing he saw was Conops lashed hand and foot to the mast with a gag in his teeth. He cut him loose and rushed into the cabin under the poop.

Orwic sat on the table drinking mead, surrounded by as many as could crowd themselves into the place. The remainder were in the citadel. They were roaring a long chorus about Lunden Town.

Tros stood back to the doorway, his strong teeth glinting in the light of the horn lantern, until surprise took full effect and all grew silent.

"You're a fine shipload of meat-fed* Romans with the smallpox!" he growled, grinning. "Were you going to eat Conops next?"

"Your man was too full of his own importance," Orwic drawled. "He actually knifed a friend of mine. Where's Cæsar? Are we ready to start back? Here—have some mead."

Tros drank with him. There was only one barrel of the stuff aboard, supposed to be for medicine. The best plan seemed to be to finish it.

"If you'll hold your tongues," he said, wiping his mouth on the back of his hand, "and make those young asses in the citadel douse the lights and be quiet, I'll give you a crack at Cæsar before you're two days older. Otherwise, I'll guarantee you at the bottom of the sea by midnight! Suit yourselves!"

Orwic strolled forward to the citadel, his apparently casual eyes alert for Conops, who fingered an empty sheath and glared at him. Presently the singing ceased and lights went out. Tros sat on the table, playing boon companion, for there was no other way just then of managing those gentry.

"Here's your knife," said Orwic cavalierly, tossing the thing to Conops as he came back out of the darkness. "Keep it for your equals, or your betters will have to have you whipped."

"Don't you young idiots know," said Tros, "that the gloomiest place on earth is a Roman bireme that has been two months at sea, as we're supposed to have been? The crew are always down with scurvy. You have smallpox in the bargain!

"To enforce discipline, the commander has used the scourge; he has thrown men overboard; he has chained unruly rowers to the benches. He's as sick and ill-tempered as the rest of you. He has boils on the back of his neck. The omens are all wrong; they always are when a man has specks before his eyes.

"You've been fed dry meat, which a Roman hates and moldy bread, which sickens you to look at. There are rats in the water casks, so you're afraid to drink. You're short of fuel, so you can't boil water or cook your rations.

---

* Roman soldiers and sailors usually mutinied if their rations contained too much meat. Cæsar writes of his men's heroism when, on one occasion, they ate meat for several days.

There's a curtain of weed a yard long on the galley's bottom, which trebles the labor of rowing. The bottom leaks and you have to man the buckets day and night.

"The sail won't draw, because it's full of holes, which your fingers are too swollen and cracked to mend. The ship stinks. Such blankets as you have are full of vermin. You hate one another even worse than you hate your officers.

"If those people in Caritia get a hint that you're merry-making, they'll not stop to argue. They'll know we're no Romans from Ostia! As you love Lunden Town and hope to see it, be miserable!"

He had to carry on in that vein. He had to tell them tales of Roman ships he had seen in foreign ports, coming in with a crucified* man at the masthead and the rowers so rotten with scurvy that their teeth had fallen out and the skin fell away from them like scales from a decaying fish.

"You're supposed to be feeling like that," he insisted.

And when they had finished laughing at him, being Britons, they found an entirely different reason for doing what he asked.

"You're a foreigner, so I suppose we must make allowances," said Orwic.

Tros got up the anchor and set them to rowing, lest the liburnians sneak out on him in the darkness to investigate.

The Romans were quite capable of that. Julius Cæsar had been known to swim broad rivers under cover of the night, to do his own scouting when he doubted the tales that were brought to him. But if liburnians had come, their crews would have heard such dismal groanings at the oars, such cries of anguish, as might have made them believe it was a prison ship.

Orwic, with some pitch smeared on his arms and legs to represent the scurvy, walked up and down the plank beside the rowers flourishing a cord with which he made believe to flog them, and nothing would satisfy them until Tros sent a man to the masthead to pretend he was crucified up there. Now that they were over seasickness they seemed to understand no middle course between comedy and mutiny.

Tros, forgetting that man at the masthead, for he soon

---

* The victim was hardly ever nailed. He was tied with rope, and left to suffer from sun, flies and thirst. The same form of punishment was used by armies in the field as recently as 1918.

grew tired of groaning, steered the galley slowly toward Hiram-bin-Ahab's ship, arriving within easy hail about a minute before the liburnians came thumping through the night. Then he implored his crew to be silent, gesticulating with both fists, and the Britons leaned on the oars to listen, not that they could understand a word of Latin. There was nothing visible except the dim, shadowy outline of the Phœnician's ship.

"Here's your man!" cried some one.

"What is his name?"

That was Hiram-bin-Ahab's voice, wheezy and suspicious.

"Perseus."

"Is he alive? I won't take him if he's dead."

"Yes, he lives. Come on, throw a line! And hand over that written order!"

"There goes the line—catch! *Yarrh*—what duffers! Throw again there, you. Now. What's that? No! I'll throw you down the writing when I've seen the man. Put the rope under his armpits. Gently now—haul away—gently, gently, gently!"

Silence, in which everybody held his breath. Then the Phœnician's voice:

"All right. Here is the writing. Catch."

Tros sighed relief. The Britons, all eyes on his silhouette against the poop rail, saw the shoulder movement and sighed with him, swinging the oars for the dip. The man at the masthead heard that, and accepted it as leave to play the idiot—he had a gallon of good mead under his painted leather armor.

"Wow!" he yelled. *"Hoi!* You here, Romans! Tell Cæsar, next time he tries to conquer Britain—"

"Silence!" Tros thundered, but too late.

There was a roar of laughter from the hold. The liburnians came hurrying to investigate, their oars churning the water in short, sharp strokes.

Their officers knew Gaulish when they heard it, even if they had not caught the words. Hiram-bin-Ahab, making no sound, let his ship swing slowly on the tide. There came the sudden creak and rattle of his mainsail going up, and a man in one of the liburnians shouted to him to drop anchor.

"Poseidonius! O Poseidonius!" cried a voice from the other liburnian, nearly alongside.

Tros did not answer. He pounded the drum and the oars began to thump in unison. But he had to swing the ship before he could hoist sail. There was hardly any wind at that, and the liburnians could out-row him two for one. A low, dark, skillfully maneuvered vessel shot in under his stern, and again a voice hailed him:

"Hey, there! Poseidonius!"

"Drown him!" yelled the Britons. "Plug him full of arrows!"

The man at the masthead offered himself for a target to the Romans, waving arms and legs and caterwauling. Tros had to make the best of it.

"Come aboard," he suggested in his choicest Latin, speaking drily, imitating Cæsar's voice as nearly as he could. Then:

"Stand by that arrow-engine, Conops. Man the crank there, you! Come aboard, Centurion! Did you hear me? Come aboard!"

He beckoned. Orwic and a dozen Britons left the oars and crouched under the bulwark. The liburnian had come in under the galley's counter, too close for the arrow-engines, its bow nosing in under the starboard oars. The other liburnian was keeping a safe distance.

Tros lowered a thick rope with knots in it. The centurion, half curious, half conscious there was nothing else he could do unless he chose to be shot or sunk, came up hand-over-hand.

He was allowed to reach the poop before the Britons pounced on him and took his sword away. He offered no resistance so they let him stand, with Orwic close behind him and two others ready to jump on him if he should move. He stood like a man, with his chin high and a short, stubby, pugnacious beard sticking out under it.

"What is this?" he demanded.

He was not afraid. He was scandalized that a foreigner should dare to take such liberties with Rome. Tros loved him.

"Centurion," he said, "tell me first, is my father unharmed? I am Tros, the son of Perseus, Prince of Samothrace."

"So you are he?" said the centurion. "Your father has been treated as you will be, when Cæsar catches you! They who conspire against the Senate and the Roman People, all get their deserts in time!"

"Has Cæsar tortured him?"

"I believe he was racked."

Tros ground his teeth and spoke to Orwic over the centurion's shoulder.

222

"He is your prisoner. What do you wish?"

"He is yours," said Orwic. "Do what you like with him."

"Do you hear that?" said Tros. "You are my prisoner." The centurion nodded. He seemed perfectly indifferent. "Take back your sword then and obey me. Tell Cæsar, when the day comes I will deal with him and not with a centurion! Tell Rome, the Senate and the Roman People, that I, Tros, am the enemy of Rome from this day forth!"

Tros signed to the Britons to stand aside.

"No enemy of Rome lives long!" the centurion answered. "Farewell, Tros!" There was a clank of bronze as he saluted. "I will deliver your message, although I think you are a fool. Cæsar will crucify you for it."

CHAPTER XXV

"GOD GIVE YOU A FAIR WIND, HIRAM-BIN-AHAB!"

Better far the good faith of one stranger to another than a thousand times a thousand vows upon the altars of gods who look, I say, for deeds, not promises.

FROM THE SAYINGS OF THE DRUID TALIESAN

THE other liburnian tried to head off Hiram-bin-Ahab and force him to drop anchor, but the wind came athwart tide and current, lending the Phœnician heels and forcing the smaller craft to run for shelter. Tros paced the poop, fretting at the galley's slowness as he followed in the Phœnician's wake.

The Britons were all cock-a-hoop and skylarking, Orwic imitating the centurion, thrusting out his throat and chin exactly as the Roman did. And one of the others took off Tros so perfectly, hilt forward, arms akimbo, feet apart, teeth showing in a large, alert grin, that even Tros came out of his dudgeon at last and laughed.

"You young dogs! You have lost Cæsar for me! You would laugh if Lunden burned."

"Lost him? Wait and see," said Orwic.

"See? You shall see a fight, or I don't know the Romans. They can overtake Cæsar with a message much faster than we can sail to Seine-mouth. That is why I gave that centurion something for the messenger to say."

"Why then go to Seine-mouth? Why not leave Cæsar whistling?" Orwic suggested.

"I told Caswallon I will go to Seine-mouth, and I will. I told Hiram-bin-Ahab I will escort him, and I will. I told Cæsar, by the mouth of Skell, that I will go to Seine-mouth. So I will. I have promised you a brush with Cæsar. You shall have one."

He was grateful for the rising sea, that made it dangerous to approach the Phœnician closely. He did not want any conversation with his father just then, felt too sure the old man would forbid vindictiveness, with his dying breath, perhaps. Tros could not stomach such an interview. He knew that if his father should exact such a promise from him he would make it and keep it. He preferred not to run that risk.

"Let the gods attend to it," he growled, turning to face Conops at the helm. "My father and the gods are intimates. If it is right for him to bind me in his violenceless peace before he dies, let them bring us together."

Conops did not answer. He knew that mood just as well as he knew that he and Tros could cross that intervening quarter-mile of sea in a boat, if Tros cared to do it.

They had sailed much rougher seas together, in worse boats than the hide-and-wicker thing they carried. Conops, lacking an eye because he had dared to answer Cæsar pertly, also would have obeyed Tros's father if commanded with the old man's dying breath to let bygones be.

Like Tros, though, he craved no such injunction. He respected the old man as much as Tros did. Like Tros, loved him well enough to run all risks to snatch him out of Cæsar's hands. But, like Tros again, knew too well, from grim experience, that the peace of non-resistance is a warfare that does not suit uninitiated men. It is easier and more exciting to fight Cæsars than to wrestle with emotions in oneself.

So they boiled and plunged along in the Phœnician's wake, he standing well out from the shore, until dawn found them nearly out of sight of land and the gale increasing. It was almost too rough to keep footing on the deck, but Tros made Orwic drill the Britons with bow and arrow and train them at imaginary floating marks with the well-oiled arrow-engines. They grumbled because he would not let them use up ammunition, even threatened to defy him.

"Very well," he answered. "Fight with bare hands if you choose. Cæsar will be lying up for us in Seine-mouth with all the ships he can find. If we come on him at night, and see him first, we may burn his ships. If not, and if he sees us first, we shall be hard put to it to guard that old Phœnician's rear while he makes his escape homeward.

"As I know Cæsar, we will need every arrow we have, and pray for more before we're through with him!"

So they loosed bows at an imaginary mark, practising the quick combination of hand and eye at any angle that is the secret of efficient marksmanship.

"Speed," Tros urged them. "Speed! Three arrows in the air at once, and all aimed straight."

"Cæsar will have no arrow-engines," Conops reminded him. "His warships are laid up for the winter. The best he can get will be Gaulish fishermen or merchantmen, slow, slower than we are, low in the water, leaky. Give us half a gale like this one, and—"

"I know Cæsar," Tros retorted. "That fox will have a trap set."

And he paced the poop again, pounding his palm in his fist, pondering, matching his wits against the cleverest Roman of them all.

His main objective was to escort the Phœnician to open sea and safety. Would Cæsar guess that? Much would depend on what Skell might have told. If they had thrown Skell into a pest-house and conversed with him across the dung heap that surrounded it, Skell might have said almost anything.

Tros made up his mind at last that, whatever Skell had said, Cæsar would conclude now that it was all part of one and the same trick. Cæsar would learn by messenger that two ships, one a trader, one a captured Roman galley, were acting with forged documents in close coöperation. He would do his utmost to catch both ships.

And if he believed that Seine-mouth story at all, he would probably take such ships as he could get and put to sea, with the idea of bottling both in the river-mouth if they should enter. Failing which, if the whole tale were a ruse, he would stand a good chance of catching both ships in the open. Cæsar was the last man in the world likely to sit still and let things happen to him.

The second objective—and Cæsar might guess that too—was to place his father, dead or living, among friends. If he should die there were rites that he, Tros, only he, could properly perform. Dry land, Britain, Lunden, with the druids helping, was the proper place for them.

The third objective was to punish Cæsar drastically, to capture Cæsar if he could.

He finally made up his mind that Cæsar would be no

such fool as to risk his own life in a hurriedly conditioned ship, without very definite information as to where the enemy might be. He would send his men to sea, and wait for the cavalry, or whatever other troops he might have available, at some point whence he could signal and conduct the operations.

But he was sure of this: That wherever the fighting should take place, there Cæsar would arrive, if it were possible, to take command if his men were having the worst of it and to seize for himself the credit in any event.

High noon saw Tros still thinking and Hiram-bin-Ahab hove to, waiting for him, with a big sea wetting the ships' decks as they plunged with a couple of miles between them, nearly out of sight of land.

When Tros had brought his galley within hailing distance and had quieted his Britons so that he could hear, the Phœnician's mate howled to him that the man at the masthead had reported three sails low down on the horizon near the Gaulish shore, proceeding westward. He added that Tros's father was unconscious in the cabin.

"Has he spoken?"

Tros waited for the answer with his fingers clenched into his palms, and sighed enormously when it came at last, howled through a speaking trumpet:

"No-o-o! No word!"

"Then we are not forbidden!"

He slapped Conops on the shoulder.

"Tell your master," he bawled back, "to keep behind me until nightfall!"

Then he took the lead and set full sail, in order to arrive within sight of Seine-mouth as near sunset as he could, sparing his Britons all labor at the oars, making them eat and rest, using every trick he knew to make them conscious that the effort of their lives was coming.

There was no more sign of Cæsar's ships, although he had Conops at the masthead, and Conops' one eye was worth a score of other men's. There was no sign even of fishing boats, a fact not wholly accounted for by the high sea that was running. Men who fish for a living often have to haul their nets in half a gale. The sea was empty, in the way the fields are when a thousand men lie ambushed.

He dropped anchor and lowered his sail within sound of the surf that pounded on the mud banks off the estuary, a little too near sunset to satisfy him entirely, wishing Cæsar keener vision that the eagles whose images were perched on Roman standards.

226

And there he waited, rolling comfortably in the mud bank's lee, studying the color of the water and the inshore landmarks, until Hiram-bin-Ahab came within hail and dropped anchor astern of him. Then he and Conops rowed to the Phœnician's ship.

"What now?" asked the Phœnician.

But Tros went straight to his father, down under the poop in the cabin crowded with skins, wicker baskets and a hundred other marvels for the Alexandrian trade. There were several nightingales* in a wicker cage, and a starling with a cut tongue, who could talk a dozen words.

Tros's father lay on the Phœnician's bed, calm as in death, his eyes closed and the tortured wrists crossed on his breast. His long gray beard appeared to have been combed by one of Hiram-bin-Ahab's men, and the torn skin of his ankles had been wrapped in linen.

"*Tchuh, tchuh, tchuh!* They racked his joints apart!" said the Phœnician.

Conops knelt by the tortured feet, muttering Greek blasphemies. Tros stood scowling, hands behind him, grinding strong teeth.

"Has he spoken?" he asked.

"Not a word," said the Phœnician.

But it was as if the old man had reserved his strength for what he knew was coming. His lips moved two or three times. Then the voice came, as if from another world, as if the soul had left the body and were using it for one last communication. It was so dark Tros could hardly see his father's face.

"Tros, my son, you would obey my will. But that is not my will. I, who was a fighter in my youth, ceased from fighting with men's weapons. But I, Perseus, sowed the seeds of fighting when I fathered you. And now knowing the full strength of your obedience you dread what I will lay upon you. But I forbid nothing; since the seed that may not sprout in one way breaks forth in another.

"Hear my last words and remember them. All warfare is with self. All that you know of Cæsar is your own image, cast in the reflection of your own unconscious thought. Be brave. Be noble. You shall know strange seas.

"But you shall not slay Cæsar, though you try, since that is others' destiny. Cæsar shall serve you, and you shall

---

* In Cleopatra's reign, a few years later, nightingales were plentiful in the Grove of Eleusis, near Alexandria.

serve him, each to the other's undoing, but many things will happen before that time. And now, my son Tros, I have finished with the body that begat yours and its wanderings. In your hands, Tros, I leave it. Let it not be cast into the sea or lie unburied."

So Perseus died, in darkness, in a creaking ship, the silence pulsed with heavy breathing and stirred by the fluttering of nightingales in a swaying wicker cage. After a long while Tros and Conops wrapped the body carefully and rowed it to the galley, where they laid it on the bed that had been Cæsar's and covered it with Cæsar's own cloak.

Then Tros returned to the Phœnician and said good-by to him.

"For whether I fail to-night, or whether I succeed, you must run when Cæsar's ships come hurrying in on the tide. Your man saw three ships. There were likely six or seven; maybe more. Cæsar has seen us anchor here. He will think we await the tide to take us up the river.

"I am sure that beacon, yonder to westward, where a hill looms back of the coastline, is his signal to the ships to come out from their hiding place and follow us up-river.

"So now you and I put to sea again, showing no lights, and when the last of Cæsar's ships puts in, I follow! But you turn homeward. God give you a fair wind, Hiram-bin-Ahab! And may we meet again!"

CHAPTER XXVI

"NEITHER ROME NOR I FORGIVE!"

Speak not to me of forgiveness until ye first learn to forgive yourselves for all the treacheries with which ye have betrayed that Inner Light of which ye are the shrines, each one of you. It is a dark saying, but I tell you: None can forgive or be forgiven, who hath not learned to forgive himself his sins against himself.

FROM THE SAYINGS OF THE DRUID TALIESAN

TROS boiled with mixed emotions. Had his father, dying, not assured him he would live and know strange seas? Could this night's venture fail, then? Such men as Perseus speak prophetically on a deathbed.

Tortures such as Cæsar had inflicted flay away personal values and leave nothing in the thought but sheer fact,

228

which was why courts applied torture to witnesses. If they had tortured the judges, too, there might have been some sense in it.

He should not slay Cæsar, since that was others' destiny. Might he not capture Cæsar? He and the Roman were to serve each other, each to the other's undoing. Nothing in that about not punishing Cæsar first.

With all his heart and strength, with all his cunning, to the limit of the bold, storm-daring will that glowed behind his amber eyes, Tros burned to punish Cæsar. He was in a mood that night to kill a hundred men, if only the lean rascal who had conquered Gaul might pay the price.

And dark night favored him. Wind howled in the rigging, but there was not much weight behind it, and presently the rain came down in torrents, beating the waves flat. Tide served the Romans too, perfectly. Two hours before midnight he could count eight swaying lights to westward, and knew he had outguessed Cæsar. The Roman ships were coming into Seine-mouth from some hiding place along the coast; they were sure he and the Phœnician were up the river and that they could cut off their escape.

But the galley wallowed in the murk a good two miles to windward of them, under a scrap of sail, with the oars a-dip at intervals to keep her from drifting inshore. Farther, still, to seaward Hiram-bin-Ahab's ship lay hove to, waiting for the last Roman light to sway clear of Seine-mouth shoals and turn up-river before she filled away with the northerly wind abeam and plunged for home.

The shore line was invisible. But Cæsar had set that beacon on a hilltop to guide his own ships. Now another light appeared, up the estuary, big, low down, almost as if a house were burning near the shore line.

"Cæsar," said Tros to himself. "That's where the troops are waiting. Hah! He'll have twenty or thirty boats there, hidden among the reeds. And he's as sure I'm up the river as I'm sure— Conops," he exclaimed, taking the helm himself, "tide's been making four hours. We've got until it turns—not a minute longer! Up-river, at grips with Cæsar —out again on the flow at daybreak."

"And the dirtiest mess of mud shoals ever a ship sat on!" Conops retorted. "Wind enough to drive her beak in as if she'd grown there! A heavy sea astern!"

"Make sail," Tros answered. "Then get forward and take soundings. Keep on crying me the cubits until I say

'Cease.' If we do hit bottom, hurry aft and stand by me."

Came the creak and groan and thunder of a mainsail rising, impatient shouts from Conops; then the galley heeled and headed straight for Seine-mouth with a burst of rain behind her, that curtained everything except a glimpse of foam boiling in the pitch dark.

Nothing but the wind to steer by; no sign of Cæsar's beacons. Thunder, solid and continuous, of surf on mud banks; then friendly thunder, from the sky, lightning, that made Tros swear at first, until he laughed aloud.

It showed him a line of white surf boiling over shoals, and Cæsar's eight ships wallowing too close to it. Mean little ships, Gaulish coastwise trading vessels, black with men, not too near to the shoals if given sea room to the eastward, but much too near if crowded by an enemy. White water ahead of them, where the 'tween-shoal channel narrowed.

"Orwic! Four men in the fighting top! Man starboard arrow-engines! Ten men on the citadel! Line the starboard rail. Hold fire until I give the word—dagger the man who shoots without permission!"

Flash after flash of lightning. Eight ships staggering before the wind in rough formation like a flight of geese, the shorter arm of the V to eastward. They were all too close together, aiming for a channel they evidently knew, too watchful to look behind them, or the lightning might have shown them the galley's sail in time.

"Ten!" howled Conops, pitching his shrill voice against the wind.

The galley drew seven cubits.

"Stand by! Ready, all!" Tros thundered, not changing the helm a hair's breadth, trusting memory.

"Nine!" yelled Conops.

Then three vivid lightning-flashes in succession, and Tros did change the helm—excitedly. He saw dark water, headed for it.

"Eight!" yelled Conops, as if the end of the world had come.

He was heaving the lead from the starboard chains. The galley's port side bumped the mud and her stern swung westward. But she heeled, for they did not let go the sheet, and the next wave, and the next, that crashed against the high poop drove her into deeper water.

"Ten!" yelled Conops, hurrying aft, for she had hit the

230

mud, and that was orders. "Deep water straight ahead, sir!" he bellowed in Tros's ear.

"Aye! And shallow to westward! We have them!" Tros answered.

He was laughing, not at what the lightning showed, for that was tragedy; no sailor laughs to see men drown. He was laughing at his Britons, drenched to the skin, their bow-strings wrapped dry in their cloaks, who had not even known they were in danger when they bumped the mud!

The Romans had seen him at last. They were in panic, with a boiling shoal on their right hand and an enemy coming down on them to windward. The rain ceased, but the wind rose.

Cæsar's beacon shone out of the night like something that had been asleep. There was another, lower light to shoreward of it. Tros guessed they showed the channel and set his course straight for the two, keeping them in line, with the wind on his port quarter, racing to crowd those eight ships on the shoal to westward of the channel, where the estuary curved to the eastward. He had the wind of them and, slow though the galley was, she could outsail any of those eight.

Three ships clawed around and tried to beat to sea again. He could hear the thumping and the shouts as they struggled to man the oars. One ship's sail went with a crack as if her mast had gone, too. One was swamped within a bowshot of the galley's bows.

Tros beaked the third, driving the great iron-shod ram into her broadside, rolling her over and sinking her as the galley pitched on a wave.

The Britons squandered arrows, orders or no orders, Orwic with the rest of them, smiting Conops on the mouth, backhanded, when the Greek tried to pull him away from the poop arrow-engine. Then arrows began to rain on the galley's deck from the five ships that struggled with wind and tide like dancing phantoms in the wedge-shaped channel entrance.

One of them went aground and the waves burst over her with a din like thunder. Four, under staggering oars and badly handled sail, raced neck and neck, masking one another's fire, Roman-fashion, risking all in one supreme effort to grapple and have the fight out on the bireme's deck.

Tros beaked the nearest as she swung, with her sheets let go, but a dozen Romans leaped into the bireme's bows,

231

where they were massacred with arrow fire from Orwic's engine, that came near cutting down the Britons who rushed to use their swords.

There was no discipline. No order, no command could have been heard above the shouting and the crash of breaking ships.

Two more of Cæsar's ships collided, and Tros beaked them both, breaking the first on the bows of the other and leaving both to drift on the deafening shoal. But their arrows swept the citadel, and the shock of collision had stopped the bireme's way, nearly splitting the sail.

Conops let both sheets go in the nick of time to save the bireme from capsizing. And before they could get the mainsail sheeted down again, with ten of Orwic's Britons dragged and driven aft to help the sailors, the last of Cæsar's ships had crashed alongside.

Grapples struck into the deck and pierced the bulwark. Fifty of Cæsar's legionaries leaped up the bireme's side, and the fight was on in darkness, with the two ships grinding together in the trough of steep waves.

Then the beacon lights went out, or else were screened. The wind increased to a full gale, and though the moon showed once or twice between the racing clouds there was nothing to show the channel's course. The Romans, silent, shoulder to shoulder on the heaving deck, were driving the Britons fore and aft in front of them.

Tros trusted then to the gods, and his father's prophecy, and the strength of the Roman's grappling chains. He put the helm hard up, until the small ship struck the mud and the bireme's weight hammered her into it.

Then he sprang from the poop, let go the sheets and, with a shout that the Britons heard above the din of sea and crashing timbers and loose sail, plunged into the fight.

Part of the bireme's bulwark broke away. She swung down wind in mid-channel, anchored by the other grapnel to the wrecked, swamped, smaller ship, tugging at it like a hooked sea monster, until none could keep his footing and Tros nearly rolled through the gap in the broken bulwark, at grips with a Roman centurion.

Blood and spray churned into scum. A dozen Britons, cornered in the bow, loosed flight after flight of arrows humming through the darkness, so that both sides struggled for the shelter of the citadel. And it was there that Tros's long sword began to turn the tide of battle, for he

232

caught the stoutest Roman of them all and skewered him through the throat against the bulkhead.

Then Orwic sprang beside him from the shadow, dripping blood from scalp wounds—his Roman helmet had gone overboard—and Conops found Tros, guarding his back with a flickering two-edged knife. They three swept that section of the deck, rallying other Britons to them, until Tros thought of a ruse. But as he thought of it the bireme broke the grapnel chain at last and plunged up-channel, beam to the waves and swaying drunkenly before the wind.

So he seized Orwic's quivering arm and tugged him—no need to signal Conops, who was like a dog at his master's heel. They three, and a dozen after them, sprang for the poop, where Conops took the helm and tried to keep mid-channel. Tros stood sword in hand at the edge of the poop bull-bellowing, in Latin, lungs out-thundering the din:

"Omen! An omen! Cæsar's eagle, falling from the sky!"

His voice burst on a pause. Briton and Roman were gathering for another rush. The Romans, superstitious about omens to the verge of madness, turned to look at him.

The eagle they saw was Tros, feet first, leaping on them from the poop. He landed on two men, ran a third through the head, and vanished scrambling away into the darkness of the scuppers. Orwic came next. Almost before the Briton's feet touched deck Tros was up beside him and they two charged forward, bellowing:

"Lud of Lunden! Lud of Lunden!"

The Britons rallied to that cry until all the deck was clear, except of dead and dying, and there were only half a dozen Romans left to deal with, who had fought their way into the citadel and held it.

Tros left the Britons to attend to that. He looked for the crew, and found them at last, below-deck, hiding among water casks. He hauled them out of darkness one by one, cuffed them and drove them on deck. The bireme had worked under the lee of a low hill and was turning slowly in mid-current, drifting toward unimaginable mud banks over which the waves were gurgling as a river gurgles when it overflows the fields.

Tros left Conops at the helm and drove the crew forward, where he belabored them until they dropped the heavy anchor overside and the bireme came head to wind at last.

For a while he waited in the bow, watching to discover whether the anchor dragged or held; but there was nothing to judge by; he could see no land-marks, only gloom, and beyond it a long, deep shadow that was land.

The Britons were busy stripping Romans of their armor; he heard them drag the last one from the citadel; heard the splash as the body went overboard, then Orwic's voice:

"Nine-and-forty! Not bad! How many have we lost?"

There was a long pause, full of murmurings. Tros sat down on the bitts, rubbing bruises thoughtfully, feeling himself from head to foot, his spirits falling, falling as the minutes sped, and the count was not yet done. At last Orwic's voice again:

"Are you sure that's all? Seven-and-twenty dead. How many hurt?"

Again a long count, interspersed with argument as to whether or not a sword slash was an injury. Then an answer:

"Two-and-thirty."

"Almighty Zeus!" Tros murmured. "One-and-forty of a hundred fit to fight, and Cæsar waiting for me down the river! Cæsar with eight ships and about four hundred men! Cæsar with wind in his favor and dawn to see by! Cæsar and all Gaul to draw from! Hah!" he laughed, heaving himself to his feet, "but I'll con the channel seaward by the bones of ships! By Cæsar's grief, I'll find the way!"

No lights. He did not dare to show a light, not even in the hold among the water casks where they laid the wounded, with a few men who could crawl around to serve out water to them, binding wounds by the feel with thread-drawn linen that Caswallon's wife had sent aboard.

The dead they laid on the deck in one long row, face upward, and covered with the spare sail. Then Tros cast about for the strongest men and sent them to the benches, fifteen to each side.

There were scarce two hundred arrows left of all the thousands they had brought with them, and though they added to the number scores more that the Romans had shot into the woodwork, there were even then not more than ten or eleven excited Britons could use up in as many minutes.

Then a leak to plug, below the water-line, where one of the ships the bireme beaked had opened up a seam;

234

thereafter, the scared and sulky seamen to be driven into the rigging to patch that, and to get the sail rebent where the wind had wrenched it from the spar.

Then gray dawn; sea-birds crying over wastes of marsh; gulls screaming where a corpse lay drifting in the mist; wind still in the north, but less of it; a great swell rolling up the estuary and lumping where it met the tide that had begun to flow down-river.

"Up anchor, Conops!"

Oars, and only thirty weary men to man them, the bireme beginning to feel the flowing tide, but prone to swing before the wind, and bucking on the lumpy water so that the oarsmen repeatedly missed stroke.

No drum for fear of warning Cæsar. Groans from the dark hold, as discouraging as the chilly daybreak, but a fog coming in on the wind in hurrying gray wisps, with patches of clear air between, for which Tros thanked the gods of Gaul.

"If only Cæsar sleeps."

The wish was father to that thought, as always. Tros's eyes were heavy. Every fiber of him ached from too much strain and no relief. His head swam and things multiplied themselves. He had to look three times to see a land-mark once. The wrecks of Cæsar's ships, glimpsed between scurrying drifts of gray, seemed never in the same place twice.

But minute by minute the tide flowed faster, the wind lessened and the fog increased. There was no sound but the surge of water, the muffled thump of oars, and the cry of sea-birds. Tros could sense a coming shift of wind, and he knew he had twice as much sea-room as the night before, because the tide was higher.

"All's well, master! We have given him the slip!" said Conops as the first wreck loomed in the fog for a moment and vanished astern.

He was heaving the lead from the poop, lest the sound of his voice should carry as he cried the changing depths.

But Tros knew Cæsar was the last man in the world to leave an outrage to the Roman dignity and eight vessels unavenged.

"Drum now!" he ordered. "I want every last tremble of speed!"

Speed now. Nothing else counted. If Cæsar was not in the neck of the channel waiting for him, all the warning in the world would reach the Romans too late. If he were there, nothing mattered but the impact.

There was only one way that Cæsar could prevent him from escaping. Somewhere, somehow he might have collected small boats and have moored them across the channel, using a stout cable anchored at both ends.

That was what Tros argued he would have done in Cæsar's place, with every available man who could be crowded into the boats, ready to jump aboard the bireme when she struck the cable.

"Faster! Faster!" he commanded, peering forward on the port side for a glimpse of wrecks, stamping his foot to set time for the drum.

"Zeus!" he exclaimed suddenly.

He swung his whole weight against the steering oar, as a shower of arrows and a dozen javelins twanged aboard out of the fog.

"Row, you Britons, row!"

There were boats alongside, crowded with men. Cæsar had outguessed him! Straight ahead, moored beam on to the channel, rolled two of the wrecks that had been floated in the night, and only Cæsar would have thought of that! Cæsar, and only Cæsar could have done it. Only in the nick of time Tros saw the movement as they wallowed in the swell, and knew they did not mark the channel but obstructed it. In another second he would have struck the mud bank to the right of them. Their decks were black with men, and as he swung the helm he caught one glimpse of Cæsar's scarlet cloak, on the left-hand ship. Then the mist, and a hail of arrows whistling through it.

"Row!" he ordered, his voice cracking with excitement.

For a marvel his eleven Britons had not fired an arrow. Orwic jumped to the port-side arrow-engine just as the bireme's beak struck Cæsar's floated wreck amidships and the crash threw every rower off his bench.

"Drum! Drum!" Tros thundered. "Back to your benches! Row! For Lud o' Lunden—row!"

He heard the cable break, and through the ghosting mist he saw one hulk go swinging toward the mud to starboard, a volley of arrows from her rattling into the bireme's bulwark, short by the length of the swing.

But Cæsar's hulk was on the ram, transfixed by it and sinking, holed under the bilge. Nine-tenths of the way was off the bireme. She was down by the head and refused to steer. The crowded boats were overtaking her. Unless the heave of the groundswell should shake off the wreck from her ram, the game was up!

"Orwic! Lay your arrow-engine forward! Cæsar is on that wreck ahead of us!"

But Cæsar was not. He was over the bireme's bows already like a god out of the opal morning in his scarlet cloak, alone, and beckoning to his men. Orwic fired point-blank at him, and missed with all twelve arrows. Before he could load again there were a dozen legionaries on the bow, shields locked and Cæsar in their midst.

"Row! Row!" Tros thundered.

He did not dare let go the helm. The pursuing boats were thumping through the mist and the air was whistling with arrows. But one of Cæsar's legionaries blew a trumpet blast. The arrows ceased. Then Cæsar's voice, calm, with a hint of laughter:

"Tros! I believe you know me. I advise you to surrender at discretion."

Tros swung the helm. He had a chance yet. Conops hurled his knife at Cæsar, but it clanged on a soldier's shield. Ten Britons clustered beside Orwic, crouching, forgetting bows and arrows, ready with their swords.

"Come on!" cried Orwic, and led them, all leaping from the poop and rushing forward past the citadel.

Marvel of all marvels, the thirty oarsmen never missed a stroke! The bireme was gaining headway, lurched, shook herself, buried her bow as a heavy wave passed under her stern, shook the wreck free from her ram and crushed it on the down plunge.

The shock of that sent the charging Britons staggering in a heap against the citadel, but the Romans, shoulder to shoulder with locked shields, contrived to keep their footing. Then the oars struck wreckage. An oar broke.

"Drum! Drum!" Tros thundered. "Slow beat! One—two! One—two! Stick to it, you Britons!"

Then, as they cleared the wreckage—

"Conops, take the helm!"

He drew his sword. A Roman hurled a javelin at him, but he dodged it. Orwic and his ten were out of sight beyond the citadel. Tros knew where they were by the eyes of the Romans, who were watching them, alert to repel the expected charge.

Cæsar seemed to be listening for the oar-beat of his own boats, but the wind, that had fallen calm, began to shift to westward, blowing the mist along in front of it. A sudden vista between hurrying fog banks revealed the fleet of small boats scattered hopelessly astern.

"Cæsar!" said Tros, laying his left hand on the arrow-

237

engine. "I believe you know me. I advise you to surrender at discretion!"

Cæsar laughed. Less than a second later Tros knew why. Orwic chose that instant for the charge. He and his ten Britons leaped up on the bow and hurled themselves against the locked shields, with their own backs protecting Cæsar and his men from arrow-fire.

The Romans were past masters at that kind of fighting. The shields rose and fell almost leisurely, blocking attack, wearing down the adversary. Tros could see Cæsar's lips move as he spoke to his men in low tones, and though they stood the Britons off with shield and sword they made no effort to force them backward off the bow. Orwic's point slew one man, but the locked shields merely closed the gap.

"You are a bold rogue, Tros!" said Cæsar, in his pleasantest, amused voice that carried the effortless vibration learned in Rome's schools of oratory.

A Briton hurled a short spear at him, but he ducked it without taking his eyes off Tros.

"To-day, it would appear you have the best of it. To-morrow—who knows?"

Orwic pulled his men off. He knew no Latin, thought all this was talk about surrender. But the Britons were still in the way of the arrow-engine's fire. Tros whispered to Conops and signaled, trying to catch Orwic's eye but it was Cæsar who saw the signal. He made a superb gesture to Orwic, as if about to surrender to him. It deceived Tros for a moment, and it was to him, not to Orwic, that Cæsar spoke:

"I don't doubt, Tros, you are a man of discrimination, who will realize that Cæsar's ransom is worth more to you than Cæsar's dead body. Whereas you are worth nothing to me, dead or alive. And there is no one, Tros, whom I will crucify with less compunction when the proper time shall come!"

His eyes were on Tros, so he did not notice Conops signaling to Orwic. Orwic whispered to his men, but apparently Cæsar was unaware of that, too. He went on speaking:

"I advise you, Tros, to think of your predicament, since it is dangerous to be the enemy of Rome, fatal to be the foe of Cæsar! Neither Rome nor I forgive! Farewell!"

Almost without a gesture he turned and dived into the sea. The Britons sprang aside. Tros loosed a flight of arrows, but they clanged against raised shields, piercing them, sweeping down three legionaries.

Two followed Cæsar, plunging after him feet first, but their armor dragged them under. Orwic and his Britons slew the rest, hacking them down as they tried to re-form the broken line.

"Arrows! Arrows!" Tros roared, reloading the arrow-engine, watching the waves.

Cæsar's bald head, and the scarlet cloak behind it, appeared after a moment. Tros fired, but Cæsar ducked, and all twelve arrows missed.

Cæsar shook off the scarlet cloak and towed it, breasting the waves like a grampus, plunging into them and swimming under water when the Britons took pot shots at him, until he disappeared into the mist.*

There was too little sea room, too much fog and tide to turn the bireme and pursue him. His cold, amused laugh mocked Tros across unseen waves.

"By Lud of Lunden, that's a clever fellow who ought to have been born a Briton!" said Orwic, with the end of a cloth in his teeth as he was bandaging a sword slash in his arm.

"By Jupiter of Rome, he will become one by conquest!" Tros retorted savagely, hating himself, above all hating deathbed prophecies, that undermined a man's nerve, and created indecision.

Prophecy or not, he told himself the gods had delivered Cæsar into his hand. He, Tros, had failed them.

"Conops!" he roared. "The crew are skulking in the forehold. Rouse them with a rope's end! Make sail! Easy now, oars! The wind and tide serve."

-END-

* Cæsar was an extraordinarily strong swimmer, and a more than usually bold one, in spite of vicious self-indulgence that should have ruined the physique and nerve of any ordinary man. He often swam wide rivers, whose current was strong enough to hold up the engineers and their pontoons. The best known of his recorded swimming feats is the incident at Alexandria, where he was caught on the mole between forces advancing from either end. He escaped by jumping into a rough sea and swimming, dodging missiles and dragging his cloak after him, until picked up by a ship.